When Midnight Comes

When Midnight Comes

BERYL MATTHEWS

Allison & Busby Limited
12 Fitzroy Mews
London W1T 6DW
allisonandbusby.com

First published in Great Britain by Allison & Busby in 2018.
This paperback edition published by Allison & Busby in 2018.

A CIP catalogue record for this book is available from
the British Library.

10 9 8 7 6 5 4 3 2 1

ISBN 978-0-7490-2350-8

Typeset in 10.5/15.5 pt Sabon by
Allison & Busby Ltd

The paper used for this Allison & Busby publication
has been produced from trees that have been legally sourced
from well-managed and credibly certified forests.

Printed and bound by
CPI Group (UK) Ltd, Croydon, CR0 4YY

Chapter One

Camden, London 1856

'But my dad's funeral isn't until Friday.' Chrissie Banner looked at the rent collector in dismay. 'Can't I stay until that's over?'

Jack Porter's heart ached for the young girl in front of him. What he had been told to do was cruel, but he was lucky to have a job. There were plenty more waiting and willing to take over from him. He needed this job. 'I'm sorry, but the landlord has tenants waiting to move in and he wants you out by tomorrow.'

'Has he got a heart?' she asked with a grim smile on her tired face. 'Dad never once got behind with the rent and I've kept the place clean and free from bugs. That ain't easy in this slum.'

'You're a good girl.' Jack's mind was working quickly, trying to find a way to help this girl he had come to like and respect. Whenever he came to collect the rent it was always handed over with a smile. Her mum had died some years ago and then a couple of months ago her dad became ill and couldn't work. He knew it had been a struggle for her, but she had never complained.

'Could I stay if I paid for the next four days?'

He knew the landlord was only interested in money, so he nodded. 'That would be all right, but can you afford it? I know you haven't been able to do the rounds with your dad so ill.'

She shrugged. Poverty was a way of life to her, but it was no good crumbling under the strain. Her dad always said she was a survivor and she hoped he was right. 'How much would that old skinflint of a landlord want?'

Jack studied his book. 'Sixpence.'

Hiding her distress she drew out some coins from her pocket, reluctant to part with her last few pence, but there wasn't any choice. She had been hoping the landlord would let her stay for a few extra days as they had been good tenants, but that was too much to ask. She handed over the coins and replaced the last remaining one back in her pocket.

'How are you going to manage?' he asked as he reluctantly took the money from her.

'I'll have to sell the horse and cart.' Her eyes misted with tears at the thought. Dear old Bessie had been with them for a long time and it would be hard to part with the faithful horse. 'Bob, down the street, is interested in taking over the round, and I know he'll treat Bessie kindly.'

'But you and your dad are well known in this area, and you're a strong girl so I thought you would carry on with the rag-and-bone business.' Jack was dismayed.

'How can I? What do I do – leave Bessie in the street and sleep in the cart?' She shook her head. 'The dear animal deserves better than that.'

'So do you,' he said gently. How he hated this job, but it was all he could get, and he was lucky to have it. At least he could feed his family, which was more than some of the poor devils round here could do. 'What are you planning to do?'

'I need a roof over my head and food in my stomach, so I'll have to go into service, I suppose.' She gazed along the street of slum houses and her mouth set in a determined line. 'I've got the chance of a new start so I ain't staying in this disgusting place. If I have to scrub floors, then I'll do that to earn some money, and then I'm gonna find somewhere in the country where there are trees and open spaces round me.'

'I wish you luck with that, but you be careful.'

Her smile lit up her weary face, and her dark eyes flickered with amusement. 'Don't you worry about me. I'm taller and stronger than a lot of men. I can take care of myself.'

He nodded. 'I'll be at your dad's funeral.'

'Thanks. I'd like him to have a good send-off.' Her mind went back to the man she had loved so much. He had come from Romany Travellers stock, but after marrying a girl outside of the group, he had settled down in one place and started the rag-and-bone round. He had been a good man, and she was going to miss him so much.

She went to the yard and gave Bessie the last of the feed she had left. After paying for the extra days' rent there wasn't anything left to buy more, and it was no good putting things off, she thought sadly. She would have to go and see Bob. Of course, she wasn't going to get much for Bessie and the round because he didn't have any money. Jobs were hard to come by for the likes of them, but at least he would be able to feed his family if he took over her dad's business. They'd always managed until he had become too ill to work. She took Bessie and the cart out now and again, but never seemed to do well. Not like her dad. He had a voice that could be heard several streets away, and he was well liked. She gave the animal a pat on the rump and headed for Bob's house just three doors down.

He'd seen her coming and was waiting, worry etched on his face. 'Saw the rent man at your place. Are they turning you out, lass?'

'Yes. They wanted me out before the funeral, but I couldn't have that, so I had to pay for a few days extra.'

'Our landlord is a bloody disgrace!' he declared angrily. 'You've got your dad in his coffin there, so what the hell did he think you was gonna do with him until the funeral?'

She shrugged. 'He's an unfeeling sod, but Jack was kind. You could see he didn't like doing it, but it's his job and he has to do as he's told.'

'Of course, and he can't risk being sacked.' He looked hopefully at the tall girl in front of him. 'You made up your mind, Chrissie?'

'Yes, you can take over from Dad. Come and get the horse and cart whenever you like. I've just given her a feed. I know you ain't got much, but can you give me anything?' When she saw the worry on his face, she said quickly, 'If you ain't got nothing then that's all right. I understand.'

'All I can rake together is sixpence, but once I get going I'll give you a bit more.'

'No, you keep that to feed the kids. I don't want nothing, and Dad wanted you to have the round. Just take good care of Bessie and I'll be happy.'

'I'll do that, lass, and thanks. What are you going to do? Have you got family you can go to?'

'No, I'm on my own now.' She gave a strained smile. 'I'll be all right, though. I'm gonna get away from here and make a new life for myself. I've got to earn some money first, but then I'm heading for the country. There's bound to be posh houses there where I can get a job.'

'I hope it works out for you. Will you write and let us know how you're getting on?'

'I'll do that.'

'We'll all be at the funeral. I'll come and get Bessie and the cart right now, if that's all right. Her shed's all ready and nice and comfy. I'll go out today and see if I can pick up anything.'

'Good idea. She'll enjoy an outing.'

Chrissie kept away from the yard, but knew the animal had gone when she heard Bob shouting, 'Rag an' bone!' With tears streaming down her face she went and cleared out the shed and swept the yard, telling herself off for being a sentimental fool. Handing her over to Bob had been necessary for the animal's sake. He was a kind man and would take good care of the horse. After all, his livelihood depended on her now.

* * *

Friday dawned a dull overcast day with a fine drizzle soaking everything. It was a depressing September day and Chrissie hoped it wouldn't keep people away. She wanted to do right for the dad she had loved, and it would be upsetting if only a few attended. She had been able to pawn a couple of things to buy bread and put on a modest spread for after the funeral, and there were a few bottles of beer for the men.

The undertaker arrived to collect the coffin and she walked behind the horse-drawn cart to the church. People began to fall in behind her and by the time they reached the church there was such a large crowd that every pew was taken, with many standing at the back. This gave her some comfort and showed just how much her dad had been liked and respected.

The service went well and Chrissie was glad she had been able to scrape enough money together for what she considered to be a proper send-off for him. He'd had the penny insurance everyone took out no matter how poor they were, but it hadn't been enough to cover everything. It had left her broke, but as she looked round she felt it had been worth it. All the neighbours were there, so were his friends from the pub, as well as many who had known him from his rag-and-bone rounds.

Just about everyone came back and crowded into the small house and she worried that there wouldn't be enough food and drink for them all. While she was in the scullery boiling water to make the tea, the back door opened and she watched in amazement as one woman after another came in carrying a plate of something; when two men arrived from the pub with a barrel of beer, she couldn't help brushing away a tear. If her dad was watching from on high he would approve of this, and she could almost hear his amused chuckle.

It turned out to be quite a wake, with a real knees-up going on and spilling out in the street. The party didn't break up until midnight, and after the last person had left she collapsed in a chair, exhausted. It was only then the realisation hit her that she was now alone and tomorrow she would be homeless. All the money she had left was tuppence and that wasn't going to get her far. The furniture belonged to the landlord so that couldn't be sold. Everything her dad had collected on his last round had been sold to help with the funeral costs, and they didn't have anything of value she could use to raise money. She wandered round the squalid house but there were only a few battered pots and pans, and Bob could have those. They might bring him in a few coppers.

She sat on the edge of the bed frightened about the future. What was she going to do?

When Chrissie opened her eyes she shot straight up in bed. It was light! What was she doing sleeping so late; there was such a lot to do. The first thing was to see to Bessie. Her hand was on the bedroom door when she stopped suddenly and looked down at herself. She was fully clothed. Then the memories flooded back and she gasped in pain. Her father was gone, Bessie was gone, and she had to get out of the house today. For a moment she nearly crumpled where she stood, but that couldn't be allowed to happen. Still holding on to the door for support, she took a deep breath to try and clear her mind. Be strong, she told herself. If you keep calm and think clearly you will get through this. Think of those open spaces and green fields you have always longed for. Keep that as your goal and you'll fight for it knowing your Romany heritage is calling you to a new life – grasp it. You're a survivor, remember.

In control of her emotions again she opened the door and made her way down the narrow staircase. There was work to be done this day, and as painful as that would be it had to be faced. Her first concern was money and she gathered together anything she could sell or pawn, but there wasn't much for they had never been ones for possessions. The only thing she had of value was his silver pocket watch and chain that had come down through the family, and that was something she hoped she would never have to part with, no matter how bad things became. The bedlinen could be pawned and she might get a few coppers for that. It was clean and in good condition, but that was about it. Her dad had been buried in his only good suit and Bob could have the rest of his old clothes.

After having a quick wash she packed her few belongings in a bag, then gathered up the other bits and pieces and headed along the road.

Bob's wife, Gladys, opened the door and reached out to help her with the things about to topple out of her arms. 'Thanks, Glad. I thought Bob might be able to use this lot.'

'I'm sure he could. He's getting the horse and cart ready to do a round this morning. Come in, ducky, and have a bit of breakfast with us. I don't suppose you've had anything to eat.'

'I haven't had time as I slept late,' she admitted. 'But I can't take your food.'

'Of course you can. Letting us have the round has given us hope for the future, and Bob's a different man already now he has a way to provide for his family.'

'That's right.' He strode in to the scullery, followed by all six of his excited children.

'We've been feeding Bessie and making her coat shine,' the eldest told her proudly, 'and I'm going with Dad so I can help.'

'My goodness, she'll love all that fuss,' Chrissie replied, hiding her grief at losing the animal by giving the boy a bright smile. As she looked at the happy smiling faces around her she knew she had done the right thing. 'I've brought you this. They ain't worth much, but you might make use of them.'

The children swooped on them. 'Can we put them on the cart, Dad?'

He smiled and nodded, and when they all disappeared, laughing and running down the yard, Bob turned to Chrissie. 'I've made a little bit already, so I'll give you sixpence for the lot.'

'No.' She held up her hands in horror. 'Come on, I know what things are worth and it ain't that much. I've got a few things to pawn, so I'll be all right.'

'You sure?' He studied her carefully. 'You ain't lying to me, are you?'

'Course not, I've got plans. I come from a line of Travellers, as you know, and I'm gonna live in the country as soon as I can. As soon as I've saved enough money I'm leaving all this behind.'

He still looked doubtful. 'I don't like the idea of you out there all on your own. If you can't get a roof over your head by tonight you come back here. You can stay with us until you're settled in a job.'

'Thanks, but I'll be all right.' She gazed around this already overcrowded hovel and knew she couldn't burden them like that.

'Promise you'll come back here,' he told her sternly, guessing her thoughts. 'We'll manage.'

She reached out and grasped his hand in gratitude and made the promise, knowing she wouldn't keep it. When she saw the concern leave his face she excused herself the lie.

'Do you want to see Bessie before you go?'

'Better not. She's settled in with you and the kids making a fuss of her, and it might disturb her. I said my goodbyes to her yesterday, now I'd better go. Jack will be coming for the keys and to inspect the house.'

'Keep in touch and let us know how you're getting on,' Bob called as she hurried away.

She turned and waved, and then ran to do a final tidy-up of the house before leaving it for the last time.

Chapter Two

The pawnbroker hadn't given her much for the things, but she hadn't expected him to be overgenerous. Still, she had a few pennies in her pocket now and that was enough to get her to the posh part of London.

After visiting six large houses she was losing hope. It was late afternoon and she was getting desperate. Someone must need a servant, she thought as she made her way around the back of another house. Taking a deep breath she knocked on the servants' door, and when a young girl answered it Chrissie smiled. 'I'm looking for work.'

'I'll ask if they want anyone,' she said.

'Thanks.' She waited, praying they had a vacancy. At least she hadn't been turned away immediately this time, and when a footman came to the door and told her to come in, her hopes rose.

The footman gave her a saucy wink and opened the housekeeper's door for her. A severe woman was sitting behind a desk and didn't look up for a while, her attention on the ledger in front of her. Finally she glanced up and studied the girl in front of her.

'What is your name?'

'Christine Banner, ma'am.'

'And why are you looking for work?'

It didn't enter her head to gloss over what had happened and she told the housekeeper exactly what the situation was. 'So you see, ma'am, I need a job desperately. I can't burden my neighbours, willing though they are, cos they have problems enough without me dumping myself on them.'

'Wouldn't the landlord have let you stay in the house if you paid the rent?'

'No, ma'am. He's a tight old sod, pardon my language, and he had a family willing to pay more. I kept it nice, you see, and free from bugs, which wasn't easy in that dump.' She gave a hopeful smile. 'I'm really good at scrubbing, and you won't be disappointed if you take me on.'

'Don't you have any family who can help you?'

'Not that I know of, ma'am. It was just me and my dad.'

'Not that you know of? Explain.'

Chrissie sighed inwardly. This woman wanted to know a lot, but if there was a job at the end of it she would answer her questions politely. She explained about her dad and the situation she now found herself in by his death.

'You're part-Romany?'

'Yes, ma'am.' Chrissie tilted her head at a proud angle.

She wasn't ashamed of her heritage and wasn't going to let anyone belittle her because of it. Her dad had been a decent and hard-working man.

'We have need of a scullery maid,' she said briskly. 'You will get a half-day a week off, and be expected to work late when there are guests in the house.'

'Hard work don't worry me, ma'am,' Chrissie told her, relieved to be offered a job. 'I'd be happy to take the job.'

The housekeeper's expression softened, and she almost smiled. 'You address me as Mrs Conway; only the lady of the house is ma'am. When can you start?'

'Immediately, Mrs Conway. I ain't got nowhere else to go.'

The housekeeper stood up and swept out of the room calling for Pat, and a young girl who couldn't be more than fourteen rushed up, still holding a scrubbing brush. 'Take Christine upstairs to the room next to yours.'

'Yes, Mrs Conway.' The girl hastily dried her hands on her apron and gave Chrissie a shy smile as she reached out for her bag.

'I can manage that,' she told her. 'You lead the way.'

They walked up the winding servants' stairway to the attic rooms and Pat opened a door for her to enter. 'This is yours, and I'm right next door. There's a pot in the cupboard by the bed in case you need it in the night. I'll bring up hot water in the morning for you to wash with.'

Chrissie studied the room, turned back the blanket and examined the bed. It was spotlessly clean and she smiled at Pat. 'Much nicer than sleeping in the street, and that is where I could have ended up if I hadn't got this job. What's it like here?'

'Hard work, but we get good grub and the rest of the staff are nice.'

'What about the family?'

The girl hesitated and then shrugged. 'The Hamlins are all right, I suppose, but we don't see much of them.'

'You don't sound too sure.'

She shrugged again. 'Well. The son has just come home after travelling a lot and he's always staring at me. He frightens me a bit, but I expect it's my imagination.'

'Maybe, but if he gives you any trouble let me know and I'll sort him out.'

'Oh, no! If we cause any trouble we'll lose our jobs.'

Pat looked so horrified that Chrissie was sorry she had said anything. She laughed. 'Don't worry; I'll behave myself as long as I'm not pushed too far. I'm not used to being a servant so I'll be relying on you to show me what I should do.'

Pat relaxed then and looked much happier. 'Do you want to unpack now?'

'No, I'll leave it until tonight. I haven't got much.'

'We'd better get back, then. Mrs Conway will have jobs for us to do.'

As they made their way downstairs Chrissie knew this wasn't going to be easy for her. She had always spoken her mind when she came across things she didn't agree with, and was going to have a struggle to stop herself from answering back. She needed this job, though, so perhaps that would keep her in order.

Chrissie soon found out just how hard the domestic servants worked, but that didn't worry her. She had a roof over her head and plenty of good food from a cook who was proud of her talent. The long days filled with constant activity also helped her to come to terms with the loss of her dad. He had brought her up from the age of ten by himself when her mum had died, and she had loved him dearly. Her mum had died far too early, but she could remember them together, and it had been a happy marriage. Now that was all gone and it hurt her so much to think of her parents, Bessie and the business. They'd had such fun and laughed a lot.

She was scrubbing the entrance hall with determination when the front door opened and she was looking at a pair of wet, muddy riding boots as they left dirty prints all over her clean floor. She glared up at the man. He hadn't even wiped his feet on the mat on the step! It was an effort not to tell him off, but she remembered just in time that she was a lowly servant. This was the first time she had seen the master's son, and she took an instant dislike to him. Sitting back on her heels she held his gaze, her dark eyes showing her annoyance, and when he laughed and began to make even more mess she could have hit him. She studied his retreating figure as he walked away, still laughing. There was no doubt that this was the man Pat was afraid of and she could understand the timid girl's worry about him.

'What a mess!' Mrs Conway exclaimed. 'How did this happen?'

'The son marched in with muddy boots and made as much mess as he could. He thought it was funny.'

The housekeeper looked furious. 'Visitors are expected within the next hour so clean it up as quickly as possible.'

'Yes, Mrs Conway.' It took three buckets of clean water

to remove the mud and by the time she had finished she was fuming. That spoilt brat had better stay out of her way or she might give him the thrashing he deserved. She was tall and strong, and from what she had seen of him he was a weakling. Bullies always were, and coming from the slums she had dealt with a few in her time.

In less than an hour the hallway was spotless and the tiles gleaming brightly.

'That's an excellent job,' the housekeeper said as she inspected Chrissie's work. 'Take a break now, you have earned it, and Cook has just taken a lovely fruit cake out of the oven.'

'Thank you, Mrs Conway. I'll empty the bucket first.' She stood up and took a critical look at the floor, nodding in satisfaction. Then she hurried back to the scullery anticipating a lovely slice of hot fruit cake.

The rest of the staff had heard about the incident and showed their disapproval. 'That young man needs his backside walloped,' the cook declared, handing round the cake.

'He nearly got a hiding from me,' Chrissie admitted, 'but I remembered just in time that I was a servant and he the master's son.'

'And you could have done it.' John the footman studied Chrissie with admiration. 'I reckon you're ten times stronger than him, and taller.'

The young bootboy danced up to her in a boxer's pose with a huge grin on his face. 'Let's see how tough you are. Come on, show us your muscles.'

With one quick movement she swept the lad off his feet

and tossed him over her shoulder, making him squeal with laughter. 'All right, I believe you. Put me down!'

The room was full of laughter as she put him back on his feet. This was the first time she had laughed since her dad took ill, and it felt good.

The family were entertaining that evening and it was eleven o'clock before they were able to go to bed. It had been a long day and Chrissie was asleep almost before her head touched the pillow.

What was that? She sat up in bed and listened, instantly awake. There was a muffled cry coming from Pat's room, and Chrissie's first thought was that she was having a bad nightmare. She hastily lit a candle, grabbed her robe and hurried to the girl's room. What she saw enraged her. The son was there and holding his hand over her mouth as he tried to subdue her. He half-turned as the candle lit the room and rocked back as Chrissie hit him and dragged him off the bed.

'Take your hands off her, you dirty beast!' She hoisted him up and slammed him against the wall. 'She's only a child!'

The moment Pat had been released she started to scream in terror. John, the footman, was the first one to reach the room, quickly followed by the butler and the rest of the staff.

'What's going on here?' Andrews, the butler, demanded, turning to Chrissie who now had a firm hold on the son.

'This beast was trying to rape Pat,' she told him.

'What are you doing in the servants' quarters in the middle of the night, sir?' the butler asked angrily while trying to comfort Pat.

'It's my bloody house and I can go where I like.'

'But you can't do what you like to us.' Chrissie gave him a shake to emphasise her point.

'Yes, I can. You're all just dirt.' He got one hand free and caught her a stinging blow across the face. 'Get off me, you bitch! You'll pay for this.'

When he went to hit her again she ducked and then retaliated, splitting his lip and making him groan from the blow.

The men stepped in quickly to stop the fight, took hold of the son and dragged him out of the room.

'Let's have a look at your face,' Mrs Conway said as soon as the men had gone. 'You're going to have a black eye, and are you hurt anywhere else?'

'No, I'm all right, it's Pat I'm worried about.' She sat on the bed by the frightened girl who was silent now, but shaking, with tears running down her cheeks.

Pat wrapped her arms around Chrissie and said over and over again, 'Thank you.'

'Shush. It's all over now. I doubt he will bother you again. But if he so much as looks at you, let me know and I won't hold back on my punches again.'

There was an amused chuckle from the footman as he came back with the butler. 'If you held back on that punch then remind me never to upset you.'

'That wouldn't be a good idea.' She grinned, trying to lighten the tense atmosphere. 'Where I come from you learn early in life to stick up for yourself. What have you done with that nasty man?'

'We've escorted him back to his own part of the house,'

the butler replied and sat on the bed by Pat. 'You all right, lass? He didn't hurt you, did he?'

Pat held out her thin arms and showed him the livid marks. 'He . . . frightened me, Uncle.'

'Well, he won't do that again. I'll see to that!'

'I think what we all need now is a nice strong cup of tea,' Cook declared. 'We won't be able to sleep now, so everyone down to the kitchen.'

They all sat around the large table, and while Mrs Conway was applying a salve to Pat's arms, the butler spoke quietly to Chrissie. 'You know there will be consequences from this night?'

She nodded. 'I'll take all the blame. The rest of you only arrived after it was all over.'

'Oh no you don't. We'll stand together on this, so you tell it like it is when you are questioned.'

'Let's see what happens in the morning. Perhaps he'll slink away in shame and not say anything to his family.'

'There isn't much hope of that.' He squeezed her arm. 'Thank you for saving the child from being hurt too much.'

Chapter Three

The breakfast had only just been cleared away when the butler came for Chrissie. 'We've been ordered to the master's study.'

She threw the cloth in the bucket and got to her feet. 'We?'

'You, me and Pat.'

'Can't they leave her out of it?' she declared angrily. 'The poor girl is still in a state after that attack on her.'

'We'll be with her, so she'll be all right.' His expression was grim. 'This won't be pleasant. I don't think the old man and his son have a decent bone in their bodies.'

'If they are looking for a fight then they'll get one!' After drying her hands on her apron she said, 'Where's Pat?'

'She's waiting for us in the hall.' He caught hold of her arm as she made to walk away. 'Remember what I said. Don't try to gloss over this in an effort to save our jobs. The one in the wrong here is the boy; we did nothing wrong.'

'Perhaps he just wants to apologise,' she joked.

The butler gave a grim smile and shook his head.

Pat was so frightened she was shaking and Chrissie had to support her. 'What . . . what does the master want? . . . I don't wanna go in there.' A tear trickled down her cheek.

'You are not to worry about them,' Chrissie assured her. 'We'll be with you, but it's really me they want to see.'

'Come on, my girl, dry your eyes and don't let them see they can frighten you.' The butler smiled to reassure his young niece. 'There isn't anything for you to be frightened about. Chrissie will deal with them,' he joked.

'You can be sure of that!' Chrissie guided Pat towards the study door.

The footman opened the door for them and whispered softly, 'We're all with you.'

Chrissie nodded and rolled up her sleeves, ready for the confrontation. She could take care of herself and was determined to see that the rest of the staff didn't suffer if she could help it. She was certain she had lost this job, but she didn't want any of the others to be dismissed as well.

The master was standing by the fireplace, with a thunderous expression on his florid face. His wife was seated by the window and the son was standing a few paces away from his father and looked smug. That told Chrissie all she wanted to know. The father was going to support his son, no matter what he had done the night before. But it gave her some satisfaction to note the son's swollen lip and livid bruise where she had hit him.

The master turned to Chrissie immediately and pointed

to his son. 'I want an explanation for this unwarranted attack on my son!'

So this was how it was going to be: the son had denied any wrongdoing and the father believed him. She showed no emotion when she spoke. 'Your son was about to rape a fourteen-year-old girl so I pulled him off her. He hit me and I hit him back.'

'How dare you accuse my son of such a thing!' he bellowed. 'He'd had a little too much to drink and wandered in to the servants' quarters.'

Chrissie couldn't help herself, she laughed. 'Is that what he told you?'

'He wouldn't lie to me. I believe him above the likes of you.' He almost spat in contempt.

'What Miss Banner has told you is the truth,' the butler told him. 'The rest of the staff were also witnesses to the attack and are prepared to sign statements, if necessary.'

The master turned his fury back to Chrissie. 'You're lying and have convinced everyone else that it is the truth. My son wouldn't touch dirty tarts like you and the girl!'

That was too much, and furious, she took a step forward. 'Be careful who you are calling names, sir. I come from the slums, but let me tell you something. We look after each other, and if your son had been caught by us he would never have been able to attempt such a thing again.'

He snorted in contempt. 'Violence is rife where you come from. You don't know anything about civilised behaviour.'

'Don't be so quick to condemn.' She spoke firmly and clearly. 'You are the one who doesn't have anything to be proud of. You have a son who doesn't know the first thing about civilised behaviour. He believes that because of his privileged position he can do what he likes and he knows you will support him. I think this attempted rape should be reported to the police; let them deal with him.'

'I have it all written out for the police, should we decide it necessary to report this.' The butler pulled an envelope out of his pocket and showed it to them.

'Father, don't let them get away with that!' The son sounded alarmed now.

Chrissie ignored the son and the father's stunned expression and, knowing she was certainly going to be dismissed, continued. 'Your son needs to be taught discipline and respect for others, whatever their station in life. If you put him in the army they might be able to make a gentleman out of him, but I doubt they will even take him. He will certainly end up in prison if he isn't dealt with and taught the difference between right and wrong.'

'Enough! Get out of this house at once, and take that other piece of dirt with you.' He pointed at Pat, who grabbed Chrissie's hand and looked at the butler in alarm. 'Uncle . . .' she wailed.

'It's all right, lass. I will also be leaving today.' He put his arm around the terrified child's shoulder, and then addressed the master. 'Pat is my youngest sister's child, sir, and is in my care after her mother died. I would not allow her to stay in a household where she is in danger of being molested.'

By now the master was apoplectic with rage. To have the butler accuse his son in this way was too much. 'Get out! You will all leave this house with no pay or references. I'll see that you can never get another job. No one will employ you after I spread the word about your unforgivable actions.'

'You do that, sir, and we will have to defend ourselves by explaining about your son's attack on a fourteen-year-old child. Society will react badly to such news.'

'They won't believe you!' he roared at the butler, and then stormed out of the room.

Chrissie turned her attention to the son and noted that he was now drained of all colour. When they had entered the room he'd had a smirk on his face, confident his father would deal with the situation. Now it was a different story. He was clearly shocked that servants should dare to defend themselves. They hadn't remained mute and subservient, and the butler leaving as well hadn't been expected. Three people out there who knew the truth could rip his reputation to pieces.

'Come on, my dears, let's get out of this house.' The butler took hold of Pat's arm and Chrissie followed them to the door.

'Wait.'

They turned to face the mistress, who had spoken for the first time. 'Andrews, you and the child do not need to leave. My husband will calm down and I will see that nothing like this happens again. You are an excellent butler and I do not wish to lose you.' She gave Chrissie a sad smile. 'I am afraid I cannot do anything about your dismissal, as much as I would like to.'

'I understand, but the rest of your staff are blameless and I would not like to see them suffer because of my actions.'

'I will see they do not. Andrews and Pat may stay and—'

'I'm sorry, madam,' he interrupted. 'We will be leaving with Chrissie. I am responsible for Pat and will not put her at risk by staying, and she would never be happy here again. Thank you for your kindness, though.'

They left the room then, and before the door was completely closed behind them they heard the mistress turn on her son. 'You ought to be ashamed of yourself, and your father is no better. You are a disgrace to this family, and when word gets out, as it certainly will, we shall be shunned by society.'

As the footman closed the door they heard a sound and Chrissie gasped. 'Did she just hit her son?'

'Sounded like it, and about time too. Cook's got a feast laid out for us, so let's go and enjoy it.' The footman grinned at Chrissie. 'I listened to what was said and it did my heart good to hear you both standing up to that bully. They've got another shock coming because I've been offered another job and will also be leaving.'

Cook went into a flurry of despair when she heard the news, and it took a while to calm her down. 'What are we going to do?' she cried. 'There is a dinner party for twelve this evening. How can I manage without the help of the girls and you, Mr Andrews?'

'It will be cancelled,' the housekeeper informed them as she swept in to the kitchen. 'Madam is leaving for her house in Bath today and I am to go with her.'

'But there won't be anyone to manage the house,' Cook gasped. 'Those two men won't have any idea what to do.'

The footman grinned. 'It will be chaos, unless they are going to Bath as well.'

'That house belongs to Madam, and they won't be joining her. They will have to spend most of their time at their club until they have engaged more staff.' Mrs Conway turned to Andrews. 'Madam has insisted that you all be paid in full before leaving.' She handed the three of them a packet each.

The butler tipped out the coins and frowned. 'This can't be right, Mrs Conway.'

'I was told to include the extra by way of an apology for the way you have been treated.'

'Would you please thank Madam for us?' Chrissie asked. She hadn't been here long enough to receive much, but she was grateful for the money and relieved that Andrews and Pat were being given this extra. At least it showed that someone believed they had told the truth.

It didn't take long for them to pack their belongings and leave the house. 'Do you have anywhere to go?' Andrews asked Chrissie as they walked along the road.

She shook her head and grimaced. 'No, but I'll find somewhere. I'm getting used to being thrown out.'

'Then you must come with us. My eldest sister will find you a bed for the night, then tomorrow you can decide what you are going to do.'

'That's very kind of you, but I couldn't dump an extra person on her. It wouldn't be right.'

Andrews stopped walking and faced her. 'Now you look here, my girl, we owe you for saving Pat from that boy and I won't have you wandering the streets looking for somewhere to sleep.'

'Please come,' Pat pleaded. 'Auntie Helen will be happy for you to stay with us.'

'Well . . . just for one night, then.'

'Good, that's settled.' Andrews started walking again. 'We'll do a bit of shopping so we don't turn up empty-handed.'

After buying a joint of mutton and plenty of vegetables they made their way to the house. It was small but in a much better area than the one Chrissie had come from. There was a green space across the road, and although too small and unkempt to be called a park, it gave a feeling of space when you looked out of the front window. Auntie Helen obviously took pride in keeping her home nice, and although she made them very welcome, Chrissie knew her first task the next day would be to find somewhere else to stay. She had intended to remain in London until the spring and then make her way to the countryside, but now she had lost her job it might be better to move out of London sooner than she had planned. There was no doubt that the father and son would lose no time in blackening her name and make finding another job here impossible.

There was a little money in her pocket now and she would have to see how far that would get her.

Chapter Four

When Chrissie looked out of the front window the next morning the piece of ground was filled with people, horses and caravans. 'What's all this?' she asked Pat, who had come to stand beside her.

'It's the Travellers. They come almost every year as they start their journey south for the winter. They set up stalls for a couple of days and then move on. Do you want to go and have a look? They make some nice things.'

'I'd love to.' She grabbed her coat, an idea already forming in her mind. This might be the answer to her problem.

It was a lively scene, with a lot of shouting and laughter as the locals bartered for the goods on display. None of this interested her, though, as she headed for a man selling baskets.

'Take your pick,' he told her, smiling broadly. 'I'll do you a good deal.'

She had listened to her father talking about life as a Traveller and knew who to ask for. 'I'm not here to buy,' she told him. 'Would it be possible to speak to the headman of your group?'

'And why would you want to do that?' he asked, frowning.

'I need to ask if I could travel with you for a while. I understand you are heading south, and that's where I want to go.'

He was now studying her intently. 'That's an unusual request. Most young women are afraid of us. They think we can't be trusted.'

She laughed. 'You don't scare me. I come from travelling stock.'

'Do you now. What's your name?'

'Banner.'

He nodded. 'You'd better come with me.'

When he began to walk away she glanced round and found Pat right behind her. 'I'm going to see someone, and will come back to the house later.'

Pat nodded, looking slightly worried. 'Be careful, Chrissie.'

'I will, don't you worry about me.' She had to run to catch the man up.

He looked at her and said, 'My name's Sandy, by the way.'

'Good to meet you. What are my chances of being able to travel with you?'

He just shrugged and kept on walking towards a group of horse-drawn homes. They were elaborately decorated in bright colours and a group of horses were grazing nearby. The sight of them tugged at Chrissie's heart and she hoped Bessie was happy with her new owners.

'Pa!' he called when they stopped by one of the homes. 'Someone here wants to see you.'

A man appeared at the door and jumped down the steps, extremely spritely for his advanced age. He fixed his gaze on Chrissie. 'And what might you be wanting to know?'

'I would like your permission to travel with you as you make your way south. I'm a hard worker and good with horses. I'll earn my keep.'

His bright blue eyes roamed over her. 'Why would a young, strong girl like you want to travel with us? What kind of trouble you in? If the law is after you then I'll tell you straight that we don't take in troublemakers.'

'The coppers ain't after me,' she told him indignantly. 'I'm homeless and need a job. I thought I could find a nice big country house needing a servant, but you're not as friendly as my dad always told me Travellers were.'

'Your dad knows all about us, does he?'

'Did. He died a while back.' She didn't like this man with the cold eyes and turned to walk away.

'Wait!'

She glanced over her shoulder and said sarcastically, 'Don't you worry; I'll make it on my own.'

'Stand still, girl. What's your name?'

'Christine Banner.' She called back as she started walking again. Suddenly he was right in front of her, hands on hips and blocking her path.

Furious now, she turned to Sandy who was watching

with interest. 'Tell your pa to get out of my way or I'll make him move. He's too old and rude to be the head of this group. It's time you put him out to grass.'

The man in front of her burst out laughing; in fact the two men were doubled over with mirth, which made her even more indignant.

Pa straightened up and nodded to his son, then called out, 'Ma, brew up some tea. We've got a guest.'

Chrissie turned and saw an elderly woman standing next to her son, her face wreathed in smiles.

'You'd better move, Pa,' she told her husband. 'She's big and strong enough to make you.'

He stepped aside, still grinning, and the transformation was so marked he looked like a different man. 'Wipe that scowl off your face, girl, and stay to talk with us. I was just testing to see what you were like. Banner isn't an uncommon name amongst Travellers and they have a reputation for being feisty. Let's see if we can help you.'

With a nod she turned and walked up the wooden steps in to the home. It would be daft to walk away without hearing what they had to say.

'Right,' Pa said the moment they were settled, 'tell us about yourself and your family.'

She gave them a brief account of her life so far, why she was looking for a way to travel to the country, and the reason she had left her last job.

'Sounds like you don't stand no nonsense,' Ma remarked. 'Reckon we can help her, Pa. What do you think, son?'

'We can't turn someone away who comes from Traveller stock when they ask for help.'

'I agree that wouldn't be right,' Pa told them. 'You'll have to earn your keep, girl. Everyone in this group has to contribute in any way they can.'

'I'm not afraid of hard work – and the name is Chrissie. I know I'm a girl and don't have to be reminded.'

A deep chuckle came from Pa as he glanced at his wife. 'What can we give Chrissie to do?'

'We need a fortune-teller. Elsie is too frail to do it now.'

Chrissie studied their faces, certain they must be joking.

'Good idea,' Pa agreed.

They weren't joking! 'I can't tell fortunes,' she protested. 'It would be taking money under false pretences. I don't have a gift like that.'

'Have a talk with Elsie,' Sandy suggested. 'She'll show you how to read people to tell if they are happy, worried or even desperate when they come to the tent. You'll tell them things to make them feel better and give them encouragement to deal with whatever problems they have. If you feel they've just come to you for a bit of fun – which many do – then tell them something good is coming their way.'

She pulled a face in disgust. 'Like a tall dark stranger?'

'If you think it's appropriate,' Sandy said, amused at her expression.

'I couldn't do that; it's dishonest. I'm good with horses,' she added hopefully.

'You can help look after them as well.' Pa's gaze held hers. 'You work as a fortune-teller when we stop, and care for the animals when we are on the move. Those are our conditions, Chrissie.'

'Before you refuse' – Ma placed her hand on Chrissie's arm when it looked as if she was going to leave – 'have a talk with Elsie first.'

'All right,' she agreed, reluctant to give up this chance to travel with them.

Although very advanced in years and frail, Elsie's eyes were bright and alert. When Ma explained that they were trying to get Chrissie to take over from her, she nodded and studied the girl in front of her for some moments before breaking into a huge smile. 'A good choice. Sit down, my dear, and show me your hands.'

Chrissie sighed inwardly. This was a mistake and she would have to find another way to get out of London. Not wanting to offend the older woman she smiled and started to stand up. 'I'm sorry to have wasted your time. I'll be on my way.'

'Are you too proud to hear what an old lady has to say?'

'I'm not the right person for this. I couldn't take money from people and tell them lies.'

'Indulge me, Chrissie. What harm can it do? This will just be a bit of fun between friends.'

'Come on,' Sandy urged, holding the chair for her to sit down again. 'Don't throw away this chance without finding out all you can first.'

He was right, of course, she recognised, as she sat at the table and held out her hands.

Elsie took hold of them, frowning, and studied them for a moment. 'Hmm. These are hard-working hands, and very interesting. You will eventually get what you want from life, and perhaps more than you could have dreamt of. Someone very powerful is coming to you. He will adore you and you will feel the same about him. He will have a devilish sense of humour and be hard to deal with, but his affection for you will have him bowing in submission.'

Chrissie shook her head. This was a load of nonsense! 'I suppose he will be tall, dark and handsome and we will marry.' It was hard to keep the sarcasm out of her voice.

'He is indeed tall, dark and handsome.' Elsie looked at Chrissie with a faraway look in her eyes. 'But you can't possibly marry him. You see, he is a horse.'

'A horse!' She stared at the fortune-teller in astonishment, and then dissolved into helpless laughter. It had been some time since she had relaxed and as she wiped away the tears of amusement a strange thing happened. The trauma of the last few weeks dropped away from her like a heavy cloak falling to the ground.

Elsie was watching her intently. 'You've had a tough time, so do you feel better now, my dear?'

'Yes, I do,' she admitted. 'That is the first time I've laughed like that in weeks.'

'If you had given me a coin would you have felt cheated?'

She thought about that for a moment and then shook her head. 'I'd have been amused – even entertained by the story you have just made up.'

'You think I made it up?'

'Of course, but it was very good. However, you haven't convinced me I could do this.'

'Then I shall have to try harder.' The fortune-teller then removed a cloth to reveal a crystal ball. 'Look into that and tell me what you see.'

She pulled the crystal ball towards her, prepared to play the game now and gazed at the object, scepticism apparent on her face. After a while she looked up and grinned. 'It's very pretty but it is just a piece of stone.'

'It's quartz crystal, my dear,' Elsie replied calmly. 'It's a very special kind of stone. Relax, clear your mind of all those doubts and try again.'

'This is just a waste of time,' she protested.

'Give it one more try,' the elderly woman urged. 'I'm sure you have the talent, but your disbelief is blocking it. Concentrate on looking to the middle of the crystal.'

With a shrug, believing this was a complete waste of time, she tried to look in to the depths of the crystal. 'What a shame; it's all cloudy inside, and I didn't notice that the first time,' she exclaimed, not taking her eyes from the ball.

'What is in the mist?'

'Nothing . . . Oh, there's a big house there,' she laughed. 'That's clever.'

'Look again.'

She did as asked and shook her head. 'I can't see it now. How did you do that?'

'I didn't do anything. That was your future you saw.'

'Well, I'll certainly be kept busy scrubbing all those floors,' she joked. 'This has been fun, but if you will excuse me, I have to find another job.'

Elsie put her hand on her arm to stop her leaving. 'Tonight we will be moving on and won't make camp again for another three days, so give me that time to show you the art of telling fortunes. Then do one session with the public, and if you still feel the same after that you needn't do it again. I am sure Pa can keep you busy with other things while we are travelling.'

Chrissie glanced across at Pa and then back to Elsie. 'I was told I couldn't travel with you unless I took on the fortune-telling.'

'Don't take any notice of Pa,' she waved a dismissive hand. 'This is between you and me. No one will force you to do anything you don't want to. All I'm asking is that you try it once at our next stop. What do you say?'

'I'd be willing to do that.' She looked hopefully at Pa again and was relieved when he nodded. This was her chance to get out of London and she had to take it.

'Good.' Elsie was clearly delighted. 'Go and get your things. You can share my home. I'll be glad of the company.'

Chapter Five

After saying goodbye to Pat and her family and wishing them well, she went back to the field just in time to help them pack up. There was a lot to do so they would be ready to move off first thing the next day.

She slept well in Elsie's cosy home and in the morning enjoyed helping to hitch up the horses. Sandy was driving the caravan as Elsie was no longer able to do this for herself, and Chrissie was excited as they started their journey. She was going to get out of London now, and in a way she would never have imagined. A slight smile appeared on her face as she wondered what her dad would think about this. He would be laughing, she was sure.

'I used to drive the horse and cart for my dad sometimes,' she told Sandy. 'If you would show me how to manage the caravan it would save you doing it.'

He immediately handed the reins over to her and began giving instructions. They had been on the road for two hours when they stopped on a spare piece of ground.

'Time to water the horses and ourselves. Put the kettle on, Elsie,' he called as he jumped down. He held out a hand for Chrissie and grinned. 'It's always the animals before us. Without them we would be stuck in one place.'

That was the routine for the day, and by the time they camped for the night Sandy declared she was a natural and could handle the caravan on her own. It was very different from the horse and cart, and she was quite proud of the achievement.

Over the next three days she saw the scenery begin to change from crowded London streets to open spaces, and the autumn colour of the trees made her stare in wonder at their beauty. She had learnt so much in a very short time and the children had even taught her to ride bareback whenever they took the horses to a stream to drink. Much to her surprise she found it easy and soon tried to compete with the youngsters in their races and games. They thought that was huge fun and shouted encouragement as they urged her on, laughing as they ran to her help whenever she came off – which wasn't rare at first. She would have been completely happy if it wasn't for the fortune-telling hanging over her head. Elsie instructed her every night and gave her high praise, but she was not happy about attempting it; in fact, she was dreading the next day. She had made Elsie a promise, though, and wouldn't let her down. Still, it was a comfort to know it would only be the one time, because she was certain she was going to be terrible at it. Once that was over she could relax and enjoy the journey. This was the first time she had been out of London and there were so many new wonders to see.

'Will you go through it all with me again?' she asked Elsie that evening, a worried frown on her face. They had designated stops where they set up their stalls, and one was nearly here. She didn't feel at all prepared for her first outing as a fortune-teller.

'We will do better than that,' she replied. 'I've asked a few of the group to come and let you tell them their fortunes.'

'Oh, no!' Chrissie was horrified. It would be bad enough trying this with strangers, but worse with people she had come to know. 'I can't do that.'

'Don't worry, my dear, you'll be all right. Just remember what I said. Study them as they come in and tell them only things that will uplift and intrigue them. No bad news; you want them to leave you happy and full of hope.'

Chrissie nodded but was extremely apprehensive. She couldn't understand why they were insistent she become their fortune-teller during the journey south, but she didn't have time to worry any more as the first person arrived. Elsie had been so patient explaining everything, so she put aside her doubts and plunged in, hoping she didn't make too much of a fool of herself.

The next two hours flew by. As soon as one person left another took their place at the table, giving her no time to panic.

'Quite remarkable,' Elsie said when they were finally alone. 'You have a nice way with you and they were all smiling as they left.'

'I'm happy you are pleased, but I was just telling them

whatever came in to my head, and it doesn't sit easy with me to be fooling anyone. I'll be even more uneasy when it is people who pay.'

'We'll see how it goes tomorrow.' Elsie put a cup of tea in front of her. 'Drink that and I'll give you a reading.'

Chrissie sat back and ran a hand over her eyes, feeling suddenly drained.

'It takes it out of you, doesn't it? That's why I can't do a long session any more.' She pulled Chrissie's hand towards her and gazed into the crystal ball. 'By the time the trees are beginning to bud you will leave us. We will be sorry to see you go, but there will be a job you want to take, and life on the road is not for you. I don't usually do this, my dear, but I'm going to give you a warning. There is a rough journey in front of you, where you will encounter sadness and disappointment. Things will be unpleasant for a while, but no matter how bad things are, all will be resolved and your future happiness assured.' She looked up and smiled. 'And don't forget that horse because he is there.'

Chrissie laughed and shook her head. 'That was a good fairy story, Elsie. I'll never be as good or as inventive as you.'

Elsie patted her hand, still smiling. 'Why don't you have an early night? It will be a long day tomorrow.'

'How did she do?' Pa asked quietly as he looked in Elsie's door.

'Very well. Everyone was happy with the readings she gave them. They all gave me a nod of approval as they left. She has the gift, Pa, but doesn't know it and doesn't want to know. She thinks it's a load of nonsense, but she's worn out and fast asleep now.'

Pa came in, sat down and spoke in a whisper. 'If she's that good do you think we can persuade her to stay with us? She does come from Traveller stock and this might be the life for her.'

Elsie shook her head. 'She'll stay with us until the spring and then be on her way. Her destiny is in a different direction.'

'I'm sorry to hear that. Some of us have become rather fond of her. It doesn't matter what there is to do she just pitches in without being asked, and I'd swear she's as strong as some of the men.'

Elsie looked pointedly at Pa. 'I know how you feel, but she won't be staying, no matter how much we'd like her to.'

He nodded and stood up. 'I believe you, but that won't stop us trying to keep her. See you in the morning. You'll watch over her while she does her first session in the fortune-teller's tent?'

'Of course, and I'll step in if she becomes flustered, but I'm confident that won't happen.'

'Take your choice.' Elsie spread out an array of bright and beaded shawls and shirts.

Chrissie eyed them with dismay. 'Do I have to wear things like that?'

'The people who come to you do expect it, but you don't have to dress up if you don't want to.'

'I'd rather wear my own frock.'

'Hmm.' Elsie studied Chrissie carefully. 'We must put on a bit of a show, so how about a compromise? You stay as you are and we'll drape a shawl over your chair.'

'All right, but not that one.' She pushed aside the gaudy one Elsie had given her and picked up one with blue and green swirls on it. 'I think this will be better. When Mum was alive we went to the seaside once and I'll always remember it. This pattern reminds me of the waves rolling in.'

'In that case, my dear, it's the perfect choice. Help me to the tent and we'll get it all set up for you.'

Chrissie's insides churned as she thought about the day to come. She really didn't want to do this, but she had given her promise and there was no backing out now. 'Will you be close by in case I need you?'

'I'll be behind a curtain the whole time, but you don't need to worry, you'll be quite all right.'

'I wish I had your confidence,' she declared when they reached the tent.

There was plenty of room inside, with a table in the centre covered with a plain soft-green cloth, the crystal ball on top and two chairs. The inside was draped with various gauzy curtains and a place behind one of them for Elsie to sit comfortably unseen. She was pleased to see it wasn't festooned with bright colours and strange symbols. It was rather dim in there, though. 'Can we have more light?' she asked. 'I want to be able to see the people clearly and for them to see me.'

'You can have whatever you like.' Elsie peeped out of the tent and called for Sandy.

He arrived at a trot. 'What can I do for you?'

'Chrissie wants more light in here.'

He looked around, frowning. 'The only way to do that will be if we pull the flap right back and drape thin gauze over the entrance.' He set to work and when finished he turned to Chrissie. 'Is that better for you?'

The filmy curtain was blowing gently in the breeze and the sun was filtering through to light the interior. 'That's much better. Thank you.'

'My pleasure, madam . . .' He grinned. 'What do we call you?'

She frowned, puzzled. 'Chrissie, you know that.'

'No, you need an exotic name we can put on the board outside.'

'Can't I use my own name?' she asked Elsie.

'Well, Chrissie or Christine doesn't sound right. Do you have a middle name?'

'I do, but I never use it. It's awful.'

'What is it?'

'Gloria.'

'Perfect.' Elsie and Sandy said together. 'Madam Gloria it is, then.' Sandy left whistling happily.

'Oh dear,' she groaned. 'This is going from bad to worse. You never told me I needed another name.'

The elderly woman laughed at her expression of dismay. 'I was about to mention it, but Sandy got there first. Sit down, people will be arriving soon. One of the young boys will stand outside and show the customers in one by one.'

She waited, secretly hoping no one would want their fortunes told, but that hope was soon dashed when the curtain was lifted and a woman took the seat opposite Chrissie.

For the rest of the day it was one customer after another and she was surprised to see how many people wanted to consult a fortune-teller, and it wasn't only women. As each one came in she took note of how they were dressed and the way they approached the table. It was evident that for many it was just a bit of fun, but others were more serious, and one or two badly needed their spirits lifted. A woman arrived at the end of the day when they were going to pack up and Chrissie was feeling quite drained after such a long day. The woman was quite smartly dressed but her clothes had seen better days and it was clear she had fallen on hard times.

'I know you are getting ready to finish for the day,' she said, hesitating at the door, 'but could you give me a reading – or whatever it is you do?'

Ah, she doesn't believe in this, Chrissie recognised, and had probably been driven here by desperation. The woman's next words confirmed this when she was asked to sit down.

'I don't know what you charge, but this is all I have.' She placed a penny on the table.

Chrissie didn't touch the coin, but just reached out for her hand and studied the palm. Then she did something she hadn't done all day and pulled the crystal ball towards her, gazing at it intently. 'There is a welcome change on the way for you – in fact, it is very close. You must be careful not to miss the opportunity, though. Look down at the right time, and the key to opening a better life for you is honesty.'

'But you do see hope for the future?' the woman asked.

'Yes, I do.' Chrissie picked up the penny, placed it back in the customer's hand and curled her fingers around it. 'The reversal of your future starts now, but remember honesty is the key.'

The woman smiled as she stood up. 'I don't understand

what you have just said, but thank you for talking to me. I do feel a glimmer of hope now.'

When she had left, Chrissie rested her head in her hands, exhausted. That woman wasn't the only one who didn't understand what that was about – she didn't either!

Elsie came out from behind the curtain and sat at the table. 'You didn't take any money from her. Why?'

'I couldn't after telling her such a load of nonsense. It was all she had.' Chrissie shook her head wearily. 'I can't do this again; I'm worn out.' A tear trickled down her cheek and she wiped it away quickly. She never cried, and to do so now when there wasn't any reason was just stupid.

'You've drained yourself, that's all, my dear. The same thing happens to me after a day of trying to lift hopes for those in need. You've done an excellent job, but the amount of people coming has been too much for you. I'll get Sandy to limit it tomorrow. All you need now is sleep and then you'll feel better in the morning. I've listened and watched you all day, and everyone left with a smile on their faces. You may not believe it, but you have helped a lot of people today. It will be easier next time.'

She didn't see how this could get better, but she was too tired to argue.

Chapter Six

They were all so pleased with her and grateful for the success she had made of the fortune-telling that Chrissie didn't have the heart to refuse the next day. They had also given her half the money she had earned, with the rest going to help feed the animals. This was something she hadn't expected. During the night she had thought long and hard about what she was doing and seriously considered striking out on her own again. It didn't take her long to dismiss that idea, though. She had food and a roof over her head, and all the time travelling to the country – albeit a slow journey. Once well away from London and in an area she liked the look of, she would start searching for work in a big house somewhere. Everyone here was kind and she enjoyed working with the animals and anything else she was asked to do, but this wasn't the life for her. She wanted to put down roots somewhere nice, where it would be possible to make a life for herself away from the dirt and noise of London. It wasn't going to be easy, she knew that, but at least she was moving in the right direction now.

'We've got bad weather coming in.' Sandy reached out and helped her put a cover on a mare. 'We'd better do this for all of them.'

'I was going to. It's beginning to rain already and the wind is cold for early October. I doubt if we'll get many visitors today.'

'A few will come.' He gave her a sideways glance. 'You did well yesterday and Elsie was pleased. I know you only want to stay with us for a short while, but we would all be pleased if you would join us permanently. It isn't a bad life.'

She shook her head. 'I'm grateful you've let me come along, but I can't stay. Although I enjoy being with you and seeing new things every day, I want a permanent home. I need to belong somewhere. Do you understand?'

'You would belong here, but I do understand. You are welcome to stay here for as long as you wish.'

'Thanks.' She patted the horse and sighed. 'Can you finish here for me? I'll have to get the tent ready just in case anyone does come.'

'All right, and don't look so worried. You'll have an easier day today.'

She rolled her eyes and grimaced. 'I do hope so.'

The wind became so strong during the afternoon they had a job to stop the tent from blowing away. There had only been three customers all day and now the weather was so bad they had to pack away the stalls.

'All right, my dear.' Elsie came out from behind the curtain. 'Let's get out of here before it blows away. We must let the men take the tent down before it's damaged.'

Chrissie quickly packed everything in a bag and took hold of Elsie's arm. The rain was thundering down now and she was relieved when two of the men arrived to hold a rainproof sheet over them to keep the elderly woman dry as they helped her back to her home. Once inside she made Elsie comfortable by the stove and put the kettle on to make a hot cup of tea.

'As soon as I've made the tea I'll go and see if the horses are all right.'

'The men will see to them, my dear.' She smiled and patted Chrissie's arm. 'You already do more than your fair share of the work.'

'Well I promised Pa I'd earn my keep while I'm here.'

'And you are. In the short time you've been with us you have earned everyone's affection and respect.'

The caravan door opened and two men tumbled in. 'Got any more tea in that pot?' they asked, shaking the rain from their hair.

'Plenty.' Chrissie got out two more cups for Sandy and Pa. 'Sit down, you look cold. Are the animals all right?'

'They're fine. We've found them a sheltered spot by that tall hedge. 'They'll be all right there, but we'll keep an eye on them until the storm passes.'

'Call me if you need any help,' she told them.

'Thanks, but you stay here with Elsie. It could be a rough night.'

They were right, but as the night wore on she thought

rough was the wrong word. Wild was a better description. It was something she had never experienced. There had been storms in London, of course, but living in a solid brick house was very different to this. The noise of the wind and pelting rain made the little home seem flimsy as it rocked in the storm. Elsie didn't seem concerned, though, and slept peacefully through the noise. For Chrissie there was no sleep and she was relieved when dawn came and the storm had died down.

The men and youngsters were already at work when she joined them. A couple of the homes had been damaged by falling branches and the field where the horses were was a muddy mess.

'Start moving the animals,' Pa ordered. 'Put them in the corner by the homes. It's dryer there.'

As Chrissie squelched her way through the mud, three of the boys caught up with her.

'We'll have to clean their hooves and dry them off,' young Bobby told her.

That job took the four of them all morning. The horses were precious to the Travellers and their welfare was of prime concern to everyone. By the time they had finished, the animals were clean and dry, but Chrissie and the boys were filthy.

'Good job,' Sandy told them as he inspected the animals. 'They are clean, fed and happy now, which is more than I can say for you four. There's a river over there, so why don't you all go and throw yourselves in it?'

'It's only a bit of mud,' the boys declared before running off to see what else needed doing.

'Go and get cleaned up, Chrissie, and see if Elsie needs anything. We've got quite a few repairs to do so we won't be moving for a couple of days.'

It was a busy time but everyone worked together, determined to make the delay as short as possible. On the third day after the storm they were hitching up the horses when Ma came over to Chrissie.

'Someone here wants to see you.'

She glanced up from fastening the harness and recognised the woman with Ma. There was a difference in her this time. She was smiling and the look of desperation on her face had disappeared.

'I'm so pleased I caught you before you left. I had to thank you for the advice you gave me.'

Chrissie didn't know what to say. All she could remember was telling the woman a load of nonsense.

'Everything has happened just as you said it would. The day after the storm I was walking to the village when I slipped on the mud and grabbed hold of a tree to stop myself falling. When I looked down there was something shining at my feet and when I picked it up I saw that it was a beautiful pearl necklace with a diamond clasp. My first thought was that such a find would ease my situation, but then I remembered what you said about honesty, so I took it to the local policeman. He came to see me the next day and said it had been returned to the lady who had lost it and she wanted to see me. They live in a mansion the other side of the river and she told me it was a family heirloom.' The woman beamed and caught hold of Chrissie's hands. 'They needed a housekeeper and because I had been honest and not kept the jewel for myself they offered me the job. So you see, if I hadn't returned the necklace I wouldn't have been offered the post. I can't thank you enough. You wouldn't take any money off me, but I want you to have this now.'

Chrissie looked at the sixpence in her hand and gave it back. 'I didn't feel it was right to take your money when you came to me, and I still don't want it. I am pleased everything has worked out for you, and thank you for taking the time to come and tell me. That is payment enough.'

'Well, if you're sure, but would you mind if I gave it as a small gift for the babies in your group? Perhaps it would buy a couple of toys for them.'

'I'm sure that would be appreciated.'

The woman handed the money to Ma and then turned back to Chrissie. 'Thank you again, and God bless you. I hope your life will be a happy one. You deserve it.'

'Thank you.' Chrissie really didn't know what else to say, and she watched the woman walk away quite embarrassed by the praise.

'That was nice of her to come and tell you,' Ma declared. 'Elsie said you had the gift and that proves it.'

'Of course I don't. Finding that necklace was just luck, and because it turned out well she believed I had foretold it. She made the nonsense I told her fit the situation, that's all.'

'Perhaps,' Ma said. 'One thing is for sure, though, you have made that woman very happy and you must tell Elsie. It will brighten her day to know someone came back to thank you.'

'Come on you two, stop gassing. We need to get on the

road as soon as possible while the weather holds,' Pa told them. 'What did that woman want?'

'She came back to thank Chrissie for helping her.'

'Ah, that's good,' was all he said as he strode away to urge everyone else to get moving.

In less than an hour they were on their way. Chrissie was competent enough now to drive without supervision, and Elsie came to sit beside her. 'It's good to be on the move again, my dear.'

She glanced at the elderly woman she had become very fond of. 'You don't like staying in one place, do you?'

'No, I was born to this life and I love it. There is always something interesting to see, new people to meet and a beautiful view around each corner. I would hate to live in a house and not be able to hitch it to a horse and take to the road, but I know this life is not for you.'

Chrissie nodded her head in agreement. 'I want somewhere to put down roots.'

'It's there ready and waiting for you. You are definitely heading in the right direction.'

'I'm pleased to hear that.' She laughed. 'And that reminds me, Ma told me to tell you something.' She then explained about the woman who had thanked her, making a joke about the coincidence.

'She must have been very pleased to take the trouble to come back, but even after that you still don't believe, do you?'

'I believe you taught me well, and as long as you don't make anyone unhappy then it's just a game.'

'If that's the way you like to view it, then that's all right.'

Elsie patted her hand. 'Next time we stop, try including the crystal ball more often in your game.'

'You still haven't told me how you made that picture appear, and I feel silly gazing into a piece of glass.'

'Crystal, dear,' Elsie reprimanded gently, 'and it's no trick, but I don't think I'll ever convince you of that.'

'I doubt it. My dad was a good rag-and-bone man, laughing and joking with everyone on his round, and now I know where he got that flair for showmanship from.'

'You miss him,' Elsie remarked softly.

'Yes, him and Mum and Bessie. I always will, but they are gone and I can't live in the past. I have to make a new life for myself. I'll admit it's hard without them, but I'm determined to try. I don't want to look back in a few years' time and regret not trying to fulfil my dream of living in the country.'

'Well, in that case you are doing the right thing. The journey ahead will have many ups and downs for you, but at least you are following your heart's desire. You mentioned Bessie. Who is that?'

'Our horse. I gave her and the business to a neighbour. He'll take good care of her.' Chrissie's eyes clouded over for a moment as the pain of loss swamped her again, but she fought back the tears. There was a new life ahead of her, and it would be what she made of it.

'Well, by summer you'll have another horse in your life to love.'

The pain and grief faded to be replaced by amusement, as she remembered what Elsie had told her. 'Ah, yes, big and black with a sense of devilment.'

'That's right, and when he appears you try to let me know. You have a record of our proposed route.'

'I'll do that, but you'll be waiting for a very long time,' she teased.

'We'll see.' Elsie got to her feet. 'This is a nice smooth stretch of road so I'll make us a cup of tea, then I'll read your tea leaves.'

Chapter Seven

Spring was nearly here at last, and Chrissie wandered along a narrow country road marvelling at the sight of snowdrops and wild flowers growing along the verges. The hedgerow was bursting forth in a myriad of colours, and birds were singing in celebration, it seemed to her. She had never seen such beauty and the slow journey with the Travellers had been worth it. After her father had died she had expected to spend a lonely Christmas, but it had been just the opposite, and she'd thoroughly enjoyed herself. The frequent stops, however, had been frustrating and a couple of times they had been delayed by snow. The group seemed to take it all in their stride, but she wanted to move on, longing to get as far away from London as possible before she left them. When they reached the New Forest she hadn't been able to believe her eyes. There were so many trees all growing wild, and how the others had laughed as she'd darted in and out of them, touching as many as she could. They had been ready to burst forth into leaf and she could only imagine what a glorious sight it would be in the summer. They had only moved on about three miles since then, and the feeling had grown inside her that this was the place to settle down. What she needed was to find a job of some sort, and she didn't care what it was as long as it wasn't fortune-telling!

She laughed out loud. What a game that had been. She had quickly realised that most of the people who came to the tent were only doing it for a bit of fun, and didn't believe a word they were told. That made it easier for her, and she was very careful what she said to anyone who showed they believed it. Elsie had soon stopped coming to the tent and that meant she didn't have to take it seriously, but was careful not to make too much fun of it in front of the elderly woman. Elsie was so kind, and she wouldn't do anything to hurt her.

Something caught her attention and she climbed up a small bank to look over the hedge. 'Hello,' she said softly. 'Isn't it a lovely day?'

A startled rabbit stared up at her for a frozen moment, and then took off as fast as it could.

'Don't run away!' she called. 'I won't hurt you. Isn't the country a wondrous place?' But it was gone.

She shaded her eyes to see what was on the other side of this field. Horses, and that meant there must be a house somewhere nearby.

It took her less than half an hour to find the gates, and at the end of a long treelined road she could just see a house, and her heart soared at the sight. What a wonderful place to live, surrounded by such beauty. The gates were locked and she searched for a way in. There was a door in the wall a few feet along, and much to her delight it swung open when she turned the handle. There didn't appear to be anyone around to stop her so she walked up the road, her head tipped back to gaze at the huge oak trees, their branches reaching across to touch those on the other side. When the house was in full view she stopped and gasped in wonder. It was enormous and breathtakingly beautiful, and she couldn't even imagine what it must be like inside. It would be a pleasure to scrub floors here.

The servants' entrance was always round the back and she made her way there, only to be distracted by a paddock with four of the most magnificent horses she had ever seen. This day was full of wonders!

'What are you doing here, miss?'

Chrissie spun round to face the man who had come up behind her. 'I'm looking for work, sir, and was on my way to the servants' entrance when I saw these beautiful horses. Aren't they big? I've never seen anything like them before.'

'They are destriers – warhorses. We breed them for the cavalry.'

She sighed. 'It's sad they have to go in to danger.'

One of them began to come towards them and she held out her hand. 'I wish I had a carrot for him.'

The man caught her arm and pulled her away from the fence. 'Careful. They aren't pets. They are born to fight and will bite if you get too close.'

'They won't hurt me.' She stopped suddenly, remembering she was here to apply for work as a servant. 'I do beg your pardon, sir. I should not have spoken to you like that. I meant no disrespect.'

'I was not offended.' He smiled then. 'Most people are afraid of them, but you are obviously not. Are you used to being around horses?'

'Only workhorses, sir. I've never seen the likes of these, and I can't believe they are dangerous.' She pointed to the chestnut-coloured animal. 'He's very calm, and if you look closely in his eyes there is sadness there.'

He looked surprised and studied her intently for a moment. 'That is one of the master's favourite destriers and I don't think he's sad, he's just wondering what mischief he can get up to.'

Without thinking she stepped forward and began speaking softly. 'You're a very beautiful animal and I'm sure you don't want to hurt me. I don't know why there is a hint of sadness in your eyes, but come closer and show me how friendly you can be.'

The animal lowered his head and she reached up to kiss his nose. Hearing a sharp intake of breath she turned and smiled. 'He's happier now.'

'How on earth did you do that?' He was shaking his head in bewilderment. 'You had better come away before you try to do that to one in a bad mood. You said you were looking for work. What kind?'

'Anything, sir. I'll do anything and I'm a hard worker.'

'Come with me and I'll take you to see if any jobs are available.'

'Thank you, sir. Er . . . I thought you were the owner.'

'I'm Carstairs, the estate manager. What's your name?'

'Christine Banner – Chrissie.'

'Right, Chrissie, let's see if we can get you a job.'

They walked in to a huge kitchen full of the mouth-watering smell of food being prepared and it made her realise just how hungry she was.

'What have you got there, Mr Carstairs?' the cook asked, smiling at Chrissie.

'I found her petting the horses,' he replied dryly.

'I saw her!' A young boy was jumping up and down in glee. 'She kissed Red and he didn't bite her head off. How'd she do that, Mr Carstairs? He won't let me near him.'

'It was lucky she caught him on a good day,' he replied with laughter in his voice.

'Nah, he don't have good days. He thinks it's fun to push you around, but he don't realise how big he is.'

The estate manager chuckled under his breath at the boy's remarks. 'Don't you go trying it, Sid.'

'Not likely. I ain't daft.'

'Ah, here's the housekeeper, Mrs Baxter.' He pulled Chrissie forward. 'This girl is looking for work.'

'We have a full staff at the moment. I can't offer you anything.'

'I'm sorry to hear that, cos it's lovely here.' She found it hard to mask her disappointment. When she had walked up the treelined entrance she had fallen in love with the place, feeling deep inside that this was what she had been looking for, and when she'd seen the horses had known it was more than she could have ever dreamt of. Her dad had drummed into her that she must be polite at all times, no matter how she was feeling, so she smiled. 'Thank you for seeing me, Mrs Baxter, and you, Mr Carstairs. You've been very kind.' She went to walk out of the kitchen when the estate manager caught her arm.

'Don't give up yet. I said I'll take you to see Lord Frenshaw. He might be able to find you something as long as you don't mind what you do.'

Her face lit up. 'Do you think he would? I'll do anything.'

'I'm not making any promises, but we can try. Come with me.'

He took her through a magnificent hallway and rapped on a door, opened it and ushered her inside. The room was large and the walls were lined with shelves holding books of all shapes and sizes. The carpet under her feet was soft and matched the green leather of the chairs. She turned slowly, gazing at everything in wonder. There was a lovely smell of leather and books and the colours in the room gave it a restful atmosphere. How beautiful, she thought. It was a world apart from the dirt and grime of where she had lived.

'And who is this, George?'

The man's voice snapped her back from her inspection of the room and she remembered her manners. The man studying her intently was elderly, but not as old as Elsie, and he was tall and upright. He still had a full head of hair but it was sprinkled with grey, as was the neat moustache. Apart from that he was clean-shaven.

'This is Christine Banner, your lordship. She's looking for work and I thought you might be interested in seeing her.'

Chrissie curtsied as elegantly as possible, hoping this was the right thing to do. She'd never met a lord before.

'And why do you think I would like to see her? Mrs Baxter does the hiring.'

Her heart plummeted again.

'The housekeeper doesn't need new staff at the moment. I found her looking at the horses in the paddock, and not only did Red come over to her, he even allowed her to touch him and kiss his nose. She told me she is used to horses and appears to have a nice way with them – something they respond to. We could use a stable lad, your lordship, especially one who isn't afraid of the warhorses.'

'Highly irregular to have a female stable lad.' His lordship pursed his lips. 'What made you foolhardy enough to pet Red Sunset, young lady?'

'He looked sad, sir.'

'Very perceptive of you – we are all sad, but that animal doesn't understand why he's been abandoned by his master.' He paused and gazed out of the window and sighed, then turned back to face her. 'Tell me about yourself.'

'I was born and bred in London.' She then told him what had happened after her dad had died. There was no point hiding anything, including the episode at her last job, because if he contacted them they certainly wouldn't recommend he employ her.

'Hitting the master's son was not a wise thing to do.'

'He was the worse for drink and he hit me first, so I hit him back, sir—your lordship,' she corrected.

'I see.' His mouth twitched as he tried to control a smile

of amusement. 'So you decided to leave London. How did you get here?'

She then explained about joining up with the Romany Travellers.

'You don't want to stay with them?'

'No, your lordship. Although my dad came from a Romany family my mum didn't, and travelling all the time is not for me. I want a permanent home.'

'You are part-Romany, then?'

She nodded. 'They treated me like one of their own, but I don't want that kind of life.'

'I assume you have had to work while you are with them. What do you do?'

'Anything that's needed: looking after the horses, cleaning, chopping wood and driving an elderly woman's home . . .' she tailed off.

'And?' he prompted.

She took a deep breath and blurted out, 'Fortune-telling, but it was only in fun, your lordship. They said I couldn't travel with them unless I did that as well as the other jobs.'

'Fortune . . .' He glanced quickly at his estate manager who was having great difficulty controlling himself, and then asked, 'Were you any good at it?'

'They said I was, but I think they were just being kind.' She shrugged and grinned. 'I never could get the hang of the crystal ball, though.'

That was too much for the men and they roared with laughter. When his lordship had controlled his mirth he turned to the estate manager. 'Do you think she will fit in as a stable lad?'

'I'm sure she would, and from what we've heard she is quite capable of looking after herself.'

His lordship chuckled as he recalled her story about the trouble she'd had at the London house. 'Quite. I don't think I would like to get in a fight with her.'

Chrissie listened with mounting hope. 'I'd love to work with the horses, if you'll give me the chance. I won't let you down, sir—your lordship.'

'Very well. I think you deserve a chance. When can you start?'

'Today.' She beamed at both men. 'I just need to collect my things and say goodbye to everyone.'

He nodded. 'Go with Carstairs and he will take you to the head groom who will explain your duties. On second thoughts, I'll come with you. I must see his face, George, when you give him a girl as a stable lad.'

The head groom could not hide his disbelief when he was presented with a girl as a stable lad. He looked from the estate manager to the master, and blurted out, 'But what am I going to do with her? She can't bunk in with the other hands, and if she has a room in the house I can't go running there in the middle of the night if help is needed.'

The man was horrified and Chrissie knew she had to find a solution quickly. She looked up and saw a trapdoor in the roof of the barn. 'I could sleep up there on a nice bed of straw. It would be warm and comfortable.'

'She can't sleep up there! It wouldn't be safe for a young girl.'

Seeing the man wasn't going to give in easily she went

over and shook the ladder. It was loose. 'I'll be quite safe. Once I'm up there I can pull the ladder up, and if you put a bell at the bottom you can ring it if you need me.'

His lordship still hadn't said anything, but it was clear he was enjoying this.

'Well, I suppose that would work,' the head groom admitted reluctantly. 'But a girl still can't be a stable lad. There's a lot of dirty jobs and mucking out to do and her skirts will be dragging in the muck all the time.'

'Oh, that's easy,' she declared. 'I'll wear breeches like everyone else.'

'There you are, then, that's settled, and you have your new hand,' his lordship said, somehow managing to keep a straight face as he turned to his estate manager. 'George, see the loft is made into a safe, habitable place for Miss Banner, and ask the housekeeper to provide suitable bedding. I don't know what we can do about the breeches, though.'

'That's all right, your lordship.' She grinned, so happy they were giving her a chance. 'I've already got some when I needed to ride bareback with the Travellers.'

'Splendid. That's all problems taken care of.' His lordship turned away and as he made his way back to the house they could hear him laughing.

The head groom was shaking his head and looking bewildered. 'I don't know what the other hands will say about this. But I tell you one thing, Mr Carstairs, that's the first time his lordship has laughed for quite a while.'

'Yes, it's good to hear.' He smiled at Chrissie. 'Go and collect your things and come straight back, and then I'll introduce you to the other hands. We'll see to everything while you're gone. How long will it take you to say goodbye and get back here?'

'Two hours, maybe less.'

'That will be fine. Off you go.'

Chapter Eight

She was so excited she ran all the way back to the camp, but was quite aware how hard it was going to be to say goodbye to everyone. They had been very kind and she was grateful to them, but she didn't belong with them, and she'd told them from the start that her stay would only be temporary. She couldn't believe she had got the job, and had taken an instant liking to his lordship. The moment she had seen the place and the magnificent horses she had known that was where she wanted to be, and to work with the animals was the best job they could have offered her. It would be much better than being at the beck and call of everyone in the house and scrubbing floors. Mucking-out stables was much more appealing to her. Perhaps if she worked hard they would let her ride one of the beautiful animals one day. Her mind was racing with wonderful possibilities, and any spare time she had, there were miles and miles of lovely countryside to explore. The forest wasn't far away, either, and she would be able to see it when the trees were in full leaf. Bursting to tell everyone her good news she ran full pelt into the camp.

'Careful!' Ma said when Chrissie nearly crashed in to her. 'What's the rush?'

'I've got a job!' She stopped and took a deep breath after running so far. 'I can start straight away and must tell Elsie before I say goodbye to everyone else.'

'Ah, I'm pleased for you, but we will miss you. I'll get everyone together, shall I?'

'Yes, please.'

Elsie already had a pot of tea made when she arrived, and smiled at the excited girl who tumbled into her home. 'So, you're leaving us.'

Chrissie nodded. 'There's a big house not far from here owned by Lord Frenshaw and he's such a nice gentleman. They breed warhorses for the cavalry and I've got a job in the stables. They are beautiful animals, but the one I made friends with is a bright chestnut colour, not dark and handsome,' she teased. 'In fact, I didn't see a black horse there.'

The elderly woman laughed but said nothing.

Hearing the familiar laugh, a worry crossed her mind. 'I've become very fond of you, Elsie, and I'm wondering who will look after you now.'

'Don't you fret. It has already been arranged while you were out this morning. There are plenty of willing hands and we are family. No one here is ever left to cope for themselves.'

She frowned. 'I've only just got the job, so how did you know I would be leaving today?'

'I knew days ago that we were approaching the place where you would leave us.'

'Did you see it in your crystal ball?'

'No, I saw it in your eyes as you studied this area, and change is written in your hand. After all you've done over the last months you still don't believe, do you?'

Chrissie grinned and shook her head. 'Though I did come to quite enjoy the game and see the customers enjoy the experience, even if it was just for fun.'

'Although you believe it's all nonsense I want to give you a gift.'

'Oh, I don't want anything. You have already given me so much. You took me in when I had nowhere to go, and have been like a mother to me.'

'That's kind of you, my dear, but I think grandmother would be a better description.' She picked up a brightly coloured wooden box and held it out. 'It would make me very happy if you would accept this with my blessing for a happy future. It was my grandmother's and she would be pleased to know you have it.'

Whatever was in the box belonged to Elsie's family, and that made her hesitate to accept such a precious item. 'It must mean a lot to you. Are you sure you want to give it to me?'

'Positive. If I told you my grandmother said it belonged with you, would you believe me?'

'You know I wouldn't.'

'Well then, *I* believe it belongs with you.' She placed the box in Chrissie's hands. 'Your time here has been a blessing to all of us.'

Knowing it would hurt Elsie if she refused, she took the box. 'I will treasure it and it will be a reminder of the happy times we have spent together. Can I look inside?'

'Not now. Look at it before you settle down to sleep tonight.' She glanced outside. 'Everyone is gathered to wish you well.'

She had known leaving them wasn't going to be easy, but it turned out to be harder than she had imagined. They considered her to be one of them now and were reluctant to see her go, and by the time she had spoken to everyone she had an armful of gifts. A lucky horseshoe from the young boys she had helped with the animals, a colourful scarf from Ma and Pa, a small embroidered tablecloth and practical things from the others, like pegs to hang out her washing and a basket to put everything in. She was quite overwhelmed by their kindness and obvious affection for her, and she felt the same about every one of them. Her words of gratitude for all they had done for her seemed so inadequate, and for the first time in her life she was lost for words.

Pa smiled as she stumbled over what to say and bent to kiss her cheek. 'You know where we're travelling, Chrissie, so if you need any help you come and find us. We always look after family.'

To hear they now considered her to be family was nearly too much and she fought back tears as doubts rushed in. Was she making a mistake leaving them? She was safe here, had plenty of food, good friends, plenty to keep her busy and new places to see. But it wasn't what she had planned for herself. When she had joined them she hadn't anticipated becoming this fond of everyone and this was the reason for her doubts, she realised.

Elsie clasped her hand and nodded as if reading her mind. 'This is what you have set out to do, my dear, and I know it is something you must do, and remember to keep a watch out for the black horse because that is important. It could bring your destiny with it.'

The doubts melted away and she laughed. 'Once I'm settled in I'll search the stables for him.'

'He isn't there yet.' She patted the hand she was still holding. 'He's on his way, though, and will need your love.'

'Oh, Elsie, I'm going to miss you.' She gazed at the people surrounding her. 'I'll miss you all.'

'There will always be a place for you with us if things don't work out,' Ma told her, and all the others nodded in agreement.

'Thank you, that's comforting to know. I'll always remember my time with you as something special. Now I must go. They are waiting for the new stable lad.'

Before leaving the camp she changed into breeches and rolled her hair up under a cap, packed her belongings and set off for her new life. Excitement was tempered with apprehension and one thought was uppermost in her mind: if she was making a mistake there would be somewhere to go this time. They would be moving off today, but they travelled slowly so it should be possible to catch up with them, or wait for their return journey.

The moment the house came into view she stopped and

gazed at it for a while. It was so beautiful here and she sincerely hoped it would turn out to be the fulfilment of her dream of life in the country. It had to work. She would make it work. There couldn't be a better place to put down roots than here, surely?

The head groom nodded approval when he saw she was sensibly dressed for the work needed, and after one of the boys put her things in the loft, he put her straight to work mucking out the stables. She set to it with a smile on her face. They had given her a job with the horses and what more could she want?

She could feel that all the other stable hands were doubtful about her, but during the afternoon, as she joked with them and did as much, and even more than them, they began to act more friendly around her. It was clear they had been worried she wouldn't do her share of the work and they'd have extra to do. That fear was soon dealt with and the evening meal was a relaxed affair. By the time she climbed the ladder to the loft she was happy the way things had gone, and when she saw what they had done to the loft she couldn't believe her eyes. Instead of a pile of straw to sleep on there was a bed with clean sheets and blankets, a colourful rug covered the rough floorboards and there was even a small table and comfortable chair. For light there was a lantern for safety with a candle inside. All the items would have squeezed through the trapdoor except the bed; that must have been made up here, she realised. A lot of trouble had been taken to make a comfortable room for her, and she was determined to thank everyone in the morning, especially his lordship for there was no doubt in her mind that he had ordered this to be done for her.

She sat in the chair with a contented sigh and began looking at the gifts the Travellers had given her. There was already a nail sticking out over the bed and the lucky horseshoe went there perfectly, and the cloth looked nice on the table. The last item was Elsie's gift and she gasped in astonishment when she opened the box. 'Oh, Elsie, you shouldn't have parted with this,' she exclaimed. 'It must be very precious to you.' Tears filled her eyes. 'I know now why you told me not to look at it until tonight, because you knew I would have insisted that you took it back. You are travelling now and I have no choice but to keep it.'

Reaching in the box she carefully removed the contents and placed it on the table, then brought the lantern close, making the light sparkle from it. This wasn't the one she had used in the tent; this was clearly special and must be valuable. What a gift! But why had Elsie given her such a thing of beauty, especially as she had made no secret of the fact that she didn't believe in fortune-telling? She had to admit, though, that some strange things had happened while she had been masquerading as a fortune-teller.

Unable to resist she ran her hands over it and bent to kiss it. 'Thank you, Elsie, I'll keep it safe.'

The crystal ball seemed filled with stars of light as if pleased by her acceptance.

Chapter Nine

'How much longer are you going to keep me from my inheritance?' Edward Danton glared at his uncle, exasperated.

'You cannot lay claim to the estate until it is proven that Harry is dead. That is stated clearly enough in his will, as you well know. Until I have irrefutable proof that he is not returning I will continue to see that the stud farm is run as it should be.'

'But it is over a year since the Crimean War ended. If Harry had, by some miracle, survived the Battle of Balaclava and the massacre of the Light Brigade, he would have been back by now. He's dead, Uncle, and it's time you faced that fact!'

Lord Frenshaw rose to his feet. 'I have told you time and time again I will not accept that without proof. The only report I have received is that he is missing – no body has been found.'

Edward thumped the desk. 'Is that surprising? Can't you imagine the chaos there must have been out there?'

Charles Frenshaw would not let his nephew see the pain his remarks had caused him. He deeply regretted that this was the only family heir – the only child of his sister. She had been a fine woman but had always indulged her son. If he wanted anything she made sure he received it. He had always coveted this estate, and that brought out the selfish streak in him. He knew, of course, that he couldn't keep waiting for his son to return and would soon have to hand everything over to his nephew. That worried him because among Edward's many faults he was known to be an addicted gambler, and the longer he could keep this place out of his hands the better. He would continue to remain stubborn.

'I'll hold the reins efficiently, as my son wanted, until such time as we receive official news.'

Edward snorted in derision. 'I would hardly call engaging a girl as a stable lad efficient. It is not seemly to have her walking around the place wearing breeches, of all things. And have you seen her riding those beasts bareback? Whatever possessed you to do such a thing? You couldn't have been thinking straight.'

That was too much. 'Are you accusing me of not being in full command of my senses?'

Edward took a step back when confronted with his uncle's fury. He was still an impressive man. 'It was perhaps a moment of hasty decision on your part, that's all I'm saying.'

Charles drew in a deep breath as an idea came to him. It was no good losing his temper, as he knew from experience with his nephew, so he spoke softly now. 'Let me tell you something about that girl. She comes from the slums of London and when her father died she was thrown out of her home by a greedy landlord. She was determined to get out of London and that journey has not been without hardships, but she has strength of character and did not allow anything to deter her from realising her dream of coming to the country. She works hard, taking on more than her fair share of the tasks and has gained everyone's respect – including mine.'

'That may be so, but she's still a girl doing a man's work,' Edward protested.

It was no good trying to explain anything to this boy; he only had thoughts for himself and what he wanted. He picked up the bell from the desk and rang it. The butler appeared immediately. 'Ah, Dobson, would you send someone for Banner and tell her I'd like to see her?'

'At once, your lordship.'

'What are you up to, Uncle? I know that look on your face. It's the same one Harry always had when he was up to no good.'

'Wait and see. There might be a way to settle our argument.'

In less than ten minutes Chrissie arrived, slightly out of breath from running and wiping her hands on her breeches to clean them a little. 'You wanted me, your lordship?'

'Yes, my nephew and I have a disagreement and I wondered if you could help settle it for us?'

'Me?' She frowned, puzzled by the strange request.

'Yes, I'd like you to do a reading for us.'

That rocked her back on her heels and she opened her mouth to refuse when she saw him give her a sly wink. Ah, so he was playing some game, but what was he up to? Well, he'd been good to her, so she would go along with this and hope she said the right things. If this was a game, then she would play it with a flourish. 'I would be happy to, if that is your wish, your lordship. Would you give me a moment to get something from my room?'

'Of course, and thank you.'

Chrissie ran full pelt for the barn and scrambled up the ladder to her room, her mind racing. What did his lordship want her to do? He knew she couldn't really read fortunes and yet he was asking her to do just that to settle an argument with the other gentleman. How could she when she didn't have any idea what this was all about? Taking a deep breath she told herself to calm down and hope he'd give her some clue along the way. Elsie had taught her well and she must use that knowledge she had been given. After all, she managed as a fortune-teller on the journey here, and she could do it again as it was probably important to his lordship. Suddenly she saw the humour in this situation and grinned, feeling relaxed now.

Carefully holding the precious box and a bright cloth she made her way back to the library. The other man was staring out of the window and she could tell by the way he was holding himself that he was angry. His lordship, on the other hand, appeared quite at ease.

'May I use that small table?' she asked.

'Of course.' He removed a pile of books and watched with interest as Chrissie covered it with the cloth and removed the crystal ball from the box.

She glanced up at him and he gave an almost imperceptible nod of approval, and that was a good start. Once everything was ready she asked, 'Would you both sit opposite me, please?'

'This is preposterous!' the other man declared, remaining where he was.

'If you want this argument settled, then you will go along with this. And don't pretend outrage because I know you have been to a seance more than once.'

Making no further argument he sat down, and Chrissie watched the movements and expressions carefully. That remark about the seance was interesting. They were both looking for answers to something – but what?

'Give me your hands, please.' She examined the lines on both but said nothing, trying to clear her mind as she had been taught and allow thoughts to flow in freely. For some reason she turned away from the other man quickly, spending more time on his lordship's hand. She could read the lines, but that wasn't what these men were looking for. Turning her attention to the crystal ball she concentrated on its depths.

'What do you see, Chrissie?' his lordship asked softly.

Suddenly Elsie's words came into her head. If that horse was coming to her, then it was coming here. It was nonsense, of course, but that was the only thing in her head. 'There's a big horse, black, and he's coming this way.'

A sharp intake of breath came from his lordship. 'Who is riding him?'

'A soldier – and they've been travelling for a long time.' Why on earth did she add that last bit?

Lord Frenshaw reached across the table and caught hold of her hand. 'How far away is he?'

'Nearly here – a week, maybe. I can't be precise.' She had made that prediction without thinking. 'That's all I can see. I'm sorry I couldn't help you.'

'But you did, Chrissie. You have just given me the news I have prayed for over these long months.'

'I did?'

'Yes, my son is alive and nearly home!' He turned to the other man. 'You have your answer. Harry is alive, as I've always believed.'

'Really, Uncle, I grant you she put on a good show, but you don't really believe what she said, surely? Even supposing some of what she told us happens to be true, that military man could be someone coming to tell you, officially, that he died in the Crimea.'

His lordship was shaking his head. 'It's Harry and he's riding Midnight. Now you can stop pestering me!'

The nephew glared at Chrissie, and pushing the chair back stood up and stormed out of the room, and she knew she had made an enemy. He would have to be watched because there was something about him that made her uneasy.

His lordship came and sat beside her. 'I thought you told me you couldn't use that crystal ball or tell fortunes.'

'I can't. If you had told me why you wanted me to do this I would have played the game better. I didn't know your son was missing. No one has mentioned it to me.'

'He's an officer in the Light Brigade and was in that disastrous charge at Balaclava. We have not heard from him or the military and have no idea if he's alive or dead. I have been distraught by the uncertainty, and it is never mentioned here out of consideration for me. My nephew is the only heir to the property, but I have refused to hand it over to him until I receive official confirmation of Harry's death. You have just given me hope and I am very grateful.'

'I'm pleased to have helped lift your burden a little, but please don't—'

He put his hand up to stop her. 'Whatever you believe about your abilities I choose to believe what you said is true and my son is nearly home. Go to the kitchen now and Cook will make you a good strong cup of tea and we will talk again tomorrow. Bless you, my child, for what you have just done.'

Worry gnawed away at her while she packed up her things. It had started out as a game, but whatever she had said was now being believed. She respected this kind man and hoped sincerely that she hadn't added to his worry about his son.

The butler had arrived to take her to the kitchen and she followed him, pausing at the door to cast one more anxious look at Lord Frenshaw. What was going to happen when his son didn't arrive as predicted? He would be devastated, and if that other man took over then she would definitely lose her job. The thought of leaving these beautiful animals was upsetting, but the knowledge that she might have given him false hope made her feel sick. Again Elsie came to her mind when she had told her to believe that her predictions would come true, and if she believed hard enough things would work out the right way. Suddenly a sense of calm swept through her as she pictured the horse and rider coming this way. Close – so close – arriving in less than a week.

'His lordship said Chrissie must have a strong cup of tea,' Dobson told the cook when they reached the kitchen. 'I'll have one as well.'

Cook ordered one of the maids to make the tea and hurried over to Chrissie. 'Do sit down, my dear, you look so pale. Are you unwell?'

Chrissie shook her head and sat down, not wanting to talk.

Cook glanced at the butler. 'What's happened?'

'I don't know, but his lordship was looking very happy and it has wiped ten years off him.'

'Well, there's only one thing that would do that.' Cook studied Chrissie with interest.

The back door burst open and the head groom rushed in. 'There's a chance Master Harry will be home within the week. His lordship is rushing around to make sure everything is in perfect order.'

'Oh, dear God, what have I done? Please help!' Chrissie groaned in despair. *He really believes what I told him. Please – please bring him home quickly. I never wanted to do that – I never wanted to hurt anyone. It was just supposed to be a game.*

The excited chatter in the kitchen was deafening and she quickly finished her tea and stood up. She had to get out of here and nearly bumped in to one of the stable hands who had also come in.

'Red's playing up something terrible,' he told the head groom. 'We can't calm him down and he'll hurt himself if he doesn't stop.'

The attention turned to Chrissie but she was already running. The thumping could clearly be heard and she hurtled in, dumping her things by the ladder and running to Red's stall, shouting, 'Stop that, Red! I'm coming.'

When she entered the stall she had to dodge the flaying hooves to get to him, and reaching out she wrapped her arms around his neck, speaking softly. 'What's the matter, my lovely boy? You tell me all about it.'

It was quite a tussle, but he eventually quietened as he listened to her soft voice, although he was still tense.

'Well done,' the head groom told her. 'Are you hurt at all?'

'No, he wouldn't harm me. He needs to be in the paddock so he can run off what is troubling him.'

'We've been trying to do that, but he wouldn't let us move him.'

The animal allowed her to lead him out, and once in the field he began to gallop round, kicking his legs. Eventually he ran over to her, snorting and his sides heaving. When she asked him if his tantrum was now over he shoved her so hard she nearly lost her balance.

Laughing, she turned to the head groom. 'He's all right now.'

'That's a relief. Perhaps he knows his master is nearly home.'

In the struggle to calm down Red she had quite forgotten about that and it felt as if a bucket of ice-cold water had just been thrown over her. The next few days were going to be a nightmare for her.

And it didn't help when a couple of days later the nephew came up to her, gloating that he would soon be in charge now, and his first task would be to dismiss her.

Chapter Ten

'How is Red Sunset now?'

Chrissie spun round to face Lord Frenshaw. She had seen him the day after that disastrous game with his nephew, and she had tried to convince him that although what she had said appeared to fit his son, it was merely a coincidence, but to no avail. He was still convinced his son was on his way home. She turned her thoughts back to the horse and answered the question. 'He's all right as long as he's in the field. He complains when we bring him in, though.'

'Hmm. Perhaps he needs a mate?'

'Maybe. We've checked him over carefully and can't find anything wrong with him.'

He looked at her intently. 'Are you all right?'

'No, I'm not,' she answered without hesitation. 'I'm going to lose my job, and I don't want to leave here.'

'Why do you think you are going to lose your job?' He frowned at the puzzling remark. 'I am the only person who can do that, and I haven't any reason to take such action. You work hard and have earned the respect of the other hands.'

'When your son doesn't come home in the next few days you will be angry and tell me to leave.'

'I most certainly will not! You have made it quite clear that you don't believe you can tell fortunes, but there is no mistaking that what you said was uncannily accurate and it has given me hope.' He studied her unhappy expression and something dawned on him. 'Has my nephew been threatening you?'

She nodded miserably. 'He came by yesterday when you were away from the house and told me that as soon as he takes over I will have to leave. And he said that thanks to my reading it will be very soon, because you will have to hand over the estate now without delay.'

'I'll deal with him!' He turned to walk away and then spun back to face her. 'Your job here is secure for as long as you want. What you did was at my bidding. I was tired of his continual pressure to hand the estate over to him, and although you had no idea why I made such a strange request, you did a remarkably good job. It will keep him away from me for a while and give me time to see that he never becomes master here. When my son comes home he will deal with this.'

'But, your lordship—'

He held up his hand to stop her. 'I know how you feel about this, Chrissie, and I apologise for causing you so much worry. However, be assured that whatever the outcome you will not be dismissed while I have any say in the matter. You have my word.'

The relief was immense as she watched him walk away and it felt as if a great weight had been lifted from her. He was a strong, determined man, and would not give up easily. He also knew that the chance of his son arriving soon was doubtful, but to hold on to the belief that he was returning had given him some comfort – short as it may be.

The spring was back in her step and she set to work mucking out the stalls with a smile on her face.

Charles returned immediately to the library and began to compose a legal document. He sent for his lawyer and by the time it was finished he had arrived, and it was then duly signed and witnessed.

'I'm not sure you would win if your nephew contests this,' the lawyer told him. 'You could end up with a long battle ahead of you.'

'I am aware of that, but it would at least delay his claim to take over. It needed to be done while I am still legally in charge of this estate according to my son's will. If he should be declared dead, then I will have little choice in the matter, but I will delay as long as possible.'

'You understand that if your son does return, then this document will be useless.'

'When that happens I shall have great pleasure setting fire to it, but in the meantime my concern is to protect this estate and its workers. Since the unfortunate death of my eldest nephew, who was Harry's stated heir, that has placed

Edward in line to inherit and he is determined to do so.'

'That was your eldest brother's son?'

'Yes, and unfortunately both died in a carriage accident a year ago. My son doesn't know that, so is unaware that Edward is now in line to inherit.'

'You obviously don't trust this nephew.'

'I happen to know he has huge gambling debts, although he thinks no one is aware of that, and my fear is that if he gets his hands on this estate he will sell it to pay off those debts. I can't let that happen.'

The lawyer nodded in understanding. 'I can see your dilemma. If you get any trouble, then call me. We could probably string this out for some time.'

'That's what I wanted to hear.' Charles smiled then, feeling much relieved. 'I've managed to shut him up for a while. Thank you for coming so quickly.'

When the lawyer left Charles put the document in a safe place, quite aware that this was a desperate act on his part, but hopefully it would cause a delay in Edward making a claim to the estate. All he needed now was Harry to return. Where are you, son? he murmured to himself. We need you.

After her talk with Lord Frenshaw, Chrissie was much happier, and as she cared for the animals she adored, the days slipped by. There hadn't been a sign of the other man and everyone seemed pleased about that. When she mentioned this to one of the hands he told her the nephew was not liked and didn't have the first idea about caring for such strong, unpredictable animals. 'They need a strong hand with love behind it, and that's where you excel. You have earned their respect. We've never seen anyone ride them bareback before, and they don't even try to toss you off.' He laughed.

She grinned. 'I think they are awfully tempted, though.'

Two weeks went by and Chrissie was completely happy to see his lordship was still smiling, and that assured her she hadn't done any harm. She would have been dismayed if she had caused him more distress. With his son missing he must be suffering enough.

'Chrissie!' the head groom called. 'Where are you?'

'Laying fresh straw in the mare's stall.'

His head appeared over the door. 'Leave that. The blacksmith is trying to change Red's shoes and he's having trouble with him. Go and tell the animal to behave himself, will you? You're the only one he listens to. It's no wonder the master didn't take him to join the Brigade. He can be so difficult.'

They had their own blacksmith and she hurried over to the forge to find the man standing in front of Red Sunset with his arms folded and they were glaring at each other. 'You've lost one of your damned shoes and another is loose. I've got to put new ones on for you, and you'll feel much more comfortable after that – you stubborn beast.'

'Having trouble, Bill?' she asked, holding back her amusement.

'Thank goodness you're here! Tell this cantankerous animal to behave himself. He's already tried to knock me over twice. I've told him we'll send him off to the cavalry instead of keeping him for stud, but it hasn't made any difference.'

She made the blacksmith stand away, and reaching out

she rubbed Red's nose, speaking softly. 'Now what's this all about, my beauty? You've got to let Bill work on you because if you keep throwing these tantrums they will send you off to some war and you might get killed. That would break my heart, and I know you wouldn't want to upset me, would you?'

He pushed his head into her hands and she nodded to Bill. He approached carefully and when there was no move to stop him he got on with his work while Chrissie stayed where she was.

When he'd finished he nodded with satisfaction. 'I fear he is getting worse than his half-brother, Midnight. The master was the only one who could control him, but they are probably both dead by now – more's the pity.'

'No, no.' She shook her head emphatically as denial swept through her. 'We mustn't give up hope. They are alive.'

'We all hope that is true, but it's been too long without news of any kind.' His sad smile told her he didn't hold out much hope. 'Take Red back to the paddock for me.'

She led the animal outside, and with a bunk-up from Bill, leapt on to the horse's back. He trotted happily to the paddock, and as she left him and closed the gate, there came the call, 'Rider approaching!'

This was her order to run to the front of the house and take care of the visitor's horse. When she saw the animal she was horrified. His head was drooping in exhaustion and looked as if he was unable to take another step. With her whole attention on the animal she grabbed his reins, completely ignoring the rider, so angry by what had been done to this horse. Cradling the horse's head she told him gently that he was safe now and she would look after him. Oblivious to what was going on around her she led him to the stables.

Her first task was to feed and water him just a little at a time, and then she began to brush the dust of the journey from him. It was while she was doing this she saw the scars on his body. 'Oh, you poor darling!' she cried. 'What beast has treated you so cruelly? No wonder you are in such poor condition.'

When he was clean he took another drink of water and, unable to stand any longer, he settled down on the fresh straw. Not wanting to leave him, she sat next to him, watching and ready to run for help should it be needed.

She stayed there all night, refusing to leave him, and by dawn he was on his feet again, his head up and looking round with interest. 'Feeling better now, are we?' she asked him as she set out his feed. 'You eat up and get your strength back. I'll see what I can do to get you away from your cruel master.'

'And how do you intend to do that?'

She spun round and had to look up at the tall man who had just walked in.

'No animal should be treated like this,' she said defiantly, unable to hold back her anger.

He was staring at her, his pale-grey eyes raking over her as if he couldn't believe what he was seeing. In one swift movement he swept the cap from her head and watched in disbelief as her dark hair tumbled loose around her shoulders.

'What the hell are you dressed like that for?'

'I'm a stable lad and can't do the work in a frock.'

He shouted for the head groom, and pointing to Chrissie, demanded, 'Explain what a girl is doing working in the stables.'

'Lord Frenshaw engaged her, sir, and she's the best stable hand we've ever had. Her love and understanding of these difficult animals is amazing. She can control them when everyone else is having difficulty. She has been with your horse all night, refusing to leave his side. That's how concerned she has been for him.'

With his mouth set in a grim line he began running his hands over the animal, inspecting him thoroughly.

Chrissie watched, eyes narrowed and ready to step in if he did anything to hurt the poor animal. The horse didn't seem to mind; in fact he even nuzzled the man when he rubbed his nose. She was puzzled. Why would there be such affection between them if he had mistreated the horse? Had she been hasty in her assumption that he was to blame?

The head groom was smiling. 'Midnight looks much stronger today, Major Frenshaw.'

Those words nearly knocked her off her feet with shock. She hadn't noticed. Her only concern had been for the welfare of the suffering animal and nothing else had mattered. He was jet-black and even the scars hadn't made her realise the truth. 'Oh,' she gasped. 'He was hurt in battle. I do apologise for my harsh words, sir. That was unjust of me.'

His only response to her apology was a brisk nod. 'We can put him in the paddock now.'

'No, sir, he needs rest and quiet for at least another day. He feels safe and happy in here for the moment.'

The major glared at her and then asked the head groom for his opinion.

'I would agree with Chrissie's opinion, Major. Another day of quiet will not do any harm.'

'Very well. Where is Red Sunset?'

'In the paddock, and he will be pleased to see you. He has become increasingly difficult to handle, and if it hadn't been for Chrissie being able to control him, he would have been sent to the cavalry by now.'

'I see.' Without another word he strode out of the stable and headed for the paddock.

'He doesn't like me.' She watched the tall man walk away and her heart was troubled. 'I could feel the anger boiling within him.'

'You came as a shock to him.' He gave her a wry smile. 'You came as a shock to all of us, but I think his anger stems from what happened at Balaclava. From the condition both Midnight and himself were in, I would say they've had a very bad time. They will both need time to recover. Don't look so troubled. Your prediction that he would return has come true.'

'That was just a lucky coincidence.' She turned back to Midnight, pleased for his lordship that his son was finally home, but she couldn't shake off a feeling of foreboding.

Chapter Eleven

'You're going to do what?' Charles asked in disbelief. 'You've only been home for a week and have hardly recovered from the arduous journey, son. Don't you think you need more time to think this through?'

'I've done nothing but think about it ever since that damned Crimean War. I won't breed more animals to be slaughtered like that.'

'That won't happen again. Lessons will have been learnt.'

'Will they?' Harry spun away from the window to face his father. 'I have my doubts, and that is why I have resigned my commission. From now on the estate will be my life and I am going to make changes.'

'I understand your need – but racehorses . . .' Charles saw how determined his son was, and asked, 'What are you going to do with the destriers you have? They are only fit for cavalry horses.'

'That's where they will have to go, but they will be the last they get from me.'

'All of them?'

'All except Midnight. He will stay with me. I owe him that.'

'What really happened out there?' he asked gently. 'You haven't said why it took you so long to return home, or why the military didn't know if you were alive or dead.'

'Because it was bloody chaos, and I don't wish to talk about it. One thing I will talk about, though, is what possessed you to engage a girl as a stable lad?'

'She came looking for work and that was all we had available.'

'Well, she will have to go. I won't have a girl working for me dressed in such a disgraceful manner.'

'She's good with the animals,' Charles protested.

'I saw that with my own eyes, but she can't stay. What were you thinking?'

Now Charles was angry. 'Let me tell you something about that child. If it hadn't been for her help you wouldn't have a damned estate to come back to. With the blasted legal mess you left behind while you were off to fight in your war, Edward would now be the rightful owner. Before you go making radical changes and sacking people, put your own house in order. I have had to endure that boy's continual badgering to hand over the estate to him, but Chrissie put a stop to that long enough for you to arrive back. She shut him up and gave me hope that you would return soon. And she was right!'

'What is she, some fortune-teller?' he asked, making it sound insulting.

'Yes! And I gave her my word that her job here was secure.'

Harry sighed in exasperation. 'I'm sorry about your brother and my cousin's death, and for the legal mess it left you with, but I'm back and the decisions are mine. I'll make any changes I deem necessary, and that girl has to go.'

Charles stormed out of the room. This wasn't the son he remembered. They had always been able to talk and work things out between them, but not now, and he was wasting his breath trying to reason with him. It was going to be hard watching him ruin a profitable business – one his grandfather had set up, but now Harry was back he had no say in the running of the estate. He had fought so hard to keep the place out of a gambler's hands, only to find his son risking everything because he was angry. Whatever the truth about that disastrous campaign, and the long delay in his return, it had changed his son. Difficult as it was, he knew he must step back and let him work his way through the mental turmoil in his own way and time.

'What's going on?' Chrissie rushed up to the estate manager. 'Why are all the horses being rounded up?'

'They are being sold and the cavalry are taking most of them.'

'All?' she gasped in dismay. 'Does that include Midnight and Red Sunset?'

'I believe Midnight is staying but, yes, Red is going.' He looked at the agitated girl with sadness. 'The major has also given me orders to dismiss you by the end of the week. I'm sorry, lass, you've been an excellent stable hand.'

Chrissie thought her heart would break at that moment. She loved it here and had hoped to stay for a very long time, but putting aside her own grief her thoughts turned to the animals. Midnight was staying, so he would be all right, and because of his injuries he was no longer fit to be a military horse again, but Red mustn't be sent to face the same fate. That couldn't be allowed to happen!

'I understand that I will no longer be needed,' she told the estate manager. Then she ran to the barn, clambered up the ladder and began to gather together anything she had that might be worth something. All she possessed was a small silver locket that had belonged to her mother, her father's pocket watch and one shilling. She didn't know how much these animals cost, but what she had wasn't nearly enough, of that she was sure. Her gaze rested on the box containing the crystal ball and she picked that up as well. Elsie would understand.

Clutching her precious items – precious to her – she went to the house and caught the butler. 'Please, I have to see Major Frenshaw urgently.'

'He's in the library. Come with me and I'll ask if he will see you.'

'Thank you.' She followed the butler and waited anxiously outside the room. She breathed a sigh of relief when he came out and beckoned her in, then he left, closing the door quietly behind him.

The major was standing by the window staring out and, without turning, said, 'Well?'

'I want to buy Red Sunset, please, sir.'

He spun round with narrowed eyes. 'How is someone like you going to pay for him?'

His tone was insulting, but she held her temper – just – and placed her things on the small table beside him, determined not to let him intimidate her.

His laugh was devoid of humour. 'Don't be ridiculous. These paltry items wouldn't even buy one leg of such a fine animal.'

Her head came up in defiance. 'They may seem paltry to you, sir, but they are treasured items to me. Surely the fact that I am offering everything I have in the world means something?'

He reached out to open the box and see what was inside when a stern voice ordered, 'Put that down, Harry.'

Lord Frenshaw strode in to the room, picked up Chrissie's things and thrust them into her hands. 'I know they mean a lot to you, so you keep them.' Then he rounded on his son. 'One day I hope you will understand that some things are beyond price. Not in monetary value, but in sentimental value. What the child was offering you is of more value than this entire estate. I have just heard what you are doing, and I think it is ill-advised and cruel, so I will return to my own neglected estate and take Chrissie and Red Sunset with me. Don't worry; I'll give you a fair price for the animal. Name it.'

The amount the major quoted made Chrissie's head reel.

'Done. Go and get your things,' he told her. 'We leave in an hour.'

They were about to walk out of the library when the major called, 'Father.'

His lordship turned his head.

'That price I quoted was too high. I don't want your money, just take him with you.'

'You will get the price I agreed to,' he told his son sharply.

Chrissie was suddenly overwhelmed with a sense of foreboding and she faced the tall man, clutching the box to her. 'Sir, you are surrounded by danger. Please be alert.'

Once outside the room his lordship asked, 'What did you mean by that warning?'

'I don't know. There was a feeling of danger and I spoke without thinking. It was probably the danger he faced in the past still clinging to him.'

'Or maybe not. You are uncannily perceptive.' He patted her shoulder and they continued walking. 'I'll have a word with the estate manager before we leave.'

'Thank you for taking Red Sunset, your lordship, and for the offer of a job with you, but I couldn't accept. You have been very kind to me, and I have loved working here, but that is finished now.' Tears filled her eyes and she swiped them away. 'I need to make a life for myself and my attempts so far have not gone well. I feel as if I am being pushed from place to place, and this isn't what I had planned for myself. I want something permanent; somewhere I can belong and put down roots. I had hoped it was here, but it isn't and I must continue my search.'

'You can have a permanent position on my estate. I'll find you something to do you are happy with.'

'I don't know how to explain this, your lordship,

but I will try. Where I come from taking charity from someone is a dirty word, and the prospect of being sent to the workhouse is terrifying for the poor. Most cling on to as much independence and dignity as possible in the slums, but it is a daily struggle, and a few sink under the burden. I come from that background and my dream has always been to get away and make a better, cleaner life for myself. If I come with you it will feel as if I am taking charity. I am sure you don't need more servants, and I would never be happy knowing I was taking advantage of your kindness. This isn't the right place for me, after all, and I must pursue my dream, however long and bumpy the road.' She gave him an imploring look. 'That is a very muddled explanation, but it is the best I can do, and I hope you understand.'

'I can see what you are saying, but at least come with me until you find another position. I can perhaps help with that.' The look on her face made him hold up his hands in surrender. 'I know, that sounds like charity as well. You are too independent, child, and clearly too proud to accept help when it is offered.'

'Yes, I am, and that's a fault, I know, but it is the way I am.'

They had reached the stable block now and he shook his head in sorrow. 'My son is a damned fool. This isn't the way his homecoming should have been.'

'Be patient, your lordship. Your son is greatly troubled about something, and until he comes to terms with it, his mind will be in turmoil. I know you are angry about the things he is doing, but please keep an eye on him. He is going to need your help and support for a while.'

'You are a wise girl who is good with horses and people, and it will be a loss not to have you in our lives, but I do understand your need to make a new life for yourself. May I ask you one thing?'

'Of course.'

'Keep in touch with me.' He handed her a visiting card. 'That is my address and if you ever need anything you can contact me. Promise?'

'I will if I can; I can't promise you more than that. I was told to leave at the end of the week, but I'll make a quick break and go now. It's better if I don't prolong the agony and go at once. Goodbye, it has been a pleasure to know you, your lordship.'

He looked alarmed at her determination to leave at once. 'But where will you go? Have you got any money?'

'I'll find somewhere, and I do have a little money I've saved. Don't worry about me.'

'I suppose it's useless me trying to give you money to help you on your way?' When she shook her head he ran a tired hand over his eyes. 'And it's no good you telling me not to worry about you, because of course I will, and for my son as well. Are we all going to be all right?'

She smiled. 'I don't know. I'm not a fortune-teller.'

When he gave a short laugh she left him and went to the barn to collect the rest of her things and change into a skirt. It didn't take long, and without saying a word to anyone she walked away from the place she had come to love. Thrown out again.

* * *

Harry watched the girl walking towards the gate, carrying her few belongings, and frowned at his father as he entered the library. 'I thought you were taking her with you?'

'She wouldn't come. Chrissie has her pride and my offer was too much like charity to her. Dammit, Harry, you've just broken her heart.'

'Where is she going?'

'What do you care?'

'I don't.' He spun away from the window. 'Take Midnight with you as well. He will be happier with his half-brother, Red Sunset.'

'How much is he going to cost me?'

'Nothing. I don't want anything for either of them. Just take them!'

Seeing how distressed his son was, and uneasy to leave him like this, he asked gently, 'Would you like me to stay a while longer?'

'I am not fit to be around, and I might do or say something that will leave our relationship beyond repair. I don't want that to happen, so it's for the best that you go back to your own place now. Solitude is what I need at the moment.'

'That's how I see it as well.' Charles walked towards the door with a heavy heart. 'Take heed of Chrissie's warning. There is an aura of danger and violence emanating from you even I can feel. When you have dealt with your demons, then come and see me.'

'I will.' He watched his father leave, turned sharply and threw the glass he was holding at the fireplace, then he swept out of the house, calling for the head groom.

'Major,' he rushed up to him.

'Saddle me a horse.'

'Midnight, Major?'

'No, any mount will do.'

Within a few minutes Harry was in the saddle and galloping across the estate, hoping the exercise would help him deal with his demons, as his father called them. In fact, it was grief and anger at the senseless loss of life he had witnessed, both of men and beasts. He had been down, unable to move, Midnight badly wounded, and he didn't believe he would ever forget the sight of his friends and colleagues spread out all around him, dead or dying. When the carnage was over they had come to collect the wounded, and if he hadn't been conscious they would have shot Midnight. That he would not allow and had struggled up to urge the animal back on his feet. When his own wounds were dressed he kept close to his horse, fearing even to sleep in case they shot Midnight. Somehow he had survived and he had been determined that both he and his horse were going to walk away from there and return home. The days that followed were a blur as he nursed the horse until some of his strength had returned. Midnight had still not been able to travel when the Brigade had moved on, so he had stayed behind, and if it hadn't been for his friend Joe remaining with him, he didn't think he would have survived. The journey had been a nightmare and many times he doubted if they were going to make it back. But by some miracle they had.

He pulled up on a rise and gazed at the estate spread out before him. The dream of this place kept him moving and what had he done since returning? Destroyed the business that had the reputation for providing the finest destriers, alienated his father who had struggled so hard to keep it out of Edward's gambling hands, and that girl – what had he done to her?

What a mess he had made of what should have been a joyful homecoming. He should be ashamed of himself, but at the moment he was just numb; his feelings shut down with a lingering exhaustion. That would pass, he knew, but for now he had to manage as best he could.

Chapter Twelve

Chrissie had been walking for over an hour, not knowing where she was going, and beginning to feel desperate. She had been so upset about leaving the estate that she had acted hastily instead of pausing to think things through. Her father would have caught her arm and told her to stop for a moment before making a decision, but he wasn't here now. She was on her own and had to do what she felt was right at the time and, right or wrong, that was what she had done. When there were signs of habitation and perhaps a village ahead, she headed for that, relieved to see houses. This was such a sparsely populated area and there were not many opportunities to find work. It felt as if the heart had been wrenched out of her as the place she had loved on sight receded in the distance, never to be seen again, she was sure. She hadn't dared to look back at what she was leaving. The people, the animals and the beautiful estate had been everything she had dreamt about, and she had so wanted to stay. It wasn't to be, though, and her search must continue to find a place where she could belong and make her home. When she had joined up with the Travellers, it had seemed so easy. She would find a place she liked and that would be her home for the foreseeable future, but it was turning out to be a very difficult thing to achieve.

She stopped for a moment to watch cattle grazing on lush grass, then turned away and continued walking. Many would consider her foolish to turn down the offer from Lord Frenshaw, and perhaps she was, but she just couldn't take it – she just couldn't. There were many reasons, but the main one was he didn't agree with his son's decision to dismiss her, and as he had engaged her he was trying to find a way to put that right. She wasn't a fool and knew he didn't need another servant. The talk amongst the stable hands was that his lordship had been able to stay at his son's estate because he had a team of excellent staff who could successfully run his estate while he was away. He clearly felt bad about his son's actions, but he wasn't responsible for her, he had enough problems with a son who had not yet recovered from his ordeal. The horse and rider had been at the point of collapse when they had arrived. Both had been badly wounded and she couldn't even imagine how hard that journey must have been. Her heart ached for both of them, and if she had been allowed to stay she might have been able to help. It was no good wishing, though, because there wasn't anything she could do now. They had to deal with their own problems, and so did she.

She rounded a corner and thankfully there was a village, making her quicken her stride as it came in to view. It was late in the afternoon and the main street was quiet. A job and somewhere to sleep tonight was urgent and she must find someone who could help her if possible. Thankfully she had a little money, but she must be careful with it because it wouldn't last long. Her thought went to the lovely cosy room they had made for her in the barn loft, and she pushed the thought away immediately. It was no good dwelling on the past, lovely while it had lasted, but that was now gone and must be put behind her.

The butcher's shop was still open and she went in.

'Ah, you're just in time; we were about to close.' The man smiled at her. 'What can I get you?'

'I haven't come to buy anything. I'm looking for work and a place to stay tonight. Do you know of anyone who needs workers? I don't mind what I do.'

He pursed his lips. 'The only place you might get work is at the Edmonds' farm about two miles further along this road. He's got a strawberry harvest ready for picking.'

'Oh, thank you. I'll go there straight away.'

'Why don't you leave it until the morning? If you don't mind me saying, you look worn out, and the inn a few doors down will probably have a room for the night.'

'Thank you, but I can't miss the chance of work so I'll go now, and come back to the inn if I can't find anywhere else to stay.' She headed for the door, anxious to be on her way. If there was a chance of a job and somewhere to sleep then she mustn't waste any time.

'Wait! Bobby,' he called and a young boy appeared from

the back of the shop. 'Hitch up the cart and take Edmonds' order tonight instead of in the morning. This young girl will go with you, and bring her back if she needs to return here.'

She sagged with relief at the offer of a ride to the farm; it felt as if she had been walking all day. 'That is very kind of you, sir.'

He waved away her thanks. 'We've got to go there, and it will save you another long walk, because I imagine you've already covered a fair few miles today. Bring the cart to the front, Bobby, and here's a nice pie for each of you to eat on the way.'

It was only then she realised how hungry she was, and dived into her pocket to pay the butcher.

When she held out the money he smiled and shook his head, refusing to take the money. 'You keep that towards your bed for the night. Now, off you go, the pair of you, and enjoy the pie. You won't get finer.'

Chrissie was grateful for the lift when she saw just how far away the farm was. The butcher's idea of about two miles was way out. If she'd had to walk it would have been dark by the time she got there, and she'd have probably been faced with the prospect of sleeping in a field somewhere. The young boy was obviously glad of some company because he never stopped talking, and that suited her just fine, because she was still hurting from leaving the estate and her two beautiful horses. Midnight had quickly recovered from his ordeal and had been a real handful, taking great pleasure in teasing her by dodging out of her range when she was trying to do something for him. She smiled at the memories. It was as if he had been smiling with her, and Red joined in the fun, spurred on by her laughter. She hoped the major would find a way to keep them together. They had been so happy to be reunited.

'Here we are, miss.'

She was jolted out of her reverie, not realising they had entered the farm gates.

'They usually give me a glass of home-made cider, so you go and see if they need any more workers. I'll wait and take you back if there's nothing here for you.'

'That's kind of you.' She jumped down, wondering, not for the first time, if she had done the right thing by coming to the country. There were lots of big houses in London needing staff, but here you had to travel miles to find one. She gave a mental shrug. Well, she had made her decision, and right or wrong she was here now, so there was little point worrying about it. And really, after seeing the beautiful countryside and the vast expanses of open space, she knew she would not be happy returning to the crowded streets of London.

'Got company, Bobby?' A man of around fifty walked up to them. He was of average height but stocky and strong-looking.

'Yes, Mister Edmonds. This is Chrissie and she's looking for work and a place to stay. Dad told me to bring her and see if you needed anyone.'

'You go to the kitchen and get your drink, then, while I talk to Chrissie.'

The boy winked at her and dashed off.

'I can't help you,' he said at once. 'We don't need anyone in the house.'

'I'll do anything', she told him, trying to keep the tone of desperation out of her voice. 'I'm strong and can work on the land. I was a stable hand in my last job.'

'Were you really? Where were you and why did you leave?'

She explained what had happened and he was clearly surprised.

'Major Frenshaw is alive? We felt sure he had been killed in the Crimea.'

She nodded. 'He's suffered, though, and is having problems. He didn't like to see a girl working in the stables, so I had to leave. I need work and somewhere to sleep. Bobby's dad mentioned you had a strawberry harvest to get in.'

'Well, I suppose another hand would get the harvest in faster. That job will only last for a week, but if you work hard I might be able to find you something else for a while.'

'Thank you, sir.' The relief that swept through her was enormous. When she looked around there was nothing here but field after field with not another house in sight.

'The only accommodation I can offer is in the barn, and not really suitable for a girl, but it's warm and dry. If you can make do for tonight we'll see if we can sort out something better tomorrow.'

'That's all right, sir, I'll be quite happy with that. I slept in a barn at the Frenshaw estate.' She didn't mention that they had fixed it up as a cosy room with a proper bed in it.

'Right, then, if you're happy sleeping there you can stay right away. Dinner will be in an hour and you will eat with the rest of the workers. My wife will sort you out some bedding to make it more comfortable for you.' He gave her a speculating look. 'I think there's more to your story than you told me, and I look forward to hearing the rest of it.'

He walked away just as Bobby appeared. 'Did you get the job?'

'Yes, thank goodness, and a place to sleep. Thank your dad for me when you get back, and tell him he was right, that was the best pie I have ever tasted.'

'I will,' he smirked. 'Dad's proud of his pies. I'll get your things from the cart. Where are you going to sleep?'

'In that barn over there.'

'Ah, that will be nice and cosy, and better than sleeping in a field.'

'Much better.'

'I must get back now. 'Spect I'll see you around.'

'Thanks for bringing me out here.'

'Glad of the company.' With a wave he climbed back on the cart and trotted away.

Picking up her belongings she went to inspect the barn, and while she was sorting out the best place to sleep, the farmer's wife arrived with an armful of blankets.

'You're a girl!' she exclaimed. 'Stan never told me that. You can't sleep out here. Didn't he tell you that a couple of miles down the road there's a woman who takes in lodgers? Her rates are reasonable.'

'He didn't mention it, but I wouldn't have gone there, anyway. This will be just fine.'

'It will be more comfortable there,' she insisted.

'I can't afford to spend what little money I have on lodgings,' she admitted. 'I must have something in my pocket when I leave here.'

'Things are that bad for you, then?'

'I'm afraid so.'

Her expression softened. 'Well, then, let's make you as comfortable as possible. Gather all that straw together so we can make a bed on top of that.'

While they worked, the farmer's wife chatted away. 'Stan told me you'd worked at the stables on the Frenshaw estate, and that's why I thought you were a lad. He also said the major is back.'

Chrissie nodded.

'Such a nice boy, but a bit of a handful when he was younger, just like those great horses they breed there. Always kind and considerate, though, and I can't imagine him dismissing you when you had nowhere to go.'

'I'm afraid he has returned a troubled man, and he disapproved of me working as a stable lad, although everyone else was pleased with my work.'

'That doesn't sound like him, and all I can say is that he must have changed while he's been away.'

'I think he has a lot on his mind, but he's a strong man and will work through his problems.'

'Let's hope so.' She studied Chrissie carefully. 'You don't sound bitter about the way you've been treated.'

'What would be the point of feeling like that? He did what he thought was right. I do admit to being sad and upset, though, because it was a place I had hoped to stay for a long time.'

The farmer's wife patted her arm in sympathy, and changed the subject. 'You can use the outhouse, and when you are ready you can join the others for supper. I expect you're hungry.'

'I am. Thank you.'

'The other workers all live locally and go to their homes after we've fed them, so you will be the only one here at night. However, you can slip the bar across the door and that will make it secure for you. Wish we could offer you better, but this is all we have as you need to stay.'

Later that evening, after having a substantial meal, Chrissie settled down to sleep, and as her thoughts turned to Midnight and Red Sunset, and the happy times she had spent on the estate, she allowed a few tears to fall. Just a few, though, not allowing herself to wallow in self-pity.

Chapter Thirteen

Two weeks had dragged by and Harry was still suffering. His nights were troubled with nightmares and the days filled with doubts. He felt as if he was being buffeted by a strong wind, unable to gain his balance. He had acted completely out of character since his return by making hasty decisions, and he now knew that clearing the estate of destriers had been a mistake. With the estate manager, Carstairs, he had looked at dozens of thoroughbreds without purchasing even one. It was hard to imagine riding one. He loved the size, strength and power of the warhorses and he missed them, especially Midnight and Red Sunset. Thank heavens they were safely with his father. He desperately wanted to go and see them, but after behaving so abominably to his father, frankly he was ashamed to show his face. He ran a hand over his eyes. What a mess he had made of everything by allowing grief and anger to consume him. He had to start pulling himself together – and fast!

'Have you decided on any of these horses, Major?' Carstairs asked, breaking through Harry's troubled thoughts.

He shook his head as his gaze swept over the animals being paraded for him at yet another sale.

'They are fine animals, and that grey is outstanding. These are some of the best we have seen yet.'

'I agree, but they are not for me.' He politely complimented the breeder on his excellent horses, and as they rode away he looked at his estate manager. 'You've been very patient with me, George, but we both know I have made a mistake.'

'Not irreversible, though, Major. Lord Frenshaw still has two of the finest destriers. Their bloodline is impeccable and I am sure he will allow you to use them to start again.'

'No doubt, but I am through with making hasty decisions. I'll sleep on it.'

'Good idea, Major.'

When they arrived back Edward was pacing around and looking at the empty stalls. The moment Harry arrived he strode up with a smile on his face. 'Good to see you home safe and sound, Harry.'

'Don't pretend pleasure at seeing me, for I've heard what you have been up to, so know you are not happy I have survived.'

'Ah, I was told you were not in the best of moods, and that is why I have stayed away.' The smile was still on his face but didn't reach his eyes. 'Where are all the horses?'

'Sold.' Harry marched towards the house, needing a strong drink.

'All of them?' Edward had difficulty keeping up with his cousin's long stride. 'What are you going to do, then?'

'Start again.' He swept in to the library and headed straight for the decanters. 'Why are you here, Edward?'

'I came to see how you are. Is that a crime?'

'As you can see, I am strong enough to survive for many years yet.'

'I'm pleased to hear that.'

Liar, he thought, as he handed Edward a drink out of politeness. Edward had never been his favourite cousin. As a child he had been sullen and envious of Harry, knowing he was going to inherit this estate, and as an adult he had mixed with the wrong crowd of young men who spent their time gambling. The one who should have been in line to inherit was James, who had unfortunately been killed while Harry had been away. He could only imagine how devastated his father had been at losing this favourite nephew, and having his son missing at the same time.

'Thanks.' Edward took the drink. 'When I saw the empty stalls I thought you might have decided to turn the estate over to cattle and crops. People have to eat, and such things are always in demand.'

'I'll probably make some changes in that way. There is plenty of land not being put to good use, but horses are my first love.'

'Of course.' Edward downed the drink in one go.

'What have you been up to, apart from pestering my father to hand the estate over to you?'

'No one thought you were coming back, and after the

118

death of our cousin I am the rightful heir, so I had every right to claim the estate. Your father stubbornly refused to declare you dead.'

'He had no proof that I had been killed, and he was right to wait for definite news. You were premature with your claim to the estate.'

'That has turned out to be true,' he admitted rather reluctantly.

'It has, and that won't happen again. I am out of the army now, and intend to put my affairs in order.'

'What do you mean by that? You do not have other heirs.'

'Then I had better see about marrying and having a clutch of children.' That remark clearly rattled his cousin, much to his satisfaction. 'Want another drink?'

'No, thanks. I just popped in to see if you were all right.' His cousin then strode out of the room.

Almost immediately the estate manager arrived and remarked, 'Mr Edward didn't look too happy.'

'He's just found out I am fit and well.'

Both men grinned.

'He did make one suggestion that has merit, though. We have a lot of land not being put to good use, so what do you think about turning some of it over to crops and cattle?'

'Some is only suitable for grazing land, but there are a lot of acres to the south which could be used for crops.'

'Let's go and have a look at it. I like this idea.'

As they walked to the stables, George asked, 'Are you dismissing the idea of raising horses?'

'I have decided against those thoroughbreds, but we'll go

back to what we know best and breed warhorses. I need to see if my father will let us have the two he took with him.'

'I'm sure he will, and be pleased with the news. Those two stallions will be a perfect foundation for a new herd.'

Harry mounted his horse, feeling as if the life was creeping back in to him. There was a lot of work to be done and this was just what he needed. There was a farm to set up and two suitable mares to be purchased. It was good to be home.

They mapped out the proposed farm, and then took their time returning as they talked over what had to be done. They could get local workers to erect fences where needed, and then engage an experienced man to run the farm.

'I expect he will have a family, so we could build a house by that stream,' George suggested, 'and he could employ his own workers.'

'My thoughts exactly. First thing tomorrow we'll start engaging men and get the land cleared and fences erected.'

'And you'll see his lordship about the horses?'

Harry nodded, and reined in when he heard noise coming from the stables. The two men looked at each other and spurred their mounts forward. It was chaos as they approached the house. There was a great deal of shouting and men running around waving their arms about.

'What the hell!' Harry leapt from the saddle the moment he reached the yard. 'What's going on here?' he bellowed.

'Oh, Major, thank goodness you're here.' The head groom was sweating from running around. 'Midnight and Red Sunset are here and we can't control them.'

'Has my father returned them?'

'No, Major, they came on their own.'

'What! Where are they?'

'They're in the barn at the moment, but they've been running around and we haven't been able to catch them.'

Alarmed by this, he ran to the barn and found the two warhorses had pinned one of the stable lads in the corner of the barn. Every time the boy tried to get past them he was pushed back against the wall again. 'Keep still, lad,' he told him softly. 'They won't hurt you.'

'I know that, sir, or they'd have finished me off by now, but they sure are mad about something.'

'Midnight, Red!' he said in a commanding voice. 'Come here!'

Both animals turned their heads at the sound of his familiar voice, came straight to him, and nuzzled their master.

He rubbed their necks. 'It's good to see you as well, but what are you doing here? Are you all right?' he asked the lad as he walked away from the wall.

'No harm done, sir.'

At that moment they heard the sound of a horse approaching fast, and shortly after that Lord Frenshaw rushed in to the barn. 'Oh, thank heavens they are here. I'm sorry, son, but they jumped the fence and took off on their own. I don't think they are happy with me. They want to come home.'

'It's all right.' He smiled, pleased to see his father. 'They are wilful creatures and can stay here, if that's all right with you?'

'Of course. This is where they belong.'

'I'll buy them back.'

'You will not! Those unpredictable animals belong to you and always have done. I happily return them to you – free of charge.'

Red Sunset began stamping his feet and milling around again, then Midnight joined in. They moved to the middle of the barn and stood there looking up.

'Now what are they doing?' Harry was perplexed. He knew these animals well, and they could be difficult, except in battle when they never hesitated to obey a command. However, the way they were behaving now was inexplicable.

'Oh my goodness.' Charles began to chuckle. 'They've found you and I do believe they are now looking for Chrissie.'

'Who the hell is Chrissie?'

'The girl you dismissed. Don't you even remember her name?'

'That is ridiculous. You are letting your imagination run away with you. They don't care who looks after them as long as they get what they need and are well treated.'

'One never knows what those two are thinking. Now that scare is over I could do with a drink.'

'Good idea. I've got a lot to tell you.' He turned his attention back to the horses. 'Come on, boys, let's get you in a comfy, secure stall,' he commanded.

They turned and followed him without any further bad behaviour, much to everyone's relief.

'You're looking better,' Charles told his son when they were settled in the library with large drinks in their hands. 'How are you sleeping now?'

'I'm getting some sleep, but the nightmares are still there. They've changed, though.'

'In what way?'

Harry grimaced. 'I'm still in the front of the charge, but instead of guns I see that girl glaring at me and shouting danger and I'm yelling back that I know it's bloody dangerous. I wake up in a sweat and wondering how the hell she got in my dreams. Even when I'm awake, if I look out of the window I can see her walking away carrying her few possessions in her hand. It's ridiculous. I've dismissed servants before and it's never haunted me like this. My mind still must be in a mess.'

'I liked that girl and she's worrying me as well. You shouldn't have sent her away like that. It was unjust. You didn't even take the time to get to know her and find out how good her work was with the horses.'

'I know that now, but I wasn't thinking clearly when I arrived home. I took one look at her and wanted her out of the way. Goodness knows why. Have you any idea where she is now?'

Charles shook his head. 'I tried very hard to keep her with me, at least until she had found another position, but she's an independent girl and won't accept help if she thinks it comes out of pity, or the slightest hint of charity.'

'Do you think she would go back to London?' he asked as he refilled their glasses.

'I really don't know, but she might have, I suppose. Work as a servant would be easier to get there, but there isn't anything we can do about it now. She's gone and all we can hope is that she is all right.'

Harry nodded. His father was right, and there was no point worrying about it. What he had done had been thoughtless and unkind, and that was something he would have to live with – along with all of his other nightmares.

'You said you had something to tell me,' his father prompted.

He leant forward, enthusiasm lighting his eyes as he explained his plans for the estate.

'Good, good,' his father nodded approval, relieved to see his son almost back to his old self. Even as a child he had been a force to be reckoned with, and had grown into a dynamic man. That was why the military had beckoned him, but that was over, thank goodness. Now he was free to put his energy and talents to better use.

'Oh, and Edward came to see me,' he added.

'Ah, I thought he might show up soon, just to check that you really had survived. I suppose he was delighted to find you fit and well.'

'That wasn't the impression I got from him.'

Both men looked at each other, and lifting their glasses, burst out laughing.

Chapter Fourteen

The strawberry harvest had lasted longer than expected, but now it was over and Chrissie really hoped the farmer would find her another job. It was near the end of June now and working in the fields was not to her liking, but she couldn't make up her mind what to do next. In her spare time she had searched the area, but there wasn't any work around here. Her options were to set out and try to find the Travellers again, or return to London. Neither of those things appealed to her. The Travellers would be miles away by now, and wouldn't be returning this way for several months, and the thought of going back to London made her feel sick. No, she couldn't throw away her dream just because of a setback. That would be weak of her, and she wasn't going to give up so easily. She would have to find a way to stay in the country, no matter how difficult it would be.

'Ah, there you are.' The farmer walked across the field, now completely cleared of fruit. 'You've worked well, and I can give you something for another week if you are prepared to help dig up the first crop of new potatoes. It's hard work, mind you.'

'I'd be happy to do that, sir.' She smiled with relief. It wasn't long, but it meant another week where she had food and somewhere to sleep. 'Thank you.'

He nodded and made his way back to the house, and when he was out of sight she spun round and round drinking in the beauty of the countryside. There wasn't a piece of concrete anywhere, and she knew that whatever happened, the country was the only place she wanted to be. Work on the farm was hard and the days long, but here she felt free. She was aware that was a strange way to look at it when her future was so uncertain and she still didn't have anywhere to call home, but she belonged here – of that she was sure. And there was always hope that the farmer would keep her for longer than the promised week.

Harry surveyed the scene in front of him with satisfaction. There were men working everywhere, and in only two days fields were being cleared, fences erected and the house was already under way. 'You've done well,' he complimented his estate manager. 'Where did you find all these men?'

'They are all local and grateful for the work, Major. Many have asked if they can stay and work on the farm when it's ready. I've told them we will need workers, but I don't know how many until we decide on crops and cattle.'

'Take all their names.'

'I have already done so.'

'Looks as if those men could use some help with those fence posts.' He shrugged out of his jacket and strode over to the workers, and without saying a word he began to work with them, much to their surprise.

'This hole needs to be deeper, otherwise the first strong wind and it will tumble,' the man in charge of fencing said as they heaved the thick pole out again.

Harry grabbed the shovel and began enlarging the hole. 'How far down?' he asked.

'Er . . . another foot, but we can do it, sir.'

He looked up and grinned. 'Of course you can, but I'm quite capable of digging holes. You tell me how deep you want them and I'll go along the line while you erect the fence. A bit of physical exercise will do me good.'

'Well, if you're sure, sir, only we heard you'd been hurt bad fighting in that war.'

'I'm quite fit now.'

'Glad to hear that, sir.' Then turning to his men he shouted, 'All right, you heard the major. Let's get this fence up.'

They didn't pack up until around seven, and mounting Red Sunset, who had been happily grazing nearby, he headed back to the house. The horse wanted to stretch his legs so they began to gallop. As they rode towards the stables something hit Harry and he fell out of the saddle and crashed to the ground. Winded and dazed he wondered what he was doing there. When he tried to sit up he was even more confused to find that he couldn't, and turning his head, he saw blood beginning to soak his jacket. Red had stopped and came back to look down at him, clearly agitated.

'Don't mill about like that, boy, you'll hurt me more if you step on me.' He tried to put as much command into his voice as he could. 'Go to the stable. Go!'

That last command had taken all of his remaining strength and he sighed with relief when the animal took off, heading in the right direction. He was fighting to remain conscious, trying to recall what had happened. They had been moving quite fast and there had been a sound – a sound he was familiar with. He had been shot, and whoever had done it was a damned fine marksman. Hitting a moving target wasn't easy. One memory came to him as he drifted in to unconsciousness, and it was that girl again, telling him to be careful because he was surrounded by danger.

Red Sunset thundered in to the yard, foam flecked and obviously upset. A stable hand tried to restrain him while yelling for the head groom. 'He's come back on his own, and look, there's blood on the saddle. The major's in trouble.'

'Everyone, mount up!' the head groom ordered, and the yard was soon a mass of milling horses and men as they prepared to go to their master's aid.

'What's going on?' The butler arrived on the scene, breathless from running, having heard the commotion.

'Red's come back on his own and there's blood on the saddle! Send someone for Lord Frenshaw, and get the doctor as well.' He leapt on to his horse and joined the other six who were ready, including two young stable lads, and they left the yard at full gallop.

They knew the direction their master would be coming

from, and it didn't take them long to come across him sprawled on the grass with an alarming amount of blood soaking his jacket.

'Oh, he's hurt bad,' one of the young lads murmured, as he watched the men rush to aid the injured man.

'We've got to stop the bleeding before we can move him.' The head groom was already at work.

'Is he alive?' someone asked.

The head groom nodded. 'But he won't be for much longer if we don't get him to a doctor quickly. Help me remove his jacket and get that towel out of my saddlebag.'

The lad rushed to find the cloth and then handed it to the men working desperately to staunch the flow of blood. They tore his shirt into strips and bound the wound as tightly as they could.

Everyone was asking and wondering what could have happened and were horrified when told that it looked as if he had been shot.

Afraid that the wound might open again if they put him on a horse, they hurriedly made a stretcher using wood from the nearby trees and carried him back to the house as carefully as possible.

Lord Frenshaw and the doctor were already waiting, and the kitchen was a hub of activity, boiling water and arranging bandages, in case they were needed. The moment the doctor saw the condition Harry was in he began barking out orders and had everyone running around to help as much as they could.

The estate manager had stayed much later at the farm and had just arrived. He jumped from his horse and ran over to his lordship. 'What has happened?'

'It looks as if my son has been shot.'

In a flurry of anxious activity, Harry was carried to his room and the doctor ordered everyone out apart from a maid who was to assist him by collecting water and anything else he needed.

Charles refused to move and the doctor relented and allowed him to remain in the room as long as he kept out of the way.

The temporary dressing was removed and the wound cleaned before the doctor was able to probe and remove the bullet. 'Thank goodness he stayed unconscious for that. I don't think anything vital has been damaged, though it was a close thing. Another couple of inches and he would have died instantly.'

'Is he going to be all right?'

'It's hard to say at the moment, but with rest and care he should recover well. I will have to wait to do a closer examination, though, until the bleeding has stopped.' The doctor washed his hands in a bowl of clean water. 'He must be kept absolutely still. The next few hours will be crucial, so I will stay with him tonight. You get some rest, your lordship, and I will call you if there is any change in his condition.'

'I'll have a meal sent in for you, and anything else you need.'

'That will be welcome, thank you.' The doctor pulled a comfortable chair up to the bed, and settled down to watch over his patient.

'How is he?' George wanted to know the moment

Charles came out of the room. 'Everyone is worried. Can we give them any good news?'

'The doctor is hopeful. I'll talk to the staff, and then we must discuss what to do about this.'

With the staff reassured that the major stood a good chance of recovering, the two men settled down with a strong drink, and George asked the question they all wanted to know. 'Who would want to kill the major?'

'One person comes immediately to mind – Edward. But we need proof, and how are we going to get that? There wasn't a witness to the shooting, and we must be careful about accusing him.'

'Would he be capable of such a shot?' George asked.

'I wouldn't have thought so, but he could have paid someone else to do it. However, there isn't anything we can do tonight, but first thing in the morning we will go and search the area for any clues.'

'Would you like me to stay within calling distance tonight, your lordship? I doubt any of us will sleep much now.'

'I agree, but the doctor has ordered me to get some rest, so you do the same. He'll call us if we are needed.'

Dawn was just breaking when the butler woke Lord Frenshaw, who was still in the armchair. 'The doctor said the major is awake and asking for you.'

He hurried to his son's room, relieved to see him propped up against pillows with his eyes closed. 'How is he?'

'Better than expected,' the doctor told him. 'He's a strong, determined man.'

'And I thank the Lord for it.' He sat on the edge of the

bed. 'I'm here, Harry. The doctor said you've been asking for me. We'll find the person who did this to you.'

Harry opened his eyes. 'Find that girl and bring her to me.'

'What are you talking about?' He shot the doctor a worried glance. 'You think the girl shot you?'

'Don't be ridiculous.' He gave a weary sigh. 'I want to see that girl I sent away.'

'I don't know where she is.'

'Then find her.'

'Why?' But he didn't receive an answer; his son was asleep. 'Are you sure he's all right, Doctor? He isn't making much sense and sounds delirious to me.'

'I'm confident that he is in his right mind, but he's been asking for a girl, whoever she is, from the moment he regained consciousness. I wondered if perhaps it was his intended and that it might mean something to you.'

'I know who it is, but she isn't someone he even knows very well. It doesn't make sense. His attention should be on discovering who tried to kill him.'

'There's only one person it could have been, and you damned well know it!'

Both men spun round to face the bed again, surprised to see the patient awake. Not only awake but with eyes glinting with rage. 'I can't do anything stuck in this bed, so I'm relying on you to find proof. But before you do anything I want that girl found and brought here.'

'Why?' his father asked, thoroughly confused and worried by his son's strange behaviour.

'Mind your own bloody business.' Then he was asleep again.

Charles grinned at the doctor. 'Ah, that sounds more like my son.'

'Yes, I would say he is in full command of his faculties, but just who is this girl he wants you to find?'

'Christine Banner. She was working here as a stable lad when he arrived home, and he didn't approve so he dismissed her. What he did was unjust and I think it must have been playing on his mind. Having this brush with death has probably made him want to right a wrong.'

'Maybe.' The doctor looked doubtful.

'My son has always been a kind person,' Charles pointed out, 'and the way he acted when he returned was out of character. He came home a grief-stricken and angry man.'

'Then she had better be found. It might make him rest easier.'

'I agree, but I don't have the faintest idea where she is now. I'll put one of the men on to tracking her whereabouts, but I don't hold out much hope. She could be anywhere.'

Chapter Fifteen

'How is he?' the estate manager asked the moment he walked in to the library.

'The doctor assures me he is going to be all right, but it will take a while before he's up and about again. He's angry, though, so we had better find out who the culprit is or he will be moving around before he should.'

'The place to start will be from where the shot was fired, and hope we can find some clues.' George pursed his lips. 'We have our suspicions, of course, but proving it won't be easy.'

'Edward,' Charles said through gritted teeth. 'That boy has been nothing but trouble from the moment he could toddle. He really wants Harry out of the way, but is he desperate enough to try to kill his own cousin?'

'That is what we have to find out, and as quickly as

possible, because until someone is caught, your son will not be safe. They have failed this time, thank heavens, but they could try again and make sure they don't fail.'

Charles gave a weary sigh. 'This is twice I have nearly lost my son. By some miracle he returned from the Crimea, only to be shot at his own home. How much more grief does a man have to take?'

'We'll keep him safe, your lordship. Every worker on the estate is alert and watching for anything unusual happening around the place.'

'Yes, I know, and that is a comfort. There is another task my son has set me, and that is to find Chrissie and bring her back here. I need someone who will search for her.'

'Adam is a sensible lad and he would be happy to do that, I'm sure. Have you any idea where he should start?'

'The village is the logical place to start. She might have gone there first.'

'I'll send him straight away and then meet you at the stables when you are ready.'

'I'll see you there in fifteen minutes. I must see Harry first and let him know what we are doing.'

The young boy was soon on his way, happy with the task of finding Chrissie, who he had liked very much. Then a group of six men rode out to search the area where Harry had been shot. They soon found the spot where the assassin had waited, and although they searched it inch by inch, the only indication that anyone had been there were broken branches and flattened grass.

After two hours, Charles called off the search, disappointed not to have found even one small clue.

Whoever the culprit was, he had been careful not to leave anything behind.

'What can we do next?' the estate manager asked.

'I shall have to pay my club in London a visit. It's also where Edward spends a lot of his time, and I might be able to gather some news there. My son and I both believe he is the likely candidate for this crime, and we have either got to prove it or eliminate him and look elsewhere. Let's return to the house and I'll discuss it with Harry, if he's up to it.'

Harry was awake and anxiously waiting for news.

'The search was fruitless, I'm afraid,' he told his son. 'The spot he used to conceal himself was clear; he was careful not to leave anything behind, not even a cigar end we could have used to identify the make.'

'I'm not surprised. Whoever did this knew what they were doing. You'll need to find out if Edward is a good enough shot to hit a moving target. If not, he might have engaged someone to do it for him. I can't think of anyone else who would want me dead, and I did make it clear to him that I would take steps to see he couldn't inherit the estate. That might have made him desperate enough to try and get rid of me before I took any action on that.'

'On reflection, telling him was perhaps unwise.'

Harry snorted. 'Add that to the list of mistakes I've made since arriving home. And talking of mistakes, what steps have you taken to find that girl?'

'Will you stop calling her "that girl"? Her name is Chrissie, and the lad, Adam, is out there now trying to trace her.'

'She can't have got far.' Harry sighed and rested his head

back against the pillows. 'What are you going to do next about Edward?'

'I'm off to London in the morning to pay a visit to our club. I haven't been there for some time, but I know a lot of the members and they do love to gossip. If Edward has been up to anything unusual they will know.'

'Good place to start.' Harry moved to get more comfortable and winced.

'Try and rest. I know how frustrating it must be for you to be confined to a bed, but you have to leave this to us. Everyone on the estate is willing and anxious to help.'

His son nodded. 'Thank them for me.'

There was a quiet knock on the door and the head groom looked in. 'I thought the major would like to know that the two mares he bought the other day have arrived.'

Harry was immediately alert. 'Come in and tell me what you think of them. I purchased them on impulse.'

'They are beautiful, Major.' The head groom smiled excitedly as he stood at the end of the bed. 'I've never seen a colour like the golden one, and the other is so black she shines blue in the sunlight. They will be perfect.'

'That's what I thought when I saw them, and I had a job making the man part with them.' He gave a rumble of laughter. 'I didn't go out to buy horses, but when the owner saw how much I wanted them the price kept going up.'

'Well, they could turn out to be worth every penny you paid for them. Midnight and Red are already showing an interest in them.'

'Don't let those two near them yet. They need to settle

in. Damn! I wish I could come down and see them. Who have you got looking after them?'

'I'll do that myself, but if Chrissie was still here I would have given that job to her.' The head groom smiled at Charles. 'You know what a special feeling she had for the horses.'

'Yes, quite remarkable how quickly they responded to her when they were in a fractious mood. You will be pleased to know that we are trying to find her and bring her back.'

'So I heard, and that is good news.'

Charles glanced at his son and saw that his eyes were closed and there was sweat on his brow.

The doctor was already bending over the bed, and then spun round to face the men in the room. 'Out! Everyone out.'

'What's the matter?' Charles rushed to his son's side, but the doctor made him move away.

'It looks as if he is developing a fever. I feared this might happen. Send the maid to me.'

Just then there was a rap on the door and Adam looked in.

'Out!' The doctor raised his voice this time.

The lad flinched, but remained where he was. 'I was told to come up here,' he protested.

'Let him come in,' Harry said firmly. 'I give the orders around here, Doctor. Have you found her?' he demanded as Adam sidled into the room, keeping a wary eye on the doctor.

'She went to the village, sir, and then to a local farm. I went there and found out she's been helping with the strawberry harvest and potato crop, but they're finished now and the farmer had to let her go. He doesn't know where she went. I'm sorry, sir, I haven't found her yet, but I'll keep looking. She's only been gone from the farm for two days so she can't have got far.'

Harry was clearly disappointed. 'Thank you, Adam. Do your best to find her for me.'

'Yes, sir.' The boy bowed slightly to his lordship and left the room.

'That's enough, Major. You are exhausted and have all the signs of a fever developing, and we must deal with that at once.' The doctor ushered the two men still in the room towards the door, and said quietly, 'Send me a man to help as well as the maid. I want plenty of water up here – hot and cold. We must get that fever down quickly, but your son is a strong man and a fighter.'

'I know what you're saying, and I'll stay with him.'

'No. I mean no offence, but I need a young man who is strong enough to help me lift him. Your son is a big man.'

'I understand,' Charles agreed reluctantly. 'I'll send the footman.' He hurried from the room to make sure the doctor had everything he had asked for. A fever was the worst thing that could have happened, and the next hours could be desperately worrying. It didn't matter how much he told himself that Harry was a tough man and could fight off anything, he was frantically concerned. His son had somehow survived that war, only to have this to deal with. If he ever came face-to-face with the criminal who had done this he wouldn't be responsible for his actions. And if it did turn out to be Edward – well . . .

'Bad business, your lordship,' the estate manager said, 'but the major will overcome this.'

139

The manager's voice cut through his troubled thoughts and he dredged up a semblance of a smile. 'Of course he will. Will you go and ask Cook for the water the doctor needs, and I'll send the footman upstairs, and then I'll have a look at those mares.'

With everything done he went out to the stables, knowing he had to keep his mind occupied. He wanted to be in the room with his son, but he knew he would only get in the way. He had known Doctor Carter for many years and he was a competent physician. He would do everything in his power to see Harry survived this crisis. What he had to do was find some good news to help his son's recovery.

The hours stretched from late morning to evening, and all Cook's efforts to tempt him with food were useless. Charles paced the library, unable to settle. The house was silent as if holding its breath as everyone waited, their attention focussed on the room upstairs.

It was nearly midnight when the doctor came downstairs. Charles was waiting for him at the foot of the stairs the moment he had heard him, and he hardly dared ask.

'The fever has broken and he is sleeping peacefully at last.'

'Oh, thank God!' He had to grab the banister to support himself, the relief was so immense. 'Does this mean he is out of danger?'

'He now has a very good chance.' The doctor smiled, took his arm and guided him back to the library. 'Let us get you a brandy, and then you can go upstairs and see him.'

The footman was still there, and he stood up the minute Charles walked in to the room. 'Go and get something to eat, John, and I'll stay with my son for a while. Thank you for all you've done.'

He bowed and left, leaving father and son alone.

'Are you awake, Harry?' he asked softly. When his son opened his eyes and gave a weary smile, he let out a silent sigh of relief. 'You've got to stop this, you know.' He sat on the edge of the bed. 'I'm too old to cope with the fright of nearly losing you twice.'

A deep rumbling laugh came from the patient. 'Don't try and fool me, Father, because you are tougher than any of us. Now, if I remember correctly, all investigations so far have been fruitless. What are you going to do next?'

'Now you are out of danger I'm going to take that trip to London to see if I can unearth any gossip about Edward. If anyone knows it will be the members at the club who, as you know, keep a sharp eye on what everyone is doing. We have to find out quickly if he is responsible, because if not then you have another enemy out there.'

Harry said under his breath, 'Be careful. You are surrounded by danger.'

He had spoken softly but Charles heard Chrissie's last words to him, but he didn't remark on them. 'I saw the two mares you bought and they are magnificent. They should produce fine colts.'

'I agree. I had to negotiate hard for them because I wasn't the only buyer interested.' He looked pointedly at his father. 'What is being done to find that girl?'

The quick change of subject showed Charles just what was really on his son's mind. 'Adam is continuing his search, and her name is Chrissie,' he reminded him. 'Will you tell me why you are so insistent she is found? You were appalled to find a girl working as a stable lad and didn't hesitate to send her away. Why this sudden interest in finding her?'

'I was wrong, and you know I don't admit that lightly. That picture of her walking away wearing her own shabby clothes instead of those breeches is haunting me. It surprised me, because I thought she was going with you, but she didn't. She was alone with nowhere to go, and even knowing that she warned me of danger – a warning I ignored. If I had treated anyone else like that they wouldn't have given a damn what happened to me, but do you know what I saw in those dark eyes at that moment?'

'What?'

'Concern – concern for me. When I was on the ground with a bullet in me I heard her words and finally realised what a wrong I had done her. I've got to put that right or I'll never sleep easy. That's why I want her found.'

Seeing his son was getting agitated, he grasped his arm. 'You stop fretting and get your strength back. We'll find Chrissie, and the devil who tried to kill you.'

Chapter Sixteen

The attic room was dark and cramped, with only room for a single bed and nothing else. Chrissie sighed and sat on the edge of the bed. The farmer's wife had told her this family might want some help, so with a packet of bread and cheese and water to drink, she had set out for the ten-mile walk. It had taken her most of the day, and when she had finally arrived her instinct had been to keep walking, but the sun was beginning to set and she didn't relish the thought of sleeping in a field. Weary in both body and mind she went to the servants' entrance and knocked. The housekeeper who spoke to her said the only position available was for someone to help nanny with the three children.

She liked children and had been happy to accept the job – until she had met the children. There were two girls and one boy with ages ranging from three to ten, the boy being the eldest. The two girls were not much trouble, but the boy was rude, arrogant and had taken an instant dislike to her. He needed a firm hand to keep him in order, but no one bothered, and he was allowed to run wild. She had only been here for one day and didn't know how long she would be able to stop herself from giving him a clip round the ear. His mother called him her little darling, but she could think of a more uncomplimentary description for him. Another worrying thing was Chrissie sensed there was something wrong with the mistress of the house, but couldn't quite decide what it was. She ought to have followed her instinct and kept walking. This was not a happy house.

She stood up and braced herself for another difficult hour as they got the children ready for bed.

'She's not helping me!' the boy declared the moment she walked in to the room.

'I've no intention of doing anything for you,' she declared. 'You are old enough to look after yourself, and you should be spending your time at your studies and not running riot in the nursery disturbing your sisters.'

'The last tutor left after four days,' he sneered. 'None of them stay long.'

'I'm not surprised. They are educated people and don't have to waste their time on a bad-mannered child.'

'You can't talk to me like that,' he shouted. 'I'm the oldest son and you are nothing but a servant. I'll tell my father what you said and he'll throw you out.' He stormed out of the room, slamming the door and making the house rattle.

'Oh dear,' the nurse moaned. 'And I was so hoping you would stay.'

'He needs taking in hand. How do you put up with his behaviour?'

'Because I have to. In his mother's eyes he can do no wrong. I can't understand it; she never used to be so withdrawn and oblivious to what is going on around her. All of her attention is on that one child.'

'What about the father? I haven't seen him yet.'

'He's away a lot, but returned just an hour ago. I have heard him reprimand his son, but he's never here long enough to straighten the boy out. He works hard and I think he likes a quiet life while he's home.'

'What does he do?'

'He's a lawyer – barrister, I believe, and works in London.'

Chrissie nodded and let the subject drop. She would no doubt meet him soon, when he dismissed her.

As soon as the two girls were safely tucked up in bed Chrissie made her way up to her room. When she opened the door she was horrified to see the boy in there. He had pulled her belongings out from under the bed and was holding the box containing the crystal ball.

'Put that down,' she demanded.

He opened his fingers and let it crash to the floor, and then laughed, dancing up and down as if it was a huge joke.

She scooped it up and her eyes clouded with distress and anger when she saw the box had split down one side, and she was afraid to look inside. If this monster had damaged Elsie's precious gift she would give him the hiding he deserved and take the consequences for her action.

'What is going on here?' A man caught hold of the

145

laughing, prancing boy and demanded, 'Be quiet! Your noise can be heard all over the house.'

'Send her away, Father. I don't like her.'

'I told you to be silent.' The man turned his attention to Chrissie. 'I would like an explanation, please.'

This was clearly the master of the house and she had been surprised by the word 'please'. He was quite tall and rather imposing-looking, with an air of authority about him. Feeling for sure she was about to be sent on her way – again – it didn't enter her mind not to tell exactly what had happened. 'I discovered your son in my room, sir, and he was holding this box. When I asked him to put it down, he just dropped it on the floor.'

'What were you doing up here?' he asked the boy.

He shrugged. 'Looking round and I wanted to see what she had. That box is too good for her. I bet she stole it.'

'I didn't, sir,' she protested, unable to keep the distress out of her voice. 'It was a gift to me from a lovely woman.'

'And therefore very precious to you,' he said softly.

She nodded. 'And now the box is broken and I'm afraid to look inside. It's very old and had been in Elsie's family for a long time.'

He held out his hands. 'Let me see.'

She handed it over very carefully, and watched as he removed the crystal ball from the broken box. When she saw it was undamaged, she gave a huge sigh of relief.

Turning it over and over in his hands, he said, 'It's beautiful.'

The boy was staring at it in wonder. 'A servant can't own a thing like that. She stole it, Father. She must have.'

146

The look he received shut him up immediately. 'I'll hear the young woman's story, and if you have done wrong, which I firmly believe you have, I will deal with you later. Now, I don't want to hear another word from you, and I won't tell you again.'

'I didn't do anything wrong. She's only a servant.'

'Don't you dare defy me, young man! I told you to be quiet and I mean it. I will decide who is in the wrong here.' He handed the crystal ball back to her and began to examine the box. 'I know an excellent handyman and he will repair this for you. Will you allow me to take it to him?'

'Thank you, sir, but I will try and fix it myself. I can't pay for it to be repaired.'

'My son damaged it, Miss Banner. You must allow me to cover the cost of the repairs.'

'Thank you, sir. I would be grateful.' She had been surprised by the generous offer, and the fact that he knew her name when he must have only returned a short time ago.

'Tell me about this kind person who gave you this lovely gift.'

'She's a fortune-teller.' Chrissie smiled sadly as she remembered the happy times she had spent with Elsie and the Travellers. 'This belonged to her mother, grandmother and even further back, I believe.'

'And why did she give it to you?'

'It's a long story, sir.'

'I have plenty of time.' He smiled, looking relaxed and not at all angry with her.

Seeing his reaction and feeling he was genuinely interested, she began with her dad's death, leaving nothing out.

When she came to the end of her story he shook his head. 'You have had a difficult time, and I apologise that you have had to endure more distress in my house. I will make certain that nothing like this happens again. I know the Frenshaws and am pleased to hear that the major has returned safely, but astonished he dismissed you. That does not sound like the man I know well.'

'He was in a poor way when he arrived home, and not himself, sir. I don't blame him. He didn't like a girl working as a stable lad, and he does own the estate.'

'It is unusual, I must say.' He smiled again.

'I love horses, sir, and those warhorses are a real handful at times.'

'So I believe.' He picked up the box. 'Now, if you will permit me, I will see the damage my son has caused is repaired.'

'You're not going to take her word for it, are you, Father?' his son protested. 'You heard her, where she comes from. She's a Gypsy and can't be trusted.'

'And who told you that?' her father demanded.

'I heard Mother talking about it one day when she was having tea with her friends.'

He pulled a face in disgust. 'You shouldn't be listening to idle speculation by people who have probably never seen anyone who doesn't belong to high society. I can see there are some family matters to sort out. Now, apologise to Miss Banner for causing her such upset.'

He pouted and looked defiant.

'Do as I say,' his father told him in a tone of voice only a fool would disobey.

'I . . . I'm sorry I broke your box.'

'If you are truly sorry, then I accept your apology.'

The master caught hold of his son's shoulder, gave a slow bow to Chrissie, and left the room.

Their footsteps echoed on the wooden stairs and she listened until they faded away, then she sat on the bed hugging the crystal ball. Sir Stuart Gretham had been kind, but from what she had seen of his wife she doubted she would be as understanding. It was her adored son being disciplined, and as Nurse had said, in her eyes he could do no wrong. She bowed her head in worry. Tomorrow could see her wandering the countryside in search of work again. Oh, Dad, she cried silently, you know how I've always wanted to get out of London, but after all the trouble I've had I'm wondering if I've done the right thing. Perhaps I should have given up this idea of finding a permanent home in the country and stayed with the Travellers.

'Ah, there you are.' The nurse came into her room, and when she saw Chrissie's stricken expression she sat beside her. 'Are you all right? We heard all the commotion. You haven't been dismissed, have you?'

'Not yet, but I expect I will be in the morning.'

Nurse Benson patted her arm. 'Let's hope not, but in the meantime we have the children to look after.'

'Of course.' She tucked the crystal ball in the bed for safety and stood up. 'Will you deal with Robert, please, and I'll see to the two girls.'

'He's still with his father. Will you tell me what happened? When I heard shouting coming from your room I was on my way up to see what was going on when I heard the master telling his son to be quiet. Then I turned round and went back down, knowing he was dealing with his son.'

'That was the boy dancing around and enjoying himself. I'll tell you about it later.'

'All right, my dear, you talk about it when you want to. I can see you are still very upset.'

An hour later they were free of any chores and Nurse said, 'I'm ready for a nice cup of tea now.'

'Me too,' Chrissie agreed.

While making their way to the kitchen the scullery maid caught them, agog with excitement. 'There's been a terrible row. I've never heard the master raise his voice before; you know how calm and composed he always is. Robert has been crying and the mistress has taken to her bed, distraught.'

Chrissie's heart plummeted, knowing she had been the cause of this unpleasant situation. The last thing she ever wanted to do was cause trouble for anyone, but it had happened yet again to her.

'Did you hear what was being said?' Nurse asked.

The maid nodded, hardly able to contain herself. 'The master said he's taking his son away in the morning to the same boarding school he went to, where he would be taught some discipline and good manners.'

'Good, that's just what he needs.' Nurse smiled with satisfaction. 'The boy should have gone there some time ago, but I know the mistress objected. It looks as if the master has decided it can't be put off any longer. Anything else?'

'The master then lowered his voice so it was hard to hear,

but I think he told his wife the child had been thoroughly spoilt and was out of control, and no son of his was going to behave like that. I'm not sure, but I believe he threatened to divorce her and take the children away from her if she didn't do as he said.'

Chrissie gasped. 'You must be mistaken, Lilly; he would never do such a scandalous thing.'

'You're right,' Nurse agreed, giving them a knowing look. 'But he might say something like that if he wanted to make sure she obeyed him. Let's get some sleep. We'll find out what all this is about in the morning.'

It would be her dismissal, Chrissie was now sure.

The moment the children were up and had their breakfast – except Robert – Chrissie was called to the library. She paused at the door and took a deep breath, determined to face another dismissal with dignity, knowing she had not done anything wrong this time or the last. Once she felt composed enough she tapped on the door and entered.

The master was seated behind a large desk and rose to his feet the moment she walked in. He glanced across at his son who was sitting by the window. 'Robert. It is polite to stand when a woman enters the room.'

The boy opened his mouth to protest that she was only a servant, but the expression on his father's face made him change his mind and he stood up.

Stuart Gretham nodded and turned his attention to Chrissie, and smiled. 'Your box is being repaired and will be returned to you by this evening. The craftsman assured me that you will not be able to see where it has been broken, and I believe him. He is excellent at his trade.'

'Thank you, sir.' This evening? So she wasn't going to be sent on her way immediately.

'I am taking my son to a good school noted for its discipline – in fact, I attended there myself, at the same time as Harry Frenshaw. I have called you here to let you know that the only person in this house who has the authority to dismiss you is me. I shall be away for a few days and if anyone – *anyone*,' he emphasised, 'tells you to leave, you are to ignore them.'

Chrissie didn't know what to say, she was so shocked. She had been ready to leave, and now she was being told that no one could dismiss her but him.

'Is that clear?' he asked, when she didn't answer.

'Not really, sir,' she admitted. 'You can't mean Lady Gretham as well?'

'That does include my wife. If I return and find you are not here I shall be very angry. However, if you decide to leave after the disgraceful way you have been treated, I ask you to wait for my return and talk to me first. Will you do that?'

'Yes, sir.' She let out a silent breath of relief. The thought of roaming the countryside trying to find work and a roof over her head again so soon did not fill her with pleasure.

'Thank you. My other children like you very much and will be happy to know you are staying. Nurse also speaks very highly of you.' A slight smile crossed his face. 'They said you tell good stories and make them laugh. I understand you ride, so would you teach them? It is time they got used to being on a horse.'

'I would be happy to do that, sir.' A bright smile lit up her face. 'But I ride bareback and in breeches.'

He tipped his head back and laughed. 'I think we had better start with saddles for the children or they will be tumbling off the animals.'

'Of course, sir.'

'Come, Robert, we must be on our way. I'll see you in a few days, Miss Banner.'

Then they were gone and she was standing in the same place, unable to believe what had just happened. She walked slowly out of the room to find Nurse waiting anxiously for her. 'What happened?'

'I am still here and cannot be dismissed by anyone but the master himself. What an extraordinary thing to happen.'

'That's wonderful news! The girls will be delighted, and so am I. You're the best helper I've ever had.'

The rest of the day was relaxed, there was no sign of the mistress, and even the children appeared happier without their older brother tormenting them.

When it was time for bed, Chrissie felt almost happy. The crystal was back in the expertly repaired box, and she still had a job. She was grateful for that, but her heart was, and always would be, at the Frenshaws' estate and her beloved horses.

Chapter Seventeen

'What the hell do you think you are doing?' Charles strode in to his son's room and caught hold of him as he struggled to stand upright. 'Get back in that bed!'

'I can't stay here; there's so much to do.'

'Everything is being taken care of, as it was while you were away fighting in that damned war. We need you fit and well, but if you try to move around too soon it will only delay your recovery. I got you back when it seemed impossible, and I don't want to lose you now, son.'

'I'm sorry. You are right, of course, but it's so frustrating not being able to do anything.' He settled back in the bed with the help of his father and grimaced. 'I seem to be causing you nothing but grief.'

'Indeed you are,' he replied teasingly, 'but none of it is your fault. Now, I want you to stop causing us trouble and regain your health and strength as soon as possible. Trust us, Harry. Everyone is working to sort out this mess. If you will give me your word that you will behave yourself and do as the doctor tells you, then I intend to leave for London this morning to see if I can find out who wants you dead.'

'I promise to do as I'm told, but I wish I could come with you. You'll have to be careful not to alert Edward to the fact that he is our prime suspect.'

'I am discretion itself.'

Harry gave a snort of amusement, and then concern crossed his face again. 'Any news of that girl?'

'Not yet. She won't be easy to find. If she's joined up with the Travellers again she could be anywhere. We'll keep looking, but I don't hold out much hope. You have to forget about her because we might never see her again. You made a mistake, Harry, we all do, but you have to put it behind you now.'

'I won't accept that she can't be found. The look I saw in her dark eyes when I sent her away is haunting me. It was as if I had ripped her world from under her feet, and I have since discovered how much she loved it here. I can't put it behind me until I've seen she is all right.'

'I understand how you feel. You acted completely out of character, but what is done is done. You have to accept that and move on.'

Harry shook his head. 'I've got to right that wrong. If I'd had a good reason to dismiss her, then I wouldn't have given it another thought, but I've been told just how good she was with the horses. What I did was not only unjust, it was cruel and completely unjustified. I've never acted like that in my life before, and it rankles. She must hate me.'

'That may be true, but not enough to have you killed,' Charles pointed out firmly.

'Of course not. In my opinion the only candidate for that crime is Edward.'

'Agreed, and I must be on my way.' Charles stood up. 'My main concern is to find whoever the would-be assassin is, or he could try again when he discovers you are still alive.'

'Edward hasn't been round to enquire about my health?'

'Not a sign of him, but I have written to his London address to let him know that you are gravely injured and your life is in the balance. We've also done our best to spread the word, because the villain is probably waiting to see what happens. If I can't discover who attacked you, then I might try to make him reveal himself by announcing that you have died. I don't want that to be true, so for goodness' sake stay in that bed.'

'That's good advice, Major, so take it.' The doctor entered the room and studied his patient carefully. 'What's he been up to?' he asked Charles.

'I caught him out of bed and trying to stand up.'

The doctor raised his hands in exasperation. 'I'd better have a look and see if he's done any damage.'

'Keep an eye on him. I will be away for a few days.'

'I'll see he is guarded all the time.'

Charles ignored the sound of disgust that came from his son and left the room, anxious to be on his way. He knew his son and he wasn't going to stay in that bed a moment longer than absolutely necessary. For his safety the culprit had to be found and detained, and if it wasn't Edward then the task was even more urgent.

He hadn't been to the London club for quite a while and was greeted warmly when he walked in. They were all eager to talk to him and he was soon seated with a group wanting news about his son. This was just what he needed, and made it easy to slip questions into the conversation. These men knew everything that was going on and loved to gossip.

After hearing the remarks of pleasure at Harry's safe return from the Crimea, Charles was surprised that news of the assassination attempt on his son had not yet reached these gentlemen. That left him free to turn the conversation round to his nephew.

'Is Edward here?' he asked.

'Haven't seen him yet,' one man answered. 'But he will probably be here later.'

'Ah, good, I might catch him, then. I haven't seen him for a while. What has he been doing with himself?'

'Gambling. He likes the tables a little too much, but you already know that.'

'I was hoping he had mended his ways. A spell in the military would do him good. Not cavalry, of course, he's not a proficient enough horseman, but perhaps a rifle brigade.' He pursed his lips thoughtfully. 'Though I don't suppose he knows one end of a gun from another.'

Some of the men laughed, but one said, 'I believe he does. My son is a member of a shooting club and has seen him there quite often. He told me he's a remarkably good shot.'

'Really?' Charles expression remained passive, showing only slight amusement. 'He's never mentioned it to his family and that isn't like him. He does like to brag about any new skill he might have.'

'I wouldn't say it was a new thing for him. My son believes he's been a member there for at least two years.'

'My goodness,' Charles exclaimed. 'Does your son know him well?'

'He's only met him a couple of times, that's all. They don't have the same interests, you know.'

'You mean your son doesn't gamble.'

'He does not, and that's a blessing when so many young fools are losing their inheritances on the turn of the cards.'

'A sad state of affairs, indeed.'

The subject changed to more general topics and Charles sat back to listen, satisfied that he had the information he needed. He would follow it up by visiting the club to find out exactly how good a shot his nephew was. He had to be very good to hit a moving target, and knowing his son, he doubted he was moving at anything less than a full gallop. He had to admit this news about Edward's proficiency with a rifle had surprised and disturbed him. In his heart he had hoped the culprit was a nameless person with a grudge against Harry. It would have been so much easier to deal with emotionally, but to suspect it might be a member of your own family was very distressing.

Charles stayed the night at his club and then left early the next morning to visit the gun club. There was a chance they had not been talking about Edward, as the information had come from a young man who had only met his nephew a couple of times. It was worth following up, though, because if it was him he must be stopped, however painful that would be for Harry and himself. It saddened him to suspect his dear sister's boy was capable of such an act, and it was a blessing his parents were no longer alive. His sister had died many years ago in childbirth, and her distraught husband had neglected his duties as a father, leaving Edward without a strict enough upbringing. He had passed away with a heart attack some ten years later, and Edward had gone to live with a relative of his father. They had been good people, but unable to control the young man who quickly became addicted to gambling.

The club was busy when he arrived and asked to be shown around, pretending to be interested in joining.

During the tour he questioned them about the different targets they had, such as instructions on how to fire at moving targets.

'We do teach that skill here, your lordship. Many young gentlemen come here to become proficient before joining the military. Perhaps you would like to meet our instructors?'

'I would, indeed.'

There were two of them, obviously retired soldiers, and Charles spent some time with them. They were extremely interested when he told them his son had been a cavalry officer in the Crimean War, but had survived. By now he had their full attention and asked casually, 'I believe my nephew, Edward Danton, is a member here.'

'Lord Danton comes regularly and is a remarkable shot.'

Lord? So the boy was passing himself off as being titled. He hid his surprise and asked, 'Is he good enough to hit a fast-moving target?'

'Yes, your lordship. He has a good eye.' Knowing they were talking to a relative of Edward's they were eager to praise his abilities.

This news confirmed that the boy was almost certainly the culprit, and the disappointment Charles felt at that moment was crushing, but he knew, family or not, he had to be dealt with. Harry was his loved son and he would do anything to protect him, even if it meant turning in one of his own family to the law.

He spent another night at his club, and headed for home at dawn the next day without seeing a sign of Edward.

The moment he arrived home he went straight to his son's room and was relieved to see him looking more rested with a little colour in his face.

'What news?' he demanded immediately, and listened with a grim expression to what his father had found out. He laid his head back, looking stricken. 'Damn! I'm sorry. I was really hoping it wasn't Edward, but it must have been him.'

'I'm afraid so, and now we have to prove it, which isn't going to be easy.'

'And if we can't, what do you intend to do, Father?'

'I don't know.' He ran a hand over his tired eyes. 'But the blasted fool must be dealt with somehow. If he's tried to kill you once, we will never be sure he won't try again, and you will spend your time looking over your shoulder.'

Seeing his father's anguish he reached out and squeezed his arm. 'We could confront him and threaten him with prosecution if he tries anything like this again.'

'No, I couldn't risk that. From what I heard he is

desperate for money and needs you dead before you change your will.'

'He's too late. I did that while you were in London.'

'That's a relief. Can I ask what you have done with the estate?'

'I've bequeathed it to someone who loves the animals and, I believe, would take good care of the place.'

'Oh, and who is that?'

'I won't tell anyone, not even you, because that would put them in danger, and if you know it could also put your life at risk.'

'I understand.' Charles went to stand up when there was a gentle rap on the door and the butler looked in.

'Mr Edward is here asking for you, your lordship. Will you come down, or shall I send him away?'

'Well, I'll be damned. He's got a nerve.'

Harry was grinning now. 'He's come to check up on me.'

'He mustn't know you are on the road to recovery, or he will surely find another way to get to you. We must convince him you are gravely ill. I'll come down,' he told the butler.

'Bring him up here.' Harry reached out and dabbed water on his face and then settled against the pillows, eyes closed. He opened one eye. 'How is that?'

'Not bad, but I'll dim the lights, though, and draw the curtains a little more, so he can't see you too clearly. And send up one of the maids to sit in the room. It would look strange if someone wasn't with him all the time,' he told the butler.

Once everything was in place, he hurried down to see his nephew.

'Uncle, I've just heard the terrible news about the attack on Harry. No one here will tell me anything. How is he?'

'The prognosis is not good, I'm afraid. This injury on top of those he suffered in the war could prove too much for him.' Charles let his eyes cloud with moisture. 'I was in London for a couple of days on business and hoped to see you at the club.'

'Ah, I'm sorry; I have been in Bath for two weeks so didn't see your letter until I returned to London. May I see Harry?'

Charles hesitated as if unsure. 'I suppose you could, but I must ask you to be very quiet. He mustn't be disturbed.'

Edward agreed and followed his uncle up to the bedroom. He walked straight up to the bedside and studied the still figure of his cousin for some moments. 'Is he conscious?' he asked quietly.

'He hasn't regained consciousness yet.' Charles took hold of Edward's arm and indicated that they should leave. 'The maid will tell us if he wakes.'

Back in the library Charles offered his nephew a drink, which he declined.

'I can't stay, Uncle. I came as soon as I read your letter. It doesn't look good.'

'We haven't given up yet. We have an excellent doctor tending him, and he has kept him alive so far.'

'Hmm. It's going to take a long time, though. He's only been home a short time so if you need any help with the estate I would be happy to stay.'

'Not necessary, but I appreciate your offer. I'll let you know when there is any news.'

'Do you have any idea who did this?'

Charles shook his head, knowing it was important not to let Edward know he was a suspect. 'Not yet, but we will find him; you can have no doubt about that!'

'You said "him", but have you thought it might be a woman? That girl you had working as a stable lad could have hated him for sending her away.'

'Chrissie? Good heavens, she wouldn't know how to fire a gun, let alone hit a moving target. That takes a skilled marksman.'

'I wouldn't rule it out,' he persisted. 'She spent time with some Travellers and they must have guns to hunt for food. Rabbits are very fast-moving targets, and they might have taught her.'

'That's a possibility, I suppose, but highly unlikely, and she has left the area and is probably back in London again by now.'

'Well, let me know if I can help at any time.'

'I will, you can be sure of that.' Charles watched Edward mount up and ride away, and then he went back to his son and dismissed the maid.

Harry sat up. 'Did we fool him?'

'I think so, and he wanted to stay and help with the estate. I expect he believes you haven't been home long enough to change your will.'

'He would have been correct if that bullet had killed me. Tell me everything he said.'

When Charles had finished, Harry looked thoughtful. 'Sounds as if he came to set up an alibi by saying he was in Bath at the time of the shooting. That needs to be checked.'

'I'll send someone to the gaming houses he frequents. He was very keen to put the blame on Chrissie, but she would never harm anyone.'

'You have great faith in her character, and I'll take your word for it.'

'It's obvious he's trying to turn our attention away from himself. I hate to suspect he did this but everything we've found out so far points to him.'

'I agree, and I wish it were otherwise.'

'Yes, it is a sad state of affairs, and we must be very careful, Harry. If he believes for one moment that we are investigating him there is no telling what he might do.'

'I'll send for a man who was with me at Balaclava. No one knows him and he is a fine investigator, and he can be trusted. Without him I would never have got back to this country.'

'Good idea. We really need help.'

Chapter Eighteen

The last week had at least been peaceful, even though the mistress had shown her hostility to Chrissie by making her work from early morning till late in the evening doing all manner of unnecessary jobs. It was clear she blamed her for her son being sent away to a boarding school, and was showing her frustration at not being able to dismiss her.

Chrissie scrubbed the long hallway until it gleamed, determined Lady Gretham wouldn't be able to find fault. If she hadn't given her promise not to leave before Sir Gretham returned she would have walked out days ago, but she tried never to break a promise, and she didn't know where else she could go.

'What the blazes are you doing?'

She spun round at the sound of the angry male voice and hurriedly stood up. 'Scrubbing the floor, sir.'

'Why?'

'Because I was told to, sir.'

'By whom?'

'Lady Gretham, sir.'

'That is the scullery maid's job. You were engaged to help look after the children.' He dropped his case on the floor, and when she went to pick it up, he said sharply, 'Leave it.'

'I was going to take it up to your room, sir.'

'What you are going to do,' he stated furiously, 'is take that bucket back to the scullery and resume your proper duties.'

'I haven't quite finished the floor and Lady Gretham will be angry if it is left like this.'

'And I will be even angrier if you continue, Miss Banner.' He moderated his tone. 'Now, do as I say.'

'Yes, sir.' She picked up the bucket and scrubbing brush and hurried back to the scullery. The young maid was waiting and took the cleaning things from her.

'I'll finish it, Chrissie. It's my job, anyway. You should never have been told to do it.'

'My, my,' the cook declared, 'there's going to be trouble, and just wait until the master finds out how you've been treated while he was away.'

'I'd better go and collect my things together ready to leave. I can't stay here when I'm only causing upset.'

'Oh, don't leave,' Nurse told her. 'He's a good man and he'll deal with this. He has married below his station and the marriage has only lasted because he spends so much time away.'

Chrissie shook her head. 'That is none of my business. I must move on.'

'But where will you go?'

'I'll find somewhere.' She smiled sadly and made her way up to her room, sick at heart. What was the matter with her? She always tried to do whatever she was asked to do, never complaining, and yet she didn't seem to fit in anywhere. That wasn't quite true, of course. She had been completely happy at the Frenshaw estate with those beloved horses, and his lordship had been a real gentleman. She had honestly believed that was the right place for her – until the son had arrived home.

She pulled the box from under the bed, opened it and gazed in to the crystal ball. Her mind was so full of memories of Midnight and Red Sunset that she actually saw them gazing at her with sad eyes. She closed the lid quickly, the image too painful to look at, then did something unusual for her, she began to cry in great sobs of loneliness and grief for what might have been.

It took a while to compose herself, and then she was ashamed of her weakness. Feeling sorry for herself would not solve anything, in fact it would only add to her problems. After splashing her face with water from the bowl in the room she tidied her hair and resolved not to be so silly again.

'Chrissie!' The butler called her from the bottom of the stairs. 'The master wants to see you.'

'I'm coming,' she replied, hurrying down the servants' stairs to the library, where she hesitated. He had been very angry and she was sure she was about to become homeless again.

She tapped lightly on the door and walked in when he said 'Come'.

He was sitting behind a large desk and rose to his feet when she entered. 'Sit down, please, Miss Banner.'

She did as ordered, and waited.

'Can you read and write?'

That wasn't what she had expected at all, and for a moment she hesitated. 'Yes, sir.'

He pushed a pen and paper towards her, and then handed over an official-looking document. 'Copy the first paragraph of that for me, and make it as near to the original as you can.'

Completely at a loss to understand what this was about, she set about the task of copying from the document. When finished she replaced the pen in its holder and handed him the sheet of paper.

He studied it for some time, and finally looked up at her. 'That is an exact copy. The lettering is almost identical to the original. Where did you learn to write like this?'

'I went to school, sir.' What on earth was he doing this for?

'That is obvious, but that is not what I'm asking. Who taught you to write such beautiful script?'

'My dad showed me how to do it. The Travellers have their own teachers, and my dad used to do all the notices because he was good at fancy writing.' Her smile was wistful. 'After the day's work was done we used to play a game to see who could make the best copy of each other's writing, or draw the best picture. He always won.'

He stood up and went to the bookcase, searching for a

particular volume, and when he found it he opened it at a page showing a picture of a bridge. 'Copy that for me.'

Thoroughly confused by now she set about the drawing. From a young child she had been able to draw, and had never thought much about it.

He waited patiently, not speaking while she worked. After examining the finished work thoroughly, he slapped it down on the desk and got to his feet, walking over to stare out of the window.

Suddenly he spun round. 'What the devil are you doing working as a servant?'

'Sir?'

'You have a talent. Why aren't you using it?'

This was getting silly and she was losing patience with all this talk. What did a man like this, born to privilege, know about the life of the poor? 'Sir, I was brought up in the slums of London where every day is a struggle to keep a roof over your head and food on the table. It doesn't matter how bright you are, no one's going to give you a good job. Society thinks all we are good for is scrubbing floors and being treated like the dirt we come from.' Her eyes turned almost black with defiance. 'Well, some of us are not ignorant or dirty, but it's bloody well impossible to get away from that, as I am finding out. I have always dreamt of coming to the country and making a good life for myself, but it's no different here. I'm still that girl from the slums.' She stood up. 'I'll get my things and be on my way.'

'Sit down. I haven't finished talking to you yet.'

'I think you have, sir. You are about to tell me Lady

Gretham doesn't want a troublemaker in her home, so you don't have to bother. I already know.'

'Is that what you think this is about?'

'Of course. What other reason could there be for calling me in here?'

'Sit down again and I'll tell you.'

Reluctantly, she did as ordered. He had moderated his tone again, and what did she have to lose by hearing what he had to say?

'I apologise for raising my voice to you, Miss Banner. I was not angry with you, but I get angry when I see anyone being denied a decent life just because they were born poor. You may not believe this, but I do understand the struggle some have to drag themselves out of the gutter. But let me tell you, it is possible. I am involved in helping the underprivileged with talent towards a more productive life. I have one such boy working for me in London.'

She sat up straight, suddenly interested in what he was saying.

'I noticed from our first meeting that you are bright, and even though life has not been kind to you, you kept on trying to improve your life. I believe the severe setbacks you have encountered have not dimmed your resolve. Now I have discovered you have a talent that can be put to good use. I need help and will promise my support to see you get the kind of life you yearn for. Will you agree that we will help each other?'

She leant forward, intrigued but suspicious about what this handsome, successful man wanted from her. From what she had seen of his marriage it wasn't a good one, and she wasn't daft or ignorant about the ways of some men, especially the upper class. She knew of several young girls who had been taken advantage of while in service, and then abandoned. Nothing like that was ever going to happen to her!

'Well?' he raised an eyebrow, waiting for a reply.

She sat back and folded her arms. 'State your case, sir.'

He laughed. 'I see you want me to plead my cause.'

'If you would, please, sir.'

'Very well. First, I must say that you have a very expressive face and I can quite easily guess what you are thinking. I have no intention of taking advantage of you, and I am certain you would not allow it anyway. There are one or two ladies who would be willing to pamper to my needs, should I so wish it, which I don't,' he told her bluntly. 'What I am looking for is someone to copy documents that must be done by hand. If you will agree to do this for me I will see what I can do to advance your standing in life.'

'How can you do that?' Hope and excitement was building inside her, but she wanted to know more.

'You will work on an urgent document here first, then once my local business is finished, I will take you to my London chambers.'

'Chambers?'

'Offices. Your duties will be to copy documents when necessary, run errands, and any other tasks that need doing.'

'Scrubbing floors?'

A slow smile crossed his face. 'Certainly not. I have a cleaner to do that.'

'I don't want to go back to London. I have struggled hard to get out of that place.'

'It will only be for a week or two at the most, and then you can come back here.'

'Where would I stay while in London, sir?'

'You will lodge with my colleague and his wife. You will be quite safe.'

She looked down at her shabby skirt and then back at the man behind the desk. 'What will they think about taking in a girl from the gutter, as you so vividly described it?'

'I will see you are dressed appropriately for your new position.'

'And what will that cost me?'

'Nothing. Accept it as a token of my gratitude for the help you are about to give me.'

'I won't accept gifts from any man, sir. If I need new clothes I will have to be able to buy them out of any money I earn. I assume I will be paid for this work?'

He inclined his head. 'Of course. You will be in my employ and will be paid in accordance with the position of office junior. I admire your caution.' He wrote down something and pushed the note towards her. 'That will be your salary.'

'Is that for a year?'

'You are still thinking like a scullery maid,' he chided. 'That will be your salary for a month.'

Her mouth dropped open and she shot to her feet. 'A month! You're joking.'

'I'm perfectly serious.' He was having difficulty controlling his amusement. 'Is that acceptable to you? Do we have an agreement?'

'You do, sir,' she replied with as much dignity as she could muster.

He stood up and reached out to shake her hand. 'Welcome to the Gretham firm of lawyers.'

'Thank you, sir. I won't let you down.'

'I am aware of that, Miss Banner, or I would not have considered employing you.' He gave a deep laugh. 'After these negotiations I think you would make a fine lawyer.'

'Oh, they would never allow a woman to do that.'

'One day it will become quite normal, along with other professions like doctors, politicians and many more. At the moment, too many men think women should be confined to the home – I don't.'

'Is that why you are giving me this chance?'

'That's one reason, but there is also a selfish one. I am in need of a good copier, and you have the skill. I don't employ anyone on a whim. They must be capable of doing the work required, and you have proved to me that you have the skill needed for the job. The fact that you are a woman makes no difference to me.'

'You are an unusual man, sir.'

'So I have been told on numerous occasions. Now, I'd like you to start on the document on my desk immediately. I will need it by midday tomorrow. You can work in here and I will see you are not disturbed. You will break for mealtimes, and work no later than six in the evening.'

'What about my other duties, sir?'

'From now on you have no other duties. You work for me and no one else.' He smiled at her. 'I will leave you to your work. There is plenty of paper and ink on the desk.'

She watched him stride from the room, took a deep breath and hoped her dad was looking down, unable to believe that the games they had played with writing and drawing had led to this. 'Dad, what do you think of this? I'm going to work in an office for a while.'

Settling at the big desk she put the first sheet of paper in front of her. It was a lengthy document and she would be very careful with it, because it needed to be perfect.

Two hours passed without her noticing when there was a quiet knock on the door. It opened and she watched in amazement as the maid wheeled in a trolley. 'The master said you are to be given refreshments.' The girl did a quick curtsy and giggled.

Chrissie tried to remain serious, but couldn't, and laughed along with the young maid. She was being waited on!

Chapter Nineteen

The doctor changed the dressing and nodded in approval. 'You heal quickly, Major. You may get up today, but only to sit in the chair. I expect you can do with a change of scenery.'

'I certainly can.' Harry was already on his feet with the aid of the doctor.

'Let's get you dressed and I will help you downstairs, but I want your word you will not go wandering around outside.'

'I'll make sure he doesn't.' Charles entered the room, delighted to see his son making good progress now. The change in him over the last few days was remarkable.

With one man either side of him, Harry made his way to the library where he could look out on the paddock and watch his horses. His favourite green leather chair was pulled up to the window and he sat down with a grunt of relief. 'Just look at those two mares I bought. Aren't they magnificent, Father?'

'Prime specimens.'

'Ask Bert, the head groom, to come and see me—'

'No!' both men stated at once.

'In a day or two you can start ordering people around,' the doctor told him. 'Today you must remain quiet, or I'll have you back in bed.'

Harry grimaced. 'Good thing I didn't have you at Balaclava, Doctor, or I would never have arrived home. I was travelling with injuries worse than this, and so was my brave horse.'

'Quite frankly, after seeing the scars on you and your horse, I don't know how you survived. That disaster took its toll on you, though, and we don't want to take any chances you might still be in a weakened state. If you do as I say, then your complete recovery will be all the faster, but be patient.'

'All right. For today I will be content to just look.' He gave both men a determined glare. 'But tomorrow I shall expect to become involved in the running of the estate again. There is a lot to do.'

'No riding until you are strong enough to stay upright on a horse.'

'I'll wait a couple of days.'

The doctor sighed and turned to Charles. 'I'm beginning to think I should have tied him to that bed. Please don't let him do too much the moment my back is turned.'

'I'll do my best, but you know how stubborn he can be.'

'And thank the Lord he is. I'll be back this evening to help him up the stairs and back in to bed.'

'I'm not a baby. I can look after myself now.' He watched the doctor head for the door, and when he was about to leave, Harry called, 'Doctor, thank you for all you've done. I do appreciate it.'

'I know you do, Major, and you haven't got rid of me yet. Your recovery still has a way to go, so behave yourself – if that's possible.'

'Everything is possible.'

It was the middle of the afternoon when the clatter of someone arriving woke Harry from a doze. After a few minutes the butler arrived.

'There is a Captain Joseph Taylor asking to see the major. Are visitors permitted, your lordship?'

Harry hoisted himself out of the chair. 'Send him in.'

'At once,' the butler answered when Charles nodded to him.

The man who entered was dusty from travelling hard. He was of stocky build, with fair hair and alert blue eyes, which gleamed with pleasure when he saw Harry.

He marched in and saluted smartly. 'Your message sounded urgent, Harry, and I came as soon as I could.'

'Ah, it's good to see you, Joe, and thank you for coming. This is my father.'

Joe bowed quite elegantly. 'It is a pleasure to meet you, your lordship. Harry spoke of you often while we were travelling back.'

Charles shook the captain's hand, liking him instantly. 'Please sit down and I'll order refreshments. I expect you would also like a drink to wash down the dust.'

'That would be very welcome, your lordship.'

'We don't stand on formality here, Joe, so please call me Charles.'

He inclined his head and his eyes narrowed as he watched Harry make his way to the drinks table. 'You're hurt!'

'Yes, that's why I sent for you. Someone shot me and I need your help to track him down.' He handed his friend a large whisky, then poured a smaller one for himself and his father before sitting down again.

'Before we start on my story, tell me what you've being doing since we arrived back.'

'Like you, I have resigned my commission and have applied to join the London police, and they've accepted me.' Joe grinned. 'It seemed the logical thing to do.'

'Excellent.' Harry turned to his father. 'If we ever needed to find out what was happening in a certain area, or track something down, we always sent Joe. He's as good as a bloodhound.'

'He's just the man we need, then.'

Joe emptied his glass and watched as a trolley was wheeled in piled with food. Once the maid left, he asked, 'So, I assume you need to track down the devil that shot you?'

'We have an idea who it is, but we need proof.'

'Tell me the whole tale.'

It took a while to explain everything, and when Harry finished, his friend looked grim. 'As this is a relative of yours, what do you intend to do when you have the necessary proof?'

'If there isn't a shadow of doubt that he is guilty then he will have to be handed over to the law,' Charles told him.

'That will be a tough decision for you, but I'll see what I can find out.'

Charles sighed in relief as a weight lifted from his shoulders. Harry had been right to send for this man.

'Thanks, Joe,' Harry told him. 'We can't do this ourselves, because if we start investigating news will likely get back to Edward, and we are concerned what he might do then. As you know only too well, a cornered man is the most dangerous. If he finds out a stranger is asking questions about him he will probably think one of his debts is being chased.'

'Don't worry. He won't even know I'm on his tail.'

Harry laughed. 'I don't suppose he will. You've had plenty of experience slipping in and out of places unseen. You'll make a good officer of the law.'

He winked, showing he knew what his friend was hinting at, and then got down to business. 'Have you got a likeness of this man?'

'Only a miniature.' Charles retrieved it from the drawer of the desk and handed it over.

The captain studied it for a while, and then handed it back.

'You can keep it for reference.'

'Not necessary. I'll recognise him if I see him.'

'Joe never forgets a face,' he told his father. 'That image is now firmly fixed in his mind.'

'Ah, that's a useful talent.'

'I have found it so. The place to start will be Bath, to find out if the man was really there when he claims he was. Even if he was that doesn't rule him out, because he could have hired someone to kill you, Harry. Though considering his financial situation, such an arrangement could have been too costly for him, but we mustn't rule out any possibility.'

'We did consider he might have hired someone, until we found out he's an excellent shot and quite capable of hitting a moving target. From what my father has told me, Edward wants this estate quite desperately.'

'He does seem to be the most likely candidate, but I must ask you, is there anyone else you can think of who wants you dead?'

'None who would stoop to killing me on my own land . . .' His words tailed off.

'I need to know all the facts, no matter how unlikely,' Joe urged his friend.

'There is something I haven't told you.' He then explained about the girl he had dismissed, her background and how Edward was attempting to throw suspicion on to her.

The captain fixed his gaze on Charles. 'You know her the best. Is there any possibility she could be involved?'

'None at all. The idea is not even worth considering,' Charles declared firmly.

'I understand. Do you know where she is now?'

'We've been looking, but haven't been able to find her,' Harry admitted. 'I'm worried that Edward mentioned her. I don't trust him.'

'I'll see if I can find her. What does she look like?'

'Taller than the average girl, maybe five feet eight or nine inches, dark hair, dark eyes, slim and strong for a female,' Charles explained.

'Well, her height will single her out. However, our

first task must be to find out who fired that shot.'

'Agreed.' Harry laid his head back and closed his eyes.

His father was immediately at his side. 'You've been up too long for your first day. Help me get him back upstairs, Joe.'

Harry didn't protest and was soon back in bed and sleeping peacefully.

The two men left the room quietly and returned to the library.

'There is a room being prepared for you, and we dine at seven. Please join me before then for a drink. The butler will show you to your room.'

'Thank you. That will give me time to freshen up after the journey.'

Charles found Joe an interesting dinner companion and the conversation flowed easily. 'My son told me he would never have made it back here if it hadn't been for your help and support.'

'I'm sure he would have managed, but we've been friends for some time, and I couldn't leave him. When the regiment was preparing to move out neither Harry nor his horse was in any fit state to travel. He could have gone in the wagons with the other wounded, but that would have meant shooting the horse, and he wouldn't allow them to destroy him. I was a good scout and could find the safest places for us to camp. Once they were fit enough we started back, but it took some time to reach these shores again. It was a hell of a journey as I watched both Harry and the animal fighting with determination to keep moving. You can be proud of your son.'

'I am, and I owe you a debt of gratitude.'

'You don't owe me anything. I was the one repaying a debt. I wouldn't have survived that carnage if it hadn't been for Harry's bravery, but that is another story.' He changed the subject. 'I had the impression he's very worried about this girl. What else can you tell me about her character? Can you start from the moment you met her and why you gave her a job here?'

Charles smiled gently as he remembered the day a young girl walked in, and he began to tell the story.

Joe listened intently, his whole attention focussed on Charles.

'She wasn't at all afraid of the huge horses, and when she saw the condition Midnight was in she refused to leave him. She stayed in his stall until he had recovered.' Charles laughed quietly. 'She used to ride them bareback.'

'And they let her?' Joe exclaimed in amazement.

'She had a wonderful way with them and they liked her. In fact, I believe they still miss her.'

'If she was so good, why did Harry dismiss her?'

'I really don't know, and we had quite a row about it, but when he saw a girl working as a stable lad and wearing breeches he sent her away immediately.'

'Well, I would say he's sorry now. I like the sound of the girl and will see if I can find her once we have settled the question of who fired that shot.'

'Yes, my son could still be in danger.' He went to the desk and took out a packet from the drawer. 'You will need money if you are to blend in with the gambling crowd at

Bath. Edward will be at the tables if he's there, and even if he isn't the best place to glean information will be with the gamblers. If you need more then let me know.'

Joe looked at the money and shook his head. 'This is more than enough. I rarely lose, unless I want to.'

'Really? How can you be sure of winning?'

'I can remember every card that has been played – and no one can detect when I'm cheating.' Joe laughed. 'I was taught by the best card sharps in the brigade, and that's why I never gamble. However, I may need to use those skills if I am to get the information we need.'

'Do be careful. Hardened gamblers can be dangerous.'

'I'm always careful,' he assured Charles. 'That's why I'm still alive. I will be leaving at first light, so if you will excuse me, I will retire early.'

Chapter Twenty

It was an anxious ten minutes as she watched the document she had copied being examined. It hadn't been easy because she didn't know what many of the words meant. It had been like a foreign language in places, and each letter had to be done with great care.

'You have done well,' Sir Stuart Gretham finally said. 'I will be returning to London tomorrow and will take you with me. How do you feel about that?'

'To be honest, not very happy, sir. I have no desire to see London again.'

'It will only be for a short time and then you can come back to the country again. You might find it exciting. I have a court case and I'll see you have a seat in a good position so you can watch the proceedings.'

'I'm sure that will be very interesting, sir.'

He laughed then. 'From your expression I can see I haven't convinced you.'

'It will be a new experience for me, but it's the thought of going back to London I don't like.'

'I won't keep you there any longer than necessary, but I have work for you to do. Even my experienced clerk can't copy documents as expertly as you. Now, come with me. I want to see how well you can ride.' He began to walk towards the door, and then turned a frown on his face. 'You are quite happy to ride for part of the journey, I take it?'

'Yes, sir.'

He nodded and she followed him to the yard where a groom was holding a mare and a boy was there ready to help her mount. 'Er . . .' she stared, puzzled. 'What's that on her back?'

'A saddle.'

'But it's facing the wrong way.'

'It's a lady's side-saddle, miss,' the groom told her. 'Haven't you seen one before?'

'No, and I can't use that. I ride bareback.'

The master gave a spluttering laugh. 'Give the saddle a try. I'm told it is quite comfortable, and you will soon get used to it.'

She tried – she really did, but the next few minutes were hilarious, and in the end the men had to admit defeat. 'Can't I try an ordinary saddle? I'll be much happier if I'm facing the right way.' Chrissie stroked the horse's nose. 'Don't you get upset about this. It isn't your fault. That saddle is ridiculous, don't you agree?' When the animal tossed her head up and down, she stroked its nose and turned back to the men. 'There you are, she agrees with me.'

'But, miss, you can't ride astride. Ladies use this kind of saddle.'

'That may well be, but I'm not a lady.'

The groom gave his master a helpless look. 'She can't ride astride, sir. It isn't possible with a skirt.'

'That isn't a problem.' She smiled happily at the men. 'I have some breeches.'

The groom looked scandalised, and the master was roaring with laughter. 'That would really make a stir if we rode into Southampton to board the locomotive to London with you astride and wearing men's breeches.'

'I could wear them under a full skirt, and when I got off the horse no one would see them.'

Alerted by all the laughter, Nurse had brought the children out to see what was going on. They were staring at their father in wonder, and Chrissie guessed they were not used to seeing him laughing like this.

'Get rid of that saddle,' he told the groom, still having trouble controlling his amusement.

'That's better,' she said as soon as the mare was unsaddled. 'Give me a lift up,' she asked the boy, and mounted eagerly. Delighted to be riding again, she urged the horse to a canter and then a gallop around the field. She trotted back, face glowing, and slid to the ground.

'How do you stay on without a saddle?' The groom couldn't believe what he had just seen. 'No lady would ever ride in such a way, without a saddle and her skirts billowing around her legs.'

'The Travellers taught me. It's easy.'

'You can certainly ride, there's no doubt about that, but how do I get you to London in a dignified manner?'

'You could take the carriage, sir,' the groom suggested.

'I thought of that, but it will slow down the journey.' He turned and beckoned Nurse over. 'Can you find Miss Banner a very full skirt by tomorrow morning?'

'We should be able to manage that, sir.'

'Good. That is what we will do. You stay here and get used to a proper saddle, and then tomorrow you will wear your breeches concealed under a suitable skirt. We will leave at eight o'clock.'

'I'll be ready, sir.' She watched him walk over to the children and swing the youngest up in the air, making her squeal in delight. The other one danced around him as they made their way back to the house.

'Ah, that's good to see.' Nurse sighed. 'Come and see me when you're free, Chrissie, and we will find you another skirt.'

She spent a happy half an hour getting used to the saddle, and although she preferred bareback, she decided it would be all right to use the saddle for the journey. Then she went to Nurse to see if they could find her something suitable to wear for the trip.

The next morning, attired in a voluminous skirt made out of two old garments, her breeches underneath, and a hat borrowed from Cook, Chrissie set off with Sir Gretham. The children waved until they were out of sight.

'It must be hard for you to be away from your children so much, sir.'

'It is, but my wife won't live in London. She tried for a while, but she is of a nervous disposition and couldn't stand the noise and crowds there.'

'That's a shame. I'm sure she could have a good life there, with more friends than she has in the country. It was different for me. I left after my dad died because I wanted to get out of the slums, and I always dreamt of open fields to run in.'

'You'll find the London I'm taking you to very different from the one you left behind.'

'I don't doubt that,' she laughed. 'You're upper class and have probably never seen the slums.'

'As a matter of fact I have, and it makes me angry that people should have to live in such appalling conditions.'

'When you are born into that kind of situation it's a struggle to get out of it. Many just give up hope and stop trying for a better life.'

He cast her a thoughtful glance. 'But not you.'

'Things haven't gone the way I expected or wanted, but I'll never go back to living like that. I'm out now and intend to keep trying to make a new life for myself – even if I have to leave a little bit of my heart in some places.'

'And where did that happen?'

'The Travellers and my last job.'

'The Frenshaw estate?'

'Yes, I thought I had found my place, but it wasn't to be, so I have to put it behind me and move on – again.' Her smile was tinged with sadness. 'Now you've given me this chance, and I can't refuse it even though it's taking me back to the place I never wanted to see again.'

'The time will soon go, and I promise to return you to your green fields.'

'Thank you, sir, and your promise is the only thing that made me decide to come. Where exactly are we going?'

'To Gray's Inn.'

'A pub?' she asked in surprise.

'No, it is a legal institution. I'm a barrister and have my chambers – offices – there.'

'It sounds posh. I'll have to remember to keep my mouth shut in case I embarrass you.'

'You could not embarrass me, Miss Banner. I do not judge people by their accent, although you speak very well considering your upbringing. Do not label me as a man who turns away from those less fortunate than myself. I don't only have wealthy clients. If a worthy case comes to me from someone who desperately needs legal help but is unable to pay, I act for them free of charge.'

'That's good of you, sir.'

'Not at all. Everyone is entitled to the protection of the law, no matter what their station in life. Ah, here is a hostelry I always visit. We will stop for refreshments and water the horses.'

The moment they entered the yard people came running to take the horses, and inside they were shown to a private room. She watched the activity with interest. She was usually the one hastening to look after the wealthy, and it was strange to be on the other side.

'Sit down,' he told her, holding a chair for her.

Her expression showed how doubtful she was about this. He was still standing, and a servant didn't take a seat first.

'You are my clerk,' he told her softly, 'and not a servant in my house. Therefore, you will be treated as such. Please be seated.'

'Thank you, sir.' She reluctantly did as she was told.

Then he settled himself at the other side of the table. 'Don't be apprehensive about the sudden change of rules. I will guide you through it. You are bright and intelligent, and I am sure will soon adjust. Now, the food here is good, so eat well. We still have a long way to go. Have you been on a train before?'

'Yes, me and my dad did try it once. It was so crowded and not very comfortable.'

'You will notice a difference this time because we are travelling first class.'

Of course they would be, and that would be another glimpse into the world of the wealthy. She was certainly learning a lot since her dad had died and she had struck out on her own.

Chrissie couldn't believe what she was seeing. She'd known the place he worked would be posh, but this was more than expected, and bewildering. The place was bustling with men dashing around with piles of papers in their hands.

'Brian!' he called the moment they walked in.

A young boy came running. 'Sir, so glad you're here. Everyone's asking for you. The case has been brought forward and starts at ten o'clock tomorrow.'

'All right. No need to panic. We're almost ready, but first I want you to get hold of Mrs Trent. Tell her it's urgent.'

'I'll fetch her right away, sir.' The lad was gone in a flash.

All the time he had been writing, and he handed her the note. 'I have to leave you for a while, but when Mrs Trent arrives give her that note, and do as she says.' He gave her a stern look. 'And don't argue about it.'

'I wouldn't dream of it, sir,' she joked.

'Huh! You don't expect me to believe that, surely?' He swept out of the room.

'What do I do now?' she asked the empty room, wishing she hadn't agreed to come. This wasn't what she wanted at all, but had been swayed by his persuasive manner. I'll bet he's a demon in court, she guessed. After the struggle to get out of London, she was now back, and it was the last place she wanted to be. Stupid, she told herself. That damned curiosity of yours is a blasted nuisance, but she would have been just as stupid to turn away from this chance to do something different. Living the way she had, her knowledge of life outside of the slums had been limited, and her experiences so far had certainly opened her eyes to a different kind of life. It hadn't always been the pleasure she had imagined, and to be truthful it was turning out to be damned hard. Coming up against one setback after another, she had been trying to survive with no clear idea what to do next, so it wasn't surprising she found herself here without knowing why she agreed to this.

She wandered over to the bookcase, examined the leather-bound volumes, and chose one. It was detailing past cases, and she settled down to read. Some of the words she recognised from the document she had copied, but still didn't know what they meant. There must be a dictionary on the shelves, and was about to look for one when the door swung open and a woman marched in.

Chrissie leapt to her feet.

'Where is Sir Stuart Gretham?'

'He isn't here. Are you Mrs Trent?' When the woman nodded Chrissie handed her the note. 'He left this for you.'

The woman read the note, looking up now and again to study the girl standing in front of her. When she'd finished reading the note she tucked it in her pocket and shook her head. 'One never knows what he is going to do. With his liberal views he is considered eccentric and comes close to overstepping the bounds of society at times.'

'I beg your pardon?' Chrissie was astonished by the woman's outburst. She hadn't read the note so didn't know what Mrs Trent had been asked to do.

She glared at Chrissie. 'What he's asking me to do in such a short time is not possible. I would need at least a month to make you look presentable.'

Chrissie bristled with indignation, but just managed to hold her anger in check. 'It only takes you five minutes to be insulting, though. I'll tell Sir Gretham that you are not up to carrying out his wishes. Goodbye, Mrs Trent.' She held open the door.

'You'll tell him no such thing. I'll do what I can. Come with me.'

'I said goodbye,' she told her coldly, still holding the door for her to leave. 'You have insulted both of us and I would not go anywhere with you. I may have come from a poor family, but you are the one whose manners need a polish. Now you will leave.'

'Really! I've never been spoken to so disrespectfully by someone like you.'

'Then I would say it is long overdue.'

Still complaining bitterly, Mrs Trent swept out of the room nearly knocking the young boy over who was hovering in the passage.

Brian stopped and looked in, grinning. 'Wow, you've really upset that stuck-up bitch. Pardon my language, miss.'

'Don't worry. I know a lot worse than that, and some you've probably never heard before. Who was that woman?'

'A high-class dressmaker. She dresses all the rich and famous.'

Now she was even angrier. She had told Sir Gretham that she wouldn't accept gifts from men, and yet he had ignored her wishes. She would have a few words to say to him as well. Brian was still standing there so she reined in her anger. 'I hope she's more polite to her wealthy customers. Is she any good?'

'They say she is, but I wouldn't know.'

'No, of course not. While you're here could you help me to find a dictionary? I've started reading about trials and I don't understand some of the words.'

He went straight to the book, handed it to her, and she settled down again.

'Er . . . I was coming to see if you would like tea, and I couldn't help overhearing what was being said. Would you like tea?'

'Yes please.' She grimaced. 'I expect I've caused trouble by sending that woman away.'

'Nah. The boss ain't like that. He'll more than likely think it's funny.'

'What's funny?' he asked, striding into the room. 'Where's Mrs Trent?'

'I sent her away. The idea of making someone like me look presentable was beneath her. She was insulting.' Chrissie turned away from him, her anger rising again, coupled with disappointment. She had liked and respected this man. He had shown her kindness and she had believed he was really trying to help her. All she had been asked – no ordered – to do in the past had been menial tasks like scrubbing floors, but this man of high birth had been different, or so she had thought.

'Tell me exactly what happened.'

She turned slowly to face him again. 'I told you plainly that I do not accept gifts from men, no matter who they are, and yet you send a woman to me who must be hugely expensive, someone I could never afford. You knew that, but you completely ignored it. I am disappointed you should do such a thing.'

'I asked you a question, Miss Banner, and I expect an answer.' When she didn't answer, he turned to Brian. 'Did you hear what was said?'

'Yes, sir.' He then related the entire conversation, word for word.

His expression didn't change as he listened, but by the time the boy finished, his anger was visible. 'I apologise for ignoring your wishes, but I thought you would be more at ease with a new skirt and blouse. That would have been a mere trifle to me, and my only intention was to help you. I was wrong and I apologise. However, I will not have a member of my staff insulted in that way. Stay here, both of

194

you. I'll deal with this.' He spun on his heel and stormed out of the room.

'Oh-oh.' Brian grinned. 'By the time he's finished she'll be grovelling for mercy and begging forgiveness.'

Chrissie was studying the boy intently. 'How did you remember what had been said so accurately?'

'That's easy. I've always been able to do it. I've only got to read or hear something and it's in here.' He tapped his head. 'I come from a dirt-poor family, like you, but I wanted to get out somehow. I came here looking for work and Sir Gretham talked to me. When he saw what a memory I had he gave me this job. I sit in the court and listen to cases, and then go through them with him afterwards. He's a good man, miss, and the only reason he brought you here is because you have a talent of some kind.'

'I can make good copies of documents,' she admitted, her anger fading away.

'There you are, then; you can help him and he can help you.'

'I'm also outspoken, and he will probably send me away after the things I said to him.'

'Nah. Justice is his life, and he knows that woman was in the wrong. He won't tolerate that. It will be all right, you'll see.'

She wasn't so sure, and as the time ticked away she began to worry how she was going to get back to the country house.

Nearly an hour passed before he swept back in to the office. 'That's settled now. If you've forgiven me for my presumption, Miss Banner, you can have the desk by the window, and Brian, I need you to read through the trial notes for me. Mrs Trent has apologised for her unkind remarks,' he added.

Without further explanation he handed documents to both of them and settled down at his own desk. Glancing across at Brian, she mouthed the words, 'Is that all he's going to say?'

He nodded, gave a wink and also began working.

She would never understand this complicated man, but it looked as if the incident had been dealt with to his satisfaction and dismissed.

Chapter Twenty-One

'I'm getting stronger every day, so you don't have to stay here any longer, Father.' Harry paced over to the window, restless now he was well on the way to full recovery. 'You have already neglected your own estate for long enough in order to help me.'

'I have an excellent estate manager, as you know, and he will inform me of any problems. I don't want to leave until the culprit has been caught.' He studied his son with pride and relief. When he had returned home he had been grief-stricken and angry, but he had worked his way through those emotions and was, once again, the son he remembered.

Harry turned and smiled. 'I must admit it is good to have you here, but stay only if it is all right.'

'We'll see this through together, just as we have always

done. I wonder how Joe is getting on?'

'Waiting is hard, but Joe is the best there is at this kind of thing. I'm certain he will come back with some useful information.'

'This is a nasty business when there is a suspicion that one of your own family is trying to kill you.' Charles grimaced. 'But if it isn't him, then I don't know who it could be. What we need is Chrissie here with her crystal ball.'

'You don't really believe she can tell fortunes, do you?'

'I keep an open mind. All I know is she told me you were nearly home, and before leaving she warned you of danger. You know when I first spoke to her I felt there was something special about her. Life must have been hard for her, but she was not ashamed of her background. You accepted her for what she was. Can you imagine what it must have been like for her when her father died, and she was turned out of their hovel with no money and nowhere to go? But she had a dream to live in the country, and she set about getting here any way she could. What a brave, remarkable girl.'

'And I turned her away. Adam hasn't been able to find her. He tracked her to that farm, but after that it is as if she just vanished. She's either a long way away by now or right under our noses and we are not looking in the right places.'

'Perhaps Joe will have more luck once he's gathered what information he can from Bath.'

'Maybe.' Harry ran a hand through his hair and sighed quietly. 'I'm going to have a look at the horses.'

'I'll come with you.'

He grinned at his father. 'I'm not going to ride yet, I promise.'

Both men walked out to the stables, and all the staff stopped and smiled with pleasure at seeing Harry up and about again.

'Good to see you, Major,' Bert said. 'The mares have settled in. They are magnificent animals and we should get fine foals from them.'

'I'm sure we will. How are the two boys behaving?'

'Oh, well, you know what they are like. They know the mares are here and are getting a mite impatient to see them.'

'You can put Midnight with the black one and Red with the pale mare. Let's see what we get from those pairings.'

'Yes, Major. Do you want to have a look at them now? Red was troubled after the shooting and he'll be pleased to see you. They both will.'

Over the next three days Harry's strength slowly returned, and he became more active, involved once more with the plans for the estate. The farmhouse was nearly ready and they were considering who to take on. They wanted a family man, and there was no shortage of applicants. He was in the process of interviewing hopeful farmers, and this was keeping him occupied.

On the other hand, now his son had taken over again, Charles had only one job and that was to see he didn't do too much. The doctor was pleased with his progress, but it had been a close thing and they didn't want to take any chances of a relapse.

Joe had been away for five days and they were both becoming concerned, knowing that what they had asked him to do for them could prove to be dangerous. Late one evening, Charles was just deciding to go to Bath in case his son's friend was in trouble when they heard a horse gallop in to the yard.

Both men were immediately on their feet and were relieved to see Joe stride in.

'Ah, you are looking much better,' he said the moment he saw Harry.

'I'm well on the way to full recovery. We are pleased to see you. Do you have any news?'

'I do, but I'm not sure you are going to like what I've discovered.'

'You must eat first.' Charles summoned the butler and ordered food, then poured a brandy for each of them. 'Sit down, Joe; the news can wait until you are refreshed after your journey.'

Half an hour later they waited eagerly to hear what Joe had discovered.

'Start at the beginning,' Harry told him.

'When I arrived I immediately began to search out the serious gamblers, looking for the high rollers, and joined their games. There was no sign of Edward Danton, and I had begun to think it was a wasted trip, when he turned up after two days. I spent a long night watching him at the tables. He won a little and was in a good mood, but he is a hardened gambler, and when someone like that gets desperate you don't know what they will do. The next day I bumped in to him, accidently, of course, and he was happy to meet a fellow gambler. We became quite friendly and dined together, but he didn't talk about himself. I decided he needed to be thrown off balance, and the best way to do that was to see he lost heavily. After dinner he invited me to join a group that evening. I agreed, and when I met them I knew I would have to be very careful. This was the first time I had seen any of them in the short time I had been there, and they were serious gamblers, so I was going to need all my skill.' Joe grinned. 'It was quite exciting.'

'I hope you were armed,' Harry said, frowning.

'I had various weapons hidden on me in case I had to fight my way out. Anyway, for the first hour I lost and won a little, and no one noticed anything wrong, so I began to make sure the main loser was Danton. The others were coming out more or less even.'

'You must be exceptionally good to be able to influence a game like that,' Charles remarked.

'I've been taught by the best, and I have a good memory, able to track the cards that have been played. It also helped that Danton is not a skilled player. He is too emotional and easy to read. One by one the others dropped out, leaving the two of us to fight it out. I gave Danton the chance to stop, but he wouldn't hear of it. After a long night I took everything he had, and ended up with several markers.'

'How much for?' Charles wanted to know.

Joe handed the markers over and Charles gasped, showing them to his son.

'Where is he going to get this kind of money from?' Harry knew his cousin liked to gamble, but this was reckless.

'I asked him that, and he said he was about to inherit a large estate from a cousin who had been mortally wounded. I questioned him further by asking how sure he was that his cousin was going to die. He said he'd seen him and was certain he couldn't live much longer as the bullet was close to his heart. At the mention of a bullet I feigned shock and the others who had been watching our game gathered round with interest. He now had everyone's attention and I could see he liked being the centre of attention, so I pressured him again for details. When he said the shooting had occurred while you were riding across your estate and the shot had thrown you from your horse, I pointed out that the marksman must have been an expert to hit a moving target. By now Danton was revelling in the attention and I was hoping he would slip up and say something incriminating.'

Harry was leaning forward as he listened. 'And did he?'

'That's for you to decide. We were all discussing this, and everyone said it must have been someone very expert because they certainly weren't capable of being that accurate—'

'Just a minute,' Charles stopped Joe. 'I never told Edward that Harry had been hit with one shot only, and I don't think anyone else but the doctor knew that fact.'

'Ah, then you will need to ask everyone here if they spoke to Danton. If they didn't, then that hints at his guilt, along with his boastful declaration that he was an excellent marksman, and could hit a moving target – even a cavalry man at full gallop.'

'He admitted that?' Charles was astonished his nephew could be so foolish.

Joe nodded. 'I don't think anyone believed him, though, and I smirked along with the others. Then I threw out a challenge and invited him to show us his skill with a rifle the next day. He said he would be happy to but, unfortunately, he was returning to London at first light. The game broke up after that.'

'Damn!' Charles swore. 'I had been clinging on to the hope that he wasn't involved.'

'I'm afraid he is so desperate for money that I would consider him quite capable of doing something as extreme as this. Once I had his markers for such a large amount, no one thought it unusual when I began asking questions about him. The other gamblers were quite free with their information, and I was able to find out the time of his visits. He wasn't there the day Harry was shot, but arrived the next day.'

'Everything is beginning to point in his direction.' Harry shook his head in sadness. 'We grew up together. How could he do such a thing?'

'Addicted gamblers will do anything to obtain money for the next game and the next.' Joe pulled an envelope out of his pocket and handed it to Charles. 'There's your money back. Thank you, but I didn't need it.'

'Keep it as payment for what you have done for us.'

'That is generous of you, but I won't take money for helping out a friend. What are you going to do next?'

'Well, we still don't have anything but gossip and suspicion, so let's approach this in a military way. How do we back him into a corner and convince him there's no escape?'

Joe considered this for a moment, and then said, 'Again you need someone outside the family. Do you know anyone connected to the law? Someone with enough authority to make him believe there is enough proof to take him to court.'

'Someone like a barrister?' Charles asked.

'As long as he's a tough prosecutor.'

'The man I'm thinking of has that reputation.'

'Then have a talk with him and see what he thinks.'

'Who are you thinking of?' Harry asked his father.

'Stuart Gretham. He's a barrister now.'

'Is he? I haven't seen him for years. But would Stuart go along with this? We really don't have a lot, do we, and Edward could come up with a reasonable explanation why he wasn't in Bath when he said he was. Stuart wouldn't be able to prosecute without definite proof of some kind.'

'You need a confession.'

Father and son looked at Joe in disbelief.

'How do we make him do that?' Charles asked. 'Edward is a hardened gambler, but he's not fool enough to admit to attempted murder.'

'If he is faced with a barrister he might really believe he has been caught and panic. Would this man you know be prepared to suggest to him a more lenient sentence if he confesses?'

Harry looked at his father. 'Do you think he would do something like this for us?'

'I really don't know. The only thing we can do is tell him what we suspect and ask for his advice.'

'That will be the way to approach him. If he can't help then I will have to confront Danton for payment of his debts, and see if I can trick him into a confession.'

Harry grimaced. 'I'm still reluctant to believe he did this. You're a good judge of character, Joe, so what's your honest opinion?'

'He's your man, and once he realises you are fully recovered he will try again,' he stated without hesitation.

Charles began to pace the room. 'In that case he must be told he will not inherit the estate. That might remove the danger, Harry.'

'And place it on whomever will inherit,' Joe pointed out.

'No one knows who that is. My son won't even tell me who it is, and I agree that the fewer people who know the better.'

'Agreed. Now, I suggest you have a talk with your friend before I start pressuring Danton for payment of his debts. This barrister is in London, I presume?'

'He works there, but he does have a home some ten miles from here, where his wife and children live all the time. I'll send a message and ask when he will be there, and if he would see me on a legal matter. Let's keep this official to begin with.'

'Good. There isn't anything else we can do at the moment. I will take lodging at a local inn in the village in case Danton comes here and sees me. He mustn't know I am a friend of yours, Harry.'

'Keep in touch, and while we are waiting will you see if you can trace that girl?'

'Chrissie,' Charles reminded his son. 'Why do you still insist on calling her "that girl"?'

'Perhaps because I need to remind myself that she really is a girl.' He winked at Joe. 'The only time I saw her she was working in the stables and wearing men's breeches.'

Joe grinned. 'So you said before, and I'm looking forward to meeting her. It would help if I knew what you intend to do when she is found. Will you give her the job back?'

'Certainly not. I have not changed my opinion that it is unseemly for a female to be working as a stable lad, but I will find her something else if she so wishes. However, there are two reasons I am anxious about her, and one is that I acted unkindly, without thought, and that does not sit well with me.'

'You said two reasons,' Charles prompted.

'Did I? It must have been a slip of the tongue.'

Chapter Twenty-Two

She'd been here a week, and although it was interesting she couldn't wait to leave. No more had been said about new clothes for her, but the Martins she was staying with had given her an old but smarter skirt and blouse to wear. They had also given her a lovely room, not in the servants' quarters, which had surprised her, but she took her meals with the servants. She had spent all day yesterday in court and watched Sir Gretham in action. It had been exciting and somewhat confusing, but the way the lawyers fought the cases was astonishing, and her sympathy went out to some of the witnesses as they endured cross-examination by both sides. The prosecutor – who was Sir Stuart Gretham – had won the case, and the next one didn't start for two days.

Brian bounded in to the office, a broad smile on his

face. 'Wasn't that terrific? Anyone who finds themselves prosecuted by our boss doesn't stand a chance.'

'Even if they are innocent?' she asked.

'If we take on a case they are never innocent. We make quite sure of that before the trial.'

'We?'

'The law firm of Gretham and Gretham. The boss had an older brother, and after he died he kept the name. I expect he's hoping his son will join the firm one day.'

Oh dear, she thought silently. From what she'd seen of the boy there wasn't much hope of that happening. The child must be a big disappointment to him, and he had been right to get him away from his mother in the hope the school could straighten him out.

The door opened and Stuart strode into the room. 'I have to return home, but will be back in time for the next trial. I want you to remain here and finish those documents,' he told Chrissie.

Her disappointment showed. For a moment she had believed she would be leaving with him. 'Can't I come with you and bring them with me?'

'No, Mr Martin is going to stand in for me in case I'm delayed, and he will need you here.'

'I didn't know he was a lawyer.'

'He is, and a very good one. Brian, you know what to do while I'm away. Will you go now and purchase my usual ticket for the train?'

'Yes, sir.'

'Why do you have to rush home?' she asked, wondering if there was a family crisis, or something.

'I have received a message from an old friend of my father's who needs to see me on a very urgent matter.' He glanced at the clock on the wall. 'I must clear up a few things and then I'll be on my way, but I'll be back as quickly as possible.'

She watched him go and yearned to be leaving with him. It was ungrateful of her to feel like this, she knew, because by giving her this job he had given her a lift up in life. There was only one thing she really wanted and that was to be with her beloved horses. It was silly to be so attached to them when it was unlikely she would ever see them again. She wondered if they were missing her as much as she was missing them.

Pushing aside the sadness she picked up a pen and began working on the documents he had left for her to copy. There was a job to do and it must be done well to show appreciation for the chance he had given her. She must move on, but one thing she was absolutely certain of, she wasn't going to stay in London for much longer. Regardless of all the trouble and heartache she had experienced so far, her desire to live in the country had not diminished one tiny bit.

Stuart's country home was in a rural area and the London train only went part of the way, but it did speed up the journey, and he collected his horse for the rest of the way. He was intrigued by the urgent message he had received from Lord Charles Frenshaw. He hadn't seen him in years, and couldn't imagine why he wanted a meeting with him on a legal matter. He could have asked him to come to his chambers, but as there was a delay in the next trial he had decided to come back. It would give him a chance to check that his son was settling down at the school, and see his two delightful little girls. There was no eagerness to see his wife, which was sad, but once they were married she had changed, and he quickly realised she was not the girl he had been fooled into marrying. She was selfish and, quite frankly, not very bright. He had wanted and needed someone by his side who would mix with, and entertain, friends and associates. Once the first child had been born, she had insisted on retiring to the country, and had resisted all attempts to make her join him in London. How different it would have been if he'd found someone like Christine Banner. All right, she came from the slums, but her dark eyes shone with intelligence, and she had spirit. He didn't doubt she could be shown how to mingle with society. That was another reason he hadn't wanted Charles to come to his chambers, as he felt there was a chance he would try to take her back. He didn't want that, and refused to look too deeply at his reasons for feeling that way.

He rode straight to the school and saw the principal. 'How is my son getting on?' he asked.

'Very well. He's bright and gets on well with the other boys. They are on the playing field at the moment. Would you like to see him?'

'Please.'

The noise coming from the game was deafening and Stuart smiled, remembering his own bruising games. Robert was in the thick of the ruckus, laughing and shouting as loud as the others. When he spotted his father he ran over with a huge smile on his face.

'Father! I didn't know you were coming.'

'This is just a quick visit to see how you are. You look as if you are enjoying yourself.'

'I am. It's terrific here. Thank you for bringing me. I know now why I misbehaved so much at home. I didn't have anyone of my age there and the lessons were too easy. I was bored and didn't know what to do with myself. Mother kept fussing over me, as well, and I got angry at times.'

'You should have told me how you felt.'

'I know, but you are away such a lot.'

Stuart felt guilty, but his work was in London, and he couldn't do anything about that. 'I must try and spend more time at home. You are happy here, then?'

'I love it. Do you know there's a picture of you here as one of the past students who have achieved something in life?' He gave a cheeky grin. 'My aim now is to get my picture next to yours one day.'

Relief swept through him as he looked at his son's animated face. The school was doing what he had hoped, and was giving his son a sound purpose in life. 'Well, my firm is still called Gretham and Gretham, and waiting for you to join it if you should feel like studying law.'

'I've already started.'

'Excellent. That pleases me very much. I can't stay now, Robert, but I'll come and collect you at the term break. Now, you'd better go and get cleaned up.'

His son giggled when he looked down at the mud and

dirt on his boots and clothes, then he threw his arms around his father. 'Thank you for coming.'

Quite shaken by the show of affection, he watched his son tear off with the other boys. What a difference from the sullen boy he had brought here. He must make sure his other children didn't suffer as Robert obviously had.

The next day Stuart waited for Charles to arrive, and went out to meet him the moment he rode up to the house.

They exchanged greetings and he studied the magnificent horse his visitor had arrived on. 'What a beautiful animal,' he exclaimed.

'This is Red Sunset, but we just call him Red.'

The horse lowered its head and looked straight in to Stuart's eyes. 'What's he doing?' he asked Charles.

'Don't ask me,' he replied dryly. 'The only person who could understand what the warhorses were thinking was a girl who used to work for us. I swear they could communicate with her.'

Red snorted and gave Stuart a slight push, making him step back.

'Behave yourself, boy,' Charles scolded, 'or I won't bring you out again.'

A stable boy had arrived and was studying the animal with some alarm. 'Is he safe, sir?'

'Completely safe. He's just playing. Be firm with him and you won't have any trouble.'

The expression on the lad's face said he didn't quite believe that was true as he led the animal away.

'It's good to see you, Charles. Come in and tell me what the problem is.'

One room in the large house had been converted in to an office, which Stuart kept locked because of the important documents he kept there. It was only cleaned while he stood and watched. It was crammed with shelves, books and cupboards, but on either side of the window were two comfortable leather chairs and a small table.

When both men were settled with drinks in front of them, Stuart said, 'I heard that Harry returned safely from the Crimea. That must have been a great relief to you.'

'It was, but I nearly lost him soon after. Someone shot him.'

'What, here? Is he all right?' Stuart sat forward, eager to hear about this astonishing incident.

'Yes. But it was desperate for a while and that's why I am here. I'm afraid that if the person who did this finds out he has survived he might try again.'

'Do you know who the felon is?'

'Only a suspicion.' Charles took a sip of his drink, and then put the glass down again, clearly worried. 'We need advice.'

'Tell me everything, even the smallest detail. Start from the moment Harry returned home, and earlier if you think it's relevant.'

It took a while to explain everything that had happened, and when he'd finished, he sat back with a sigh. 'We are hoping you can advise us on how to proceed.'

Remaining silent as he digested all the information he had just been given, Stuart stood up and gazed out of the window, deep in thought. Eventually he turned back to the man waiting patiently for his opinion. 'It seems highly likely that Edward is the culprit, but you don't have enough proof to have him arrested for the crime. In fact, you don't have anything but suspicion. If you did get him to court no prosecutor could hope to win the case, and he would walk free.'

'Even if you took the case? I hear you are one of the best in the business.'

Stuart gave a wry smile. 'I have had some success, but I couldn't prosecute with such flimsy evidence. The fact he wasn't in Bath when he said he was means very little. If he is guilty then I am sure he has already set up a good alibi for that time, and the fact that he admits to being a good shot is of little use. Many men could claim the same talent.'

'So, you're saying we don't have a chance of bringing him to justice.'

'I'm sorry, Charles. The only way to do that would be with a confession.'

'I know him well enough to be certain he would never do that. What the devil can we do? I fear for my son's life.'

'You said Harry has changed his will so that Edward can't inherit. Has he been told?'

Charles nodded. 'I have written to him, but there remains the fear that he will now try to kill Harry out of rage at being disinherited.'

'That would elicit some response, I imagine, and as you say it could still put Harry in danger.' Stuart lapsed in to thought again for a while, then said, 'Would you be content if he left the country for somewhere a long way off, like America or South Africa, or a similar country of his choice?'

Charles sat upright in astonishment. 'I never thought of that. But how would we make him agree?'

'First you would have to offer him a sizable amount of money to enable him to start a new life.'

'He could have as much as he needed. But suppose we did this and it isn't him? That would mean the criminal is still at large.'

'That's the difficult part. Before you hand over any money he must admit to the crime, apologise to Harry in writing, and sign a document admitting his guilt in my presence.'

'Knowing Edward, he would confess to this just to get the money.'

'I agree, and before you confront him you need to be absolutely certain he is guilty.'

'How? We've been over and over this, and honestly don't know what we can do.'

'Talk it over with Harry and his friend. As things stand at the moment, taking him to court is out of the question. If you do decide to offer him a way out by leaving the country then I will help you all I can. Having me present in my official capacity might frighten him in to believing you have enough evidence to convict him.'

'I like your idea because the thought of sending the son of my sister to prison, no matter what his crime, would hurt me for the rest of my life. I know it would also upset Harry. They grew up together, and it is sad Edward should have strayed so far off course. How do you propose we go about this, providing Harry agrees, of course?'

Stuart then outlined his plan and had Charles agreeing. 'I have another trial, but should be back here within two weeks. The moment I'm back we'll arrange to meet with your nephew.'

'Agreed. In the meantime we can continue our search for Chrissie.' Charles smiled, relieved to at least have some plan of action. 'What we need is Chrissie and her crystal ball to put the frighteners on Edward. She can be very convincing.'

'You told me Harry dismissed her when he returned, so why are you looking for her now?'

'It was obvious my son had suffered in the Crimean War, and he wasn't himself. He sent her away without giving it proper thought, or consulting any of us, and now he's sorry. I think he just wants to know she is all right.'

'I see.' Stuart stood up. 'I must return to London now. Tell Harry to be careful and we'll see if we can find a solution to this problem.'

'Thank you for seeing me. I feel a little more hopeful about this terrible situation now I've spoken to you.'

He watched Charles ride away. What an extraordinary story. The last time he had met Edward they had all been young boys of about ten. Harry had become a cavalry officer, he a barrister, and Edward a gambler and possible criminal. What different paths they had all taken.

Back in the house he ran up the stairs to his room and began to pack for the journey back to London. He'd been interested to hear they were still looking for Chrissie, and Charles clearly liked her. It would have been a kindness to tell him where she was, but he hadn't. It was inevitable now that they would soon discover she was working for him, and when they did he would lose her, he was sure. That was sad because she was the best copier he had ever had, and he liked and respected her as well. Did she have that effect on everyone who got to know her?

Chapter Twenty-Three

When Charles arrived back Harry and Joe were waiting anxiously to hear what Stuart had said.

'Did he have a solution to the dilemma?' Harry asked.

Charles took the drink his son handed him. 'With the lack of evidence it would not be possible to win a case against him in court. He did put forward another suggestion, though.' He then told them what had been discussed, and when he finished there was silence for a while.

Harry sat back and gazed into space for a moment while he considered the idea. 'Sending Edward abroad might help him straighten himself out, and I do prefer that solution, but how the hell are we going to convince him we can prove he was the one who shot me?'

'Lie.'

Both men stared at Joe.

'Tell him you have a witness who saw him leaving the scene with a gun in his hands.'

'He'd never believe that,' Charles declared.

'He would have to if your barrister waved a document in front of him saying it was a signed statement by the witness.'

'Would Stuart do that, Father?'

'I'd have to ask him, but I very much doubt it. He has his professional reputation to consider. He won't be back for a week or two, so we can't do anything until he returns.'

'I'll be fit enough to go and see him myself by then. Joe, you come with me, and see if you can convince him to help us in that way.'

Joe grinned at Harry. 'Why me? He's your friend, not mine.'

'You are the one who came up with the idea that we lie, and you're used to underhand dealings.'

'Where did you ever get that idea from?'

The friends looked at each other and grinned.

At that moment there was the sound of a horse approaching fast and Charles went over to the window. 'It's Edward. He must have received my letter. You'd better hide, Joe.'

'Come with me.' Harry stood up. 'You can wait in my room. I'll show you the way.'

Charles was alone when his nephew stormed into the library waving the letter.

'What's this all about, Uncle?'

'Are you referring to the letter I sent to you informing you about the change to Harry's will?'

'You know damned well I am! How can the estate go

to someone else? I am the only eligible relative.'

'He can leave it to anyone he wishes. It doesn't have to be someone from the family – and don't you want to know how he is?'

'Well, from this I assume he is recovering.'

'I am indeed, and it's so kind of you to enquire about my health,' Harry remarked sarcastically as he strode back in to the room.

Edward was clearly surprised to see his cousin looking upright and strong once again. 'Last time I saw you it didn't look as if you would survive the night.'

'It would take more than one bullet to finish me, no matter how good a shot the criminal was. So, how are you, Edward?'

'Bloody furious. Why would you take my inheritance away from me?'

'Because of your addiction to gambling. I love this place and struggled hard to get back here. I was injured and so was my horse, and the only thing that kept me going was the thought of reaching home. If this estate came to you it would be gambled away within a week, if it isn't already,' he told him pointedly.

'I am not addicted to gambling! I like a game now and again, that's all, and I would never risk the estate.'

'Don't lie to me. I have the feeling you would go to any lengths to obtain such a valuable property – a property you care nothing for except its monetary value.'

'That isn't true, and you can't leave it to someone outside of the family.'

'I can, and it is going to someone who loves it as

much as I do and I know will take good care of it.'

'Who?'

He gave a grim smile. 'No one knows, not even Father. After all, I wouldn't want them to get shot as well, would I?'

A brief moment of alarm showed in Edward's eyes as Harry stared suspiciously at him as he spoke. 'Are you hinting that I was the one who shot you? If so I am bitterly disappointed you should have such a low opinion of me.'

'Ah, well, taking a bullet to the chest makes me suspicious of everybody. You can understand that, I'm sure.' Harry draped an arm around his cousin's shoulder. 'Let's forget all this unpleasantness. Are you joining us for dinner?'

'Thank you, but I can't,' he replied stiffly. 'I have another appointment this evening.'

They watched him leave and Charles pursed his lips thoughtfully. 'That was interesting.'

'Very, and did you notice he didn't deny it?'

'I did. Let's get Joe down here and tell him what has just happened.'

'Everything is pointing to Edward, but all we have to do now is prove it,' Harry remarked dryly.

The journey back to London gave Stuart plenty of time to think. The atmosphere at home had been strained. His wife, Angela, had not forgiven him for sending their son away to school, and had hardly spoken to him. He had an important function to attend in two weeks, and he had intended to try and persuade her to accompany him, as all the wives would be there. It was tiresome always arriving alone with the excuse that his wife was indisposed, but it had soon become clear that no amount of pleading would make her join him in London. Somehow he was going to have to find the time to sort out his marriage, and had thought of doing it while he had been home this time, but she had been even more withdrawn and did not appear to even hear what he was saying. However, things couldn't continue as they were, so he would have to do something about it – soon.

When he arrived back Chrissie was working hard and hadn't heard him come in. He stood watching her for a while. Sara Martin had found her another skirt for the office and she was wearing a white blouse with it. The white against her dark colouring was stunning, and he couldn't help wondering what she would look like in a fashionable gown. An idea crossed his mind, and he thought, why the hell not. That was if he could persuade her to do it, of course. He doubted it would be possible, though, even with his powers of persuasion, because she was not the kind of girl who could be flattered or pushed into doing something against her will. Nor would she be influenced by social standing. There was no shame when she talked about her upbringing, either. She spoke openly, hiding nothing, as if to say – this is me, accept it or walk away. Her openness was refreshing.

She looked up then and smiled. 'Oh, you're back. Mr Martin has left a file on your desk for you. How was your trip? Were you able to help your friend?'

'Not as much as I would have liked.' He walked over to her desk. 'How are you getting on?'

'I've finished all the work you left me so I've been helping Mr Martin.'

'You are doing well and pick things up quickly. Do you like working here?'

'I don't want to sound ungrateful, but I can't say I do. You've been kind to me and I can't lie to you. The work is interesting and I'm learning lots of new words, but I want to go back to the country.'

'That's a shame because you would make a welcome, permanent addition to my staff.'

'I'm sorry, but I won't stay in London, sir.'

He sat on the edge of the desk. This girl had nothing, and yet she was turning down the chance of a prestigious job. Her dream of living in the country must be very deep-rooted. 'I tell you what, I will take you back to the country when the next trial is over, and find you work to do at the house.'

'Helping with the children?'

'No, you will not be a house servant. I will leave you work to do for me.' He smiled at her. 'You will be my assistant in the country. How does that appeal?'

'I don't think your wife would like that,' she told him, showing her doubt about such an arrangement. 'She already blames me for her son being sent away to school.'

'No, she won't object. I've made sure she knows what really happened.'

'Well, if that's the case, then I will agree to work for you there.' She hesitated a moment. 'However, I won't stay where I'm not wanted. It would upset me if my being there caused trouble with your family.'

'I understand and appreciate your sensitivity, but you don't have to worry. I have a matter to deal with at home, which may take a while, so I'll be there for longer than usual. I visited Robert while I was there, and he's doing well, by the way, and enjoying life at the school.'

'I'm pleased to hear that. I felt he was bored at home and needed to be with children of his own age.'

'You are quite right. He was, and told me so the last time I saw him. Now, leave what you're doing and come and help me with whatever Bill Martin has left for me.'

Later that evening Stuart and Bill were discussing the coming trial, and catching up on what had been happening while he had been away. They were enjoying a brandy after dinner in the Martins' smoking room.

'How did you get on with Chrissie?' Stuart asked.

'Well enough. She's bright and willing to learn, and her copying is excellent. You cannot fault her manners, either.'

'Yes, she's been brought up well. I've been considering taking her to the judges' function. I am tired of always arriving alone, and she would look quite the part in a suitable gown.'

'Stuart, you can't! I don't doubt that she would look beautiful in a fashionable gown, but the moment she speaks her heritage would be revealed. It's quite acceptable to have her in the office because everyone knows you try to help those not so fortunate, but you can't take her to something like that. Tongues would wag, and your reputation would suffer. And we are not just talking about you. Think what you would be doing to that girl. She is probably innocent and unworldly enough to go along with you if you ask, but the moment she steps inside with you her reputation will be in shreds. Is that what you want?'

Stuart shook his head. 'Lord, no. She's had a tough enough time as it is.'

'Are you in love with her?'

'I am intrigued by her, and do wonder how far she could go if given the chance.'

'Hmm, that's a diplomatic answer, and I suspect the truth is rather different. Send her away and try to sort out your marriage. You were happy together at one time. Find out why Angela has become so withdrawn and difficult. I know many men take mistresses, but if you are considering that then forget it. That girl would never consent to such a life.'

'You have presented your case well, my friend, and you are quite right on all points except one. I will not send her away, but I will keep our relationship on a purely business basis.'

'See you do, for both your sakes.' Bill refilled their glasses. 'You have worked too hard to get where you are to become embroiled in a scandal.'

'Of course.' Stuart lifted his glass to Bill. 'It was a moment of madness after a not-too-pleasant visit home. It wouldn't have worked anyway, because I will lose her soon.'

'Oh?'

'A family friend has asked for my advice on a problem, and I have agreed to help if I can.'

'A legal matter?'

'Yes, an attempted killing, and they are sure they know who it is, but don't have any proof.'

'So the culprit can't be brought to trial, but what has this to do with Chrissie?'

Stuart then explained her connection to the Frenshaws. 'Harry now regrets his hasty action and they are looking for her.'

'You haven't told them she is working for you?'

'No, and that's another selfish act on my part. I was afraid if they knew they would take her away, but I will be spending some time with them and they will see her soon, because she won't stay in London.'

Their conversation was halted when Sara and Chrissie came into the room.

'Chrissie has been helping me choose a suitable gown for the judges' function, and likes the dark blue on me best. What do you think, dear, shall I wear that one?'

'You always look charming and elegant, my dear, so whatever you choose will be perfect.'

'Flatterer.' She laughed. 'I persuaded Chrissie to try one on, but nothing fitted her. She is slender, but with her height nothing reached the ground.'

'That was fun,' Chrissie told them, a broad smile on her face. 'But I couldn't possibly wear anything as elaborate as that. When I was with the Travellers, Elsie tried to make me wear bright clothes with beads and embroidery all over them, but I persuaded her to let me just throw a shawl over the back of the chair.' She laughed at the memory. 'It was all right, because people still came anyway.'

'Stuart told us you have a beautiful crystal ball. Did you bring it with you?'

'Oh, no, I left it at the house, and Nanny is looking after it for me.'

'What a shame. You could have told our fortunes.'

'I can't do that. It's only a game.' She did a little curtsy. 'Thank you for letting me see all your beautiful clothes, Mrs Martin. Now, if you will excuse me I will go to bed. Goodnight, sirs and Mrs Martin.'

When Chrissie had left them, Sara looked at the men and said, 'What an extraordinary girl. There wasn't a sign of envy when we spread the expensive gowns out for her to see, and to be honest, I don't think they even interested her. She joined in, making it fun, but I felt she was just tolerating a whim of mine, and I couldn't help thinking how stunning she would look attired in a glorious gown.'

Stuart began to laugh. 'She would probably wear her breeches underneath.'

This caused much laughter, and then Sara kissed her husband. 'I think I will also retire and leave you gentlemen to your brandy.'

Bill gave his friend a knowing glance when they were alone again.

'I know,' Stuart exclaimed. 'It was a crazy idea, and already forgotten.'

Chapter Twenty-Four

It was the height of summer as they rode up to the house, and Chrissie lifted her face to the warm July sun, sighing with pleasure. They should only have been in London for two weeks at the most, but the last trial had dragged on for two more days. All the way back she had kept her eyes open for any large houses in case she needed to move on again, because regardless of sir's assurances, she had her doubts and would not stay if it was going to cause trouble. It was strange; her intention had been to find a permanent place to live, and all she had done was move around. Somewhere to settle was eluding her – no that wasn't exactly true, she had believed she'd found the place of her dreams, but it was not to be. She just had to keep searching and not give up hope. There was a place for her somewhere, and she just had to find it. The one thing she was sure about, though, was that the Grethams' was not that place. However, she owed it to Sir Gretham to stay a while and see how it worked out.

When they rode in to the yard the staff ran to take care of the horses. The children erupted from the house and ran to their father, who scooped them up, pleased to see them again.

He put them down and turned to Chrissie. 'Take the rest of the day off, and we'll start work in the morning.'

'What time, sir?'

'Ten o'clock will be early enough.' He then walked towards the house with the children dancing and chattering beside him.

Chrissie greeted Nurse. 'It looks as if you've lost your charges.'

'We will have a little time to ourselves, and I'm eager to hear all about your time in London.'

'I'm glad to be back,' she admitted. 'How have things been here?'

'Peaceful. Come along, you must be ready for a nice cup of tea.'

'Let me wash off the dust of the journey and change first, and then I'll join you.'

Much to Stuart's surprise, Angela came to meet him and smiled when the children told her excitedly that Father was home to stay for a while. He kissed her cheek. 'You look better, my dear.'

'I am not feeling so tired. I've ordered tea in the drawing room for all of us.'

'I had better change first.'

'Don't bother with that or the tea will get cold.'

That was another surprise, and he was curious to know what had brought about this welcome change. They enjoyed a lively tea together as a family, and then the children went back to Nurse.

Stuart sat back, feeling relaxed, and closed his eyes for a moment.

'You've had a busy time and a long journey. You must be tired.'

He opened his eyes and nodded. 'The last case was difficult and it's good to be home.'

'I count myself fortunate you even bothered to return again, after the way I have been behaving.'

'Did you think I would leave you and the children?' he asked.

'Many men wouldn't have put up with a sullen wife. After you left I knew I had to change if I wasn't going to lose you, so I went to see our doctor and he gave me a tonic. He wanted me to go and see another doctor, but I told him that wasn't necessary. I have been suffering from depression, that's all. I soon began to feel much more like myself and went to the school to see Robert. He's a changed boy and so happy there. He told me what had happened and that it was his fault when that box was broken. He did it deliberately, he told me, and was now ashamed of the way he had behaved.'

'He's a bright boy and didn't have enough to occupy his mind here.'

'I can see that now.' There were tears in her eyes. 'I'm so sorry, Stuart. I haven't been much of a wife for some time and should have joined you for that important judges' function. I really don't know what has been wrong with me.'

'I went with Bill and Sara Martin.' Relief swept through him that he hadn't taken Chrissie with him. Although his wife was claiming she was better, there was still something about her that didn't seem quite right to him. She appeared mentally fragile – he didn't know how else to describe it – and any unpleasant gossip getting back to her about him would not be a good thing. Bill had stopped him making a terrible mistake that would have affected all of them. He wasn't going to deny that he was attracted to Chrissie, and no longer had any deep feelings for Angela, but if she continued to improve it looked as if their marriage could be saved for the sake of the children.

'I treated that girl abominably and I owe her an apology, but to be truthful the thought frightens me.'

'Why? She is kind and would understand, but I don't think that is necessary. I would ask you to be friendly now, though, because she has told me she will leave if you don't want her here.'

'You want her to stay?'

'I do, for the time being. She is intelligent and the documents she copies are faultless. I would have kept her in the London chambers, but she won't stay in London. Her desire is to live in the country, and I don't think anything will change her mind.'

'Not even a prestigious job with you?'

'No, position and prestige mean nothing to her.'

'What a remarkable girl.'

'Indeed, she is. I am pleased we have had this talk, my dear. Now, will you make me a promise?'

She nodded.

'If you are troubled about anything at all, no matter how small, you tell me. Whatever it is we will work it out together.'

'I promise.'

'Stuart's back at last.' Charles handed his son the message. 'He would like us to see him at three tomorrow to discuss the situation.'

'Good, and I think we should take Joe with us. We are no further forward with this, and it will be interesting to see if his legal mind can find a way to get Edward out of the country. I'm tired of feeling I am being hunted in my own home.'

'Yes, we have got to find a solution soon. Although Edward now knows he cannot inherit, I believe he could be angry enough to try again out of spite. We've got everyone on the estate keeping watch for him, or any other intruder, but I'm still nervous for all of us. The boy is clearly in financial difficulty and that makes him unpredictable, not to be trusted. I'm glad you haven't revealed the identity of your heir, because that would be another person for us to worry about. Tomorrow will be the first time you have left the estate since the shooting, and I am uneasy.'

'I won't hide away like a fugitive.' Harry stood up and grimaced as he straightened to his full height. 'Joe will be with us, and we'll be quite safe. He has an uncanny ability to sense danger, and it was that talent that got us both back to this country.'

'He's a good man, I agree. Where is he now?'

'Trying to track down that girl, but even he doesn't appear to be having any luck. She must be a long way away by now, and he is extending the search area, but there is always the chance she is back in London.'

Charles sighed. 'I wish you'd stop calling her "that girl". I've told you time and time again what her name is. Why do you do it?'

'You know her, but I don't. I hardly spoke to her.'

'No, you didn't, and if you had you might not have dismissed her so easily,' Charles told him.

'Do you think I don't know that? After she'd gone I heard everyone saying how good she had been, how the horses loved her, and how everyone missed her. Never find another like that, I heard the stable hands saying, and they hoped she was going to be all right. "Special" was the word I kept hearing and I felt like a monster. I'd dearly love to find out why everyone had such a high opinion of her. No one is that perfect.'

'She isn't perfect, far from it. She knows what she wants and pursues it with single-minded stubbornness, even to the point of turning down a safe home on my estate. For a girl who has nothing that is hard to understand, even foolish, but she's prepared to work damned hard for what she wants.'

'And what is that?'

'A place she can settle down with open fields around her. Is that too much to ask?'

Harry shook his head. 'If Joe can't find her, then after we've dealt with Edward I'll track down those Travellers she was with, in case she went back to them – if not I'll keep searching. From what you've said we can rule out London. I've got to find the infuriating girl, for I do declare she is haunting me. And if another stable hand says to me "if Chrissie were here she would handle this horse with ease" I swear I'll hit him.'

Joe arrived then and Harry immediately asked, 'Any sign of her?'

'Not a whisper. It's as if she's just vanished.' Joe looked thoughtful. 'We've been assuming she is quite a way from here by now, but what if she is still close by? Have we searched this area thoroughly enough?'

'We found the farm she worked at for a while, but after that she moved on, and we imagined it was out of the area.' Charles's expression showed his concern. 'I do hope she's all right.'

'Well, forget that for the moment,' Harry told them briskly. 'Stuart is back and wants to see us tomorrow. Let's put our heads together and see if we can give him a clearer picture of what we know.'

'That won't take long,' Charles remarked dryly. 'It's all supposition and of no use to Stuart.'

'I do have one piece of information. I've been away for so long because I went back to Bath on the pretence of trying to get Edward to redeem his markers from me. He wasn't there, but gossip has it that he owes money to a lot of gamblers, and is keeping out of sight. He is not welcome at the tables now, and word has it that he is desperate.'

'Well done, Joe. That is useful.' Harry was nodding. 'That might make him more amenable to fleeing the country.'

'Maybe, but any money you promise him will have to be tied up somehow, so he can only access it once abroad,' Joe pointed out.

'Damn, this isn't going to be easy, is it?' Charles thumped the arm of the chair in frustration. 'It's one blasted problem after another, and I'm beginning to doubt we will be able to make this work. How on earth are we going to persuade him?'

'That's why we're going to Stuart. We need his legal mind to find a workable solution. Don't worry, Father. If he won't cooperate I'll set Joe on him. That will frighten anyone.'

His friend smirked, raised his eyebrows, but said nothing.

The next afternoon they set off for their appointment with Stuart. Harry was riding Red and Joe was on Midnight. Charles was riding his own, slightly smaller mount. The energetic warhorses were not content with the steady pace and were eager to gallop, but the two men were superb horsemen and kept them under control. Charles was clearly nervous when they came to any spot a marksman could hide, and Joe often went on ahead to check the way was clear.

'Relax,' Harry told his father. 'No one knows we will be riding this way today, and if anyone is lurking Joe will spot him.'

'I know, but I still keep expecting to hear a gunshot ringing out.'

'Not a chance and it is good to be out riding again.'

Joe appeared at a canter. 'The way ahead is clear, so how

about letting these animals run off some of their energy?'

'You go ahead, and I'll catch up with you before we reach the Gretham home.' Charles watched them take off and they were soon out of sight. His son had been like a caged animal as his strength returned, and he hoped he wouldn't do any damage to himself. He wasn't a fool, though, and would stop if he felt any discomfort.

Fifteen minutes later he heard the thunder of hooves as the two men raced back to him, laughing as they tried to beat each other. Charles couldn't help remembering his son as a young boy riding like that, with sheer pleasure on his face. Whatever horrors he had experienced in the Crimea were now obviously fading, and he had his son back. All they had to do now was remove this other threat to his life.

Chapter Twenty-Five

'I won't need you this afternoon, so why don't you go for a walk? It's a lovely day.'

Chrissie looked up from her work, surprised. 'I haven't finished this document yet, sir.'

'Leave it until tomorrow. You deserve some time to enjoy the country after spending more time than anticipated in London.'

'Thank you, sir. Are you taking the afternoon off as well?'

'No, I have a meeting here which could take some time.' He glanced at the clock. 'Off you go, and enjoy yourself.'

'I will.' When she left the library the mistress was coming down the stairs. This was the first time she had seen her since arriving back and she expected to be either ignored, or snapped at. That didn't happen.

'Is my husband in the library?' she asked.

'Yes, Lady Gretham. He is waiting for visitors to arrive and has told me I can go for a walk if I want to.'

'Ah, you'll enjoy that, I'm sure. It's a pleasant day – not too hot.' She hesitated as if to say something else, but just turned and went to the library.

Chrissie watched in astonishment as she walked away. That encounter had been quite polite. Perhaps she was going to be able to stay here for a while after all.

Singing quietly to herself she made her way to the scullery to wash the ink from her fingers. While she was scrubbing away at the stubborn stains there was the sound of horses approaching. Several, she guessed from the noise, and they must be the expected visitors.

The door burst open and the chambermaid fell in to the room, her eyes wide with excitement. 'You've got to see this,' she gasped.

'See what?' Chrissie asked.

'The animals. They're huge and such handsome men riding them. I never saw anything like it in my life. Jim, from the stable, said he's seen one of them before, but not the black one.'

The girl's garbled description caught Chrissie's attention and she rushed out of the door, picking up her skirt and tearing round the corner to the yard. The sight she saw brought tears to her eyes. Two of the lads were struggling to lead the horses to the stalls and having no success at all. Oblivious to anything else she began running towards them and shouting, 'Red, Midnight.'

Their ears perked up and they broke away from the lads, hurtling towards her.

The thought of who might be riding them never entered her head, she was overwhelmed with happiness to see them again. They came to a skidding halt and she reached up to cradle each head in turn. 'Oh, my lovely boys, let me have a look at you.' She swiped the moisture from her eyes so she could see clearly, and began to run her hands over them, taking longer to inspect where Midnight had been injured. 'Good, good, you're both in fine condition. You are being well looked after.'

They began to push her playfully, showing their pleasure at seeing her again. She laughed with glee as they pranced around her.

'Er . . . miss,' the stable hands approached cautiously. 'We've got to get them in the stalls and remove their saddles.'

She expertly removed each saddle and tossed them to the lads. Without another thought she led Red to the fence, climbed up and leapt on to his back, amid gasps from those watching. 'Come on, boys, you need to be watered and fed.'

The two warhorses trotted to the stalls and entered like a couple of lambs.

Harry had a firm grip on his father's arm to keep him from moving, and they watched the scene in silence.

When they disappeared from sight, Joe asked through his laughter, 'Who the devil is that?'

'That, my friend, is the blasted girl we have been searching far and wide for, and here she is not ten miles away.' His expression was unreadable as he let go of his father's arm and without another word headed for the stables.

He entered quietly and stood where he could watch

without being seen. Both horses were in the same stall and appeared quite happy. She had a brush in her hand, and while running it over Red's glossy coat, she was talking to both animals, explaining how much she had missed them. The other hands were standing well back, and clearly worried about a girl being in with such large, unpredictable animals. Harry could understand how they felt. They had been struggling to get them to the stable, and along came this girl and they were immediately docile, following her around like puppies. He hadn't been able to believe his eyes when she'd climbed on Red and rode him bareback. He'd been told she did this, of course, but seeing it for himself still surprised him. If anyone else had tried that they would have been flying through the air very quickly. These two animals were still with him because of their unpredictable temperament. Only he had been able to control Midnight, but Red was quite another thing; you never knew what he was going to do. His father had told him she had a way with animals, but it had to be seen to be believed.

She had started on Midnight now, still chatting away to them, and oblivious to the dust and dirt beginning to cover her white blouse and black skirt. She was certainly better dressed than the last time he had seen her, looking tall, elegant and quite beautiful with her dark hair coming lose from its pins.

Suddenly she stopped and put her hand to her mouth. 'Oh, I was so pleased to see my handsome boys again I never thought to see who you came with. Is his lordship here? He wouldn't have sold you, surely. Who do you belong to now?'

Harry stepped forward and slapped Red on the rump

to make enough room for him to get in to the stall. 'They belong to me – always have done and always will.'

She looked up at the tall man and her heart plummeted, but she didn't break eye contact. 'I'm pleased to hear they are still where they belong, sir. They are in fine condition, and Midnight has fully recovered from his injuries.'

Red jostled Harry and he grimaced.

'But I see you haven't. Be still Red, there's a good boy.' She frowned, reaching out as if to touch Harry, then quickly pulled her hand back. 'You've been injured again. What happened?'

'I don't think that's any of your business,' he replied sharply. There was something about this girl that irritated him. There was an openness he was not used to seeing in a female, and when she fixed her dark gaze on him he became defensive. Why he should react in that way was a mystery.

'I beg your pardon, sir. I know you don't like me, and that doesn't bother me, because everyone is entitled to their opinion, but I only enquired out of concern.' She was still frowning and reached out again until one hand was a few inches from his side and the other one resting on Red. 'Ah, that's why Red is still troubled; you were together when you were injured.'

He was shocked by her accuracy. 'Resorting to your fortune-telling again?'

She shook her head. 'No, it's just a feeling, that's all, and my feelings are telling me you must still be careful. Someone doesn't like you, sir.'

'What, someone other than you?'

'I don't dislike you, sir. You are a fine man who has

suffered the kind of pain and grief it is hard to rise above. Trouble is still following you.'

'You would do well to take heed of what she says.' Lord Frenshaw was standing in the doorway and smiling at Chrissie.

The frown left her face and she pushed the animals aside so she could get past Harry. She then curtsied. 'I am so pleased to see you, your lordship. Are you well?'

'I am now I can see you are all right. We've been worried about you.'

'There was no need. I can look after myself, but thank you for your concern. Sir Gretham didn't tell me it was you he was expecting.'

'Why would he tell you?' Harry joined them.

'I work for him, sir.'

'Chrissie is my assistant.' Stuart strode up to them. 'I've given her the afternoon free. Are you going for your walk?' he asked her.

'I'd rather stay with the horses. I haven't seen them for some time.'

'As you please,' he replied, smiling warmly at her. Then he turned to his guests. 'Shall we see if we can find a solution to your problem?'

Harry cast a withering glance at Chrissie and then at Stuart, before making his way to the house.

Once they were settled comfortably in the library, Charles let his anger show. 'Why the hell didn't you tell me Chrissie was here the last time I came? You knew we were searching for her, and you could have let me see her.'

'No, I couldn't, because she was at my London chambers.'

'How can a girl of that background be of any help to you?' Harry wanted to know, a glint of suspicion in his eyes.

'Don't belittle her. Perhaps you don't know that I try to help those who are not as fortunate as us. Many only need to be given a chance, and Chrissie is one of those. She is intelligent and picks things up quickly.' He held out two documents. 'Which is the original?'

They gathered round and after inspecting them carefully, shook their heads.

Stuart held up one. 'This is the original, and the other is a copy made by the girl you think so little of, Harry. Not only that, she has been reading law books so she can understand the difficult words. She is also polite and good with people, and I would keep her in London if I could.'

'But she won't stay there,' Charles said.

'Unfortunately not. The country is her dream, and I have been unable to change her mind, even with the offer of a job with good prospects.' He looked pointedly at Harry. 'However, she has agreed to work for me here. Now, let us get down to business. Have you managed to unearth anything useful?'

Harry let his father and Joe do all the explaining while he studied Stuart. It was years since he'd seen him and he had grown in to an impressive, shrewd and confident man. He could imagine he would be a dominating force in a courtroom. He'd also just told him, in no uncertain terms, that the girl was his and he intended to keep her. Well that was all right with him, but he was suspicious about Stuart's motives. His father had told him there were rumours that Stuart's marriage was in trouble, so was he intending to fill the gap with this girl? He was a man used to winning, and no doubt could turn a young girl's head if he wanted to. He pondered this idea for a moment, and then dismissed it. From what he'd seen and heard about her, she was not a girl he could imagine being persuaded to do something against her will. Still, it would be interesting to keep an eye on the situation.

'I'm still doubtful we could make him leave.' Charles was shaking his head. 'What do you think, Harry?'

'I agree with you.' He snapped himself out of his reverie and tried to hide the fact that he hadn't been listening. 'It's hard to gauge how he will react to anything.'

Stuart turned his attention to Joe. 'You say you have some markers of his, so let's shake Edward up a little before offering him a way out. There is to be a function in London next week, and I have been told he has been invited. Why don't we all attend, and we can confront him, hinting that we know he is the one who shot Harry, and Joe can become menacing as he demands payment of the money he is owed.'

'I think that's the only way we can approach this,' Charles said. 'But how do we get invited to this function?'

'You can leave that to me.' Stuart closed the book he had been making notes in. 'The essential thing, though, is to get a confession, otherwise you will never feel completely safe, Harry.'

'Joe suggested we lie and tell him we have a witness.'

'What you do between yourselves is your business, but you know I couldn't be a part of anything underhand or dishonest.'

'Understood.' Harry grinned. 'We just won't tell you.

I've got to be free of this threat hanging over me and will do whatever has to be done.'

'Be careful or I could end up prosecuting you.' When they all laughed, Stuart stood up and rang a bell. 'That's all we can do at the moment. I'll arrange for you to receive invitations, and you can stay at my London home for a few days.'

The door opened and the butler appeared. 'Sir?'

'My guests are leaving. Will you see that their horses are made ready?'

'Yes, sir.'

They talked for a while longer and then walked outside. It was chaos as the hands tried to get harness and saddles on the warhorses, with Chrissie standing back and roaring with laughter. The more docile animal Charles was riding was ready for the return journey.

'My God!' Harry exploded. 'That girl is not a good influence on my animals. Midnight, Red, stop that at once,' he ordered.

The command of their master made them stand still and turn their heads to glare at him as he stormed towards them.

'What the blazes are you doing?' he asked angrily. 'Why didn't you help the men?'

She was not intimidated by his anger. 'I was going to get them ready myself, but the men wanted to see if they could do it.'

'That's right, sir.' One of the men came forward. 'We thought that if a young girl could handle these beasts, then it should be easy, but as you saw the animals had other ideas.'

'Well, you can carry on now because they won't dare disobey while I'm here.'

'Now, that's a sight to see,' Joe said to Charles as he watched Harry confront Chrissie. He was a force to be reckoned with and he'd seen many a recruit wilt under his anger, but not this girl. She didn't even flinch when he stormed over to her, but faced him, hands on hips, her expression calm.

'That's my girl,' Charles murmured. 'Don't you let him win.'

They were almost toe to toe, and what a striking pair they made, Joe noticed. She was tall, but Harry could still look down on her from his six feet two inches height.

She tipped her head to one side and smiled. 'Would you like to apologise, sir?'

'No, I damned well wouldn't.' He spun away to check the horses were ready, and mounted smoothly. 'Let's go.'

Before they moved out, Chrissie went to each horse in turn and they lowered their heads so she could kiss them, and then she moved back.

Joe winked at her as he swung in to the saddle. Charles was already on his way and cantering to catch his son.

'My, my,' Joe thought as he urged Midnight to a gallop. 'How very interesting.'

Chapter Twenty-Six

The next day, while Harry was having a pre-lunch drink with his father and Joe, the butler entered the room.

'There are two' – he hesitated before saying – 'gentlemen asking to see you, Major.'

'Who are they?'

'They wouldn't give me their names.'

'And you do not think they are gentlemen?'

'No, Major. They are dressed well enough, but I would judge them to be rather rough, and not to be trusted. Shall I tell them you are not at home?'

'We had better see who they are and what they want. Send them in.'

The butler left the room, clearly not happy about these visitors.

Harry walked over to the desk and slipped a small pistol

into his pocket, and Joe indicated that he was already armed. 'Father, would you rather leave?'

'Certainly not. I want to see what this is about, and I am quite safe with two armed cavalry officers.'

The door opened and the butler announced, 'Two visitors for you, Major Frenshaw.'

A quick look and it was clear the butler had been correct in his assessment of the two men. 'I am Major Frenshaw. What can I do for you?'

'We've come to collect a debt, sir. We have some gambling markers that are overdue.'

'Why do you come to me? I don't gamble.'

'Your name is on them as guarantor.'

'Really? May I see them?'

They were handed over and all three of them examined the markers.

'Edward!' Charles said angrily. 'How dare he.'

'Where did you get these?' Harry demanded.

'They came from Viscount Elland. We buy up markers at a reduced rate and then collect the debts.'

Harry knew there were men like this, and they were reputed to go after the debts using any method needed to collect. He handed them back. 'Then you have wasted your money.'

'We never do that.' Their whole attitude now changed. 'Payment is due, and you will settle up now!'

'Those notes were made out and signed by my cousin, Edward Danton. He is the one responsible for the debts, not I. I was not present when they were made out, and I can prove that my signature on them is forged. Therefore I am not responsible. My cousin is addicted to gambling and will say or do anything to keep on playing.'

'We are sure these are legal markers, and will not leave here until the debt is settled.'

'You are threatening the wrong man.'

Joe was leaning casually against the desk with a slight smile on his face. 'I would advise your friend to keep his hand away from his pocket . . . That is very wise,' he remarked when the man put his hand to his side.

If the situation hadn't been so tense, Charles would have laughed. He didn't doubt the two men were quite prepared to use violence if it was needed to collect a debt, but they obviously hadn't realised they would be facing two war-hardened cavalry officers. They knew now, and he could see the doubt in their faces.

'You claim these are legal documents, so would you be prepared to have a barrister, Sir Gretham, examine them? He is renowned as a prosecutor, and once he knows the facts I am sure he will be happy to take the case – against you. I can prove without a shadow of doubt that is not my signature. I never sign in that way.'

Charles moved over to the desk and picked up several papers, then held them out for the men to see. 'That is my son's signature, a simple H. Frenshaw. He never uses his rank.'

The men examined them closely, and when Harry thought they'd had enough time, he said, 'I suggest you leave now – unless you would like to take a ride to see the barrister?'

'That won't be necessary. We will sort this out with Mr Danton. Do you know where he is?'

'I have no idea. Good day, gentlemen.' Harry dismissed them firmly.

They watched them ride away, and as soon as they were through the gates, Charles exploded. 'How dare that boy do such a thing? Even if he wasn't the one who shot you, though there's little doubt about that now, he has to leave. He is a menace not only to us, but to himself as well, and if we don't get him out of the country then someone is going to kill him. What the devil has happened to him?'

'He's got himself into a real mess with no chance of getting out of it, as far as I can see.' Harry stared out of the window, shocked at how deeply his cousin was in debt. 'His compulsion to gamble must be so overwhelming it has pushed aside all common sense. I'm wondering if the damned fool will even dare to come to that function.'

'I think he will,' Joe told them. 'He will feel safe there and the gaming tables will draw him to attend.'

'Let's hope we can get to him before those men do,' Charles sighed heavily. 'One moment we are trying to prosecute him for shooting you, and now we will have to try and save the idiot's life. It is a blessing my sister isn't alive to see what her son has become.'

Harry poured his father a large brandy, seeing how distressed he was. 'Try not to worry. We'll get him on a boat quickly, you'll see.'

Charles took the drink and smiled sadly. 'The sooner the better.'

'I'll leave for London in the morning and see if I can find Danton before those thugs get to him, and I'll see you there.'

'We'll all come with you, Joe,' Harry told his friend. 'I'll send a message to Stuart to let him know we are on our way, and if those invitations don't materialise then we will invite ourselves.'

'Good idea.' Charles looked more relaxed now they were planning to move quickly. 'There are a couple of places the fool could be hiding.'

During the early hours of the morning, Harry was jolted awake and was out of bed and rushing to the window. What the devil was going on? Rain was thundering down, the wind howling, and he could just make out figures running around outside shouting to each other. The animals!

With his army training he was used to moving fast, and he was dressed and running down the stairs in double-quick time. Joe was with him as they exploded out of the house.

Part of the roof had come off the barn and crashed in to the stables, tearing a hole in the end of the stalls. The men were struggling to control terrified horses, all except Midnight and Red, who although wary were standing their ground as they had been trained to do.

'The mares?' Harry shouted.

'Can't get them out,' someone replied.

Harry and Joe began to tear away large pieces of roof, desperate to get at the two mares, knowing they were in foal. Others joined them and they eventually got inside.

'Thank heavens they are all right.' Harry began to calm them down.

'Better get them out, Major.' Joe reverted to the use of military rank. 'The whole place could come down any minute.'

251

'Give me a hand, Captain, we need to clear the wreckage away to make enough room to get them through.'

The men worked quickly and efficiently, managing to coax the animals out just in time. As they reached the yard, that part of the stables collapsed.

'Where is my father's horse?' he called.

'Safely in the paddock, sir,' a stable hand replied. 'They are now all out, and apart from being frightened, they appear to be unharmed.'

Harry wiped the rain out of his eyes as they led the rest of the horses to the safety of the paddock.

An hour later the storm had passed and dawn was beginning to lighten the sky. The stable hands were all busy caring for the horses, and Harry saw his father there, soaking wet like all of them. He must have come out as well, but amid all the chaos it had been difficult to know who was there.

'How are the mares?' he asked his son.

'They are unhurt, but we can only hope they don't lose their foals. That freak storm has done a lot of damage. We'll have to delay our trip to London, and you must see if your estate has been damaged as well.'

'I'll ride over there as soon as I've dried off and changed.'

'Do you want someone to come with you?'

'No, you are going to need all the help you can muster. Cook's already up and cooking breakfast for everyone.'

'Good, I'm starving.' Now the emergency was over, Joe grinned at his friend. 'That was like being in the thick of a battle again.'

* * *

Two days later the clean-up and repairs to the barn and stables were well on the way to being finished. The two men had their sleeves rolled up and were fitting a new door to the barn when there was the sound of a horse approaching.

When Joe saw who it was he chuckled softly to himself and nudged his friend. 'You've got a visitor.'

Harry turned his head and swore fluently. 'What is she doing here?'

'You'd better go and see.'

'I've been dogged with trouble from the moment I set eyes on that girl.'

'That isn't true. You were in plenty of trouble before then. Don't go blaming an innocent girl for everything that goes wrong.'

'You are right, of course.' He shook his head. 'But there is something about her that riles me. Ah, well, I'd better see what she wants.'

Joe followed him, not wanting to miss this encounter.

The moment she saw him she rushed over, looking very worried. 'You have damage from that storm. Are the horses all right?'

'They are not injured. Why are you here?'

'I was asked to bring this to you.' She held out an envelope. 'It's the invitations you were waiting for.'

He took it and then looked around. 'Where is your escort?'

'Escort? Why would I need an escort? I know the way here.'

Seeing his friend was about to explode, Joe stepped in. 'The major is only concerned for your welfare. It isn't the done thing for a young lady to travel the roads unaccompanied.'

She smiled sweetly at Joe. 'Oh, that's all right – I'm not a lady. If you saw where I was brought up you would know that I'm quite able to take care of myself.'

'That is just foolish,' Harry told her. 'Suppose I came across you on your own and decided to molest you.'

She eyed him up and down. 'I agree you are a strong man, but if you tried it you would not come out of it unscathed.'

'Like that man you attacked in London?'

'He was a drunken weakling and was trying to rape a child!' she told him bluntly, offended by his tone. 'He deserved a good beating.'

Harry lifted his hands in surrender. 'I apologise. That was uncalled for.'

'Indeed it was. I am not an ignorant fool, sir.' She lifted her skirt slightly to reveal a knife in a scabbard attached to her breeches. 'Now, before I leave, may I have your permission to see the horses?'

At that moment Bert arrived. 'Ah, Chrissie, I'm glad you're here. We have two mares in foal who were very frightened by the storm, and they are not eating properly. Would you have a look at them for us?'

'Poor darlings. Where are they?'

'In the small paddock.'

'Give me two more bags of food and I'll go and talk to them.'

They all followed her and watched her walk across the field, and the groom gave Harry a relieved smile. 'She'll soon settle them down. It's uncanny the rapport she has with the animals, and I think it's because she loves them and they know it.'

Half an hour later, Chrissie returned with two empty feed bags and handed them back to the groom. 'They were hungry and will be all right now. They said they were terrified when everything started to crash around them.'

'Are the foals alive?'

She nodded. 'I felt them moving, and the mares are quite calm now.'

'I saw you talking to the other two over the fence,' Bert told her, 'so are they all right?'

'They are fine,' she said fondly. 'It would take more than a storm to panic those two.'

Harry listened to this conversation in disbelief. His head groom really believed what this girl was telling him.

She turned back to Harry and gave a slight bow. 'Thank you for allowing me to see the horses, sir. I will be on my way now.'

'No, you won't.'

'I beg your pardon?'

'You will not start your journey back until you have had some refreshments. Go to the kitchen and see Cook.'

'Thank you, sir. I am rather thirsty.'

As she disappeared from their sight, Joe said, 'What a remarkable girl.'

'She's too outspoken, and did you see that knife she's carrying? A female doesn't do something like that, or speak so openly about rape.'

'You are forgetting her background,' Joe reminded him. 'Have you ever seen the slums of London?'

He shook his head.

'I have, and in her life there she will have seen and dealt with every kind of situation. It is life in the raw, and you learn fast or you don't survive. Her father brought his girl up to know what life was all about, and to fight when it was necessary. She will have seen villains, wife beaters, nasty drunks and even murderers. She knows both sides of life – the good and the bad – and I like her a lot.'

'I didn't know your tastes ran to witches,' Harry joked. 'Come on, we've got work to do so we can get on our way to London. There's that urgent problem for us to sort out.'

Chapter Twenty-Seven

The next day Charles returned; there had been some damage to his estate, but not nearly as much as Harry's. Once all the necessary repairs had been done they set off for London.

As soon as they were settled in, Charles took the opportunity to go visiting, and Joe went to see if he could discover where Edward was hiding, leaving Harry to spend the day of the function on his own.

He gazed out at the street with its carriages and fashionable people and remembered the rebuke Joe had given him about his rudeness to that girl. He was right; he had never actually seen the kind of conditions she had been born in to. He had seen and endured many rough times and places while in the cavalry, but his young life had been one of privilege and green fields, and he had never explored the less fashionable parts of the city. His father had told him of the area in Camden she came from, so he decided it was time he went to see for himself. His first thought was to take a horse, but he decided against it, and ordered a hansom cab instead.

It arrived quickly, and when he told the driver where he wanted to go, he received an odd look.

'Are you sure you've got the right place, sir?'

'Quite sure.'

The man shrugged. 'That's a rough area and I can only take you part of the way.'

'All right, drop me off as close as you can and I'll walk the rest of the way.'

'Do you think that's wise, sir?'

'Good gracious man, do you think I can't take care of myself? Drive on.' He was even more curious now. This man was frightened to drive all the way. Unbelievable.

He sat back and watched the scenery change from fine houses to modest dwellings, and then hovels all huddled together with dirt and filth littering the streets.

The cab stopped. 'If you go down this street and take the second turn on the left it will bring you to the place you're looking for, sir.'

'Thank you.' Harry got out and paid him.

'If you need a cab back I can meet you here if you give me a time, sir.'

'Two hours should be enough.'

'Right, I'll return for you then. Be careful, sir.'

He nodded and began walking in the direction the cabbie had pointed out. He soon had a gang of scruffy children following him and begging for money. After a while he stopped, turned to face them and asked, 'If I gave you money what would you do with it?'

'Buy sweets,' they chorused, apart from one small painfully thin little girl. 'I'd give it to my mum to buy food for us.'

He studied her for a moment and his heart ached for the child. She didn't look as if she'd had a decent meal in a long while. When he thought about the sumptuous tables set by the wealthy, he was ashamed. He'd known there were many poor, of course, but this was the first time he had ever seen it with his own eyes. 'Where do you live, child?'

'In the next street.'

He held out his hand. 'Show me.'

'Why?' She eyed him with suspicion. 'We ain't done nothing wrong. Are you a copper?'

'No. My name is Major Frenshaw, a cavalry officer.'

'Where's your 'orse?' one of the boys shouted and they all fell about laughing.

'I couldn't bring him down here, because he's a warhorse and would have chased you all away.'

'Cor, does he fight, then?'

'Yes, and he's very big and strong.' He turned his attention back to the little girl, who was still surveying him with caution. 'I will not harm you, so will you show me where you live now you know who I am?'

She thought about it for a minute, nodded, and came to stand beside him. 'This way.'

They walked the street with the children dancing round him and the questions came in torrents, which he answered, much to their delight. When they came to a small shop with lots of jars in the window, he stopped. 'Come on and I'll buy you all sweets.'

A cheer rang out and there was a stampede through the door.

'Quiet!' he ordered, and the bedlam ceased immediately. 'Now, I want each one of you to choose what you want.'

Such a big decision took time, and while they were trying to make up their minds he went to the fruit crates. With the shopkeeper's help he soon had a bag of fresh fruit for every child. He paid for all the purchases and handed out the fruit. 'The sweets are your treat, but I want you to take the fruit to your families so they can enjoy a treat as well. Will you do that?'

They all nodded, busy sucking their chosen sweets.

'Thanks, mister, you're a real gent,' the oldest boy said.

Some of them ran off home then, clutching the bags, eager to share their prize with their families, but the little girl and two others stayed with him. They turned a corner and walked down a narrow cobbled street, and Harry was appalled at the squalor he was seeing.

The little girl tugged at his sleeve. 'I live there.'

'And we live in this street as well,' the other two told him.

He took some coins out of his pocket and placed them in each grubby hand. 'You are to give that to your mothers – no one else – and tell her it's to buy food.'

They looked at the money, wide-eyed with wonder, and one of them said, 'No one ain't done nothing like this for us before. Thanks, mister.'

The little girl smiled shyly and they all ran to their homes.

He didn't linger and strode away at once. He still had

to find out where Chrissie had lived – and that was the first time he had ever thought of her by name, he realised. He had wandered a little out of his way with the children, but after retracing his steps he was soon heading in the right direction again. Then he heard the call 'rag an' bone!' and he stopped to wave down the horse and cart.

'Are you lost, sir?' the man asked.

'No.' He walked up to the animal and ran his hands over her. 'She's in nice condition. Is this Bessie?'

'Why yes, sir. How did you know?'

'Christine Banner told us about her.'

'Chrissie! You know her? Is she all right? We've been worried about her.'

'She's doing well and working for a barrister in a place near the New Forest.'

'That's a relief to know, and I'm not surprised, cos she always did have a good head on her shoulders.'

'I've come here because I want to see where she lived.'

'Do you, sir? Well, I'm heading for home now, so if you'd like to hop up beside me I'll take you there, though it ain't much to see, sir. My name's Bob, by the way,' he said as Harry jumped up on the cart.

'Call me Harry. Nice sturdy cart you have here.'

He nodded. 'Young Chrissie saved my life when she gave it to me with her dad's round. Has a heart of gold, does that lass. I didn't have any money to give her and she could have sold it, but she knew we was desperate, and that we'd take good care of Bessie. She left here with nowhere to go and no money in her pocket, and I'm relieved to hear she's all right. They had no right kicking her out of her home, but that bastard landlord has only money for a heart. Pardon my language, sir.'

'I was a cavalry officer and have heard worse.'

Bob grinned and pulled to a stop. 'I'll bet you have. This was Chrissie's place, though it looked better when her and her dad was here. Kept the place spotless, she did, and that ain't easy to do here.'

When Harry looked at the tiny terraced house in this desperately poor area, he couldn't find words to express his feelings. All he could say was, 'No wonder she had the dream of living in the country.'

'We'd be really grateful to hear how she's getting on.' Bob moved the cart a couple of doors along. 'Could you spare the time to have a cup of tea with us and tell us all the news? You say no if you don't want to. You're a fine gentleman and we'd understand if you don't want to come in.'

'I'd love a cup of tea. Thank you, Bob.' He leapt from the cart just as several children ran out of the house and began to unhitch the horse.

'How did you do?' the eldest boy asked his dad.

'Not bad; we'll eat for another week, anyway. Give Bessie a rub down and a bit of extra feed; she deserves it. Come and meet the wife, she'll be excited to hear your news,' he told Harry.

He followed him into the house and straight through to the scullery.

'Gladys,' Bob called. 'Put the kettle on, cos we've got a visitor with news about Chrissie.'

She stared in astonishment when Harry walked in,

seeming to fill the small space, and looking completely out of place in his fine clothes.

'This is Harry,' her husband told her.

Aware of her discomfort, Harry reached out to shake her hand, a smile on his face. 'I'm pleased to meet you, and thank you for inviting me in for a cup of tea.'

'You're very welcome, sir.'

'Harry,' he prompted.

'Please sit down, the water's nearly boiling.' She rummaged in a cupboard and found a cup and saucer, then washed it thoroughly before setting it on the table.

It was clearly the best china they had, and Harry felt honoured by the gesture.

As soon as the tea was poured, Bob asked eagerly, 'Will you tell us all about Chrissie, now?'

He talked for some time and enjoyed two cups of really strong tea. He knew most of Chrissie's story and had them laughing about some of the things she had done to get to the country, such as fortune-telling with the Travellers. The only thing he didn't tell them was that he had dismissed her when he had arrived home. That was something he wasn't proud of, and it disturbed him even more after walking the streets where she had lived. Somehow he felt he had come to know her during this trip.

'That's such a relief,' Gladys exclaimed once he'd finished telling them what she had been doing. 'We've been so worried about her. We knew she was a strong girl and well able to take care of herself, but moving away from everything and everyone she knew could have been a big mistake, and we weren't sure she knew what she was getting in to. She'd had this dream, you see, right from a little girl, and after her dad died I think she felt she had to follow it.'

Harry stood up and shook their hands. 'I am pleased to have been able to put your minds at rest. Now, if you will excuse me, I have a cab waiting for me.'

'Where's that?' Bob asked.

'About fifteen minutes' walk from here.'

'I'd better come with you.'

'Please don't trouble yourself. I'll be quite all right.'

'I don't doubt you can take care of yourself, but you can't be too careful around here. Some can get nasty when they're drunk. I'll just walk with you for a way.'

Seeing it would be rude to refuse, they walked out together. If any villains did try to rob him they would find lean pickings, because after buying the sweets and fruit for the children, he'd only had a half-sovereign, which he'd put under the saucer for Gladys, and that left just enough to pay the cabbie.

They attracted quite a lot of attention while walking, and many taunts were shouted to Bob wanting to know how much he wanted for the toff. He grinned and ignored them, still talking to Harry, eager to hear any snippet of information he could glean about this man who had taken the trouble to come and tell them about Chrissie. Even more amazing was the fact that he had sat in their scullery drinking tea as if it was the most natural thing for him to do. Bob could only imagine the fine place he lived in with servants to cater for his every need, and yet he hadn't appeared to be at all uncomfortable with them. Of course, he'd been a cavalry officer in that terrible Crimean War, so he had probably seen awful things. It was a relief to know that Chrissie had found such fine people who obviously cared about her.

Bob left him at the end of the next street, and out of the corner of his eye Harry noticed three men approaching him, blocking his way. They were clearly intent on attacking him, and he knew three against one was not good odds, but they were not big men and were clearly drunk, so he had a good chance. With his military training he summed up the situation at once and tensed for action.

'Give us your money and valuables,' one demanded.

He stood still, hands hanging loosely to his sides and shook his head. 'You don't think I'd be foolish enough to come down here with anything valuable on me, do you?'

'Don't try to kid us,' the largest of the three said, stepping closer. 'Let's find out, lads.'

Harry smiled. 'I wouldn't try that if I were you.'

'You're a big man, but there's three of us.'

'I've taken on more.'

At that moment one of them lunged at him and he sidestepped, making the man lose his balance and hit the road. The other two came for him then, but they were no match for a hardened military man, and soon found themselves on the road with their friend.

'That's him, Mum!' a shrill voice shouted.

Still keeping an eye on the would-be robbers as they got groggily to their feet, he put a hand out and caught hold of the small boy who had hurtled up to him, afraid he might get hurt by these men.

'Hey, mister, you ain't half tough.' He grinned up at

Harry. 'You moved so quick they was on the ground before they knew what had happened.'

The men were on their feet now and a woman stormed up to them. 'Get off home, you drunken louts, before this gentleman turns you over to the coppers.'

Without a word of protest the men scurried away, and Harry smiled at the boy's mother. 'Thanks, madam.'

She snorted. 'No need to thank me, young man. You don't need help from no one. My boy said you're the one who gave him the bag of fruit. Is that right?'

'Yes, I hope you enjoyed it.'

'We did, and it was a real treat, and I want to thank you. Most people tell the kids to clear off, but you was kind to them. That was good of you.'

'It was my pleasure, madam.'

She smiled at the polite form of address, as more of the children he'd seen before came running up to him.

'Right,' the woman said, 'I want you all to thank this nice gentleman and see he gets to where he's going without any more trouble.'

They all nodded eagerly, and walked the rest of the way with him to where the cab was waiting.

As they drove away the children waved until he was out of sight. He sat back and rubbed his bruised knuckles. What an experience, and it was one he wouldn't have missed for anything.

Chapter Twenty-Eight

'The mistress wants to see you in the sitting room.'

Chrissie looked up from the document she was copying and frowned. 'Did she say why?'

'No, but you'd better hurry, because she doesn't seem in the best of moods.'

She put the pen in its holder and got to her feet. 'Then I'd better not keep her waiting.'

'There you are. You took your time,' the mistress remarked sharply when Chrissie entered the room.

'I came as soon as I was told.' She had really tried to like this woman, and while her husband had been here everything had been fine, but now he was away she felt this interview wasn't going to be pleasant.

'My son will be coming home tomorrow for a short-term break and I don't want you causing trouble. My husband won't be here to take your side this time.'

It was clear now that she had held her tongue for a while, pretending to be a reformed person, but that was all it had been – a show.

'Don't stand there dumb, girl!'

'I'm not sure what you expect me to say.'

'I expect you to tell me that you will obey my orders. I object to you being here, but my husband is enamoured with you.'

'I beg your pardon?'

'You know what I'm talking about. Where did you stay while in London?'

'With Mr and Mrs Martin.' Chrissie was shocked. Where was this leading?

'You think I will believe that? You're a common tramp and no doubt used to telling lies.'

Now she was furious, but kept her anger under control. 'The Martins will confirm that what I have told you is true. Are you accusing me of wrongdoing with your husband?'

'It wouldn't be the first time a man has been taken in by a pretty face.'

'How dare you!' The anger and hurt erupted. 'Your husband has always behaved as the perfect gentleman towards me. I may come from a humble background, but I have been brought up to be a decent person, and I don't lie. Your nasty suspicious mind is stopping you from being grateful for all the blessings you have, and for your own sake, I pray you will soon see how fortunate you are.'

'I don't need the prayers of someone like you.' She was

red in the face now and shaking. 'Your impertinence is inexcusable. Get out!'

Chrissie turned briskly and left the room, relieved to get away.

Nanny rushed up to her. 'Are you all right? We could hear the shouting all around the house.'

'I think you had better ask Cook to send the mistress in a pot of strong tea. I don't think she is at all well.' She then returned to the library, wanting to be alone, and gazed out of the window in an effort to clear her head. She had promised Sir Gretham she wouldn't leave without telling him first, but the situation here was now impossible. Leaving the work she had been doing she left the house and walked, allowing the beauty of the countryside to caress her with its healing touch. Why was this happening to her? Her dream of getting out of London and making a life for herself in the country had seemed so simple. She would find a place she liked, get a job and settle down, but it wasn't turning out like that. She had been constantly moving on, through no fault of her own, and it looked as if she was going to have to do that again. It was as if she wasn't wanted anywhere, and that thought weighed heavily on her heart. What was she doing wrong? Why did people keep turning her away? Was she so unlikeable that no one could stand to have her around?

Her shoulders were slumped in dejection and her eyes downcast, then she stopped suddenly, straightened up and lifted her gaze to the blue sky. This wouldn't do! Her dad always said that allowing anyone to rob you of your confidence and self-respect wasn't right. What anyone else thought was their problem, not yours. He was right, and she drew in a deep breath, turning her thoughts to dealing with the problem that now faced her. She had to leave here, that was now absolutely clear, and get away from this area as soon as possible. The pull of the Frenshaw estate was so strong she had stayed as close as possible, but that had been a mistake. Elsie had told her things would be difficult. Well, she had been right about that. Her time here had been a mixture of joy, pain and disappointment, but she wasn't ready to give up on her dream. There was only one thing she could do and that was to find the Travellers again. They had said she would be welcome to join them any time, and that time was now.

Turning round she walked quickly back to the house. A letter to Sir Gretham would be her first task, and if she waited a couple of days for him to receive it, then she wouldn't be breaking her promise to him. After that she would set off to find her friends again.

Settling down at the desk she began to write the difficult letter. She didn't want to tell him what had happened, but she must give a reason for leaving, and after some thought she just said that a situation had arisen that made it impossible for her to stay, and signed off by thanking him for his kindness towards her. With the letter sealed she set off for the village to make sure it was on its way as quickly as possible.

When she returned Nurse was waiting for her and looking very worried. 'Are you all right? Come and have a cup of tea. You looked quite drained.'

She dredged up a smile as they made their way to the kitchen, where Cook made her sit down and put a large slice of fruit cake in front of her, still warm from the oven.

'You eat that, my dear. Everyone in the house heard what the mistress said to you, and it was quite disgraceful. Don't you take any notice of her rage. If you ask me she's not right in the head to shout and rave at you like that, and it's the master I feel sorry for. Such a nice gentleman. Eat your cake, dear.'

Chrissie did as ordered, though in truth it was difficult to push it down, but she didn't want to offend Cook. She listened to the chatter around her, but said nothing. Her plans were made.

When Robert arrived home the next day on a short school break, his mother fussed over him, and he got away from her as soon as he could to find Chrissie.

He opened the library door a little and looked in. 'May I come in, please?'

'Of course.' She smiled warmly as he walked up to the desk, looking rather hesitant. 'It's lovely to see you, Robert. You are looking quite the gentleman.'

'Thank you. I am going to be like my father.'

'I'm sure you will, and I expect your mother was pleased to see you looking so well.'

He shrugged and pulled a face. 'My sister, Jane, told me she had screamed at you, blaming you for having me sent away to school. That isn't true. Father told me a long time ago that when I was ten he would take me to the school he went to. I apologise for all the trouble I've caused you.'

Chrissie stood up. 'That is kind of you, Robert, but not necessary. I don't blame you at all. You were bored and didn't have enough to keep you interested here. You are a bright boy and need to have a goal in life. If you study hard, then one day you will be a great help to your father – and as famous, I'm positive.'

He straightened up proudly. 'That's what I intend. I'm pleased Father sent me to the school, but sorry I made him angry by being horrible to you and breaking your pretty box.'

'Don't worry about that. It has been repaired and is as good as new. I have forgotten all about that day, and you should also. It is in the past, and only good came out of it, don't you agree?'

'I do, and I won't worry about it any more now I've talked with you.'

'Good.'

They both spun round, startled, when the library door crashed open and his mother stormed in. 'I told you to keep away from my son!'

'Mother!' Robert raised his voice. 'I came to apologise for causing Chrissie trouble, and you are blaming her for things she hasn't done. Not once has she been unkind to me, and holds no ill feeling towards me for the things I did. If you continue to shout at her like that I shall return to school immediately and spend my free time in London with Father in the future.'

She gazed at him open-mouthed in shock, and Chrissie felt sorry for her, seeing clearly at that moment that the lady was sick in her mind. What a tragedy.

'You . . . you,' she stuttered, 'are becoming like your father.'

'I will be very happy if I grow up like him. Now, if you will excuse us, Mother, Chrissie and I still have things to discuss.'

Nurse appeared and led his mother away, talking softly to calm her down.

Robert settled himself in a chair. 'My sisters told me about the warhorses that came here, and they said you weren't afraid of them, even riding one when no one else could control them. Would you tell me about that, please?'

She sat opposite him and explained what had happened, making him laugh in delight. They talked for quite a while, and he told her about the school, the lessons and games, his eyes shining with enthusiasm. It was hard to grasp that this was the same boy. In a few short weeks he had grown and matured, intelligence shining through, and it did her heart good to see such a perfect outcome from a distressing incident, but it also strengthened her resolve to leave. This wasn't the right place for her, and it would be better for the family if she moved on.

'Robert, I have to tell you that I will be leaving in the morning.'

'Why?' He looked dismayed. 'Is it because of Mother?'

'Yes, I am making her unhappy and, hopefully, she will feel better when I've gone.'

'Does Father know?'

'I've written to him, and he should receive the letter any time now.'

'Did you tell him what was said to you?'

'No, I just told him I was unable to stay. I don't want to cause your mother any more problems. For some reason she doesn't like me being here, and that upsets me. Do you understand?'

'I can see that, but everyone here likes you and will be sorry to see you go when you haven't done anything wrong. Where will you go?'

'I don't know yet.' She smiled brightly. 'There is so much beautiful countryside I haven't seen yet.'

'Will you write to me at the school and let me know where you are and what you're doing?'

'I'll try, but I can't promise.'

'I understand it could be difficult if you are moving around, but I'd be pleased to hear from you if you can manage it.'

She just nodded, knowing that when she left it would be a clean break from everything. She had seen a lot and learnt a lot since leaving London, but she still hadn't found what she was looking for – a permanent home – so it was time to put everything behind her and start again.

Having said goodbye to Nurse the night before, Chrissie quietly left the house at dawn the next morning. The Travellers had told her they were heading for a place by the sea called Boscombe and then on to Bournemouth, and she had found it on a map in the library, making a sketch for herself. There was a little money in her pocket from the work she had done on some documents, but she would have to be careful, not knowing how long the journey would take. It would be easier if she could take a train, but this was a remote area and the lines were not near here. She was also not sure the small amount of money she had would be enough to travel that way.

Her pace was brisk as she set out for the nearest village where she hoped to get a lift if anyone was going in the direction she wanted. Every mile covered that way would speed up the journey. There was a lovely red tinge to the sky now and she tried to keep her mind on what she had to do, and not what she would be leaving behind, but the memories crept in. Why, oh why, had she allowed herself to fall in love with the Frenshaw estate, those stunning animals and the people who worked there? She had been foolish, but it had been a lesson well learnt and it wouldn't happen again, she'd make sure of that.

Lifting her face to the early morning sun, she strode on with determination. There were new things to do and see, and many more lessons to learn, she was sure. She had changed since her dad had died, and hoped she was now wiser.

The village came in to view and people were just beginning to go about their daily work, so she hoped she could find someone willing to give her a lift.

She had only ever been to the coast once, and it would be exciting to see the sea again.

Chapter Twenty-Nine

'What did you do today?' Stuart asked Harry when the men were at dinner that evening.

They listened with interest when he told them where he had been, and Joe was smiling. 'I wondered where you bruised your knuckles. They made a mistake taking you on, you can move faster than any man I've seen when you have to. Now you've seen how the people live, what's your opinion?'

Harry put down his knife and fork and gazed around the table. 'I knew some people lived in poverty, but I had never walked the streets and seen how bad it really is or how desperate their lives could be. Now I understand, Stuart, why you try to help by employing some.'

'What I do doesn't even touch the tip of the problem. It's the youngsters I'm trying to lift away from that life.

The only thing many of them want is a chance, and that is hard for them to find. Education is the answer, but getting anyone to listen is hopeless, because many of the wealthy don't want to know about such unpleasant things. I've employed one young boy and he is a good lad, eager to learn, and then there's Chrissie. She's one of the brightest I have come across, and with the right education I believe she could do anything she set her mind to.'

Charles was nodding. 'It must have taken huge courage to set out on her own like she has. She wanted something better and was determined to try. When the estate manager brought her to me, I looked at the tall, clean, but scruffy girl, and I saw hope shining in her dark eyes. I knew in that moment that this was where she wanted to be, and would work damned hard to prove she deserved a chance. I couldn't turn her away.'

When his father glanced pointedly across the table at him, Harry was shocked by the intensity of the pain that raced through him. After what he'd seen today, sending her away was a cruel act. He'd never considered himself to be a callous man, but he had been on that occasion, the only reason being that she was wearing breeches so she could do the job in the stables – the only job that had been available to her. When he looked back he didn't like the man who had done that, and he changed the subject quickly. 'What are our plans for tonight?'

'I want you two in full dress uniform, so that when we walk in everyone will notice,' Stuart told Harry and Joe. 'I take it you have brought your uniforms with you?'

'Never go anywhere without them,' Joe told him jokingly.

'You never know when they might be needed. However, if I arrive with Harry like that there is no way I can remain incognito, and if Danton is there he will recognise me.'

'That is what I want. It will unnerve him to discover the man he lost a lot of money to is a fellow officer of his cousin. If he is the culprit he will be sure Harry suspects and sent a friend to investigate.'

'So what do you plan if Edward does show up?' Charles asked.

'Take him to a side room and persuade him to tell the truth. What you say to him will be up to you. I will be with you, but standing in the background, and only introduce me in my legal capacity once he talks.'

'If he talks.'

Stuart smiled at Harry. 'You and Joe in full uniform would be enough to frighten anyone, and once Charles joins in he will want to run. I wouldn't like to have the three of you after me. Let's hope our information is correct and he is there, otherwise we will have to go looking for him.'

Stuart was right. When they walked in, the room buzzed with excitement, and mothers began assessing them as suitable husbands for their daughters.

'Mingle,' Stuart told them, not even trying to hide his amusement. 'You are the two most eligible males in this room, and will be pursued by hungry mothers. While you're enjoying all the attention, don't forget why we are here.'

'We are battle-trained officers and can handle any situation.' Harry slapped Joe on the back. 'Let's infiltrate the enemy, Captain.' Smiling politely, the two men strode forward.

Charles was laughing so much he had to turn his back to the room for a moment, and then said to Stuart, 'You did that on purpose.'

'Of course. This is a serious business, but I thought we might as well have some fun as well. Look at them, both over six feet tall and as impressive as hell. Come on, Charles, let's see what the champagne is like.'

They had been there an hour and there wasn't a sign of Edward. Harry had lost track of Stuart and his father, but Joe was close by, doing the same as him by fending off eager mothers. They had been introduced to so many people he had given up trying to remember their names. Although he came from a titled and wealthy family, they were not frequent visitors to the social scene.

The hostess approached with three more people in tow. 'Major Frenshaw, may I introduce Mr and Mrs Hamlin and their son, Walter. They have expressed a desire to meet you.'

The name immediately caught his attention. Where had he heard it before? Then it came to him in a flash. It had been mentioned when his father had been telling him what had happened to Chrissie. Were these the same people? He began to make polite conversation while studying the son carefully. It soon became apparent that the boy was brash and opinionated as he started to hold forth about the Crimean War. He looked in Joe's direction and made a silent signal with his eyes, and his friend came straight over.

'Captain, allow me to introduce you to Mr and Mrs Hamlin and their son, who has views about the Crimean War.'

'Really?'

They both turned their attention to the boy as if interested in what he had to say on the subject, and saw the fool preen visibly. They knew what he was thinking – he was going to cut these two, who were causing such a stir in the room, down to size.

After talking for a few minutes he looked mockingly at the two Light Brigade officers and said, 'Those that took part in that disastrous charge must have been fools. I'll bet you're glad you weren't there.'

'Those men were following orders.' Harry spoke calmly as he moved a touch nearer to the boy. 'And we were two of those – fools – as you so rudely put it. You have just insulted all those brave men who died in that battle.'

The Hamlins were suddenly alarmed at the blunder their son had made and stammered out an apology. 'Sirs, our son means no offence.'

'Of course he did,' Joe replied. 'He is giving an opinion on something he knows nothing about.'

Walter had tried to move away, but the officers blocked his escape route, and at that moment Charles arrived and gave his son a questioning look. 'Is everything all right? Your conversation is causing a lot of interest in the room.'

'Everything is fine, Father. Let me introduce you to Mr and Mrs Hamlin and their son, Walter. He has just been telling us what fools we are.'

'That is unwise of him.' Charles studied the boy. 'Hamlin, you say?'

'Apologise,' Mr Hamlin told his son, thoroughly embarrassed at the attention now focussed upon them.

The boy stood there sullenly, and Charles turned to his son and Joe. 'Do you think this is the boy?'

'Certain of it,' he told his father. 'I can just imagine Chrissie giving him a thrashing, and I must say he deserves one at this moment. It's a shame we are at this gathering because we would love to explain what it is like to see your friends scattered over the battlefield dead or dying. Wouldn't we, Captain?'

Joe looked at his clenched his fist. 'I would consider it absolutely necessary.'

'There's no need for that! My son spoke without thinking.'

Charles gave a grim smile. 'I understand he wasn't thinking when he went to the servants' quarters at night and tried to molest a child.'

The Hamlins, who had been in the process of trying to escape from these dangerous men, stopped dead in their tracks, and turned back to face them.

'Where did you hear those lies?' The mother had raised her voice.

'The person I heard it from is absolutely truthful, and only told me because she knew if I asked you for a reference about her employment with you it would not have been favourable.'

'That Banner girl!' The son exploded now. 'You don't want to believe anything that tramp from the slums says.'

'Be very careful, young man,' Charles said while taking a menacing step towards him. 'You have already insulted two decorated officers of the Light Brigade, and you should know that Christine Banner is a friend of ours, and

I won't allow her to be slandered by a spoilt, immoral brat like you.'

'Can I be of assistance, gentlemen?' Stuart joined them.

'I think you can.' Harry pulled him in to the group, which had grown rather large by now. 'In your capacity as a barrister, could you tell us if, according to the law, it is a punishable crime to molest a child?'

'I have handled such cases with success. Do you have someone in mind?'

'This boy is the one Chrissie stopped from doing just that. His name is Walter Hamlin.' Harry gazed around at the crowd listening avidly. 'But I think the case is already won.'

The Hamlins turned and fled, and Joe smiled with satisfaction. 'I don't think they will be receiving many more invitations.'

'I came over because I think Edward has arrived, but I'm not certain as I haven't seen him since he was a child,' Stuart explained.

'Where is he?'

'The man I saw was making his way to the games room.'

'That will be him.' Charles was already moving, and the others followed.

Before they had reached the door the flustered hostess caught them. 'I must apologise for the way the Hamlins treated you, gentlemen. I will not have the heroes of the Crimea insulted in my establishment.'

Harry bowed slightly. 'Please do not concern yourself, madam. We are the ones who should apologise for causing a scene.'

She gave a little laugh and reached out to touch his

many decorations. 'Please think nothing of it. That family are not popular, and my guests were highly entertained to see them put down so expertly. I do hope you are not leaving already?'

'Of course not.' Harry's smile worked its magic and made the colour rise in her cheeks. 'We are going to visit the games room.'

'Ah, of course, gentlemen do like to gamble a little. I wish you good luck.' She hurried away, eager to share in the gossip this incident had caused, knowing her evening was a success.

'I had forgotten you could turn on the charm with such devastating effect.' Stuart was laughing as they made their way along the passage. When they reached it, he said, 'There is a room opposite, so Harry you go in and bring him there. We will be waiting for you.'

Edward had just taken his seat when Harry strode in and gripped his cousin's shoulder. 'Good evening, Edward, we need to have a word with you.'

He looked up, surprised to see who had such a firm grip on him. Relief crossed his face when he saw that it wasn't someone he owed money to. 'I'm about to play.'

'That can wait a while.' Harry smiled at the other men around the table. 'Please excuse us, gentlemen.'

When they nodded he tightened his grip on Edward, giving him no option but to leave the table.

'What's this all about?' he demanded the moment they were outside the room.

'You are a hard man to find, and we have some questions you need to answer.' He guided him, firmly, into the next room.

The moment they entered the side room his gaze fixed on Joe, and then back to his cousin, both wearing the same uniform. 'You know each other! I demand an explanation why you sought me out in Bath.'

'I was there to see how much money I could win from you.' Joe's smile was not one you would want cast in your direction, and it clearly unnerved Edward. 'It was easy. You really are a very bad player.'

'You cheated!'

'Be very careful who you accuse. We have already been insulted this evening, and we are not inclined to let that happen again. I could make you retract that slanderous accusation.'

'You don't frighten me,' he blustered, 'and you won't get any money from me.'

'I know those markers are not worth anything because you can't possibly redeem them. How many people are pursuing you for payment?'

'That's my business. Uncle, what is this all about? If you don't explain, then I am going back to the game.' Edward turned, and only then noticed Stuart leaning against the door, blocking his exit. 'Who is this?'

'Not someone you would recognise because you were only a child the last time you saw him. You don't want to meet him now, because if he takes an interest in you that will be very bad,' Harry warned. 'Since I was shot we have discovered some very interesting facts about you, cousin. You are desperate for money, and are an excellent shot – just to mention two.'

'Are you suggesting I was the one who shot you?'

'We know you did.'

'Who's doing the slandering now? You can't prove that.'

'But we can,' Joe said. 'We have a witness who saw you.'

Edward laughed. 'You're lying!'

'Why are you so sure we are lying?' Charles asked, coming in to the conversation for the first time. 'Is it because you didn't see anyone while you waited in the trees for Harry to ride by?'

'No . . . no, I mean anyone hiding in that copse couldn't possibly have been seen.'

Charles sighed in sadness. 'How do you know the man was hiding in the copse? We never told you where the shooting took place, and you never asked.'

'You must have forgotten you told me.' He was chalk-white now and his guilt evident to all the men in the room.

'We never told you, because we suspected you from the beginning, and took steps to find out if you were capable of hitting a moving target. The instructor at that club you belong to was very complimentary about your abilities.'

He was close to tears now and shaking with fear. 'I'm so sorry. I was desperate and not thinking straight. I had been so sure the estate was as good as mine, and then Harry returned, and I panicked. What are you going to do with me?'

'We have discussed this at length. If Harry had died you would have been sent to the gallows, family or not. Thankfully, he lived, and we have come up with a solution, and you do not have a choice. You agree or go to prison for attempted murder. Our friend by the door is a renowned barrister, and is ready to prosecute – if necessary.'

'Don't send me to prison, Uncle,' he pleaded. 'I'll do whatever you say.'

Charles nodded to his son to take over, and stepped back.

'We are aware that you are in dire financial trouble, so what we propose is this. Father and I will buy you passage to a country of your choice, and a substantial amount of money will be waiting for you when you arrive. It is our hope that you will mend your ways by giving up gambling and make a new life for yourself. Before leaving here tonight you will sign a confession, to be witnessed by all of us, and this will then be placed in the safe keeping of our barrister. If you return to this country you must be a reformed man or that confession will be used against you. Is that clearly understood, Edward?'

'Yes,' he murmured, relief flooding his face. 'That is very generous of you, and I think I would like to go to South Africa. I believe there are good opportunities there.'

'That can be arranged and passage will be booked on the first available ship.' Harry produced a pen and paper for his cousin to write out his confession.

When this was done, Charles handed it to Stuart. It was a sad business, but at least they were giving him a chance to make a new life for himself, and they all fervently hoped he would make a success of it.

Edward appeared more composed now, but still obviously frightened. 'Er . . . I have people after me for money, so can I stay with you until the ship sails?'

'You can stay at my house,' Stuart told him. 'You will be safe there.'

'We will deal with all your debts, so you can leave clear of any problems in this country.'

'Thank you, Harry. That's more than I deserve.'

'Yes, it is,' Charles told him, 'but you are the son of my dear sister, and we hope you will make the most of this chance to start afresh.'

'I will, Uncle, I promise.'

For the rest of the evening Edward stayed close by their sides, showing no desire to return to the games room. Harry watched him carefully, and noted that instead of being dismayed by the prospect of leaving this country, he appeared relieved. It was also a relief to all of them, because no matter what his cousin had done, he was still part of their family, albeit one who had gone astray. They had given him a chance to reform and they could do no more than that. What kind of a life Edward carved out for himself, was now up to him, and Harry was free from that threat.

Chapter Thirty

When they arrived back at Stuart's London house they went to the lounge to discuss the evening while they enjoyed a nightcap before retiring. Edward was clearly exhausted, declining a second drink and went to the room Stuart had allotted him for the duration of his stay. They were remarking how well he had taken the idea of leaving the country, when the butler entered holding a silver tray with a letter on it.

'This was delivered while you were out, sir, and is marked urgent.'

Stuart took the letter, not paying much attention as urgent messages were not unusual in his line of work. While listening to the conversation he glanced at the writing on the envelope and recognising it he slit it open quickly. By the time he had read the short note through twice, he was seething and began to curse.

Joe smirked. 'Dear me, Stuart, even I don't know some of those words.'

'I feared this would happen! My wife was all apologetic while I was there, telling me she had been to the doctor for a tonic and was feeling much better. That clearly wasn't true because as soon as I was out of the way she has caused trouble again. How much more misfortune is that poor girl going to have to endure?' He slammed his fist on the arm of the chair.

Harry was on his feet at the mention of a girl. 'Stop ranting, and tell us what has happened.'

He took a deep breath. 'Chrissie has left my house.'

'What?' Charles exclaimed. 'Where has she gone?'

'I don't know. All she says is that a situation has arisen that makes it impossible for her to stay, and by the time I receive the letter she will have moved on.'

'She doesn't give you a reason?'

Stuart shook his head. 'She doesn't have to. My wife took a dislike to her and has done her best to make her life with us difficult. I told her that she was not to dismiss Chrissie, but she has obviously found a way to make her leave. I have felt for some time that my wife was mentally sick, but did nothing about it. Now I must.'

'You have come to know Chrissie quite well since she's been working for you, so where do you think she will go?' Charles asked.

'I really don't know. I will return home tomorrow and try to sort out this mess, and also see if I can find Chrissie.'

'I'll come with you,' Harry told him, 'and you can leave tracking down Chrissie to me while you deal with your trouble at home.'

'Thanks. Charles and Joe, you are welcome to stay here for as long as you like.'

'You two go and do whatever you have to. I'll stay here and make all the arrangements to get Edward on his way. What about you, Joe?' Charles asked.

'I have a job waiting for me, so I've spent as much time with you as I can, but I'll be in London and can help you if you need it.'

'I don't think my nephew will give any trouble. It's been good to have you with us, and you'll be welcome at the Frenshaw estates at any time.'

'I'll keep that in mind.' Joe turned to his friend. 'You'll let me know how you get on finding Chrissie?'

Harry nodded. 'I'll find her to make sure she is safe and well and perhaps persuade her to come back, if I can. The way she keeps disappearing makes me think we need to keep an eye on her. There's no telling what kind of trouble she could get herself in to.'

'I don't think she will listen to you.'

'You two are forgetting me,' Stuart remarked. 'I also want her back, and I can give her the best chance to advance in life. All you can offer is mucking out stables or scrubbing floors. She's intelligent and deserves better than that.'

Joe was shaking his head. 'And she deserves better than you three mapping out her life for her. All you can do is see she is all right, and then ask what she wants to do, but she will probably tell you all to go away and leave her alone. After all, apart from Charles, her time spent with both of you hasn't been happy for her.'

'I know when she sees me she will probably punch me

on the chin.' Harry grimaced. 'But I'll take Midnight and Red with me for protection. You wouldn't be able to come with me as well, would you, Joe?'

'Sorry, I can't. This is one mess you will have to sort out for yourself, my friend. Just remember to duck when you find her. Oh, and you can give her another option.'

'And that is?' Harry gave Joe a suspicious glance.

'It's about time I married, and she'd make a fine wife. She's got spirit and beauty, and I liked her from the moment I set eyes on her.'

'You can forget that, my friend,' Harry told him, giving a chuckle of amusement. 'You'd be asking her to live in London, and we all know she won't do that.'

'Ah, well, a man can dream.'

They were all laughing with Joe as Stuart refilled their glasses for one last drink before retiring for the night.

The next morning Harry and Stuart were on the first available train, anxious to get back as soon as they could. They didn't talk as each man's thoughts were occupied with what they had to do. Stuart was worrying about what he would find at home, and Harry was wondering why he was going to so much trouble to find someone he hardly knew. Now the unpleasant business with Edward was settled he should be relaxing and enjoying his home, instead he was about to go charging around the country to find a girl who had been working as a stable lad. He must be mad, but his father cared and he'd caused him enough grief. At least he could do this for him. And, of course, there was another reason no one knew about, and it was imperative he knew where she was.

'Would you mind if I came in and talked with your staff?' Harry asked when they reached Stuart's home. 'Someone might know where Chrissie is going.'

'I doubt she told anyone, but it's worth a try.'

The moment they rode in, Robert came running to meet them. 'I'm so pleased you are here, Father. Chrissie left after Mother was nasty to her.'

Stuart jumped down and put his arm around his son's shoulder. 'That's why I'm here, and I want you to tell me what you know.'

The boy nodded solemnly.

'This is my friend, Major Frenshaw, and he wants to talk to everyone because he is going to try and find her. But before that we need to freshen up and have something to eat and drink. Where is your mother?'

'I don't know. She left the house an hour ago and hasn't returned yet. I think she is unwell because she isn't making much sense. Nurse has been watching over her as much as she can, but Mother keeps sending her away.'

'I believe she is very sick, and I'll see she gets the best care. Now, will you run and ask Cook if she can provide us with a quick meal, then you come and join us in the library and bring Nurse with you.'

'Yes, Father.'

Harry watched the boy dash off to carry out his errand and said, 'That's a fine son you have there, Stuart.'

'Yes, he's turning out well now. Taking him to our old school is the best thing I've done.'

'They turn out fine men; just look at us,' Harry joked.

'Of course they do. They managed a barrister and a

292

military officer, to name but two. Now, we have a couple of battles to win, so let's wash up and eat before we plan our action.'

Refreshed after their journey they were joined by Robert and Nurse, listening in grim silence to the unpleasant episode that had driven Chrissie away.

'Did she tell you where she intended to go?' Harry asked.

'No, sir. I don't think she knew. She told me she was leaving because her being here was upsetting the mistress, and when I woke in the morning she was gone. She must have left before it was light.'

'Where on earth do I start? She could have taken any direction.'

'I did beg her to tell me, sir, but the only thing she said was that this area had caused her joy and pain, and as much as she loved it here this was not the place for her. The only thing she could do was take to the road again and look for another place to settle.'

The two men looked at each other, and Stuart said, 'Are you thinking the same as me?'

Harry took a deep breath and nodded. 'She certainly won't be heading back to London, that we know for sure, so the only option left for her is to find the Travellers again. But where would they be now?'

'She did tell me once that they were going to spend the summer months by the sea, but I don't know where, sir.'

'Never mind, Nurse, you have been very helpful by giving me some indication where to start the search.'

'I hope you find her, sir. She didn't deserve to be treated so unkindly. From the little she told me, her dream of living in the country has been a rocky road so far. I do hope she finds what she's looking for.'

'Thank you.' Stuart dismissed the nurse. 'Will you and Robert let me know the moment my wife returns?'

'Yes, sir.'

When they were alone again, Harry stood up. 'I'll start out first thing in the morning, but while I'm here is there anything I can do for you?'

'Thank you, but no, this is something only I can deal with. From what we've heard there is something seriously wrong with Angela. I'll call a doctor if she needs medical help.'

'I'm very sorry, Stuart.'

'So am I.' He sighed wearily. 'She wasn't a vindictive woman when I married her, but she hasn't been right since little Emma was born. I had hoped she would improve by living quietly in the country, but Emma is three now, and she is getting worse. This can't go on and I must do what is right for all of us, especially my children.'

'Of course, but do come to us if there is anything we can do.'

'I appreciate your kind offer. Let me know if your search is successful.'

'I will, and thank you for the help with Edward. That's one problem solved, and now we have two more.'

After Harry left, Stuart checked his desk and found a pile of completed documents with a note on the top saying, 'Thank you for your kindness.'

She had gone without payment for this work and his worry increased in case she didn't have enough money for her journey, wherever she was going, but there wasn't anything he could do about that now.

'Father.' Robert came in to the room. 'Mother is back and she's in the sitting room.'

'Thank you, Robert. I'll go and see her at once. Will you ask Cook to send in a pot of strong tea, please?'

As his son hurried off he braced himself for what was to come, feeling quite certain this was going to be difficult and upsetting.

Angela was sitting in her favourite chair just staring in to space, and he could see at once that something was terribly wrong with her. He sat beside her. 'Hello, my dear, did you enjoy your walk?'

'Walk? What walk? I've been here all the time.' She stared at him. 'Who are you?'

With those words he felt something crumble inside him. He'd seen this before and knew there was no cure, as the medical profession had no idea how to treat someone with lapses of memory. 'I'm your husband. We have been married for twelve years and have three lovely children.'

'Oh, have we?' She lapsed in to silence again.

He knew that questioning her about what had happened while he'd been away would be useless. She couldn't be blamed for her outburst; the outburst of rage had all been a part of the illness, and he berated himself for not recognising it long before now. He had been so tied up in his work and hadn't looked too closely, continually telling himself that she would eventually get over what was troubling her.

A maid came in with a trolley of tea, and he said quietly, 'Will you ask Nurse to come here immediately, please?'

'Yes, sir.'

She arrived almost at once, looking very concerned.

'My wife is very sick. Her memory has gone, and I would like you to care for her for a while. I'll send someone for the doctor and get some expert help for her.'

'Of course, sir.' Nurse sat in the chair he vacated and took hold of Angela's hand. 'We'll have a nice cup of tea, shall we?'

Stuart left the room, heavy of heart. She was too young for this to happen, and unless the doctors could do something for her, her normal life was over – and so was his marriage. She had given him three lovely children, though, and for that he would always be grateful to her.

When the doctor arrived he confirmed Stuart's fears and they spent quite a time discussing the best thing to do. Some of the suggestions appalled him, but he vehemently refused to have her removed from her home and children.

'I won't have her labelled as out of her mind,' he declared. 'Neither will I have her separated from everything she knows and loves. That is unthinkable!'

Finally, it was decided that the best thing for all concerned would be to employ round-the-clock nursing staff to care for all her needs. The doctor did warn that although there would probably be times when his wife was quite lucid, there was a possibility that her condition would continue to deteriorate.

'I want you to arrange the best possible care for my wife, and I will explain the situation to my children and the staff.'

'I know just the nurses to do this. They have experience of looking after such cases, and will carry out their tasks with love and understanding. This is a sad situation, sir, and will be difficult for you and your family.'

'No doubt, but at least we now know what is wrong with her, and I will do anything in my power to see she is well looked after and kept happy.'

'You are still a young man, and I have known men with an ailing wife to divorce her and marry again. It heartens me to see someone who cares deeply for her welfare.'

'Marrying again is not an option I would consider. As devastating as this is I still consider myself a fortunate man. I have three lovely children and a profession I love.' He smiled sadly. 'That will be enough for me now, and the future will take care of itself.'

Chapter Thirty-One

The next morning Harry set off riding Red, with Midnight on a rein. The search might take some time and he could change horses to give one a rest, because he had no intention of giving up until he had found Chrissie. The only hint he had was that she could have set out to join up with the Travellers again, and he would try to find them in the hope she was with them. They might be easier to track down than a young girl on her own. He still couldn't believe he was doing this for a servant, because that is what she had been, but she had clearly made an impression on his father, Joe and Stuart. Also, for some damned reason the spectre of her forlorn figure walking away from his house was haunting him. Now she was walking away again to heaven knows where and everyone was worrying about her – including him. Because of what he had done she needed to be found, and then perhaps he could get on with his life.

Every stop he made he enquired about the Travellers or a girl on her own, but always received the same response – a shake of the head. By nightfall as he settled down at an inn, he could only reflect on a frustrating day. He might not even be going in the right direction.

The next morning he was on the road again, and when he came to a crossroads he hesitated. Red stamped his feet and Harry sighed. 'It's no good you getting impatient. How about some help here, boys? I'm looking for your blasted friend, so which road do we take?'

Both animals immediately took the left fork and he didn't check them. This way was as good as any, because he didn't have a clue where he was going. When he had said he would find her, he hadn't given the search much thought, but now he was actually on the road it was beginning to dawn on him what a hopeless task this was going to be. He could be out here for weeks, and still find no trace of her.

He found another inn for the night, and after seeing his horses were being taken good care of he was looking forward to a hearty meal. The stable lad was looking at the horses in awe, but for some reason they were being well behaved, for a change. They usually kicked up a fuss if a stranger was tending them, but not on this journey and he wondered if they knew what he was trying to do. Now you are being ridiculous, he told himself. They are tired after a day's riding, that's all.

He gave the boy some coins. 'Don't be afraid of them. Look after them well for me.'

The lad looked at the money and slipped it in to his

pocket. 'I'll do that, sir, and see no one comes near them.'

'Good lad.' He patted him on the shoulder and then strode into the inn.

The bar was crowded and all eyes turned in his direction, probably wondering what such a fine gentleman was doing in their humble inn. He smiled politely and they made room for him to reach the proprietor.

'Good evening, sir. What can we do for you?'

'I would like lodgings for the night, and a meal, if that is possible.'

'No trouble at all, sir. The wife's a fine cook and will have something for you in an hour.'

'Thank you, that is much appreciated. I have been travelling all day and I'm very hungry.' When the man hurried away to tell his wife, Harry turned and faced the room. 'I am also looking for information. Can anyone tell me if a group of Travellers came this way in the last few weeks?'

'I saw them, sir.' A young lad came from behind the bar. 'They camped on the spare ground near the village for two days.'

'When was this?' Hope soared in him. This was the first news of them he had received.

'Oh, quite a while ago, sir. I think it was about two weeks, or so.'

'Do you know where they were going when they left?'

He shook his head. 'We was told not to go near them without our dads with us. Don't know why, though, cos they were friendly and had lots of interesting things to see.'

'In the last week or so has anyone seen a young girl travelling on her own? She's quite tall and has dark hair and dark eyes.'

Everyone shook their heads in denial, and he knew that was all he was going to learn here, but at least it gave him hope that he was going in the right direction.

After enjoying a substantial meal and a couple of drinks with the patrons of the inn, he retired for the night. Being a military man, he was used to bunking down in not always savoury places, but the village establishment was surprisingly clean, and the food had been excellent. Tomorrow would be a new day and he would stop at every village or hamlet to see if they could give him any information about his quarry.

Chrissie was dirty, hungry and exhausted, and couldn't believe her luck as she climbed on the cart. People had been kind, but it was harder to get a lift now she was in such a poor state. This man had taken pity on her, though, and she gave a silent sigh of relief as they set off. Every ride she had managed to get had been a help, even if it was for a couple of miles only, and she had walked for miles, as well, and the coast was getting nearer all the time, which was just as well because her meagre amount of money hadn't lasted as long as she'd hoped. The last three nights she had slept anywhere she could find, like a hayrick, an animal shelter or just a field. With no money left she had also been scavenging for food in the hedgerows or farmers' fields in desperation. It was absolutely essential that she found the Travellers soon, because she couldn't go on for much longer, and the condition she was in no one would employ her.

'There's the sea over there,' the man pointed out.

'Where?'

'Look over to your left.'

She shaded her eyes and turned in the direction he was pointing. There it was, shining in the late-afternoon sun. 'How far is that?'

'About five miles or so. I'll have to drop you here as this is as far as I go.' He pulled up by a gate.

'Thanks.' She got down, and as he drove away began walking, telling herself that she could manage these few miles before it got dark.

They were the hardest miles she had ever covered. She was weary beyond belief, and so hungry she had almost forgotten what it was like to eat; there were holes in her shoes and her usual optimism and determination were at rock bottom. She might not even find her friends, and what was she going to do then? However bleak the outlook she had to keep moving, and prayed that her friends had kept to their travel plans. They had said they would come here and stay for the month of August. That had to be true or else she was in terrible trouble.

Forcing one foot in front of the other with her head down, she kept going, feeling as low as she had ever done in her life. How had her dream ended up like this?

The sun was beginning to dip below the horizon when she heard a dog bark and that made her lift her head. What she saw in front of her was more than she could grasp, and tears of relief began to stream down her face. People were running towards her and her legs gave way, unable to hold her up a moment longer.

Everything seemed to be happening in a mist. There was a voice giving orders – a voice she knew, and she was lifted off the ground.

'It's all right, Chrissie. You've found us and you're safe now.'

She was beyond speech as she finally gave in and let exhaustion sweep over her. They carried her into Elsie's home and when she gazed around she knew where she was, relief sweeping through her. The tears came again.

'That's right, my dear, you let it all out,' Elsie told her, holding a cup of tea to her mouth. 'You drink this and then Ma and me will get you clean and comfortable.'

'I'm so hungry,' she confessed.

'There's a good nourishing stew bubbling away, and you can have a bowl now.'

It was the most wonderful thing she had ever tasted, and by the time she had wiped the bowl clean with a chunk of bread she could hardly keep her eyes open.

'Good girl,' Ma told her. 'Now, let's get those dirty clothes off you, and the shoes will have to be thrown away because they are beyond repair. How far have you walked?'

'A long way. I didn't know exactly where you were.'

'We were going to move on two days ago, but Elsie told us we must stay right here. She insisted it was important, but didn't know why, and we are glad we took notice because you couldn't have gone on much longer. My dear girl, what were you doing setting out on such a journey by yourself?'

'It was madness, I know now, but I had to get away and didn't know where else to go.'

'Well, never mind, you're here now. Can you wash yourself?'

She nodded. It was such a relief to wash in hot water and put on the clean clothes Ma had found for her. By the time another bowl of stew had disappeared, the men crowded into Elsie's home, and they were not happy.

'Who did this to you?' Pa demanded. 'We thought you were nicely settled in that job you were so excited about. Tell us what happened.'

They listened in silence, their expressions grim, and when she'd told all, she gave a sad smile. 'Things didn't work out. I think the poor lady was ill, and the major was suffering after what he'd been through.'

'That doesn't excuse what the man did, and if we ever come across him he'll be sorry.' Pa turned to the other men who all nodded in agreement. 'We won't have one of our own treated so cruelly.'

'I don't believe he's a cruel man, just a troubled one.' Feeling better now, a little mischievous smile appeared. 'You'd have a job dealing with him because he's a tough military man and over six feet tall.'

'And riding a huge black horse,' Elsie remarked.

Chrissie took hold of her hand. 'Yes, you were quite right about that, but their appearance brought me only grief.'

Elsie gazed in to the distance for a moment, and then said in a puzzled tone, 'That wasn't supposed to happen.'

'Maybe not, but it did, setting off a chain of events that brought me back to you. I was so happy there, and he sent me away.' Her eyes filled with tears again and she fought them back. It must be weakness making her so tearful.

She yawned and everyone stood up.

'We'll leave you to rest,' Ma told her, 'and we can talk more in the morning.'

* * *

304

The morning dawned bright and hot, and Ma came to cook eggs for their breakfast. 'Did you sleep well, Chrissie?'

'I did, and I don't think anything would have woken me up.'

'That's just what you needed, and we've decided to stay here for a few days to give you time to recover completely. It's a nice spot with a secluded beach not far, and has everything we need.'

'Oh, but you mustn't change your plans for me.'

'We change our minds all the time. If we like a place, we stay, if we don't we move on. There, you eat your breakfast.'

Ma's son, Sandy, looked in and smiled. 'You look better today. We found you some shoes that might fit. Try them on.'

They were a good fit. 'Thank you very much. I only had the one pair of shoes, but where did these come from? I can't afford to pay anything for them, but I'll be happy to work for whoever they belonged to.'

'Don't worry about it.' He winked at her. 'We still need a fortune-teller.'

'Goodness, haven't you found one yet?'

'Not as good as you, and you'd better stay with us this time, because you get into too much trouble on your own.'

She laughed, and it felt good to be among friends again. 'What do you want me to do today?'

'Nothing. There's a nice beach over the rise, so take a walk by the sea, listen to the waves and relax.'

'I'd like that.'

They hadn't reached a big town yet and she was grateful they had stopped here. The beach was empty and she removed her shoes so she could paddle along the shoreline. The water felt wonderful on her poor abused feet, and the gentle lapping of the waves was soothing to her troubled thoughts. The memory of the Frenshaw estate would always be with her, but she would never see it again, so that was something she was going to have to learn to live with. That was how things were and she imagined the pain and disappointment would fade in time. Working for a short time with a barrister had shown her she was capable of doing more than scrubbing floors for other people. Her love of horses would always draw her to that kind of work, but it was doubtful if anyone would employ a girl for that. One man certainly hadn't liked her working in his stables. Another option was to stay with the Travellers, but as pleased as she was to be with them again, living her life in this way didn't appeal to her.

She stopped and gazed at the sea, telling herself there wasn't any need to make hasty decisions. It was a fault of hers, and she didn't want to make any more mistakes, so any future moves would need to be given a lot of thought. She was with people who cared about her, and after what she had been through, this was enough for now.

Chapter Thirty-Two

It only took Chrissie two days to recover enough to insist she did her fair share of the work, but they watched carefully to see she didn't attempt any of the heavy jobs. She was touched by their concern, and knew they were still angry at the way she had been treated, but she assured them no one was to blame. Not everything in life works out the way we want it to, she told them with a smile. The only one she couldn't hide her sorrow from was Elsie.

'I know you don't believe it now, but everything is going to work out for the best,' the elderly woman told her over breakfast one morning.

'Of course it is,' she replied brightly.

'You can't hide your pain from me, my dear. You were forced to leave the one place you wanted to be, and that still hurts.'

She had to admit that it did. 'But I have done what I set out to do and put distance between me and the estate. It was foolish of me to get so attached to the place and the people, not to mention two special horses I loved so much. Yes, it hurts, and even my time working for the barrister didn't ease that pain. However, I'm going to have to start again, and I'm ready to do that now.'

'Good girl. Now, why don't you take an early morning walk by the sea, and don't hurry back.'

'Aren't we going to move on today?'

'No, we must stay here a while longer.'

'Why? I'm quite fit again now, and I don't want to disrupt your plans.'

'We are waiting for someone.'

'Oh, in that case I will go and have a paddle in the sea.' She finished clearing up after breakfast and set off for the beach. Her friends always left her alone when she did this, giving her the solitude they felt she needed to recover completely from her arduous journey.

It was going to be another lovely day and she sighed with pleasure as the water gently swished in and out over her feet. A pretty shell was uncovered as the water washed away and she bent to pick it up. It was conical in shape and perfect, so she tucked it in her pocket as a gift for Elsie. Suddenly a brief picture crossed her vision of black and chestnut horses galloping joyfully along the water's edge – then it was gone and the beach was empty. Placing her hands on her heart to stop it racing, she began to tell herself off. She had been plagued with a vivid imagination from a child, and it was about time she grew out of it. Picturing such things would only bring the loss to mind again, and she had to put that behind her, as she repeatedly told herself. It had been lovely, but it was gone, and she had to look forward, not back. Enough of that, she thought as she wiped the water off her feet and put her shoes back on. What she needed was some good hard work. That would sort her out.

The breeches she was wearing were damp at the ankles but they would soon dry, and she was ready to take on any job that needed doing today, she decided, as she ran over the rise to the camp.

When the camp came in sight she stopped, wondering what was going on. Everyone had gathered at the entrance, and she could hear the raised voices from where she was. Looking closer she saw a tall figure on a horse – a black horse, and with them was another one she recognised. Her breath caught in her throat. What was he doing here? And her friends were furious with him. Oh, no!

She was off and running towards them as fast as her long legs would carry her, and as she got near to them the animals began to stomp and prance, so much so the rider had to work hard to control them.

'Move out of the way,' she warned the crowd gathered there. 'They are trained to fight if they think their master is in danger.'

Skidding to a halt, she reached out to each huge animal. 'It's all right, my lovely boys, calm down now. You don't want to hurt anyone, do you?'

The rider jumped down and she faced him, hands on her hips. 'What are you doing here? Haven't you got more sense than to bring these two in to a hostile place?'

'I didn't know they wanted to tear me limb from limb. I introduced myself and politely asked if they'd seen you. The horses reacted to the shouting and hostility in order to defend me. It's what they do.'

'I know that, and you haven't answered my question. What do you want here?'

His gaze swept over her, and then back to her face. 'I've come to make sure you are all right, and to take you back with me. That's why I brought Red with me as well.'

'What makes you think I'll go anywhere with you?' She didn't have to watch what she said to him now. She didn't work for him any more.

'Because my father is worried about you, and so is Stuart, and so is every damned person back at the estate. Even Joe said you would make him a good wife, but we told him to forget that because he is based in London, and you won't go there to live again.'

Her anger drained away and she struggled to stop a smile appearing, but he noted the change.

'Now we've all calmed down, do you think we could water and feed the horses, and me? I've been travelling for days searching for you.'

She glanced at Pa, who nodded, grinned and held out his hands to give her a bunk-up on to Red, then she took hold of Midnight's reins and they trotted off to the field where they kept the horses.

The youngsters were all running ahead, eager to help with these magnificent beasts. With many hands wanting to do something for the animals, they were soon unsaddled, fed and watered, and contentedly gazing around at the new surroundings.

'Cor,' one of the boys murmured, 'we've never seen horses like these before.'

'They are special. Don't let them near your horses,' she warned, 'and don't try riding them.'

'Why? You do.'

'They know me, but they can be rough if you do something they don't like. These two are different in temperament from the others at the estate, and need to be approached with caution.'

'This one's got scars,' the eldest boy pointed out.

'He was injured in a battle and his master nursed him back to health.'

The boys gathered round to examine the animal, and one said, 'They are very quiet now.'

'That's because they have been fed, and I am here. Be careful when I leave, though, because they might bite you,' she teased, making them all laugh.

Seeing the horses were now content, she kissed both on the nose and told them to behave themselves, then made her way back to Elsie's home where everyone was clustered around. The major was sitting on the steps with a cup of tea in his hands, and Elsie sitting beside him. He was explaining something to the crowd who were listening intently.

'What's going on?' she whispered to Sandy, who was standing a little way from the crowd.

'He's trying to win everyone over to his side,' he smirked, 'and doing a good job of it, by the look of things.'

'Surely Elsie isn't taken in by him as well?'

'When we brought him over to her, she studied him carefully, the way she does, then she nodded and smiled, inviting him to sit on her steps while she poured him a cup of tea.'

'And that was already made, I suppose.'

'Of course. She's given him her approval, and everyone is now relaxed and curious about him.' Sandy gave her a sideways glance. 'Are you going back with him?'

'No,' she declared emphatically. 'He took the job I loved from me without bothering to find out if I was a good stable lad or not. He disliked me on sight and threw me out. I don't understand what he's doing here.'

'Better consult your crystal ball for the answer.'

'Not likely. I don't think I even want to know why he's been riding around the countryside with two priceless animals, and looking for me. It doesn't make sense, but I have a feeling Elsie will tell me later.'

'You can be sure of that,' Sandy chuckled, and turned to wander off. 'I think I'll go and have a look at those warhorses. I've never seen such magnificent specimens before.'

'The young boys are with them and I've warned them not to let them near your mares.'

With a look of pure innocence on his face, Sandy walked off, whistling tunefully.

'Chrissie,' Elsie called. 'Come and have tea with us, my dear.'

Torn between going after Sandy to see what he was up to, and staying, she decided it really wasn't any of her business, and made her way to Elsie and the man sitting

312

beside her – the man she had never thought to see again.

He stood up when she approached, towering over her. 'Are the horses all right?'

'They have been looked after and are content,' she told him sharply, then regretted her tone. She wasn't usually like this, but seeing him again brought back too many memories.

'Thank you.' He moved aside to allow her to get in to the home.

'Pour us all another cup of tea, my dear,' Elsie asked, smiling brightly. 'Harry is thirsty after his long ride.'

Harry? She stared at Elsie in astonishment, who just smiled back.

'You'll stay tonight, Major?' Pa asked. 'We'll put on a real feast for you.'

'I would be honoured,' he replied.

What on earth was going on? Chrissie thought as she poured the tea. One minute everyone had been ready to attack him, and now he was being invited to a feast and called Harry. In the short time she had been dealing with the horses he had won everyone over to him – except her. There was no way he was going to convince her to return with him because it would only cause her more heartache, and she wasn't going to make the same mistake again.

When the large pot of tea had been drained the men took the major away, and Chrissie helped Elsie back in to the home.

'He's quite a charmer,' Elsie declared as she made herself comfortable in her chair.

Chrissie snorted in disbelief. 'That's not what I'd call him.'

'That's because when you look at him you feel the hurt he caused you. This is a different man now, as you'd see if you would only look carefully. He clearly has a good reason for coming to find you, so don't dismiss anything he offers because you have been hurt. Listen and use your intuition, then do what you really want to. In most cases I would urge caution, but in this case, I tell you to follow your heart. Don't let the past colour your judgement or you could throw away your chance of happiness. Don't do that, my dear.'

'I know I'm being unreasonable,' she admitted. 'He was greatly troubled when he arrived home, but I'd been so happy there. Happier than I'd ever been in my life.'

'That was hard for you, dear, but you will find that happiness again, believe me. Now, what are we going to wear tonight for the festivities? I think you ought to wear a real Romany frock, and so will I. Everyone will be dressed in their brightest clothes.'

She laughed at the thought. 'That would be fun – two fortune-tellers together.'

'Exactly. Bring that trunk over for me and we'll find something that fits you.'

As evening fell they made their way to the beach where the men had a lovely fire going, and game on a spit cooking nicely. Everyone had brought food, and a table was groaning under the weight of it.

'This is wonderful,' Elsie declared. 'We haven't done this kind of thing for a long time. When I was a child we had evenings like this quite often, especially when there was something to celebrate.'

Settling the elderly woman in a chair where she could see everything, Chrissie gazed at the scene in wonder, and was shocked to see the major with his jacket off, sleeves rolled up and helping the men feed the fire. He was laughing and talking to them as if this was the most natural thing for him to do.

'He's a soldier, my dear,' Elsie said as if reading her mind. 'He's been round campfires, slept on hard ground, been cold, wet, and dirty and weary.'

'I suppose he has, but I have never thought of him in that way.'

'You imagined it was all servants, feather beds and gleaming silver services.'

Chrissie nodded. 'He was born to privilege and a titled family. It's hard to imagine him suffering hardship like that, and yet he had been fighting in a war and I should have realised.' She knelt down beside Elsie. 'I did try to understand what he had been through, I really did, but all I felt from him was anger.'

'Is the anger still there?'

She watched him in silence for a while, and then sighed. 'He's a difficult man to read, but all I can see and feel now is that he is enjoying himself.'

Sandy came to them with a wide smile on his face. 'My, don't you two look lovely, and all the girls have chosen more traditional dress for this evening. Come near the fire, because the food is nearly ready. What do you think of the major?' he laughed. 'He thinks he's back with his military pals and thoroughly enjoying himself.'

'It's good to see. Being with us might be just what he

needs to help blot out the terrible scenes he has in his head.' Elsie let Sandy support her, and Chrissie followed with the chair.

The men carved the meat and the major brought two plates over to them. He bowed gracefully. 'Enjoy your supper, Madam Elsie and Miss Christine.'

'Thank you, Harry.'

That familiar form of address still gave Chrissie a jolt, but he just grinned. His face was streaked with soot from the fire, his hair had fallen over his eyes, and he didn't seem to be the slightest bit concerned. She was certainly seeing a different side to this complex man, and she had to admit she liked him this way.

'What can I get you to drink? We have a wide selection, though I wouldn't recommend the home-made brew. It has a kick as powerful as Red when he is in one of his tantrums.'

'We'll have lemonade, please, Harry.'

'Coming right up, ladies.'

As he strode away Chrissie couldn't hide her amusement any longer, and laughed quietly. 'I would never have believed it,' she gasped. 'He's waiting on everyone like a perfect servant.'

'As I've said before, he's a charming man and quite a catch for some young girl.'

'I'm sure he has plenty of girls from titled families eager to wed him.'

'No doubt, but he's managed to avoid them so far. I'm pleased you came back, my dear, it has been a little dull without you.' Elsie beamed at her and began to tuck into her plate of food.

Everyone threw themselves into the evening, and it was full of laughter, singing and dancing round the fire. It was the kind of celebration to make you forget your worries, and that's just what Chrissie did.

Chapter Thirty-Three

The next morning there was a lot to do and Chrissie was up at dawn to help with the clear up after the celebration, making sure everything was pristine again and not one piece of litter left on the beach. Some of the men weren't at their best after drinking too much home brew, but they pitched in, knowing the work had to be done as they intended to move on the next day. The major would leave them then, and that would be for the best. The man joining in the fun last night had been very different from the one she had first met, and it would be dangerous to come to like him too much. He could now return and tell his father that she was all right, and that would be the end of it.

Gazing across the field where they had put the horses, she was surprised to see he was already there brushing the animals. They were being stroppy and she laughed to herself as they pushed and shoved him playfully.

'They are a handful, aren't they?' Sandy stood next to her, watching the scene.

'It's just their way of having fun, and they know they can get away with it because he loves them, but they immediately obey when he gives them an order in his best military voice.'

'He isn't doing that this morning.'

'Perhaps he's like the rest of you and drank too much last night,' she teased.

He grinned but didn't comment. 'Ah, looks as if he's given up and is coming over here.'

She watched him stride towards them, and couldn't help noticing how smoothly and elegantly he moved for such a big man.

'Help me exercise those beasts, Chrissie. A good gallop along the beach will settle them down.'

'I can't at the moment. There's a lot to do so we're ready to move in the morning.'

'We can manage,' Sandy told her. 'We can spare you to help the major with his horses.'

The look she gave him told him clearly that she would be having words with him later, and that made him chuckle. 'Off you go.'

'Good – thanks, Sandy.' Harry gazed down at her as she fell into step beside him. 'I take it you can ride with a saddle?'

'Of course I can. Sir Stuart Gretham taught me.'

'Hmm,' was the only reply he made.

The horses stood quietly while they were saddled, but as soon as the major gave her a bunk-up on Red, and then mounted Midnight, they pranced with excitement.

'I think they can smell the sea.' All the youngsters were running beside them, laughing and calling out to her as they cantered over the rise.

With a long stretch of sandy beach in front of them they gave the horses their heads and let them thunder along. Chrissie's dark hair was streaming out behind her and she shouted for joy at the wonderful feeling, making Red kick his hind legs in sheer exuberance.

On reaching the end they reined in and turned to make a more leisurely canter back. Halfway along the animals decided they wanted to paddle, splashing through the water's edge almost like small children enjoying a day at the seaside.

She laughed at their obvious enjoyment. 'Have they ever seen the sea before?'

'Midnight has, but only from a ship, and he didn't care for that too much. Red has never been near the sea before.'

She reached across and patted the black horse's neck. 'My poor boy, you did have a rough time, didn't you, but you're quite safe now, so you can forget all about the terrible war.'

They stopped, and the horses contentedly let the small waves splash against their legs and she gazed out to sea, drinking in the beauty and peace of this place. Being mounted on Red again only increased her pleasure in this moment.

'Come back with me, Chrissie.'

His softly spoken words brought her back to the present. Turning her head to look at him, she said, 'No.'

'Why? You obviously love the estate and adore these

animals. Talk to me and tell me your reason for refusing.'

'You wouldn't understand.'

'When I finally reached home I was filled with anger and grief, and wasn't thinking straight. I had to shut down my feelings because the pain was too great. I cared for nothing and no one, but I'm not that person any longer. I'm trying to heal some of the hurt I caused. Do you know you've haunted my nightmares and daytimes since I sent you away?'

'That doesn't make sense.' She gave him a startled look. 'You had every right to dismiss one of your staff, especially one who had been engaged while you were away. You took one look at me, didn't like what you saw, and so sent me on my way.'

'I didn't like anyone at that point, and I was even fighting with my father, and that is something I have never done in my entire life before. I took my fury out on you, a young girl who only wanted to work and make a place for herself away from the squalor of the slums. We were in London recently and I visited where you had lived.'

'Why on earth did you do that?'

'I wanted to see where you had come from, and what had made you set out on your own to make another life away from everything you had ever known. It didn't take me long to understand why. I met Bob and Gladys and had tea with them.'

She turned sharply in the saddle to face him. 'How are they? Did you see Bessie?'

'Yes.' He grinned. 'I had a ride in the cart, and Bessie's fine. The children take good care of her.'

'It's good to know I gave her to the right family.'

'You did.' He then told her what had happened when he had been walking along the streets.

Totally bemused by what she was hearing, she said, 'I don't understand why you did such a daft thing. The upper class don't visit that kind of place.'

'I wanted to try and understand you, what made you the way you are, and why you were so desperate to live in the country. My father had told me what he knew about you and I wanted to see for myself. When I left there, I had a better understanding of what was driving you.' He gave a wry smile. 'There, I've told you how I feel, so won't you tell me why you won't come back with me?'

'Because it will always be in my mind that you'll send me away again, and I'm not going to live like that. When I do stop moving on I want to be absolutely certain that I can make a home there.'

'I won't ever do that again.'

'That's a bold statement, and one you might not be able to keep. But suppose I believe you. Will you give me back my job as stable lad?'

'No.'

'A scullery maid?'

'Certainly not!'

'What then?'

'You come back and stay as our guest.'

For a few moments she stared at him in complete disbelief, and then burst in to helpless laughter. 'Oh, my, Red, your master does have a sense of humour after all.'

Still laughing she urged the horse out of the sea and trotted back to the camp.

Harry watched her disappear over the rise, and could still hear her laughter. He patted Midnight. 'Well, my boy, we made a real mess of that, didn't we? Most girls of humble birth would have jumped at the invitation to be a guest at a fine mansion. Father and Stuart were right; she isn't like most girls, and I must remember flattery will be useless, but don't you worry now. We are not giving up; we just need to rethink our strategy. I'd also better write to Father and let him know I won't be back for a while. This could take some time.'

He rode back to the camp with a smile on his face, and realised he was enjoying the challenge she presented. It was a long time since he'd felt so light-hearted.

Several of the men greeted him, clearly amused and curious. 'Enjoy your ride, Major?'

'Exhilarating,' he told them. 'Do you need any help?'

'We've got to change a wheel on Elsie's home and could use the help of a strong man.'

'I'll be right with you. Just give me time to wash the salt water off Midnight.'

'We'll do that,' three young boys called out eagerly. 'It's all right, cos he likes us.'

'Right, in that case I'll leave it to you.' He dismounted, watched them lead his horse away, and then turned to the men. 'Let's get that wheel changed.'

'Did you manage to persuade our girl to go back with you?' Sandy asked, as they made their way over to Elsie's home.

'What do you think?' he said with a wry grin.

'From the way she was laughing, I would say you failed.'

'I did. I misjudged her, but won't do that again.'

'You haven't got much time to convince her because we're moving on in the morning.'

'I'm coming with you – if you'll let me. If not, I'll just follow behind because I'm not leaving without her.'

'We'll have to ask Pa about that. Pa!' he called. 'The major wants to travel with us for a while. Will that be all right?'

'As long as you do your share of work, young man. We don't take passengers.'

'I'll be happy to.'

Pa nodded. 'Then you can come with us.'

'Thanks.'

The wheel was soon changed, and after a few more jobs everything was ready for the next day. In a smaller way it reminded Harry of preparing the brigade to move out, and he found the atmosphere and physical exercise comforting. Being here was helping to clear his mind and he hadn't even had a nightmare last night.

'Help me back in, Harry,' Elsie asked when he strode by a couple of hours later.

'Up you come,' he said cheerfully, lifting her off the chair and carrying her in to the home.

'You've been working hard, so would you like a cup of tea?'

'No, thanks, I must go and check that my horses are happy.'

'Chrissie will have made sure they are.' The elderly woman

gave him a penetrating look. 'Are you leaving tomorrow?'

'Not without Chrissie.'

'She doesn't want to go with you.'

'I know that, but I promised my father I'd try and bring her back. I made a lot of mistakes when I finally arrived home, and I'm trying to make amends, if I can.'

'The best thing you can do for our girl is ride away in the morning and leave her to get on with her life.'

He shook his head. 'I can't do that.'

'Why?'

'That is a question I can't answer. I just know I won't leave without her.'

'Then you have a problem, dear boy.'

'One of many, Elsie. One of many.'

The next morning they were soon hitched up and on the road, with Chrissie taking over again as Elsie's driver. When she looked round at the colourful procession there was a huge smile on her face, and the disappointment of the last few weeks began to fade away. Maybe all her dreams had just been silly girlish fancies, and perhaps this is where she really belonged.

'Good to be on the move again.' Elsie came and sat beside her. 'And to have you back, my dear. We've missed you.'

'It's lovely to be back, and I might be staying this time.'

'Do you think so? What about your dream of finding a permanent place to make your home?'

'I've come to the conclusion I might have been wishing for something that isn't to be, and isn't right for me.'

'I wouldn't dismiss it so easily. Why don't you just wait and see how things work out?'

She glanced at Elsie, curious. 'Aren't you going to tell me what I should do?'

'I wouldn't dream of it, my dear. You must make up your own mind.'

Chrissie laughed. 'That doesn't sound like you. What are you up to?'

'Nothing, dear,' she said innocently. 'Isn't it a lovely day? We are heading for a nice seaside town and will need a fortune-teller.'

'Ah, I wondered when that was going to come up, and of course I'll be happy to do it again.'

Elsie patted her arm. 'You're a good girl.'

'Good morning, ladies, it's another beautiful day.' The major appeared beside them, riding Red this time.

'Good morning, Harry,' Elsie replied brightly. 'It's lovely to have my driver back, and she's just told me there's a chance she might be staying this time.'

'Oh, a very slim chance, Elsie.'

'You are quite determined to take her away from us, then?'

'My resolve is unshakeable. Good morning, Chrissie,' he said pointedly as she hadn't responded to his greeting yet.

She reached out and patted the horse. 'Morning, Red, will you kindly take your master away, because he's spoiling my day.'

'It's a good thing she isn't in my brigade, or I would have to put her on a charge for insubordination,' he told the animal.

She smiled sweetly. 'Now I'm not working for you I don't have to watch my words.'

There was a rumble of laughter coming from Elsie, and

she sighed. 'Please go home, Major. You don't belong here, and you are wasting your time.'

'You don't belong here either, and in your heart you know it – and I never waste my time.' With a slight bow he urged Red forward and cantered to the front of the line.

'It's only a cold lunch today, so I think I'll go and start getting it ready.' Elsie made her way carefully inside while Chrissie stopped for a moment to allow her to move. She disappeared, still chuckling to herself.

By evening they had reached the field they always used within easy reach of Bournemouth, and they all set to work getting everything ready for the public to visit in the morning. When the tent was erected, Chrissie thought back to the first time she had done this and how frightened she had been, but she wasn't a bit concerned this time. She was relaxed and even looking forward to it again. Elsie had taught her to be observant, and it was amazing how much you could tell about a person by studying their actions and movements.

'I'll use the crystal ball you gave me,' she told Elsie.

'You should, my dear, it's yours and will respond to you now.'

She gave her an amused glance, and the elderly woman smirked. 'If you look hard enough you might see your future in there.'

'I don't want to know. I'm quite happy to let the future take care of itself.'

'It will come as a nice surprise, then. Now, we always get a lot of customers here, so are you going to wear a nice colourful outfit this time, as expected of a fortune-teller?'

'Why not? We wouldn't want customers to be disappointed, would we?'

'Certainly not. Let's go and see what we can find in the trunk for you to wear.'

Elsie had been right, and the next morning the people poured in, eager to buy the goods made by the Travellers, and see what else there was to amuse them. There was plenty. Sandy was juggling and entertaining them with card tricks, there were rides for the children on the smaller horses, and food of all kinds for sale. There was laughter coming from all parts of the field, and Chrissie was happy and relaxed when she took her place in the tent.

One of the boys standing guard at the flap poked his head in. 'You ready, Miss Gloria? There's a long queue out here.'

'All ready. Send the first one in, Pete.'

There was a steady stream of customers and she only managed to snatch half an hour for lunch. It was late afternoon before things eased off. Thinking that might be all for the day she stretched to ease the aches from sitting for so long, when Pete looked in with a huge grin on his face. 'One more for you, Miss Gloria.'

'Send them in.' She took a deep breath, hoping this would be the last customer today. When the man strode in and sat opposite her at the table, she looked him up and down. 'What are you doing in here?'

'I've come to have my fortune told, Miss Gloria.' He placed a gold coin in front of her. 'Is that enough?'

'That's too much, and I'm not going to tell your fortune, anyway.' She pushed the coin back.

'Why not?'

She sat back, closed her eyes for a moment and couldn't decide if she was exasperated or amused. He was such a difficult man to deal with, but she was certainly seeing another side of him since he had arrived at the camp. It was proving difficult not to like him, but her instincts were telling her to keep away from him because he would cause her trouble, and she'd had all the trouble she could handle just lately.

'Nice bright outfit you're wearing.'

His soft voice brought her out of her reverie, making her open her eyes and give an inelegant snort. 'You mean gaudy, don't you?'

'No, I don't. It's appropriate for what you are doing. Now, I've paid you and want my fortune told.'

Oh, why not, she thought. If he wanted to play games then she would oblige. She reached out and took his hand, studying it carefully and tracing the lines. 'You've had a lot of trauma in your life, but that is now over and from now on I can see only peace and happiness for you. There's one big decision you are going to have to make, so choose carefully because much of your happiness will depend on the choice you make.'

'When am I going to be faced with this dilemma, and what is it?'

'It is already with you.' She sat back. 'That's all I can tell you.'

'Hmm. Aren't you going to look in your crystal ball?' He pulled another coin out of his pocket and placed it on the table.

'I don't want more money, Major. You know this is only a game.'

He pushed the crystal ball towards her. 'Tell me what you see. You did it for my father.'

She gazed in to its depths with resignation, trying to clear her thoughts, knowing he wasn't going to give up. Running her hand over it she remembered Elsie giving her this priceless gift and smiled inwardly with gratitude. Then she narrowed her eyes and looked closer. 'There's a big celebration going on at your home. People are coming from everywhere and there is much excitement.'

'What are we celebrating?'

'I don't know, but it isn't only gentry there.' She covered the crystal with her hands. 'I'm sorry, it's gone now.'

'You really can see things in there, can't you? Father was right.'

'I've got a vivid imagination, and always have had.' She collected up one coin, refusing the other one. 'That's the end of your reading, sir. Thank you for coming.'

He stood up. 'Thank you, Miss Gloria. That was very interesting.'

When he ducked out of the tent she let out a pent-up sigh of relief. What a day!

Chapter Thirty-Four

Stuart's house was in deep mourning when Charles arrived. 'What's happened?' he asked the butler as he escorted him to the library.

'The mistress died suddenly three days ago, your lordship.'

When he walked in the room he said, 'I've just heard the sad news, Stuart. I am so sorry. I knew your wife wasn't well, but never expected this.'

'Neither did we. It all happened quickly. She kept having lapses in memory and moments of anger, and then fell into a coma and slipped away peacefully in her sleep. The doctors could do nothing for her.'

He studied Stuart's drawn and weary face, and asked, 'Is there anything I can do for you?'

'No, thanks, everything has been arranged. The funeral will be held in Kent where her parents live, and after that

I will be moving permanently to London. That is where my life is, and I only kept this place going because Angela seemed happier here. The journey to get back here on a regular basis has been inconvenient and time-consuming, but I had to do it to keep my family together.'

'What about the children?'

'Emma and Jane will come with me, with Nurse, of course, and Robert will stay at his school, but London will now be our home.' He ran a hand wearily over his eyes, and then looked up. 'Sit down, Charles, and tell me the reason for your visit.'

'I thought you would want to know that Harry has found Chrissie with the Travellers, and she is well.'

'Ah, that's a relief, and one worry off my mind. When did Harry arrive back?'

'I haven't seen him yet; he wrote me a letter, and said she is refusing to come back with him so he is staying with the Travellers to try and change her mind.'

Stuart frowned. 'I thought he was going to make sure she was all right, and maybe see if she would come back. If she has refused, why is he still trying to persuade her? Is he intending to give her the stable lad's job again?'

'I doubt that very much because he strongly disapproved of a girl doing that kind of work.'

'To be honest so do I. She is capable of achieving so much more in life, and I would willingly have given her a permanent job at my chambers, but she was adamant that she will not return to London permanently. Didn't he say what he planned to do if she does agree to return?'

'Not even a hint. All he said was that he wouldn't be

back without her and that could take a while. Oh, he did sign off by telling me not to worry because he was enjoying himself.'

'That's something, I suppose, after what he's been through.' Stuart gave a wry smile. 'That sounds like the school friend I had years ago, full of devilment. Would you like a drink?'

'Please. When are you leaving for Kent?'

'Tomorrow. I'll give you the address. Will you write and let me know what Harry is up to? Oh, and with everything that is happening I forgot to ask if you saw Edward safely on to a ship.'

'Yes, he went quite eagerly. I also settled his debts here, and there is money and accommodation waiting for him at his destination.'

'This has cost you a great deal of money.'

'No cost is too much to keep my son safe. Too many of my family have died and Harry is all I have left.'

Stuart nodded solemnly. 'It's hard, isn't it, but at least I have three lovely children. When Harry does arrive back you must start hinting it's time he married and had a family.'

'I know what he'll say if I try that. He'll tell me to mind my own bloody business.' Charles chuckled as he sipped his drink. 'What are you going to do with this house?'

'Sell it, if I can. When my wife insisted we buy this place she was already having problems, so it doesn't hold many happy memories for me, and I'll be glad to be rid of it.'

'What about your staff?'

'Nanny will be coming with the children, as I said, and I

have told everyone else they can stay until a buyer is found. Hopefully, some or all might be kept on with the new owners. There's a man in the village who is a retired lawyer, and he is going to deal with the sale for me, because I won't be around to see any prospective buyers.'

'And you trust this man?'

'Absolutely. I've known him for years.'

'That sounds like a good arrangement, then.'

Stuart looked more relaxed now. 'If Harry does return with Chrissie, please tell her there is a job waiting for her in London if she wants it.'

'I promise, but it's most unlikely, and if she does I doubt she would accept your kind offer.'

'I know she wants open spaces around her, but give her the option anyway. If she has too much trouble with Harry, tell her she can come and work for me.'

Charles sighed. 'I wish I knew what he was up to. She wouldn't take a job on my estate when I tried to give her one, and won't consider the excellent opportunity you have offered. She's far too independent for her own good, and look at the trouble it has caused her. To be honest, I believe he is wasting his time, but he can be very persuasive when he needs to be.'

'That may be so,' Stuart agreed, 'but after the setbacks she has encountered since leaving London, I don't believe she can be easily talked into doing something she doesn't want to.'

'She won't be so trusting, either, which is a shame, but life's ups and downs do tend to do that to all of us in time.'

'Sadly, that is true.'

Charles stood up. 'I won't take up any more of your time; I know you have a lot to do.'

'Thanks for coming, and I'll be intrigued to hear what Harry is up to.'

Harry couldn't remember when he'd felt so relaxed. This time with the Travellers was helping him to sort out his emotions and plan for the future. He gazed at the sea and felt the gentle breeze as it tempered the heat of August. He'd been with them for a week now, but all his efforts to persuade Chrissie to return with him had been met with a definite refusal. He watched her working with everyone, heard the laughter as she raced and played with the youngsters, and it made him question if he had the right to try and take her away. She was obviously happy here, and what could he offer her instead? The honest answer to that was that he didn't know, didn't even know why he was doing this. He'd found her and she was all right, so that should have been enough to ease their consciences. His, after the way he had treated a homeless girl who had nothing; Stuart, because she had been driven away by his sick wife; and his father because he liked her and was worried for her safety.

'Beautiful, isn't it?'

He turned his head to look at Sandy, who had come to stand beside him. 'Yes, it's just what I need. It's healing me, body, mind and soul, and I'm grateful to all of you for allowing me to stay.'

'You work hard and mix in with everyone. I must say you are an unusual gentleman, and you are welcome to stay for as long as you want to, but be aware we are watching you closely. If you try to hurt our girl again you will find yourself in trouble with us.'

'You can rest assured that I will not.'

'Then go home and leave her with us.'

Harry shook his head. 'I can't do that.'

'She's only part-Romany, but we still consider her one of us, so why are you set on taking her home with you? It's not the sort of thing a gentleman would do, unless he wanted her as his mistress. She's very beautiful.'

'Is that what you are all wondering?' he asked sharply. 'That is not my intention. My father told me she loves my estate and the horses we breed. She was happy there, and I took that away from her without finding out why my father had employed her. I want to correct that wrong and give it back to her. I don't harbour any evil desires where she is concerned.'

Sandy smiled then. 'Thank you for explaining your reasons for coming after her. Now, we are packing up ready to move further along the coast, so will you give us a hand?'

'Of course.'

With all of them pitching in, everything was soon ready for an early start the next day, so Harry was on his way to take one of his horses out for exercise when Elsie called him. He went over to her home. 'What can I do for you?'

'Can you spare the time to come and have a cup of tea with me?'

He climbed up the steps. 'All the work is done and I'd enjoy a cup of your excellent tea. It's a hot day.'

'It certainly is.' She looked up at him and then patted his arm. 'Do sit down, Harry. You're too big for my home

336

when you're standing. I was hoping Chrissie would come as well. Do you know where she is?'

'I haven't seen her for a while. Would you like me to go and look for her?'

'No, I expect she's still busy – or she's hiding from you.'

'That wouldn't surprise me.' He gave a deep chuckle. 'I'm beginning to understand why my father and Stuart liked her so much. She isn't afraid to speak her mind, and that's refreshing.'

'I'm pleased you find it so.' Her look was penetrating as she handed him a cup of tea. 'You look happier and more relaxed than when you first arrived.'

'I am, and I'm even sleeping well. I will be sorry to leave, but I can't stay for much longer. It isn't fair to leave my father with two estates to run; he's had that responsibility for too long now.'

'Will you be sad to leave without my dear girl?'

'I'm still hopeful she will come with me. Will she, Elsie?'

'That is something you will have to find out for yourself, but if she continues to refuse, then you must go, for both your sakes. Don't play with her emotions in order to ease your conscience, dear boy. You come from a privileged family, and her background is the opposite.'

He sat up straight, frowning at what she was hinting, and remembering what Sandy had said. They were all questioning his motives! 'I don't give a damn about background! If I did, do you think I would be here living and working with a group of Travellers?'

'A gentleman might find it amusing.'

Placing the cup carefully on the table, he stood up. 'You have all misjudged me, and I'm sorry about that.'

337

'Sit down, Harry. I did not intend to offend you, but I needed to probe your character to find out what is beneath the picture of an elegant gentleman. We all care about Chrissie and were horrified to find out she had been wandering the countryside on her own. You don't know this, but when she finally found us she could hardly stand. She didn't have any money, was filthy from sleeping rough and was starving. We hardly recognised her as the happy, laughing girl we had known before.'

He sat down again, appalled by what he had just heard. 'She didn't tell me.'

'Why should she? I don't feel now that you mean her any harm, but I've been watching you carefully, and you have become friendly – too friendly for a servant and master. If she did return with you, she could never be one of your servants again, so why are you doing this? You need to get that clear in your mind, dear boy. You come from different worlds, and the two cannot mix.' She poured them both another cup of tea. 'Unless you know exactly why you are doing this, then ride away, Harry.'

He silently sipped the hot tea, his mind reeling as he realised what Elsie's probing had brought to the surface. He had fallen in love with Chrissie. 'You are asking too much,' he told her softly.

'I was sure you would say that, but now it will be up to you to make the right decision – for both of you. You are going to have to let your head rule your heart, I'm afraid, or both of you will be hurt.'

'I'll have to give this some thought.' He drained his tea and stood up.

'You do that, dear boy. I only want what's best for both of you.'

He bent and kissed her cheek. 'You are a wise woman and I'm pleased to have had this discussion with you. It has helped to make something clear to me, and my only concern now is how to deal with it.'

'There is always an answer, Harry. You just have to listen.'

After leaving her he wandered to the beach, deep in thought, mulling over the implications of what he had just discovered, searching for the answer Elsie said was there. An idea began to form and he went over it time and time again, just to make sure it might be something Chrissie could accept. If she didn't, then he would have to follow Elsie's advice and ride away without her, as hard as that would be. He turned and walked briskly back to the camp. This had to be settled now; there wasn't any point putting it off.

He found her where he knew she would be, with Midnight and Red, and strode up to her. 'They need exercise. Shall we give them a good run over the fields?'

Her eyes lit up with pleasure, as they always did when given the chance to ride one of them, and her response gave him a glimmer of hope.

The animals were soon saddled and as they thundered across the fields her joy was infectious, and he was aware just how much depended upon what he did and said now. His feelings for her must not show or she would disappear from his life as quickly as she could. If he was lucky the time would come, but that time was not now.

Some fifteen minutes later they had reached a field with

lush grass and began to canter through it until Harry stopped. 'Let's give them a rest so they can munch on the grass.'

They found a fallen tree where they could sit and watch the horses enjoying the fresh grass.

'I've brought you out here because we need to talk. I'm leaving tomorrow, and I'm asking you again to come with me.'

'You know I can't do that. I can't be your guest because it wouldn't be right. Can you imagine the gossip that would cause?'

'I understand why you feel that way, and you are quite right. I've been giving it a lot of thought. I've given up on the idea of raising thoroughbreds, and we are going back to what we know best. These two fine animals are going to be the basis for a new breed of destriers. As you know, I've already purchased some fine mares and they are already in foal.'

She nodded; her expressive face was alight with interest. 'Yes, I saw them and they are lovely.'

He spoke slowly, choosing his words carefully. 'We are also in the process of setting up a farm to grow crops, and have cattle as well. We are making big changes, and I need your help.'

She turned to face him, a deep frown creasing her brow. 'What on earth could I possibly do?'

'Work with me to make the stud farm a profitable business again. It's going to take time, and we will have untrained warhorses to deal with, and you have a rapport with these animals that is astounding.' He smiled wryly. 'I swear you talk to them and they answer you, and they also respond to the love you have for them.'

She had gone very still and he took a deep silent breath before continuing. 'Come back with me so we can work together. What I'm offering is the fulfilment of your dreams – a permanent home on a beautiful estate, working with the animals you love.'

The silence stretched, and he waited, almost afraid to breathe. She hadn't refused, yet.

'You could dismiss me again,' she said quietly.

'No, that won't happen again. You will be working with me on the same basis as the estate manager.'

'What would the other hands think of such an arrangement?'

'They would be pleased to have you back. Everyone misses you.'

'Can I have my room in the barn again?'

'Yes, if that's what you want.' His heart jumped in anticipation.

'Can I wear breeches when I need to?'

'Yes.'

'If the time comes when you want me to leave, will you talk to me so I have time to make other arrangements? I don't want to have to walk away at a moment's notice again.'

'I can promise you that, but I can also assure you it will never happen.'

'You can't use the word "never", Major. Things change, and as the owner of that beautiful estate, you need to change staff from time to time. I know I shouldn't be asking for assurances, but the circumstances are rather different. I am not applying for work – you are offering it to me. However, it isn't clear to me just what the job is.'

'I need someone who loves and understands these animals, and isn't afraid of them. Someone who can help me buy mares, and another stallion. Someone who can oversee the training of the young horses, and isn't afraid of the rough and tumble that will involve. And I honestly believe that someone is you.'

She faced him in surprise. 'I wouldn't know how to do that.'

'I'll teach you. You have a special gift when it comes to handling horses, and that is what you should be doing. Not copying documents for Stuart, and not roaming around the countryside telling fortunes. Your real talent is being wasted.' He watched various emotions coming and going on her face, still not sure what she was going to decide. He had done all he could, though.

After a long pause, she took a deep breath. 'All right, Major Frenshaw, I accept your offer.'

Relief flooded through him and he wanted to hug her in sheer pleasure, but knew that would be the wrong thing to do. This was a business arrangement and he must keep it that way, so he shook her hand to seal the deal.

Chapter Thirty-Five

That evening the entire group settled down on the grass and listened as Harry told them they would be leaving first thing in the morning.

'You can't travel with our girl on your own, Major,' Pa told him firmly. 'Ma and Sandy will come with you as chaperones, because this has got to be done properly. We won't have Chrissie's reputation sullied.'

'I understand, and all expenses for the journey will be met by me.'

Pa nodded and turned to Chrissie. 'Are you sure you want to take a chance on this man's word?'

'I've been over it thoroughly with him, and I believe he answered all my questions truthfully. It's an opportunity I would be foolish to turn down.'

'It would seem so, but we need to make one thing clear

with the major. If we could stop our girl from coming with you, we would, but she is her own person and free to come and go as she wishes. We will give you a list of places we will be visiting and the approximate times, and if you should decide you don't want to employ her any more, you must send us word and we will come and collect her. We will not have her wandering, starving and broke, as she tries to catch up with us. Is that clearly understood?'

'Perfectly, and you have my promise that I will do as you say, but you can be sure that situation will not arise again.'

'Best see it doesn't, or you will have us to answer to.'

The journey back to the estate was slow, as Ma and Sandy's mounts did not have the speed or stamina of the warhorses. Chrissie could feel the major's eagerness to reach home, but he didn't give any indication that he was impatient with the slow progress.

When the gates came in to view she could hardly contain her excitement. She was fully aware she was taking a chance by returning, but she did love this place so much, and in the end she hadn't been able to refuse. It could end in heartbreak again, but it was a risk worth taking, and this time her eyes were wide open. If the time came when she had to move on again, she wouldn't be wandering around too upset to make sensible decisions. What she had been through had changed her and she felt she was now a much stronger person.

Sandy whistled softly as they continued towards the house, and said quietly to his mother, 'Have you ever seen anything like this?'

'Never.' She glanced at Chrissie. 'No wonder you wanted to come back.'

A crowd had gathered to meet them and she could see his lordship standing there with a huge smile on his face as he watched them ride towards him. In fact, everyone was smiling, and the feeling of being welcomed back was almost overwhelming, but she kept the tears at bay with effort.

Harry dismounted and then helped Chrissie and Ma off their mounts before going to greet his father, estate manager and all members of his staff.

'Chrissie.' His lordship grasped her hands. 'It's so wonderful to see you, and who have you brought with you?'

She introduced Ma and Sandy. 'They've been my chaperones for the journey,' she told him.

'Quite right too. Thank you for seeing Chrissie safely back to us.'

Harry strode over to them. 'Ma and Sandy, welcome to my home. You kindly allowed me to stay with you, so I hope you will let me return the favour by staying with us for at least a couple of days. That will allow time for both you and your horses to recover from the journey.'

'We would be happy to accept your invitation, Major.' Ma glanced around at the stable hands all talking excitedly to Chrissie, clearly delighted to see her again. She winked at Harry. 'It will give us a chance to make sure our girl will really be all right here. If we have any doubts we might take her back.'

'Not a chance. This is where she belongs, and this is where she will stay. Look how happy she is.'

'I grant you she's happy now, but will she stay that way?'

'Of course she will.' Harry stood to his full height. 'Are you going to make things difficult for me, Ma?'

'Me?' A slow smile spread across her face. 'I was hoping you would stay with us permanently, because we could do with some new blood in our group, and you're a fine specimen of a man.'

He tipped his head back and laughed. 'I did enjoy my time with you, but do you seriously think I could leave all this? This is where my heart is.'

'I guess you're right. It's a pity, though.'

Charles had been talking to the butler and came to stand beside his son. They were both tall, impressive men, and there was no doubting they were father and son. 'I am sure you are hungry and thirsty after your journey. There is a meal waiting for you in the dining room.'

While Ma and Sandy made their way to the house, Harry strode over to Chrissie to prise her away from the stable hands. 'There's food ready for us.'

'Oh, good, I'm ravenous.' She fell in to step beside him, expecting to go to the kitchen. Instead he took her to a stunningly beautiful dining room. The carpet and drapes were in pale green with a delicate pattern of small white and yellow flowers. The long table was polished until you could see your face in it, and the china and cutlery took her breath away.

Sandy looked at Harry with a glint of devilment in his eyes. 'This is a bit different from our celebration on the beach.'

Harry grinned, remembering that riotous evening.

The butler and two maids were waiting to serve them,

and Chrissie knew them well. Their expressions were serious until she raised her eyebrows at them and smirked, then they were struggling not to smile.

'Don't tease the staff,' Harry whispered in her ear as he held her chair for her, indicating she should be seated.

The moment he stepped away the butler came and placed a napkin on her lap. She glanced at Ma and Sandy, wondering what they thought about being served a meal in surroundings like this, but they appeared to be completely at ease. Relaxing then, she began to enjoy the excellent meal, watching carefully what utensils his lordship used. The conversation flowed as Harry told his father about the time he'd spent with the Travellers, and how he had enjoyed it.

They were on the third course and their guests were busy discussing the beauty of the china, when Harry asked his father if Edward had left without any trouble.

'Yes, he appeared quite happy to be leaving. I watched the ship until it was out of sight, so you'll be quite safe now.'

They had been speaking softly, but Chrissie heard them and frowned. 'Safe?'

'Yes, you were quite right with your warning,' his lordship explained. 'My nephew was so desperate to inherit the estate that he shot Harry.'

'Oh no.' When she had seen him at Sir Gretham's she had felt he had been hurt again and Red was troubled about something, but she hadn't known he had been injured in that way. She had assumed he'd had a bad fall. 'Were you hurt badly?'

'Just added another scar to the ones I already have,' he replied dismissively.

That wasn't much of an explanation, but she'd find out the full story later.

'Another thing you don't know, Chrissie, is that Stuart's wife died quite suddenly. She was evidently very sick. He's selling the house and moving his family back to London, and he asked me to tell you that there is a job waiting for you there if you ever want it.'

'That is kind of him, and I'm so sorry to hear his wife died. I felt there was something terribly wrong, and my being there appeared to be making it worse. That's why I left.'

The conversation then turned back to other things. Ma and Sandy were interested in the running of the estate, and Harry's plans for the future.

When the meal was over, his lordship took their guests on a tour of the house, and Chrissie ran to the barn, eager to see her room again, and hoping it hadn't been too damaged in the storm they'd had. She scrambled up the ladder and tumbled in to the loft. When she saw that it was exactly the same as before she hugged herself in delight. Someone had been to work up there already because there were clean sheets on the bed, a small vase of wild flowers on the table, and her belongings neatly placed on the bed. One thing she hadn't taken with her was the lucky horseshoe, and it was still over the bed where she had left it. Her belongings could be put away later, but now she must go and see the stables.

When nearly at the bottom of the ladder she felt strong hands grasp her round the waist to lift her down the last few steps.

'Is everything to your liking?' Harry asked, placing her on the floor and stepping back.

'It's perfect, but now I'd like to see the horses and the stables, please, sir.'

'Don't address me as sir.'

'I'm sorry; I should have used your military rank.'

'No, you shouldn't. My discharge has finally come through and I am no longer in the cavalry.'

'But I've known ex-officers who still use their rank right through life. What should I call you, then?'

'Harry.'

Her expression was horrified. 'I can't do that.'

'Why not? I thought we had become friends while we were with the Travellers.'

'That was different. You are the owner of this fine estate and I am one of your staff now, and you must be treated with the respect that is rightfully yours. I will have to call you "sir".'

Noting the determination on her face he lifted his hands in surrender. 'As you please. Now, I'd like you to have a look at the mares, Miss Banner, and tell me how you think they are getting on.'

Managing to hide her smile, she nodded. 'I would like that very much, sir.'

He muttered something under his breath, but she didn't catch it, which was probably just as well, she thought. He might be high-born, but there was a rough edge to him now and again, probably from mixing with all those soldiers.

The mares were in a field behind the stables and Chrissie was glad she was still wearing her breeches as she climbed on the gate and sat there, legs dangling. 'They look lovely, and I'm not surprised you wanted them.'

'Well, they are under your care now, so you had better go and let them know.' He leapt over the gate and helped her down.

The animals watched as they approached, and some steps away she began to talk to them softly. They had seen her before, but they still didn't know her very well and were cautious. After only a couple of minutes they walked up to her so they could take a closer look at her. 'You have done well buying these, and they like it here,' she told him.

'How do you know?'

'They've told me, of course,' she told him with a straight face.

'I am so sorry for what I did,' he told her, his eyes showing his regret. 'I sent you away from all this, when it is the only place you should be.'

'You don't have to apologise,' she told him quickly, troubled by his sad expression. 'When my father died I thought I would set out to fulfil my dream of living in the country, and imagined it was going to be so easy. It has turned out to be a long and very rough road, but do you know, I am grateful it has been like that. I am no longer the silly girl with impossible dreams. I know now that things are not always perfect, and there are many hills and valleys to travel in life. I have grown up, and that is good because the next time I have to move on, I will be able to deal with it in a more sensible way. I will not allow my emotions to get in the way again. So you see, in a way you did me a favour.'

He was silent and absolutely still for a moment before speaking. 'Are you saying that you still believe you will have to leave here one day, in spite of all my assurances?'

'I'm sure you honestly believe what you've said, but the day will come when you no longer need me. You will marry a high-born wife, have a family and you will not want a girl running around looking like a stable lad. When I agreed to return I was fully aware that one day I will have to leave here again, but I am prepared for it and intend to enjoy whatever time I have here.'

'You don't trust me.'

'No, sir, I don't, because things change and you will always do what is right for your estate and family.' She turned and smiled at the stunned man. 'Now, if you will excuse me, sir, I have work to do.'

Harry watched her walk away, shattered by what she had just told him. He had really believed that during their informal time spent together at the camp she was beginning to like him, but that wasn't the case at all. She had come back with him because she wanted to, not for anything else, and certainly not for him. Those words had cut through him like a sabre, but why was he surprised? By his thoughtless action he had caused her a great deal of worry and sadness. She was right. She had grown up because she'd had to – and he had started her on that road. In retrospect she had told him she was grateful to him, but he was sure the memory would linger. What on earth ever made him believe she would even like him, let alone love him? He needed a drink.

'Who has upset you?' his father asked when he walked in to the library.

'No one, I'm all right. Why do you ask?'

'The expression on your face tells me something has upset you.'

'I was deep in thought, that's all.' He held up the decanter. 'Fancy a drink?'

'No, thanks.' He glanced over at the mantelshelf where white cards were stuck behind the clock. 'We have been receiving rather a lot of invitations after our visit to London.'

Harry nodded. 'I must get around to sending polite refusals.'

'I think we should accept some – and don't give me that disgusted look, Harry. It's time you thought about marrying and having a family, and that's the best way to meet suitable girls.'

'There's no need to become involved in that circus because I already know who I want to marry.'

Charles couldn't hide his surprise. 'When did you meet her?'

'Oh, a while ago, and the only problem is she doesn't like me much. I will have to work hard to change her mind.'

'I'm intrigued. Who is this person?'

'I'm not ready to say at the moment.'

'I'll have to be patient, I suppose, but do make your mind up soon because you are not getting any younger.'

'I'm only twenty-nine,' he laughed, his earlier gloom disappearing.

'Exactly, and high time you settled down with a wife and family. You won't tell me who you want to marry, but now Edward is safely out of the country, will you tell me who you left the estate to?'

'Chrissie.'

'What? I would never have guessed. I thought it might have been Joe.'

Harry shook his head. 'No, this isn't the kind of life for Joe, but Chrissie loves the place and the animals.'

'I'm astonished. Does she know?'

'No, and don't say anything to her.'

'I understand why that must be kept quiet, because you will need to change it again once you marry.'

'Hmm,' was his only reply.

Chapter Thirty-Six

Ma and Sandy were treated like honoured guests for two days, and when it came time for them to leave Chrissie hugged them. 'Thank you for all the kindness you have shown me, but this isn't goodbye, as I am sure I will be with you again one day. Give my love to Elsie.'

'Why are you here if you believe you will have to leave again?' Sandy asked.

'I am here because I love this place, and I will enjoy whatever time I'm allowed to stay.' There was also another reason, but that would be kept to herself.

'That's a sensible way to look at it, I suppose, but I'm not sure you are right to put your happiness at risk again. However, there will always be a place for you with us if you ever need it.' Sandy handed her a list. 'We've given one of these to the major, but you contact us if you need help at any time. You are one of us now, Chrissie, and you come to us if you need anything.'

'Thank you, that is a great comfort. Have you got enough money for the journey back?'

'More than enough. The major and his father have been very generous with their hospitality and a gift of money.' Ma smiled and gazed around for a moment, then back at Chrissie. 'I can see why you love this place. Be happy, dear girl.'

'I will.' Another hug and they were on their way, with everyone wishing them a safe journey.

She watched until they were out of sight, and then went back to work in the stables. She was singing softly to herself as she cleaned the stalls and put down fresh straw, when suddenly the fork was wrenched out of her hands, and she looked up in surprise.

'What the blazes do you think you are doing?'

'Mucking out the stables, sir. The horses have to be kept clean.'

'I'm well aware of that, but it isn't your job.'

When he tossed the fork down and she saw his furious expression, she couldn't help thinking that her stay was going to be very short indeed. 'What would you like me to do, sir?' she asked politely.

'I want you to get cleaned up, put on something respectable and meet me back here in half an hour. There is a stallion and two mares I want you to see before I buy them.'

'Yes, sir. Will we be riding?'

'No, we'll be using the carriage.'

She nodded, turned and ran. During the morning she

had been doing every mucky job there was around and was now very dirty. He hadn't given her much time and she hoped her skirt wasn't too creased.

It was a scramble but she made it just in time. When she skidded to a halt in front of him, he eyed her up and down, and then helped her in to the carriage without saying a word. He handled it with skill, and as he remained silent she enjoyed watching the countryside pass by. Her mind wandered back to the times she went with her dad on his rounds, though the old wooden cart was nothing like this luxurious carriage, but they were good memories. She cast a quick glance at the man beside her, still silent, but looking more relaxed.

She ventured a question. 'Where are we going, sir?'

'To a farm about five miles away. The man has acquired some animals he thinks I might be interested in. He is not a horse breeder, so I have my doubts they will be any good.'

'You are an experienced and good judge of horses, so why do you need me?' She held her breath expecting a sharp response, but he answered normally.

'I can see if they are good enough for us, but I can't discern their temperament as effectively as you. Some unscrupulous sellers will sedate them if they are difficult to handle, and I'm sure you will be able to sense that. We were caught like that with Midnight and Red Sunset's sire, and we had a devil of a job trying to train them. Midnight turned out to be an excellent cavalry horse, but Red is far too unpredictable and disobedient to go to the cavalry. They need mounts that will obey their commands no matter what the situation facing them, not one who will turn round and kick to let you know he isn't going to do that.'

She roared with laughter; she couldn't help it, and was pleased to hear him join in. 'Red is a sweetie, really.'

'With you he is. I was riding him when I was shot, and when I hit the ground he nearly finished me off with his great hooves. I ordered him to go home and get help, but I had no idea if he would. He did, though, thank goodness.'

'Of course he did. He wouldn't want you to be hurt; he loves you.'

He cast her an amused glance. 'Did he tell you that?'

'He didn't have to. I can tell from the look in his eyes when you are with him.'

They pulled in a gate and she was surprised how quickly they had arrived at their destination. He helped her down as the farmer came to meet them, all smiles.

'Major Frenshaw, welcome. I believe you will like the animals I have.'

'This is my assistant, Miss Banner.'

She saw the surprise in the man's eyes, but he inclined his head politely.

'I'll see the stallion first.'

'He's ready for you, Major. Bring him out,' he ordered the man standing ready.

'Oh, my, he's almost silver,' she murmured quietly.

'Stunning, I agree, but take a close look at him before I examine him.'

He gave her a sly wink and she guessed he wanted a show put on, so she walked slowly towards the huge animal, speaking softly all the time, and he watched her every step. The man had a firm hold on him. 'Let him go,' she told him, standing about two feet away.

'Sir?' he asked, clearly doubtful about the request.

'Do as she says,' Harry commanded, and the man reluctantly released the horse and stepped away.

The animal had his full attention on her while she continued to talk to him. Eventually he walked up to her and dipped his head so she could rub his neck and nose. Taking her time to make sure there was nothing amiss with the stallion, she looked over her shoulder. 'You can examine him now, sir.'

Harry strode towards them and began a thorough examination of the animal. 'He hasn't been subdued?' he asked.

'I don't believe so, sir. He is alert and his eyes are focussed and clear.'

'He's in fine condition, but do you think he will settle in with Midnight and Red?'

A saucy smile crossed her face. 'He said that he will, and he's pleased we aren't frightened of him, because these fools are.'

'You made that up.'

'Of course I did. Anyone can see these men are terrified of him. Where did they get such a magnificent horse?'

'That's what I'm wondering.' He walked back to the waiting men. 'I might be interested, but need to know where he came from.'

'He was payment for a debt, along with two mares. The owner was Lord Hatton.'

'I know of him, but how was he in debt to you?'

'It was a gambling debt, Major.'

He made a sound of disgust. 'Let me see the mares.'

They were brought out and one was perfect for their needs, but the other one was too old.

'Don't leave her here,' Chrissie pleaded. 'There's no telling what these men will do with her, and she'll be happy with the other horses.'

He nodded and went to negotiate with the owner.

An hour later they left, and Harry was obviously pleased with the deal he had made. 'That man couldn't wait to get rid of them, and we got them for a good price. I'm having them collected in the morning. You were a great help today.'

'I'm pleased you managed to find suitable horses, but you didn't really need me for that play-acting, did you? May I ask why, sir?'

'I knew that man was a gambler before we came, and I wanted him to wonder what special skills you had and, hopefully, convince him that I had an unbeatable hand. That was inspired acting by telling them to release the horse. When the animal walked calmly towards you I heard his sharp intake of breath and knew he was impressed. That gave me the chance to get them at a reasonable price.'

'So that masquerade was to convince him it would be useless to ask an exorbitant price?'

'Exactly, and it worked beautifully.'

'I didn't realise you were quite so devious, sir.'

'That's business, Chrissie.' He shot her an amused glance. 'I think we are going to make a good team.'

She ignored that remark. 'I'm pleased you bought all three. They are fed up with being moved around and want a proper home.'

'Did they tell you that?' he teased.

'Of course. They were happy to have someone to talk to.'

A rumble of laughter came from the man beside her, and she smiled inwardly. At least he was in a good mood now – until she did something else to upset him. The first time she had met him his strong presence had almost overwhelmed her, but not any more. During their time together at the camp she had come to know his different moods and how they could change so quickly. Also, the thought of being sent away again didn't fill her with despair as it did the first time. If and when that did happen she could go back to the people who cared for her. This time she had somewhere to go, so whatever happened she was no longer alone. She glanced at him and thought with satisfaction, you can shout and lose your temper now, Major Frenshaw, and it won't bother me. Although I like you very much, you no longer have the power to frighten or upset me. I am more confident now, and I have you to thank for that.

There was great excitement when the new horses arrived the next day. The two mares were put with the others they had, and the older one appeared to be very happy to be in a lovely field with them. The stallion they put separately in a paddock where he could look over the fence at Midnight and Red.

'What are we going to call him?' Harry asked her, as they watched the stallions inspecting each other.

'Starlight,' she replied immediately.

'That sounds right. Now we have Midnight, Red Sunset and Starlight. All we need now is one named after the dawn and we have a set.'

'That will come when the foals are born.'

'Do you know, I'm never sure if you really can tell what's going to happen, or if you are playing a game with us. Elsie was convinced you had "the gift", as she called it, but you smile and deny it, saying that you make it all up. Which is it?'

'You have to make your own mind up about that. It all comes down to what a person believes, doesn't it?'

'That isn't an answer, and you know it.'

'It's the only one I have.' She turned her attention back to the horses. 'They look friendly enough with each other, so I can go back to work. If that's all right with you, sir.'

'I wish you'd damned well stop calling me that.'

'I couldn't possibly be disrespectful to my employer, sir. Servants can be dismissed for that.'

He let out a deep sigh and slapped the fence in exasperation. 'What am I going to do about you?'

She watched him spin round and march away. At that moment there was a nudge on her shoulder. 'Hello, Starlight, what do you think of this place? Beautiful, isn't it? I'm afraid I've made the master cross again, but don't you worry about him, he's really a very kind man.'

The animal nodded his head up and down, and then turned to trot back and have another look at the two stallions over the fence.

She was making her way back to the stables when a cart trundled in loaded with bales of hay, and she went straight to it and began helping the men to unload. The head groom, Bert, came over to her and shook his head. 'If the master sees you doing that he will explode.'

361

'I work in the stables and that means doing anything necessary. I'm quite capable of lifting bales of hay.'

'You're a strong lass and used to hard work, but he might sack me for allowing you to do heavy lifting.'

'No, he won't; I won't let him. While I'm here I'll do the same work as the other hands, and woe betide anyone who tries to stop me.' She grinned at Bert and hoisted a bale on to her shoulders. 'Where do you want this?'

'In the barn, and stack it neatly, then I want you to go to the blacksmith. One of Midnight's shoes has come loose, and you know what he thinks about blacksmiths.'

Her musical laughter echoed around the yard, bringing a smile to the faces of the other workers.

'Ah, it's good to have you back again,' young Adam said as she returned for another bale. 'Will you stay this time?'

'I really don't know. It all depends on how much I upset the master.'

'That's a great deal, from what I've seen,' Bert remarked dryly.

She hoisted up another bale. 'I do seem to have the habit of saying the wrong thing to him.'

Chapter Thirty-Seven

Standing out of view, Harry watched the scene, not knowing whether to laugh or explode with frustration. That tough girl was enjoying herself, knowing he had practically begged her to come back. She had completely ignored his offer of working closely with him and returned to her old position as a stable lad. There was a confidence about her that hadn't been there before, and to be truthful he liked her even more like this, but she thought she had the upper hand, and he wasn't going to allow that. I'm not defeated yet, Miss Banner, he muttered to himself. If you want a fight, then you've got one. It's what I'm trained for.

'Oh, who has upset you now?' his father asked the moment he walked in.

'That infuriating girl, of course. I offered her a more elevated post, and what does she do?'

Charles tried to keep his amusement at bay, and failed. 'I'm sure you are going to tell me.'

'She goes straight back to being a stable lad, and she's out there unloading bales of hay!'

'Have you told her that isn't her job?'

'Repeatedly! She just smiles sweetly, calls me "sir" all the time, and does exactly what she wants.'

His father was openly laughing now. 'I think she's decided that no one is going to push her around again. Good for her. I liked her from the moment I saw her.'

'How much do you like her?'

'Pardon?'

'It's a simple question, Father. Do you like her enough to accept her as a daughter-in-law, regardless of her background?'

He stared at his son in shock, suddenly realising why Harry had stayed with the Travellers for so long, and why he had insisted on bringing her back with him. He wondered why he hadn't seen that sooner. Of course, the sheltered society girl would never suit his son. He needed someone strong in body and mind who would be able to cope with this sometimes volatile man. 'I don't give a damn about her background, and I'd be proud to call her one of the family.'

'Good, because I intend to marry her.'

'Now I see why you didn't tell me sooner, but does she know about this?'

'No. If she did she'd be off faster than Red can charge. She's told me to my face that she doesn't trust me.'

'You also told me that the girl you want to marry doesn't like you either.'

Harry shrugged. 'She does really; she just doesn't know it yet.'

Charles still couldn't believe what he was being told, but he wasn't unhappy about it. Even so he felt he had to add a note of caution. 'You do know you haven't got a chance of persuading her to become your wife, don't you?'

'I agree it isn't going to be easy, but I've never backed away from a fight, and I'm not defeated yet.'

'I can understand you falling for Chrissie. She's intelligent and beautiful, but have you considered the problem such a union would cause? We are quite isolated here, but there are times when we need to mingle with society. It could be difficult for her.'

'Dressed fashionably, and with her natural grace, she would enhance any function, and I would be proud to have her on my arm.'

'I don't doubt that, but would she want to be a part of society like that? Think of her for a moment, and not what you want.'

'I understand what you are saying, but given our support I believe she could cope with anything.' He prowled over to the window. 'I have your approval, at least, so all I've got to do now is convince her she wants to marry me.'

All? Charles thought. You have a monumental task ahead of you, my boy.

'I'm going to have another look at the new stallion; want to come with me?'

When his father nodded, they strode out together as they made their way to the paddock. He was well aware of all the pitfalls that could occur from the choice he had made, and knew his father had felt it his duty to point them out. However, during the time he had spent with Chrissie, he had come to know her quite well, and was certain she wouldn't allow society snobs to upset her. There were a few young ladies who would have married him without hesitation because of his wealth and status, but not one of them had merited more than a passing glance from him. What he'd always wanted in a wife was a companion who wouldn't be afraid of the powerful horses, someone who would work with him, and above all things who wouldn't settle for less than love and respect for each other. It was a lot to ask, and he often doubted he would find such a person, but he had. Chrissie was strong, beautiful, had a sense of humour and adored the magnificent animals. She was everything he had ever wanted, and he didn't give a damn about her background. It was what had made her who she was. All he had to do now was convince her that he was the one for her, and that wasn't going to be an easy task, but he relished the challenge.

'My word, what a glorious animal!' his father exclaimed when they reached the paddock.

His father's voice cut through his thoughts and he leant on the gate. 'Isn't he perfect?'

'What is his temperament like?'

'According to our expert, it's good.'

'Expert?'

'Chrissie. I'm an expert on horseflesh, but she seems to be able to look deeper. I didn't want a repeat of the trouble we had in the past with an uncontrollable stallion, and that's why I took her with me.'

'And she liked him?'

'He walked up to her like a lamb, and she was sure he hadn't been sedated. We also bought two mares at the same time. One is suitable for breeding, but the other is too old. However, she convinced me to take all three because they told her they were fed up with being moved around and wanted a proper home.' Harry chuckled. 'She tells you things like that with a perfectly straight face.'

'I know, and it's hard to decide if she means it or not. I think she has a saucy sense of humour.' His father grinned. 'Where is she?'

'Probably doing something she shouldn't.' He turned and faced the stables and raised his commanding voice. 'Chrissie!'

She appeared at the door of the stables, fork in hand. 'Sir?'

'Put that down and come here for a moment, please.'

Doing as ordered, she came over to them smiling brightly and sketched a quick curtsy to Charles, which was more than a little comical as she was wearing breeches and had a large smudge of dirt on her face. 'Good afternoon, your lordship. Isn't it a lovely day?'

'It is, indeed.' He was struggling not to burst in to laughter. 'What have you been doing to get so dirty?'

'Don't ask, Father.'

She turned her attention back to Harry, still smiling. 'What did you call me for, sir?'

'I want to know if it's safe to put Starlight in with the other two boys yet.'

'I'll go and ask them.' She climbed over the fence and walked across the field.

Charles couldn't contain himself any longer and doubled over with laughter. 'Why doesn't she use the gate?'

'That would be too easy,' his son replied dryly.

'I take back everything I said in the library. She isn't afraid of those beasts or you, and she'd make you a perfect wife. I tell you one thing, though, my son, if you do manage to persuade her to marry you, it will not be a dull union.'

'I'm fully aware of that, and a dull marriage is the last thing I want.' He watched her walk back, chatting away to the animal as he followed her.

'Starlight said he wants to go and play with the other two.'

Harry ran a hand over his eyes. 'And what do the other two think about that?'

'It's all right. They think he's pretty.'

Charles had to turn away to conceal his mirth. She was playing games with his son, and it was clear he had met his match in her. If she had an inkling of his feelings for her, she wasn't going to make it easy for him.

'In that case you can open the gate for them.' Harry shook his head almost imperceptibly, and somehow managed to remain straight-faced.

'Right, come and meet your friends,' she told the horse and began to run towards the adjoining gate with the horse trotting excitedly beside her.

'Oh, I think I must move in here permanently, because I want to see how this works out. You do realise she's seeing how far she can push you, don't you?'

'I'm well aware what she is doing, and it gives me hope that deep down she likes me.' Harry grinned. 'What a wife she will make.'

'Look at that,' Charles exclaimed. 'She's laying down the law with those three, and I do believe they are listening to her.'

'I believe it's the tone of her voice they respond to. It's quite melodic, and have you noticed that even the London twang is hardly noticeable?'

'She does speak quite well when you consider where she comes from, and Stuart said her writing is beautiful.'

'So I believe.' Harry's gaze was fixed on what was happening in the field, and asked when she arrived back, 'Are they going to be friendly?'

'Yes, because I told them to behave themselves because I'll be watching.' She bestowed a smile on each of the men in turn. 'Is that all you need, sir?'

'No, it isn't. It's my father's birthday today, and you will join us for a celebration dinner this evening, together with the estate manager and head groom.'

'Happy birthday, your lordship.'

He bowed his head in acknowledgement.

'And do wear a dress,' Harry told her.

'I wouldn't insult his lordship by turning up in breeches. Now, if you will excuse me, I have to get back to work.'

When she was out of earshot, Charles said, 'What are you up to? My birthday isn't until December, as you well know.'

'I want to get her used to formal dining. I'll tell Cook what's needed and have a word with the other two, or they will give the game away as they know when your birthday is. See you later.' He slapped his father on the back and strode off.

* * *

The order to wear a dress presented a problem because she didn't have one. All she possessed were two skirts and two blouses, but one was freshly washed and pressed, so it would have to do. It was also customary to give gifts on someone's birthday. The only thing that might have been suitable had been her father's pocket watch, but sadly she'd had to sell that on her desperate journey to find the Travellers. It wouldn't have been good enough, though, because his lordship already had one and that was gold. Still, she ought to take something. An idea popped into her head and she ran off to find the estate manager.

He was in the kitchen enjoying a piece of Cook's fruit cake, and she sat beside him. 'Mr Carstairs, do you have a sheet of plain paper and the use of a pen, please?'

'I could find those for you. What size paper?'

'I don't mind, just whatever you have.'

He finished the rest of his cake, thanked Cook, and stood up. 'Come to my office and I'll see what we've got.'

She walked beside him, chatting away about the new horses. When they reached the office he opened a drawer, and she looked at the array of paper with longing.

'Take what you need, Chrissie.'

She chose carefully and selected a sheet. 'Could I have this and the use of one of your pens, please?'

'Help yourself. What do you want it for? Are you going to write to someone?'

'No, it's his lordship's birthday and I want to give him a gift.'

'I'm sure that isn't expected,' he told her quickly.

'Perhaps not, but I'd like to anyway. He's such a nice gentleman.'

'Yes, he is. Why don't you sit at my desk? It will be more comfortable to work at.'

'Thank you.' She sat down, thought for a moment, and then her pen began to flow over the paper. She didn't even notice that the estate manager had left the office.

When he returned an hour later he studied the picture she had just finished. 'Where did you learn to draw like that?'

'I've always been able to draw,' she told him while she studied her work critically. 'Put a pen in my hand and I'm happy, but I'm useless at sewing and embroidery. Do you think his lordship will like this?'

'I'm sure he will, but let's see if the blacksmith will make a nice metal frame for it, shall we?'

'Do you think he would?'

He picked up another sheet of paper the same size. 'I'll go and ask him.'

By the time she was ready for the dinner, the picture was in a lovely frame, and she was thrilled to have something so nice to give his lordship on his birthday. Making her way across the yard she wondered what they were going to have to eat. Something special, no doubt, and she smiled to herself. She probably wouldn't know what most of it was, but she liked trying new things.

Chapter Thirty-Eight

The butler showed Chrissie to the sitting room, announced her very formally, and then gave her a wink as he held the door open for her to enter. She stepped inside with a huge smile on her face, and stopped in delight. This was the first time she had ever seen this room, and its beauty took her breath away. It was all in pale apricot and gold, and her first instinct was to examine everything in detail, but Lord Frenshaw and his son were waiting to greet her.

She walked straight up to his lordship, dipped a small curtsy and held out her gift. 'Thank you for inviting me tonight, and I hope you've had a lovely day.'

'What's this?' he asked as he took the picture from her.

'It is customary to give a gift on a birthday, and I didn't have anything so I drew this for you. Mr Carstairs had the blacksmith make a frame, and I hope you like it.'

He stared at it for quite a while before speaking. 'My goodness, this is exquisite, and the likeness is remarkable. Thank you; this will have pride of place in my sitting room.' He stepped forward and kissed her gently on the cheek, and then moved back. 'Look, Harry, it's Midnight.'

His son, who had been greeting the other guests and handing round drinks, came over and studied the drawing. 'You drew this?'

She nodded. 'I did Midnight because he has such a noble head, and Mr Carstairs only had black ink.'

'You've done it beautifully. Stuart said you were good at copying things, but I didn't realise you had a talent for drawing.'

Delighted her effort had been so well received she took the glass he was holding out to her and sipped it cautiously. It wasn't too bad, she thought, and when she looked up he was watching her intently.

'Why are you wearing those old clothes?'

'They are all I've got, sir, and they are freshly laundered and pressed.'

'Then you must purchase better clothes.'

'I can't. I haven't got any money, sir.'

He frowned. 'Why haven't you?'

'Because you don't pay me, sir.'

'What? Why on earth didn't you ask me?'

'When I agreed to come back you never mentioned paying me. I have a roof over my head, good food and a chance to work with the wonderful horses. What more could I want? Believe me, sir, where I come from those are the most important things.'

'George!' He spun round to his estate manager. 'Didn't

I make it clear what Chrissie's position was to be?'

'You told me she would be working with the horses, so I have her down as a stable lad again. She isn't due to receive wages until the end of next month, September.'

Harry ran a hand through his hair in shock at the mistake he'd made – another one where she was concerned. 'This isn't right. I'll sort it out with you tomorrow. In the meantime, give her some money.'

'How much?'

'Whatever she needs to buy some decent clothes.'

She was looking from one man to the other, and listening to the conversation in amazement. 'Excuse me, sir,' she said clearly, 'I will not be in debt so that I can buy fripperies I will never need.'

'You won't be in debt. I will meet the cost for you. I do not like to see you walking around in clothes that clearly need replacing.'

She looked down at her black skirt and white blouse, both beautifully pressed by the maid. 'These were given to me by Mrs Martin while I was in London, and the material is of good quality.'

'That may be so, but you should be wearing a pretty frock.'

She was sure there would be other guests arriving for this birthday celebration, and was dismayed that her appearance was not considered suitable. Without further thought she curtsied to his lordship. 'I do beg your pardon for coming inappropriately dressed, your lordship. I have no wish to embarrass you or your guests.' Then she turned and walked out of the room, leaving stunned silence behind her.

* * *

Charles turned on his son, furious by what had just happened. 'You can forget any plans you had for her now! She'd made a big effort to look as presentable as she could, and in my eyes she looked quite charming. You have insulted her, and she won't stand for that.'

'Shall I go and bring her back?' Bert asked.

'She won't come back. I saw her dark eyes flashing with emotions like anger, disappointment and resignation. This will be the end for her because she won't stay where she feels she is not wanted. There's the dinner bell, so we had better go to dine or Cook will be offended after going to so much trouble to prepare a special meal at short notice.'

'Gentlemen,' Harry addressed the two guests. 'I do apologise for causing this upset, but please enjoy your dinner while I try to talk myself out of this misunderstanding.'

Charles followed his son out so they could talk in private.

'I'm sorry, Father, I was only trying to buy her some decent clothes,' Harry protested. 'I hate to see her wearing shabby clothes. She deserves better, and most girls would have been delighted with the offer.'

'In your eagerness to win her for your wife you are forgetting the harsh conditions she lived in. Where she comes from men don't give women of that class gifts unless they want something from them. What they want is not respectable, and she would never put herself in that position. Stuart fell into that trap as well, but from what he told me he managed to smooth it over without insulting her too much. Anything she needs she will work for, or go without, because that is the way she has been brought up. You have just insulted her in the worst possible way, and she will leave now. You don't deserve her, so let her go.'

'No! I was angry with myself, not her, and somehow I've got to make her understand that. I was so pleased to have her here I completely forgot to instruct George to see she was given some money in advance. I can't imagine what it's like to have nothing.'

'We have lived a privileged life, my boy, and never had to worry about money, and that is purely by accident of birth.'

'I know, and I want to give her so much, but I'm not going to get that chance now, am I?'

'I doubt it very much.'

'Nevertheless, I must talk to her.' He strode out of the house.

Charles watched him leave, knowing he was going to need all his persuasive skills to rescue this situation. Just because Chrissie had returned with him he had made the mistake of believing she was his and he could buy her things if he wanted to, without telling her how he felt. He was so wrong. Chrissie's outlook on life was naturally coloured by her upbringing. She was not like the society females with nothing on their minds but gossip and making a prestigious marriage. If Harry really wanted her for his wife – and he was sure he did – then he was going the wrong way about it by making one blunder after another. And this last one might be one too many.

Sighing deeply, he made his way to the dining room. 'We will be dining without my son. It might take him some time to talk his way out of this.'

Harry couldn't find her anywhere. He'd checked the barn first, then the stables, but there was no sign of her. Panic swept through him. She wouldn't have left already, surely? Not at night. He then hurried back to the barn, climbed the ladder and opened the hatch, giving a sigh of relief when he saw her belongings were still there. Jumping down, he went out to the yard, his gaze sweeping the area. Nothing. He wandered towards the other paddock, and when he turned the corner he saw a figure sitting on the gate. There she was, but he was going to have to be careful how he approached her. The fact that he was from a wealthy, titled family was no advantage to him with Chrissie. However, he had never been attracted to any of the society females he had met, while that girl sitting on the fence had stirred his emotions in a way he would not have thought possible. He could deal with a regiment of soldiers, but he was making a real mess of this. He should have told her sooner how he felt about her, and if he had, then this misunderstanding might not have happened. But it had, and he had probably lost any chance he might have had.

He made his way over to her, his boots making little sound on the grass. She didn't turn or look at him when he climbed up beside her.

'Peaceful here.'

She nodded.

'I seem to spend my time apologising to you.'

No reply.

'I didn't mean to insult you. I was annoyed with myself for not making sure you had some money.'

'You don't have to explain yourself, or apologise to a servant.'

'You are not a servant.'

377

'What am I then? I work for you.'

'You're a friend, and is it wrong to want to buy a friend clothes?'

'For a start we are not friends – we are master and servant. I have seen girls who have been in trouble because the master of the house showered them with gifts and flattery. I will not allow that to happen to me.'

'Now you are insulting me if you think that is my motive. I will ask you another question. Is it wrong to want to buy things for someone you love?'

'I suppose not, so long as there is a firm understanding between them.'

'An understanding like marriage?'

'That would be all right then.' She glanced at him. 'I hope his lordship wasn't too offended by my appearance. Your disapproval has made it clear that I cannot fit in with the role you have been trying to give me. To avoid further embarrassment, I'll send word to my friends and will leave at the end of the week.'

He was losing her! 'Don't do that, Chrissie. I wanted to buy you new clothes because you are the girl I love and want to marry.'

'You can't marry me.'

'Why not?'

'Because I am not of your class. You need a woman of good birth who will wear beautiful gowns and be able to socialise with your friends.'

'Can you possibly imagine me with one of them? Do you think any of them would run around in breeches and ride warhorses bareback?' He snorted in disgust. 'They'd be terrified of animals that size, and run for safety the moment they saw them.'

She giggled, and he relaxed just a little.

'You don't really believe women like that would interest me, do you?'

'I couldn't imagine it. You are a touch rough around the edges.'

'Oh, that's what you think of me, is it?'

She nodded.

'I see, now we're trading insults.' Her head was down, but he could see she was smiling.

'It's only fair. Friends can do that.'

His heart leapt with hope. They had moved from servant to friend. 'Is there any chance you could love me – even with all my rough edges?'

'I came back with you, didn't I?'

'I thought you returned because of the horses.'

'Them too.'

That word – too – told him what he wanted to know. 'Will you marry me, Chrissie?'

'I'll need time to think about it.'

'All right, but not too long, please. I don't want us to waste any more time.'

'I'll give you my answer tomorrow when I've slept on it.'

Elated that she hadn't refused him immediately, he knew he had pushed her as far as he could at this time, and he would have to be patient a little longer. 'Are you hungry?' he asked, jumping off the gate.

'Starving.'

'Come on, then.' He helped her down. 'Big decisions can't be made on an empty stomach.'

When they walked in to the dining room the men stood while Harry held a chair for her, then they all sat down again.

Charles looked enquiringly at his son and leant forward to ask quietly, 'Do we have something to celebrate after all?'

'Not yet, but hopefully we shall have tomorrow.' He turned to the butler. 'Are we in time for the main course?'

'It's about to be served, sir.'

'Good. We are both starving.'

The rest of the evening was a relaxed affair with everyone in a happy mood, and it was only later in the evening when they were alone that Harry was able to tell his father what had happened.

'It still doesn't mean she will accept your proposal,' his father told him, adding a note of caution, as he always did.

'No, it doesn't, but at least I have a chance. If she does accept then I will need you here because I intend the marriage to take place very quickly, so perhaps you should stay for a few days.'

'I have every intention of doing so.'

Chrissie couldn't believe he wanted to marry her. She'd been aware that he was attracted to her, of course, as she was to him, but she had expected a different kind of proposal. That was the reason she had felt her stay here would come to an end again. After all, gentlemen of social standing did not marry girls from the slums, and she had delayed her answer in order to give him time to change his mind. If he asked again, then it would tell her he really did love her and wanted her for his wife. She knew when she had fallen in love with him. It had been while they had been racing across the sands by the sea and laughing together with the sheer joy of it. She had come back with him because the thought of seeing him riding out of her life had been too painful. There had been no doubt in her mind that her stay would be short, but she hadn't been able to throw away the chance of a little more time with him and the beautiful horses. However, she had never expected this, and was finding it hard to believe it was real. All she could do now was wait and see what happened tomorrow.

The next morning, Chrissie was brushing Midnight when Harry joined her and asked immediately, 'Do you have an answer, Chrissie? Will you marry me?'

'Have you thought about it carefully?' she asked.

'I've thought of nothing else. I love you and want you by my side as my wife.'

'Then I accept,' she told him simply.

He breathed a sigh of relief, gathered her in his arms and swung her round while kissing her firmly on the mouth.

'People are watching,' she told him breathlessly.

'I'm too happy to care. I want the marriage to take place within two months. I think we should be able to make all the arrangements by then. What kind of a wedding do you want? A quiet one or a lively one with loads of guests?'

'I think I would like a lively one.'

'Perfect. I'll send word to the Travellers asking them to get here without delay. They can camp on the spare ground behind those trees.'

'You'd do that?' she gasped. 'Wouldn't your other guests be offended?'

'If they are then they needn't come. This will be our wedding, my love, and we will invite who we want.'

'Having them here will certainly make it lively.' She laughed. 'I'd love to see Elsie again.'

'Me too.' Harry shook her shoulder gently and grinned. 'This is the celebration you told me would take place here, isn't it? You knew this was going to happen all the time, didn't you?'

Her expression gave nothing away until he saw the sparkle of amusement in her eyes. 'How would I know that? I'm not a fortune-teller.'

As they laughed and hugged each other she knew this unconventional marriage was right for them. In different ways they had both come through hard and distressing times, but now they could move on with their lives – together.

Beryl Matthews was born in London but now lives in a small village in Hampshire. As a young girl her ambition was to become a professional singer, but the need to earn a wage drove her into an office, where she worked her way up from tea girl to credit controller. After retiring she joined a Writers' Circle in hopes of fulfilling her dream of becoming a published author. With her first book published at the age of seventy-one, she has since written over twenty novels.